P9-DNU-594

DISCOVER

READ

EXPLORE

LEARN

NEW HANOVER COUNTY
PUBLIC LIBRARY

If found, please return to:
201 Chestnut St.
Wilmington, NC 28401
(910) 798-6300
http://www.nhclibrary.org

# THE AGONY HOUSE

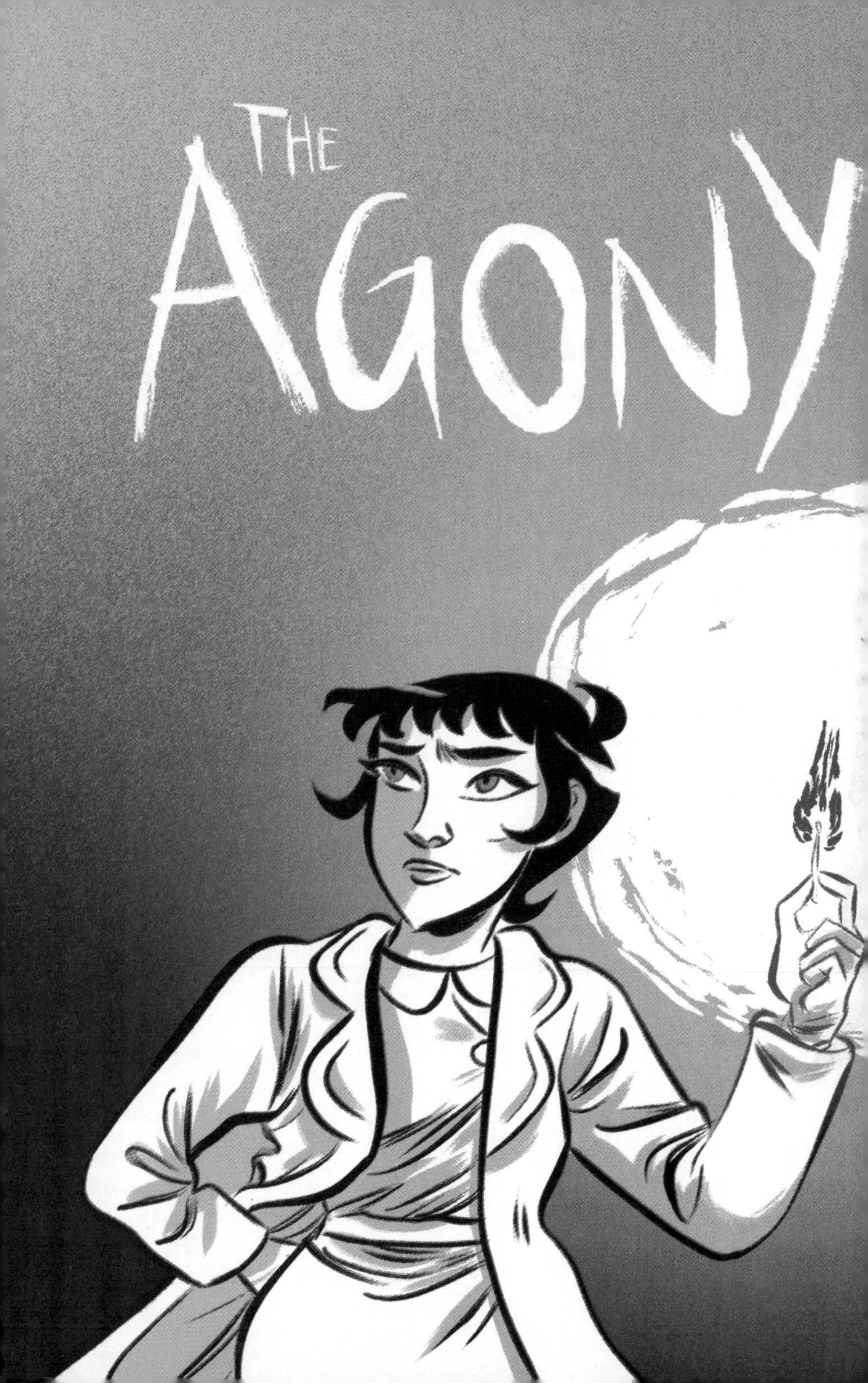
THE
AGONY

# HOUSE

BY CHERIE PRIEST

ILLUSTRATED BY TARA O'CONNOR

ARTHUR A. LEVINE BOOKS
AN IMPRINT OF SCHOLASTIC INC.

Library of Congress Cataloging-in-Publication Data

Names: Priest, Cherie, author. | O'Connor, Tara, illustrator. Title: The agony
house / Cherie Priest ; illustrated by Tara O'Connor. Description: First edition. | New York :
Arthur A. Levine Books/Scholastic Inc., 2018. | "This book contains 45 pages of interior comic
illustrations in addition to the text"--Publisher. | Summary: Seventeen-year-old Denise Farber,
her mom and her stepfather are moving back to New Orleans, into the Argonne house, which
is over 100 years old, and really showing its age, but which her mother plans to turn into a
bed-and-breakfast--but old houses have histories, and sometimes ghosts, and a mysterious
old comic book that Denise finds in the attic may hold the answer to a crime and the terrifying
things that keep happening in what she thinks of as the "Agony" house. Identifiers: LCCN
2018016855| ISBN 9780545934299 (hardcover : alk. paper) | ISBN 054593429X (hardcover :
alk. paper) Subjects: LCSH: Ghost stories. | Haunted houses--Louisiana--New Orleans--
Juvenile fiction. | Murder--Louisiana--New Orleans--Juvenile fiction. | Comic books, strips,
etc.--Juvenile fiction. | Detective and mystery stories. | New Orleans (La.)--Juvenile fiction. |
CYAC: Mystery and detective stories. | Ghosts--Fiction. | Haunted houses--Fiction. |
Murder--Fiction. | Cartoons and comics--Fiction. | New Orleans (La.)--Fiction. | LCGFT:
Detective and mystery fiction. | Ghost stories. Classification: LCC PZ7.1.P76 Ag 2018
| DDC 813.6 [Fic] --dc23 LC record available at https://lccn.loc.gov/2018016855

10 9 8 7 6 5 4 3 2 1     18 19 20 21 22
Printed in the U.S.A.    23
First edition, October 2018
Book design by Phil Falco

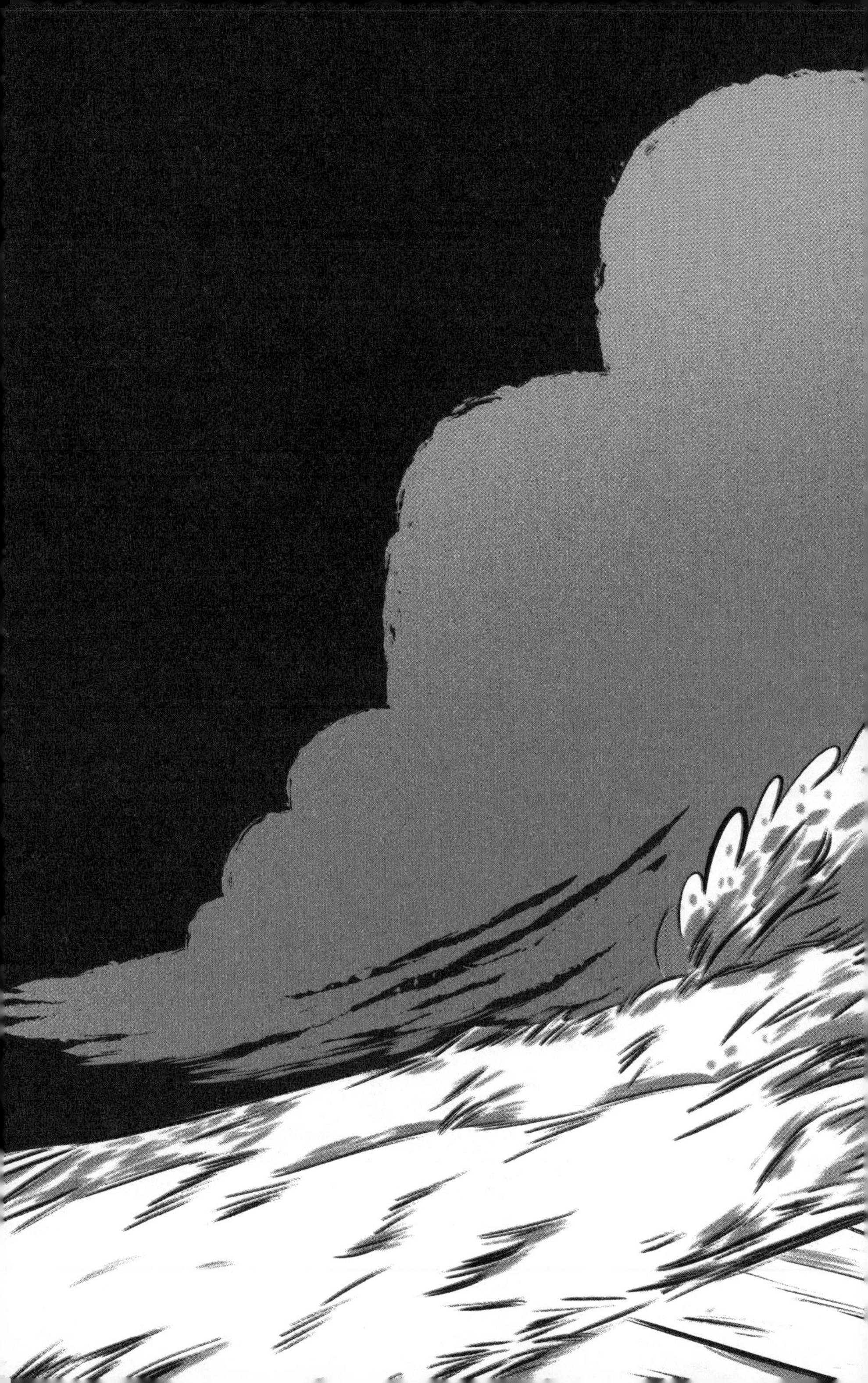

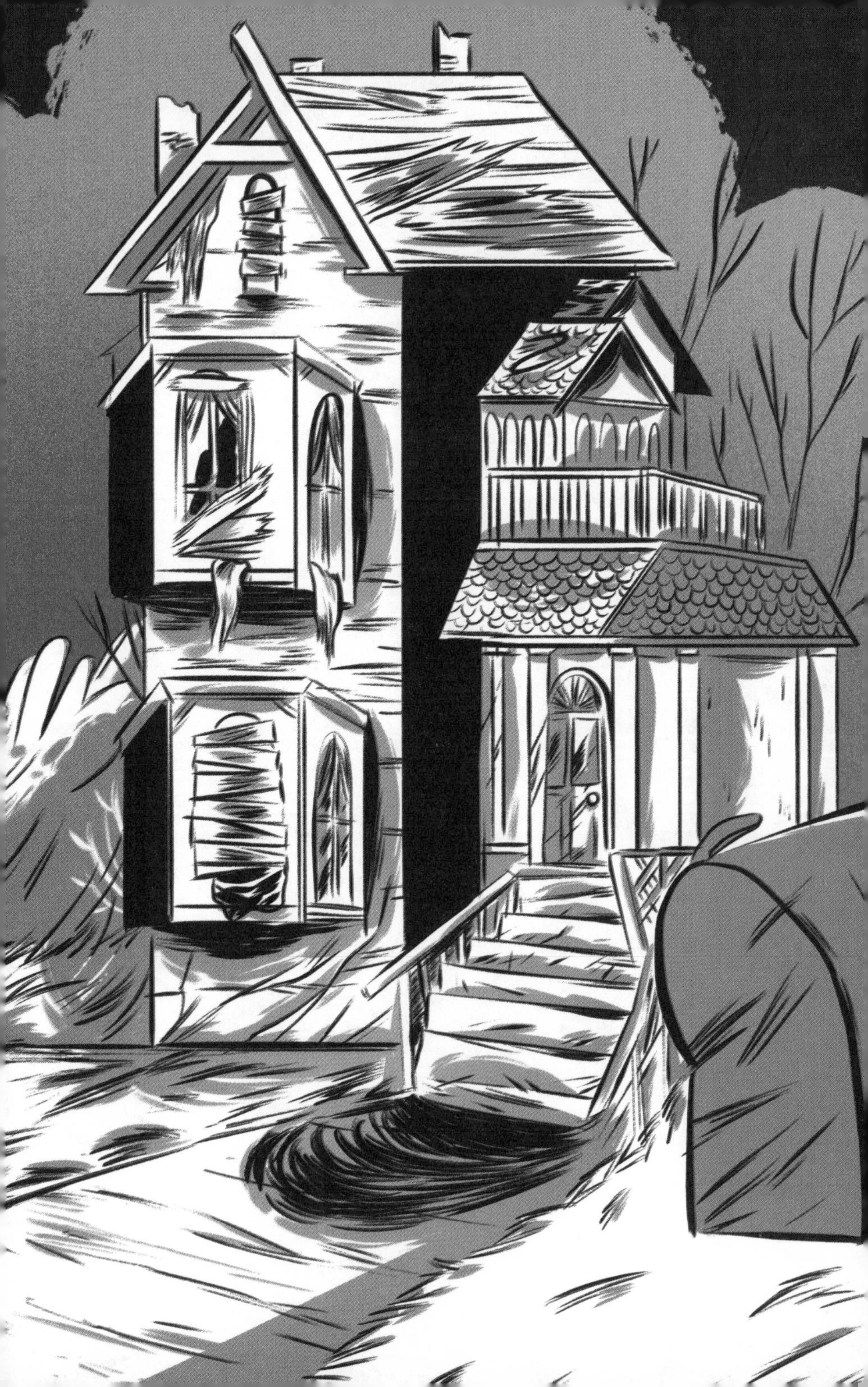

# CONTENTS

# CHAPTER ONE

Denise Farber stomped up the creaky metal ramp and stood inside the U-Haul, looking around for the lightest possible box. Her mother's handwriting offered loud hints in black marker: POTS AND PANS (no, thank you), BOOKS (forget it), and BATHROOM CABINET SUPPLIES (maybe). She pulled that last one out of a stack and shook it gently. It probably held half-full shampoo bottles, tissue boxes, and rolls of toilet paper.

The ramp squealed and groaned behind her. She looked over her shoulder. "Hey, Mike. Did you get the AC working?"

Her stepdad joined her in the truck's muggy shade. He was a bean-pole of a man, with short black hair and a sunburn that somehow made him look even more unreasonably cheerful than usual. "Almost!" he replied brightly.

Denise set down the box and used the bottom of her shirt to swab her sweaty forehead. "'Almost' isn't going to cut it."

"Yeah, I know. I called a guy, and he ought to be here in an hour or two — so let's see how much of this truck we can empty before he shows up."

"Or . . ." She raised a finger and flashed him her most charming and persuasive smile. "Hear me out . . . we could wait until we have AC, and *then* unload the truck. That way, nobody dies of heatstroke."

"Come on, kiddo. It's still early, and it's not that bad. If we all work together, the job won't take long."

"So where's Mom?"

"Good question. Sally? You coming?"

"I'm right here," she declared from somewhere outside the truck. She leaned around the ramp and waved. Her hair waved too. It was dirty blond, curly as hell, and tied up in a scarf that had no hope of containing it. "Power's still out on the second floor, and I couldn't fix it by fiddling with the breakers, so I don't know what's wrong. We'll have to call a guy."

"We're gonna need a *lot* of guys," Denise observed.

Sally ignored her. "I've opened all the windows, so at least we'll catch the breeze." Her sunglasses melted down her nose, and she pushed them back up with her thumb. "And in that box, over there"—she pointed—"the one marked OUTDOOR MISC, I packed an extension cord. One of y'all two dig it out for me, and I'll go hook up the big square fan. It'll be better than nothing."

Denise shuffled over to the OUTDOOR MISC box and punched the lid until the tape gave way. She fished out a thick orange coil, then dropped it over the truck's back bumper.

Her mother caught it before it hit the ground. "Hang in there, baby. The fun's about to start, I promise."

"Yeah, I just bet." Denise turned away, back toward the boxes. She briefly daydreamed about what would happen if she stole the U-Haul's keys out of her mother's purse and drove the truck right back to Texas, fast as can be, before anyone could catch her. Houston was almost as hot as New Orleans this time of year, and the apartment they'd left wasn't all *that* much better than this new house . . . but Houston was familiar. It had air-conditioning. It had Trish, and Kim, and Bonnie, and everybody else she was supposed to spend her senior year of high school with.

But it didn't have her. Not anymore.

She quit fantasizing and retrieved the lightweight box she'd chosen in the first place—the one that was destined for a bathroom. Sighing all the way, she trudged down the ramp and through the overgrown yard, toward the new family homestead.

312 Argonne Street was all theirs. Such as it was.

Built sometime in the late-1800s, the house was three stories tall if you counted the attic, and it wasn't very wide. It was the only building left standing on the block, surrounded by vacant lots that held overgrown grass, discarded tires, and the empty foundations of long-gone homes . . . if they held anything at all. All the flat nothingness nearby added to the impression that it had been crafted high and thin — a jumble of Victorian rooms piled up like blocks, dripping with gingerbread trim that'd gone all crumbly with rot. Once upon a time, the roof was maybe black, and the siding was maybe white. Now they were both more or less the same shade of laundry-water gray. The front porch was a ruin of peeled and bubbling paint, water damage, and missing spindles. The chimney bricks hung as loose as a first grader's teeth.

If it hadn't looked so decrepit and sad, it might've looked angry — but the Storm had washed away everything except the brittle, aching bones.

Denise stared the place down. Its front door was open, like a dare.

She adjusted her grip on the box and marched up the porch steps like she was going to the gallows, but that was an awful thing to think, wasn't it? It was only a house . . . a big, ugly house, and until she could leave for college, it was home.

Eventually, if nobody died of tetanus first, it would become the bed-and-breakfast her mom had always wanted. She was going to call it "Desa Miranda's" after her late mother-in-law, Denise's grandma who'd died when the Storm came. It'd been Grandma's idea in the first place — to take one of the big old houses that nobody loves, and bring it back to life.

Make it a destination. Put people up and feed them right, that was always Grandma Desa's big Someday Plan. Maybe she didn't plan to have it happen in what felt like a half-ruined neighborhood, scrubbed down to the studs by the Storm, but beggars couldn't be choosers. The houses that were still standing were either rugged, half-repaired survivors, or empty shells full of mold.

But this was it. This was home.

Bienvenue New Orleans.

Denise didn't remember the Storm.

She'd been a toddler when it'd hit. She didn't recall the wind or the water, and she didn't know how high the river had come when the levee failed, or how everything had smelled like death and mildew for months after the fact. For years, even. She didn't know how many days had passed before her dad's and grandmother's bodies were found, but it was at least a week. (She'd heard that much, when no one thought she was listening.)

Now at seventeen, Denise was back in the Crescent City.

She stood on the porch in front of a wide-open door, while the house inhaled and exhaled — swamp breath and rot, soaked wood and rust. Maybe somebody had died in there too. The place sure as heck looked haunted by *something*.

One grim foot in front of the other she crossed the threshold, box in arms, and stared around the foyer. Sure, the outside of the house was bad . . . but at least the inside was terrible.

According to Sally, some guy had bought the place in 2015, hoping to make a quick flip. He'd started a bunch of projects, but then ran out of money and ran out of town, leaving the bank to reclaim the property. He'd also left behind a real mess — floors half-warped and half-new, and fixtures removed for rewiring but never replaced. Ceiling medallions hung at precarious angles. The windows were missing their sills, and the remnants of old rugs had decomposed into stains. Some of the walls were open, wiring and mold exposed to the living area. Soggy plaster fell from the studs like wet cake, and strips of wallpaper curled into scrolls.

Denise sniffed and said, "*Gross.*"

"Don't be so judgy." Mike grunted past her, hauling both the box of books, and the box with pots and pans — stacked one atop the other. He set them down with a grunt, then took the kitchenware to the appropriate room, leaving the books behind. "When we get the place cleaned up, it'll look great. You'll see."

"I believe you. Thousands wouldn't." Denise looked around for a bookshelf, or a table, or any reasonably flat surface apart from the conspicuously swollen floorboards.

She peered around the corner. There, she spied a dining room table set that had come with the house. It was right beneath a hole in the ceiling where a chandelier used to be. All six of its original matching chairs were stacked beside it. Beyond them, an arc of three bay windows bowed out over the yard, offering a semi-panoramic view of the empty lot across the street.

The room was a ruin like everything else, but for the moment, the table was uncluttered and dry. It could hold a few books, for now.

She didn't want to lift the whole box, so she pulled out handfuls of paperbacks, two-fisting them all the way to the table. Some of them were her mom's mysteries, and some were Mike's military or science fiction favorites. But most of the books were hers — an odd assortment of true crime and biographies, plus a couple of nonfiction paperbacks about passing the bar exam. Denise was a good decade or so away from being a lawyer, but she'd found the books at a church swap meet for a quarter apiece, so what the hell, right?

Thirty minutes later, the air-conditioning guy showed up. Much to everyone's surprise, the unit was soon running again, as loud and wheezy as the box fan and only marginally more powerful. It blew the smell of mold and dust around the first floor, stirring the abandoned wisps of curtains and taking the edge off the heat. Kind of. A little.

The AC guy said it was the best he could do, because they really needed a whole new unit. He wished them luck as he collected his postdated check that wouldn't clear until Thursday, and then he hit the road.

By two o'clock the truck was empty — and the house contained all the stuff the old owner had left behind, and all the things the new family had brought from Texas. Once it was spread out like that, it didn't look like much. It *wasn't* much, and the house was about five times the size of their old apartment in Houston. Everything they owned would've fit into two of the bedrooms, with space to spare.

"Is that everything?" Mike asked with a wheeze. Sweat beaded up from every inch of his skin, soaking through his red Texans T-shirt and leaving a dark swath of dampness in the creases of his shorts.

"I think so," Sally said. "At this point, if there's anything left in the truck . . . Jesus. I don't care. U-Haul can have it."

Denise pushed the front door shut, sealing in the feeble draft of chilly air. "Yeah, they can have my half-drunk Coke in the cupholder."

Mike waved his hand. "No, I'll toss it out. I need to clean out the cab when I stop to fill up the tank, anyway. Speaking of, we need to return the truck before six, don't we? Why don't we go do that and you can unpack your stuff upstairs, Denise?"

"Can't I just come with? There's *real* air-conditioning in the car and I think I saw a Dairy Queen on the way . . ."

Sally smiled, but it was a tired smile. "I like Mike's idea. Especially since you haven't even picked a bedroom yet, have you? There are five in total: one down here, three on the second floor, and a big attic space that'll be a great room someday — but that one's not built out yet."

Her stepdad added, "The one down here is the master suite, and that's ours. Go pick out something on the second floor."

"So instead of five rooms to choose from, I have three. Got it."

"That's two more rooms than last time we moved. So go on, now. See what suits your fancy."

Denise strongly considered airing a list of things that suited her fancy, including such elements as air-conditioning and Dairy Queen. She could even add her old friends, her old school, and her old bedroom.

But instead of firing off at the mouth, or collapsing into sobs, or taking a plea bargain for a Peanut Buster Parfait . . . she went the dry route. "Fine. Leave me alone, in a sketchy neighborhood. In a house that's basically condemned. I'm sure I won't get murdered, hardly at all."

Sally said, "Atta girl, wiseass. And for the record, I'm less worried about you holding down the fort here, than when you had an encyclopedic knowledge of the METRO and a boyfriend out in Sugar Land. Speaking of sketchy."

"Aw, leave him out of this." Her ex, Kieron, was all right. But he was just all right, and she wouldn't fight for his honor. They'd broken up months ago, and she wasn't about to let him cause drama when he wasn't even there.

"Besides, the neighborhood isn't sketchy," Mike added. "It's . . . up-and-coming."

Denise ran the back of her hand under her nose, and behind her neck. It came back slimy. She wiped it on her shirt. "If you say so," she surrendered. She was too tired and too hot to push back too hard. "It looks run-down and empty to me. Just . . . *please.* I'm begging you: Bring me something cold."

Sally nodded and fished her keys out of her purse. "We'll see what we can find. The AC and the fan are running, and it'll cool off soon. Come on, Mike." Then, to Denise, "We'll be back in twenty minutes."

The door closed behind them with a creak and a scrape, then settled on its hinges with a miserable groan. Denise knew how it felt.

She waited until she heard her mom's car and the U-Haul pull off the two dirt ruts that served as a driveway, and into the road. Then she pulled out her phone and rubbed it on her thigh until only a faint smudge of butt-sweat remained, then unlocked the screen.

No messages, no notifications. Not even one of those stupid animated emoticons from her best friend, Trish.

But everyone knew she was on the road. Everyone knew she'd be

7

busy. They probably just didn't want to bother her. There was no good reason to feel lonely or forgotten. Yet.

Her eyes filled up, anyway.

She put the phone beside the books on the table, and wiped at her face — but that was a dumb thing to do. The salty sweat on her hands only made things worse. Her vision watered and her eyeballs burned. "Screw it," she mumbled, sniffling hard and making for the kitchen.

The kitchen wasn't very big, but Mike said that was normal for a Victorian house. It was probably somewhat *less* normal to find it out-fitted with a bunch of Formica and linoleum from the 1960s, but none of that was any uglier than the rest of the place. It was just a different kind of ugly, that's all.

Denise fished a bottle of dishwashing liquid out of a box. She washed her hands and splashed down her face, then rinsed and blotted herself with some paper towels. Briefly, she was pleased to smell the soap's "spring citrus scent" rather than the house's "perma-stink of old plaster and something dead."

She checked her phone again. She still didn't have any new messages. Not so much as a Facebook thumbs-up, or a Snapchat of Annie's cat doing something ridiculous.

She might as well take a look around.

Denise crammed her phone into her back pocket so she'd feel it if it buzzed, and glared at her shabby surroundings. Exploring was usually a good time, but maybe not here, where she was afraid to touch anything or step anywhere. A very bad feeling in the pit of her stomach hinted that nothing would *ever* be fun in the Argonne house.

"The Argonne House . . ." she said to herself, pronouncing the *e* on the end. She knew she wasn't supposed to, because it was French. In French, it was "argh-on." She grinned, but she grinned *grimly*. "More like the *Agony* House." Yes, that was better.

But Argonne or Agony, she needed to pick a bedroom.

She poked her head into the master bedroom out of idle curiosity. It was pretty big, with old-fashioned wallpaper and a door that led to a bathroom. Besides the foyer, parlor, dining room, kitchen, and master bedroom, there was also an empty room on the first floor. Denise thought it must have been an office and not a bedroom; it wasn't very big, and it didn't have a closet. The remnant of a vintage AC unit was stuck in the wall beside the door. A veil of rust-colored water marks drained beneath it, and stained the floor below.

"Yuck," she declared.

She felt the same way about a hall door that opened to a linen closet, or maybe it'd been a place where a washer and dryer went? It was hard to tell, and she didn't want to fight the fortress of spiderwebs to find out, so she shut the rattling bifold doors and tried the knob to a storage spot beneath the staircase. It wouldn't open, no matter how hard she pulled, twisted, or swore like her mother after a date with the box wine.

Giving up, Denise scaled the stairs with one hand skimming along the rail, and one hand trailing along the far wall. Most of the wallpaper had been removed, but patches of roses and vines appeared where the glue had been more stubborn than whoever had tried to get rid of it. She liked the pattern. She wished it was still there, and still bright and pretty like it must've been, once upon a time.

One by one the stairs winced and squeaked, and every few feet the temperature climbed — ignoring the ailing fan that greeted her at the top landing. It hummed along from its spot on the floor at the end of the hall, blowing manky air against Denise's bare legs.

She paused there, letting the fan dry the damp, sticky spot behind her knees.

Here on the second floor, five doors awaited. She nudged them open, one by one.

The first door revealed a long, narrow room with a broken fan dangling overhead, suspended from a frayed tangle of wires. Part of the ceiling had fallen in, and a broad, shiny stain occupied most of the floor. Denise hoped it was just an especially big water mark, but for all she knew, the place was a crime scene.

No thanks.

The next room was larger, with a broken window and a wasp nest the size of a football mounted in the far corner. She slammed the door shut and leaned against it. Her stomach flipped, because holy cow, *wasps*. One or two buzzed angrily against the door, perturbed at the intrusion.

Her heart pounded. Her mouth was dry. Her house was full of wasps.

This was her life now.

She took a deep breath and twisted the knob on the next door down the line, hoping for something less awful than wasps but not counting on it. She pushed the door open. Pleasantly surprised for once, she let the breath out slow. This room was by far the largest — even bigger than the downstairs master — and it had an oversized window like the ones in the dining room, plus an old brown ceiling fan that looked like it might actually work. But when she flipped the switch on the wall, nothing happened.

"Oh yeah, the power's not working up here," she reminded herself.

Up here, the walls were a light sky blue, and most of the paint wasn't even bubbled up with moisture. The floor was beat all to hell, but there weren't any holes or suspicious stains. Sure, the corners were full of dust bunnies, the bottom right windowpane was cracked, and the tiny closet didn't even have a door . . . but there was plenty of space and a window bench to boot.

Window benches were kind of neat, and she'd take dust bunnies over wasps any day of the week.

Back in the hall, the fan rattled away. Denise retrieved it, and hauled it toward her grudgingly chosen base of operations — but the extension cord stopped about three feet outside the door. She dropped the fan beside her foot and aimed it toward her bedroom.

She left it there, and went to check out the floor's lone bathroom.

All things considered, it could've been worse. There was a claw-foot tub, and that was pretty cool. The sink was all right too — a pedestal with old-fashioned hot and cold knobs, so you could have one or the other, but not both at the same time. When she turned the cold knob, it even spit out water that looked like water, and not like chicken soup. The tiles on the walls were minty green with black accents. Hardly any of them were chipped or broken. A bottle of half-empty liquid hand soap was perched on the sink's edge. It smelled like gardenias.

So far, the bathroom was the real highlight of the tour.

One more door to check, and her survey of the house would be complete. This last door was too narrow by half, and too tall by a foot. The knob was small and weird, and the twisty bit of hardware beneath it turned out to be a dead bolt. The screw turned reluctantly, with a grinding protest. The knob turned too, though it moaned like it would have preferred not to.

The door opened.

A dank gust of hot air belched into the hall. It tousled her hair and curled into her ears, wrapped itself about her waist, and felt around her calves. It tickled the sweaty places between her toes.

She sneezed and blinked hard, then sneezed again. She'd turned something loose into the house, and it wasn't just air — it was powder-fine dust, and particles of mold, and the odor of something that once must have been unbearable . . . and now was merely unpleasant.

The dust and the accompanying stench settled down the steps and pooled around her ankles. It slipped away; it dissipated down the hall, into the bedrooms and the bathroom. But it never quite *left*. It lingered and stank.

The grimy air made her face feel dirty, but she squinted through it anyway. Through the gloom, she saw a staircase so thin that she'd nearly have to turn sideways to climb it — and she was on the small side of petite. Always the littlest one in every grade. Always last-picked for kickball . . . but first-picked for gymnastics. You'd practically *have* to be a gymnast to navigate those oddball stairs without breaking your neck. She quietly thanked all those lessons, and all those trips to the top of the pyramid. Maybe they would come in handy after all.

"So . . . this must be the attic." Another sneeze escaped, before she could cover her mouth and nose. She wiped them both on the back of her hand, then wiped her hand on her shorts and stared at the steps.

The attic door moved.

Denise jumped back.

Maybe it had drifted in the breeze, or drooped on its hinges, or performed some other trick of very old hardware in an uneven house — but it had *moved*. All by itself.

Denise smacked the door shut. It rattled in the frame and a couple of rusty old nails rolled loose, away from the threshold.

She stood there in the hall, staring at the door and hoping her heart wouldn't pound right out of her chest. The house settled, and somewhere far away a board stretched, squeaked, and went silent. She held very still and listened, but heard only the dull roar of the box fan a few yards away. She listened harder, and heard another buzz that might've been the wasps in that other bedroom, or it might've been some other big bug brought around by the river mud and the late summer heat.

Firmly, but softly — like she didn't really want an answer — Denise asked: "Is someone inside the house here with me?" But she didn't believe the silence, so she tried again. "Am I really alone in here?"

Behind the attic door something moved, just loud enough to be felt.

Never mind the gymnastics lessons or her spirit of adventure: The attic could wait.

Quickly, she sprinted back down the hall to her bedroom. She stood in the middle and stared at the box fan, which didn't quite reach inside. Its motor turned with a crunch like a coffee grinder, and its blades did that funny thing where they made every noise sound warped and low, like it came from someplace far away. It was an illusion. It *had* to be, the way the fan blades were spitting out vowels, wide and loud. The way they were spitting out words.

Her chest was tight. Her heart stuttered. And she almost jumped out of her skin when she heard her mom's car pull off the road and up next to the house.

She darted to the window and looked down at the "off-street parking" the real estate listing had mentioned. It was only a space beside the house where nothing was built and nothing was growing, but it was big enough for Sally's old light blue Kia to camp with room to spare.

The car doors opened. Sally and Mike stepped out. And Denise could breathe again, even if she hadn't forgotten the attic door, or the smell, or the sound of something moving just out of sight. She couldn't forget any of that, but she could push it out of her head for a few minutes — because Sally was carrying three bags of Dairy Queen takeout and Mike was holding a cardboard beverage tray with three sodas wedged tightly in its grip.

So maybe the house was gross, and maybe it was practically condemned, and real talk? It was *definitely* haunted. Maybe Denise didn't have any friends at all within three hundred miles, and maybe she'd have to start school in September at a place where no one knew her name, and no one had her cell number. The situation was bad. Real bad. Wasps-in-the-bedroom bad. Crying-when-nobody's-looking bad.

But it wasn't the end of the world, because there was ice cream. It was the thinnest of all possible silver linings, but if there was chocolate fudge on it, Denise would take it.

And to hell with whatever was hiding in the attic.

# CHAPTER TWO

The next day was a whirlwind of housework and unpacking, of breaking down the free liquor store boxes they'd used, and bagging up the newspaper that had wrapped the plates and glasses. By Sunday evening, the place was almost clean . . . for a relative value of clean. A vacuum cleaner and a dustrag couldn't do much about a hole in a wall or missing floorboards, or the wires that hung loose in their frayed cloth wrappings. But they could clear out the cobwebs and the dust bunnies, and make the place feel a little less abandoned.

Still, there was always more work to be done. On Monday morning, Sally said merrily, "If you've got time to lean, you've got time to clean!"

"Kill me now."

"Oh, come on. It isn't that bad," she promised. "We're making real headway, here!"

"On *what*?" Denise asked miserably.

Mike replied, "Getting ready for the big stuff. The electrician and plumber will come around later this week, but nobody's gonna be taking down walls or anything. We're only planning a little bit of demolition, and that'll be fun. Picture it: pulling down cabinets, whacking stuff with a sledgehammer . . . it's always more fun to break things than build things."

"Says you."

"You'll be saying it too, soon enough. I bet you a trip to Dairy Queen."

"*Now* you've got my attention."

He laughed. "Good, because after breakfast . . . you can come with me to the hardware store down the street. We need a few things before we get started."

"All right. Anything that'll get me out of the house, and I've got a shopping list anyway. I think we need some light bulbs."

Mike couldn't have agreed more. "You're not kidding. Last night we were down to two bulbs down here on the first floor, and we had to move them around from room to room. I burned my finger on one."

"Very dignified."

"Don't I know it. Your old man is a real class act."

She was still getting used to hearing Mike talk like that, calling himself her dad — even in a roundabout way. Sometimes he referred to her in passing as his daughter, and that felt strange too. Not bad-strange, just . . . awkward. Even though he tried to make it as not-awkward as he could. Before the wedding, he'd gone out of his way to ask if it was okay and she'd given him the green light. Why not? It made her mother happy, and the more Denise thought about it, the more she didn't honestly care, one way or the other.

The truth was, she didn't remember her real dad. He was just a smiling man in someone else's memory, a grainy figure in other people's photos. Shorter and heavier than Mike, Billy Farber had been pale as a cave fish, with sharp cheekbones and kind eyes. If Sally could be believed, he was a Saints fan and a dog-lover — a fisherman when money was low, and a street market warrior when it wasn't. If the surviving pictures could be trusted, he was a mean cook who hosted the block's best shrimp boils. He was also a middling musician who never quite got the hang of playing bass, but enjoyed it anyway.

Then the Storm came, and the water took him. It wasn't Billy's fault that Denise hardly remembered him, and didn't love him. She just never got a chance to know him.

Now there was Mike Cooper, and Mike was pretty all right. He could call her his daughter if he wanted to, and she hoped her bio-dad — up in heaven, or wherever — wouldn't hold it against either one of them. If he was as nice as everybody always said he was, then he probably thought it was cool.

But it still felt weird.

When the remains of breakfast had been washed up or stored, Sally wished Mike and Denise good luck and said she'd stay there and wait for the city to deliver the dumpster.

"We get our own dumpster?"

"We're going to pull a lot of garbage out of this house, and it won't all fit in the bin that goes to the curb. The guy at the office said they'd bring a big one around between eight and nine, so . . . you two have fun. I'll stick around and sign for it, or whatever they want me to do."

Denise had her doubts about "fun," but she said good-bye and climbed into the Kia's passenger seat.

Mike got behind the wheel. "The hardware place is only a few blocks away. If I wasn't planning to buy stuff, I would've just walked."

She nodded approvingly. "I appreciate your laziness, good sir."

"I'm not that lazy, but it's awful damn hot."

A minute or two later they drove past a two-story building that looked brand spanking new. The sign outside read RUDY LOMBARD HIGH SCHOOL. The parking lot was big and empty, and a cluster of buses were lined up beside it — silent and still.

She didn't remember doing it, but she must've sighed and her step-dad must've heard her, because he said, "Don't be so dramatic. It looks nice. It'll be a good place to spend your senior year."

"Maybe, but I was really looking forward to *not* being the new kid, for once."

Mike shrugged. "That school's only been open for a year or two. Everybody's a new kid."

"But they're all from the same neighborhood. They all know each other already."

He didn't have an answer for that, but Pete's Notions and Hardware appeared around the corner, so he didn't need one. "Hey look. We're here."

"What's a notion?"

He pulled into a space and they both climbed out. "I think it's just another word for 'stuff.'"

It hadn't been five minutes, but Denise was pretty confident that it was already hotter outside than it'd been when they left the house. She wiped her forehead and looked around: Pete's had an empty lot on either side of it, and a gas station across the street. Both the store and the gas station looked like they'd weathered the Storm with only marginally better success than the Agony House, but there were two older black men on the front porch of the store, sipping beers and chatting about the fat old dog that lounged at one man's feet. It looked like a friendly enough spot, and through the glass front door she spied the glowing red light of a Coke machine.

Mike saw it too, and he knew who he was dealing with. He pulled out his wallet and gave Denise a couple of bucks. "Go get yourself a Coke, if you want. I won't be long, because my shopping list ain't."

"Cool, thanks. But you added light bulbs, right?"

"Top of the page, yes ma'am."

The AC inside the store wasn't a whole lot better than the one inside her house, but at least there was shade. The shelves were stacked high, and everything was crowded on top of everything else. It looked like Mike was right about "notions," because from where Denise was standing, it meant "any kind of junk or stuff that doesn't fit the description of hardware." She saw everything from pet food to suncatchers, bug spray to canned beans.

She homed in on the soda machine, a moth drawn to the lit-up logo.

She needed a dollar fifty to get the bottle of her choice. The first bill went into the slot just fine, but the second one was wrinkled. She straightened it on the machine's corner and tried it again. No dice.

"You want to trade?"

She stopped wrestling with the dollar, and turned around. Behind her, a black guy about her own age was holding out a crisper bill than the one that came from Mike's sweat-dampened wallet.

"Um . . . sure. Thanks."

They switched money, and the new bill went into the feeder just fine. Denise pushed the button for a Diet Dr. Pepper, and listened to the internal mechanisms spin up the selection. "Right on," she said. "Seriously, I appreciate it."

"No problem. And I'm Norman, just so you know."

She tried not to frown quizzically at him, but mostly failed. "Norman?" She'd never heard of a guy under the age of eighty named Norman before, but there was a first time for everything. He was beefy, like he probably knew his way around some of Pete's power tools. Maybe he worked construction in the summers. Back in Texas, she'd known a lot of guys who did that. They always came back to school in the fall looking like linebackers. He had buzzed hair and hazel eyes, and dark skin that showed a little tan line around a bead bracelet on his left wrist. "You don't *look* like a Norman."

"I was named after an aunt."

"Aunt Norma?"

He grinned. "Got it in one. And what's a Norman *supposed* to look like?"

She didn't know. "Sorry, that was a dumb thing to say."

"Don't worry about it. I've heard a lot worse. Are you new here? Haven't seen you around before."

"Um . . . I'm *from* here . . . but my mom and I left when the Storm hit. We ended up in Houston, and now . . ." She half shrugged, half gestured around at the store. At the whole neighborhood. "Now we're back."

"Welcome back, then."

"Thanks. It's been an adventure."

He leaned against the Coke machine. She noticed a camera hanging off a strap on his left side. "Good adventure, or bad adventure?"

"Let me put it this way: The house my parents bought is a *total* wreck. It's practically condemned."

He laughed. "We got a lot of wrecks around here. Wrecks, and a few houses that are so nice, nobody can afford them. But mostly wrecks."

She sighed. "Yeah, we can't afford the nice ones, so we've settled for a crappy one. Maybe if we're lucky, someday we'll be able to make it nice. But between you and me, I'm not holding my breath."

"Aw, come on. With a little time and money, you can fix practically anything," he protested. "There's life in the neighborhood yet, you'll see."

"I believe you, but this house is going to take a lot more than a little time and a little money. If we had a dump truck full of both, I'm not sure we could save it." She paused, suddenly afraid that she was being insulting. This guy obviously lived here. She didn't want to dump all over his home turf. She backpedaled a little. "We'll do our best, but I don't know."

Mike came around the corner pushing a rusty half-sized shopping cart. It was loaded up with extension cords, a massive bargain-sized box of trash bags, a roll of plumber's tape, two big bundles of rags, a pair of scrapers, and five or six boxes of light bulbs. "Hey girl, you ready?"

"That was fast." She reached into the bottom tray and picked up her cold bottle of soda.

Mike glanced at Norman, nodded, and turned the cart toward the counter.

"I'm right behind you," she promised him. Then she told Norman, "That's my stepdad."

"He looks . . . ready to light up half of New Orleans. How big is your house, that you need so many bulbs?"

"Kind of big," she admitted. Then she inserted herself into Mike's sad story about the burned finger. "And we only have, like, two bulbs that actually work. We were moving one of them around last night, from room to room."

Norman shook his head sadly. "That is just freakin' tragic."

She snorted a small laugh, right out her nose. "Like I said, we've got a lot of work to do."

"Anyway, it was nice to meet you . . . ?"

"Denise. Sorry. I'm Denise."

"All right, Denise. Catch you around."

"Yeah, it was nice to um . . . to meet you too. You're the first person I've met, actually. Since we got here." Did she sound weird? She thought she sounded weird.

"Cool. Do I win a prize?"

"My undying . . ." She stopped herself. Her undying what? Gratitude? Affection? Nothing sounded right, so she let it go with, ". . . remembrance."

He winked, and reached into his pocket for some change for the machine. "Hey, I'll take it."

Before she could embarrass herself any worse, she fled for the counter and caught Mike as he was checking out. When they were finished paying, she helped him load up the car. All the while, he very studiously avoided asking any questions. Denise couldn't stand it, so when they were inside the Kia and the doors were shut, she broke the ice. "Since I know you're dying to ask, his name is Norman. He swapped me out a decent dollar for one of your crummy dollars."

"Look at you, making friends already."

"Dude, I'll probably never see that guy again."

"He's a cute kid, though."

She rolled her eyes and leaned her head back against the seat. "Please do not ever call any guy cute again. You're making it weird. Weirder. I already made it weird enough."

"Okay, okay. I'll try to keep from making it weirder. You've obviously got that part under control."

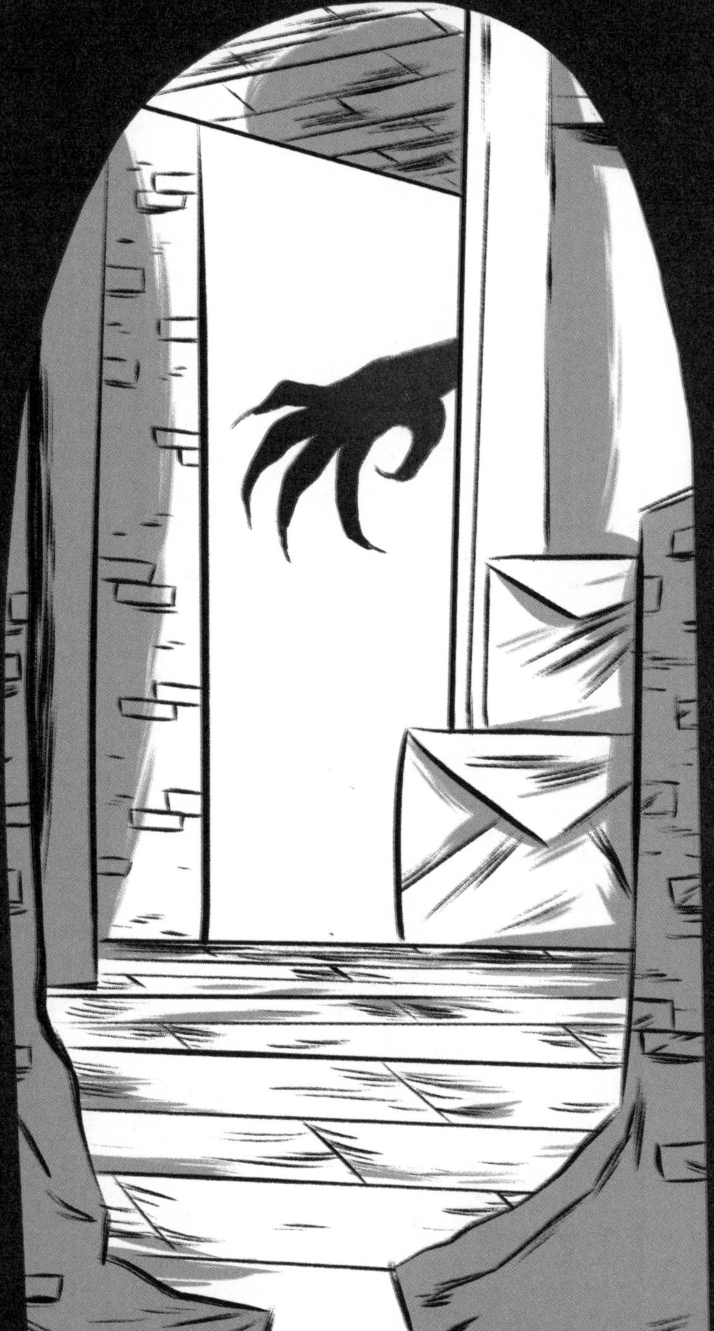

# CHAPTER THREE

The electrician came around later that day. She went on for fifteen minutes about how ancient the house's wiring was, and how many expensive-sounding code violations they would have to fix eventually — but then she flipped some breakers, tested some wires, rearranged some connections, replaced some fuses . . . and restored power to the second story of the Agony House.

Sure, they'd need another week's worth of electrical work before too long, but hey. It was a start.

With AC now wafting weakly through all the rooms, livable and unlivable alike, the small family sat down to another fast-food meal. They'd cleared out the dining room and set up the left-behind chairs, and it almost looked like civilized people lived there. The sun was going down; there was light enough to see by, but when the shadows stretched out long and low, Mike pulled out a lamp and plugged it in.

They all sat around feeling fat and almost happy, leaning back in those spindly seats and licking the last bits of chicken grease from their fingers, until Sally gestured with a french fry and warned, "You two know it won't always be like this, don't you? Enjoy the junk food now, because I'm going shopping tomorrow. We'll have real meals on a regular schedule, like normal."

Denise asked, "Will we ever get the kitchen to . . . I don't know. Work?"

"Oh, come on. It's not that bad in there," her mother scoffed. "For Chrissake, honey — it's no worse than that place on Elgin Street."

Mike frowned quizzically. He'd never seen the Elgin house.

Denise told him, "We only lived there for a year, after Mom lost that job — when the restaurant folded. It was pretty bad."

"When was this?"

She shrugged. "Not long before she met you."

It wasn't the world's most romantic meeting — trapped in a stalled and sweltering METRO light-rail train, waiting for the service crews to let them out. But love grows in the strangest places, like a bluebell on a cow pie. Or so her new Uncle James had declared in the best man's toast, when he'd recalled the story for the sake of the audience.

"No, it was at least a couple of years before Mike," her mother insisted. "Because after Elgin, we ended up a few miles away, on Burkett — and that wasn't much better, but at least it was clean. After that, we lucked into that place in Old Chinatown. That one wasn't so bad."

"What she means to say, Mike, is that we've lived in some real dumps."

Sally and Mike spoke at exactly the same time. She said, "It's not a dump!" and he said, "It won't be a dump forever!" They turned and giggled at each other like they'd done something cute.

Denise rolled her eyes. "But *look* at all this. It can't be healthy . . . ?" she tried, using a straw to point at the holes, the stains, and the dark patches they hadn't gotten to yet, all of them probably made of deathly black mold. She was sure of it.

Sally said, "We'll make it healthy. We'll do the big stuff first — the rewiring and plumbing, and then the roof. The rest of it, we can do ourselves with some elbow grease."

"And money."

Like her mom needed reminding. The loan had come with funds to fix the place up and trick it out as a proper business, ready to host and feed out-of-towners, but the money would come in bits and pieces, gradually doled out as the house was brought up to code. They could only have a chunk of it at a time. It was supposed to protect the bank from a risky investment, but it felt like a dirty trick.

"We have *some* money," Sally insisted.

Denise pushed. "But is it *enough* money?"

"It's always enough, baby. One way or another. It's always enough."

"Technically you're right. I mean, in the sense that we haven't died of starvation or exposure. Yet."

Mike laughed at the pair of them. "Denise, if your mom wanted to whip this house into shape all by herself, I do believe she could. But it's not just her, all by herself with a little girl anymore. Now it's us, all together. Three adults, more or less."

"Um, I'm eight months shy of 'adult,'" Denise pointed out. "I have eight more months to screw up big-time, and still get off as a juvenile."

Sally shook her head with mock exasperation. "What a terrible way to look at a birthday."

"It's a perfectly practical way of looking at it," she argued.

Mike rose from his seat and wadded up his trash, then stuffed it into the takeout bag. "I hope you aren't planning a last-minute crime spree. When college applications ask about your extracurricular activities, they don't mean armed robbery."

"Courts seal juvenile records, you know."

"Yeah, and I wish you *didn't*." Sally gathered her own trash and produced a plastic garbage bag to collect it all. "Here, give me your stuff. We've sat around on our butts long enough."

Together they picked up after supper, and Mike produced a speaker set for his iPhone. That could only mean one thing: a terrible evening of music that quit making the radio rounds before Denise was born. He hunkered over the screen and scrolled through his playlist.

"Mike, I love you, man — but it's been a long day, and I can't handle whatever weird old stuff you're queuing up."

"Aw, you love me?"

"Well, I like you enough to let you stay . . . but I've gotta go work on my room. Y'all have fun down here, doing the fox-trot or peace-ing out, or whatever it is you old folks do when I'm not looking."

Denise headed for the big box of cleaning supplies in the kitchen. She rummaged through it and made her selections, tossing them into the bucket. She snagged the broom too. She tucked it under her arm and stomped up the stairs, flipping light switches as she went.

It was getting good and dark outside, and after twilight, the second floor hallway was practically a tomb. It had nothing to let in natural light except a small window at the far end, so even in the middle of the day with all the doors open, it was pretty bleak. Once the sun went down, you were screwed without a lamp.

The fixture over the stairs worked, or it mostly worked. It was a square glass shade that housed four bulbs, but only one was lit up. Another lamp at the far end of the hall sputtered and warmed, but it mostly just hung out on the ceiling looking sad and yellow.

Downstairs, Mike found his groove and turned it up, sending shouty 1980s white-guy hip-hop drifting up the stairs.

Denise didn't know the group, and she was entirely unprepared to admit that it sounded kind of fun, so she disappeared into her room. The ceiling fan came on when she flipped the switch. The fan had space for three bulbs in three flower-shaped glass shades. Two of the three beat the odds and lit up on cue.

The room looked better by the dim, fuzzy light of the old-fashioned incandescent bulbs — but only a little. It was harder to see the dust bunnies and cobwebs without the sun streaming in, but Denise wasn't fooled. She still knew that it was the best of the worst, and that was all.

She heard a chime and felt a buzzing in her shorts.

She jumped like she'd been shocked, then fumbled her phone out of her back pocket. "Trish!" she yelped. The text message read: **NEW DIGS HOT OR NOT LOL?** Before she could unlock the phone for a reply, a second one landed on its heels: **y so quiet ru ok?**

Her thumbs got into gear, and she hastily replied: *I'm quiet? Haven't heard from u since I left.*

**liarpants,** quoth Tricia. **Oh wait my phone is**

Denise sat down on the floor cross-legged, and tapped back: *ur phone is???*

**I have like 50 texts dint go thru sry**

She smiled down at the screen. *Thought you didn't love me anymore.*

Then she leaned back against the wall and tried not to think of how grimy it was, or how the plaster was soft with water and mold. She settled down instead and thumb-typed at lightning speed — giving Trish a quick rundown on the move, and the heat, and the house she was now forced to call home. Then she mentioned Norman, named for an aunt. Since he was the only person she'd met so far, and she was running out of subjects that didn't sound like whining.

It was a relief to talk to anybody back in familiar old Texas, even if talking was just keyboard swiping, and trying to win a game of Who Can Find the Most Ridiculous Emoji. Poop-coil in a party hat with fireworks usually won, but Trish showed up with a brown beard smoking a cigar and holding a martini glass, and Denise admitted defeat.

*How's Kieron? Is he ok or still weird?* she asked as an afterthought.

**Not as weird as ur super-proper texts but still weird. I hrd he has a new gurl.**

*Super-proper, but u alwys understand me.* She hit SEND before either she or autocorrect caught the typo, and scowled at it, but she refused to be embarrassed about cautious texting. She'd once read about a court case that happened over a comma in a contract. You could never be too careful.

**Did u read me? Kieron has a new um-friend. Like this is my, um, friend.**

She didn't really care, but she was curious. *ORLY?*

**Sophomore. 2 young 2 no better I guess.**

Denise laughed. *She'll learn.*

**So tell me about this house of yours its haunted as crap, right**

Her thumbs hovered over the screen. She thought about mentioning the attic door, but that'd be silly. It hadn't been anything at all. What would she say? "I opened a door and it smelled bad." That wasn't a ghost story, and Trish wanted a ghost story.

*Haunted as crap*, she typed in return. *Crappy as crap, 4 sure.*

PICS OR GET OUT

She realized she hadn't taken any. She hadn't thought about it, or hadn't wanted to. Maybe in the back of her head, she was too embarrassed at the thought of anybody else seeing this place, and knowing she lived there. But she really ought to take some in the light of day — for the sake of a good before-and-after, if it all worked out someday. Or to show how narrowly she'd escaped death by debris, if it didn't.

*Don't have any.*

SNAP ME SOME. DOO EET.

*Later*, she promised. She wasn't sure if she meant it or not. *Busy right now. Unpacking. Getting my bedroom set up.*

OK BUT L8R

*I PROMISE*

When Trish didn't respond in a few seconds, she put the phone aside. Their chat had run on long enough, and the phone's battery was low — so Denise pulled the charger cord out of the messenger bag she typically used for a purse. Of the three outlets in her room, only one worked, and it took her a few minutes to find it. She chalked it up to one more thing on the list of Things That Suck About the Agony House.

Maybe she really should keep a list . . . or maybe she should make some effort to have a life, because keeping track of all the house's failings could turn into a full-time job. Technically, she could afford a part-time job. Summer had just begun.

But where would she work? Doing what? The house was sure to eat her life for the next couple of months.

Besides, come fall she'd be headed for that school they'd passed earlier today. It was one of New Orleans's new "recovery zone" charter schools, where she wouldn't know a single soul.

She sat down beside the phone and leaned her head back against the wall. She hated the thought of a new school for her senior year. It made all the celebration of her PreACT and PSAT scores feel moot. Her stellar numbers and top-notch grades had brought some great college recruiters sniffing around, but their offers would all depend on good scores on the real thing and a strong finishing GPA. Would this year be a string of easy A grades, or would it be a miserable slog that felt like a personal vendetta?

Nothing was in the bag just yet. Like her old gymnastics coach used to say, she still had to stick the landing.

She was glad to see her mom happy — she truly was, and not even in a bitter way. It felt like it had been Sally and Denise Versus the World since forever, since the Storm. But it also felt like someone had pitched a grenade into her life now, right when she was finally building up some momentum. Now it was time to start all over again.

"This is going to suck," she told the ceiling.

The ceiling didn't argue with her.

She closed her eyes and listened to the bouncy music playing downstairs, dulled by the floorboards but chipper-sounding all the same. Mike said something, but Denise couldn't make it out. Her mother laughed, and the music played on. They were definitely happy, and that was something.

It would've been really, really great if Denise got to be happy too, but she already knew the world didn't work that way. Sometimes, you had to take turns.

She gave up and got up, and used the duster to swab the fourth corner clean of spiderwebs. One spider took offense, and scuttled across the ceiling — disappearing into a crack in the plaster. Then she took the broom for a half-hearted spin around the floor, but she hadn't brought a dustpan with her, so she just turned off the box fan and swept all the dust and junk out into the hall. "Screw it," she said to the puff of debris as it settled on the floor. "Nobody cares, anyway."

The fixture at the top of the stairs rattled as if offended. Denise frowned at it, but it kept jiggling anyway — like someone was jumping up and down on the floor above it. But no one was up there in the attic, or that's what she assured herself because she sure as hell wasn't about to go look.

The glass shade trembled, and the lone illuminated bulb twitched in its socket. It flared, sparked, and went out with an angry poof.

The hallway dimmed. At the other end of the corridor, the lone yellow bulb was so dull that you could hardly tell if it was on or not. The rest of the light filtered up from downstairs or out from Denise's bedroom. She stood in the doorway, holding the broom and casting a narrow shadow onto the dirty carpet runner.

Without the weak light from the fixture, the hall felt close and crowded.

Denise listened hard, focusing on some faint noise that played above Mike's music, or around it: a low-pitched buzzing, like the sound another failing bulb (or a wasp) would make. No, not that. Not exactly. A vague rushing, like water running from a tap.

No, not that, either.

It was both quieter and more deliberate — and when Denise closed her eyes, she thought she heard a woman humming a song. She couldn't make out the tune, not with Mike's music going to town downstairs, and her mother talking and laughing. They were dancing in the parlor, she thought. Their feet were circling, jumping. Playing hopscotch with the holes in the floor.

Maybe that's all it was, rattling the lamp — only the newlyweds, being happy together.

The discordant humming grew louder, and the song came clearer — but she didn't recognize it. Was it her mother, singing along to the wrong track? She didn't think so. Louder and louder, and this wasn't Sally's voice at all. This wasn't what it sounded like when she murmured a lullaby, or the lyrics to something old and dorky.

Denise opened her eyes and the humming stopped. Just like that.

She blinked hard, and rubbed her knuckles against her eyelids. The weird singing was gone, but it'd left something behind: There, on the floor, in the dust she'd cast out of her bedroom . . . a very distinct set of marks had appeared. They marched in delicate pairs — footprints, too small to be a man's, and not small enough to be a child's. They came from the top of the stairs.

No, that wasn't true. They came from the attic door, and they pattered right up to Denise, stopping in front of her — not eight inches away from the tips of her toes.

No, that wasn't true, either. When she turned around she saw that the footprints kept going, the pointed shapes strolling into her bedroom, tracking the dust back from where it'd come.

And then vanishing.

Denise's gaze went wild, back and forth from the attic door to the bedroom — where there wasn't any dust to leave any tracks, and there wasn't anybody standing, singing a song. The room was as empty as before, and there was nowhere to hide. Only a few boxes were stacked, and those were against the wall. The closet was full of hanging clothes, and it still didn't have a door. "A door," she whispered hoarsely. It was a frantic thought, and she held it like a tiny lifeline of rational truth. "I need a door."

She needed a lot of things. She needed a glass of water and a shower. She needed to assemble her bed frame, unless she wanted to keep sleeping on a mattress and box spring flat on the floor — and maybe she *did* want to sleep that way, just for the night. When the bed was on the floor, there was nothing underneath it. When the bed was on the ground, there was nowhere for anybody to hide — even an invisible, softly singing anybody who left behind a funny smell. Not a bad one. Just a funny one.

Denise sniffed for clues and picked up something sharp but sweet. It could've been the scent of cleaning products, perhaps, or the bottle of shower gel she'd left beside the tub. The bathroom door was open, right around the corner.

She sniffed again.

No, it wasn't gardenia soap lingering in the air. It smelled more like roses, mixed with something else. Some kind of perfume, something an old lady would spritz all over herself before heading to church.

So it could've been worse, right? If you were stuck with a ghost, better a nice old church-going lady ghost than a violent murdering poltergeist. I mean, if you got to pick. Did she get to pick?

Denise glared around the room, silently daring any hypothetical spirits — old ladies or otherwise — to show themselves. She didn't really want to see a ghost; but maybe the ghosts didn't really want to see her, either.

The music downstairs played on, and the ceiling fan overhead churned — stirring the warmish air that was only half cooled by the feeble AC that struggled against the sheer volume of hot air. The house held on to it stubbornly. It was holding its breath.

Denise held hers too.

It wasn't late and she wasn't tired. She had boxes to unpack and a bed to make, even if she wasn't going to touch the frame still lying in pieces along the far wall. For one more night, she could sleep on the floor, couldn't she?

Just this one night, she could sleep knowing that nothing lurked beneath her.

# CHAPTER FOUR

The next morning, Denise came downstairs to Sally talking on the phone with one of the contractors, who was asking her a bunch of questions. "I'm not sure . . . ? Where would I look? Is that important? I couldn't tell from the fuse box."

While she nattered on, Denise joined Mike in the dining room, where he was tackling the mold they had seen the night before.

"I don't even know what to do next," she declared. Despite all their cleaning efforts, everything still felt filthy, and everything needed to be removed, replaced, or restored.

"We just have to keep plugging away," he said. "If it's broken or rotted, pull it out. Throw it away. Start yanking wallpaper — that's one of those things that'll take forever, and you might as well get started now. When you're done with that, move on to that bathroom upstairs. We're going to save the tub, but we have to clean the crap out of it first."

"Please let it be figurative crap, and not literal crap."

"I doubt anyone's been crapping in the tub, honey. It's just dirty as hell. We'll get some enamel repair stuff later. I'll put it on the list for our next trip to the store. But those shelves behind the tub are awful. Get a sledgehammer and take them down. While you're at it, let me know when you want to wreck the vanity. None of that stuff is original, and it's all too gross to keep."

"Why do I have to let you know before I sledge the vanity?"

"Because I'll need to turn off the water first. You smash it now, and you'll get a geyser — so please . . . *don't.*"

Resigned, Denise collected the cleaning supplies and grabbed a bucket. "Fine. I'll see what else can be done about my room, and then I'll move on to the bathroom."

"Thanks, trooper."

She felt more like a hostage than a trooper, but if she was going to be trapped in this place, she might as well clean it up. The only thing worse than being stuck in a craphole was being stuck in a dirty craphole.

She still didn't know where to start. She needed a plan of attack. Maybe there was more to be done on her bedroom? She could check the closet, which was full of . . . she wrinkled her nose. Spiderwebs, mostly. She'd gotten all four corners with the broom, but not the closet.

Back downstairs she went, and found the Shop-Vac, which would probably work better than a broom. Loudly she announced, "This Shop-Vac is coming with me!" because she didn't know where either of her parents were.

From the kitchen, her mom yelled, "Good to know!" Then she went back to her phone call.

Mike was outside. She saw him through the sidelight windows that flanked the front door. He was directing a truck that was hauling the dumpster, which should've arrived yesterday, but at least it'd arrived eventually.

There was no one else to protest, so the Shop-Vac was officially hers. For now.

It was a pain to get it upstairs, but it was 100 percent worth the trouble. The tall nozzle end reached up into the corners to get the very last of the dust bunnies and cobwebs, and she used the wide head attachment to do a proper job of vacuuming — probably the first one the room had gotten in years.

When she was done, the floor felt less like sandpaper and more like wood, and the last of the creepy footprints were completely gone. Like they'd never been there at all.

(It was easy to pretend they'd never been there at all.)

She was just thinking that the wallpaper was too daunting, and it might be time to move on to the bathroom, when Sally knocked on the doorframe. "Heads up," she called. "You have a visitor."

She frowned and put her hands on her hips. "I have a what-now?"

"You heard me." Over her shoulder, she added, "Come on in, honey. Denise, this is Terry Jones. He's our neighbor, down the street."

Her visitor was a freckled white boy with a glorious red 'fro. He was a little shorter than her, and a little heavy. "Hi, Denise!" he said perkily. "I'm Terry. Terry Jones. Your neighbor."

"I . . . yeah. I remember. From just now. When my mom said it."

Terry was wearing a sweaty yellow T-shirt and cargo shorts with sagging pockets. "I wanted to introduce myself, that's all. Since we're neighbors and everything."

"It's um . . . it's nice to meet you," she told him.

"Likewise." He was angling to get a good look at her room, and being none too discreet about it.

She sighed. "You can come on in, if you want."

Sally made a quiet exit, and Terry strolled inside, his flip-flops slapping loudly on the floor. Over his shoulder, he lugged a large backpack that bowed his posture with the weight of its contents.

"Man, would you look at this place!" he announced, or exclaimed, or maybe he just said everything like it thrilled him.

"Yeah, check out my five-star accommodations." She didn't get up from her spot on the mattress "Behold the peeling paint, and the plaster falling off the ceiling. You ought to see the Yelp reviews."

"Oh, please. My room is just like this, without the tall ceiling and the big fan. You're lucky," he told her. "This is the neatest house on the block."

"It's the *only* house on the block."

"Okay, then it's the neatest house in the neighborhood."

"Have you seen the whole neighborhood?" she asked.

"Most of it." Terry roamed her room like a robot vacuum, bumping off boxes and furniture. "Some of the houses are like this one." He paused to look out over the driveway where Sally's car was parked. He looked back at Denise. "But some of them have been restored, and not *good* restored. I like them better like this."

"What do you mean, 'good restored'?"

He admired the window seat covered in boxes with a hearty, "Mm, nice." Then he said, "Most flippers gut them, and put in whatever shiny junk is popular right now. They don't pay any attention to what the house wants, or what looks nice inside it. My friend Dominique calls them 'Things White People Like' houses. But you guys aren't going to do that, are you?"

"We definitely don't have the money for shiny junk, but eventually my mom wants to open up for business. Maybe we'll go shabby chic out of necessity."

"Good, good." He nodded, and dragged his fingers across the windowsill. Denise was glad it wasn't covered in dust and spiderwebs anymore. "My dad says it's a tragedy, every time they gut a place like this. He says it's a crime against history."

Denise wanted to offer him some hand sanitizer, but she didn't have any. "So . . . did you just come over here to look around inside the house?"

"Yep," he admitted frankly. "I've wanted to see inside for ages, but it was boarded up pretty good. I couldn't find a crowbar big enough to pry anything loose — not by myself."

"I'm sorry, are you saying . . . ?"

"I *didn't* break in."

"But you tried. That's what I'm taking away from this conversation."

He thought about it and shrugged. He set his overloaded backpack on the floor and straightened up, leaning his neck from left to right, and producing a good crack. "What do you care? It wasn't your house. Now that it belongs to somebody again, I knocked. No crowbars, see?"

"I don't know. Your backpack is looking kind of fat—you could have a crowbar in there for all I know."

"It's just schoolbooks, mostly."

She frowned at him, puzzled but not upset. "Are you in summer school?"

"No, but some of the teachers offer summer tutoring, over at the trailer lot. I stay late on Tuesdays and Thursdays, and help the PE lady load up her stuff. She brings soccer kits and basketballs, that kind of thing. For the kids whose homes haven't come back yet."

"Haven't come back . . . ?"

"They took the FEMA trailers out of the park and put the baseball field back in it, but that don't mean everybody's got a real roof over their heads yet. So anyway, I was walking home, and I have to go right past your place, and I thought I'd see if anyone was here. And if anyone would let me in. And if I could look around. Your mom asked if I was here to see you, so I just rolled with it."

"You're a weird one, Terry."

"I wear it as a badge of honor."

"You might as well. You um . . . you mentioned a dad. Do your parents know where you are right now?"

He sat down on the floor and unzipped his bag, then started poking through it. "I have a dad, and no mom anymore. Dad's an EMT, and he works third shift. Unless somebody tells him otherwise, he assumes I'm home safe."

"Maybe someone should have a word with him. What are you . . . Terry, what are you doing?"

"Looking for my digital recorder."

"Because . . . ?"

"Because this place is haunted like crazy. Everybody says so," he solemnly assured her. He located an old recorder and brandished it like the key to the city. Its battery compartment was held together with a strip of medical tape, wound around it twice and going gray from all the lint it'd picked up in his bag.

Denise swallowed. She'd almost forgotten the stink from the attic and the door that moved by itself (except that she hadn't), and she'd almost forgotten the old lady perfume, and the humming and the footsteps that went right through her (except she hadn't forgotten those things, either). "What makes everybody think it's haunted?"

"Because somebody famous *died* here."

She sat forward on the bed, idly wishing she could offer him a real seat someplace — but there was no place but the floor for now, or one of the dozen boxes that held her clothes, shoes, and bags that hadn't yet been unpacked. "Oh God, seriously?" She wasn't surprised, but she was definitely horrified. "Who?"

"Some writer, that's what I heard. Can't remember his name."

"Then he must not have been that famous." She flopped backwards, sprawling her arms across the blanket. "Where did he die? How did he die?" For no good reason except a grossed-out suspicion, she flashed a glance toward the hall and the creepy attic door.

Terry continued, fiddling with his gadget. "Don't know. It's just a rumor. Have you seen anything ghostly since you've been here?"

"Of course not." She didn't want to encourage him.

"Then you'll be totally fine giving me a tour of your ghost-free home, while I run my recorder and ask questions."

"Now you want to interview me?"

"Not *you*. You don't know anything. I'm going to ask the ghosts, and see if they're willing to communicate."

"With an old digital recorder?"

"So what if it's old?" He pressed the power button, and a tiny green light came on. "Old things are great. They're built to last. And things like this . . ." he wiggled it in her direction, ". . . can record things we can't hear."

"Like ghosts. Talking ghosts." *Or humming ghosts,* she did not say.

"Yep." He climbed to his feet and flashed her that undaunted, unrelenting grin of his. "I don't care if you believe me. Heck, it's probably better if you don't. That way, you won't unconsciously interfere with my results."

"You do this kind of thing a lot?"

He vigorously bobbed his head. "Every chance I get. Are you going to show me around, or what?"

"You're going to keep asking until I give up and say yes, aren't you?"

"'Never give up,' that's my motto."

"It ought to be, 'Wear 'em down until they admit defeat.'"

On that note, Denise grudgingly ran Terry through the house — pointing out such highlights as the broken windows, the duct tape repairs of yesteryear, the fixtures that didn't work, and the wasp nest that they still hadn't knocked down yet. Against her will, she started to enjoy herself. After all, here was somebody with an honest interest in the house, somebody who wasn't utterly repulsed by it. If anything, the happy little nerd was enthralled.

All around the second floor, Terry stopped and held up his recorder, asking silly questions. "Are we alone in this house?" "Are you a man or a woman?" "How did you die?"

Denise never heard anything in response, but supposedly, that's what the recorder was for.

She wrapped up the tour back at her bedroom, since they'd gotten a little warm just hiking around from floor to floor. They took a minute and cooled off under the ceiling fan while Terry went through his voice recordings — revealing nothing new as far as Denise could tell. Just awkward pauses and fuzzy static.

"Get anything good?" she asked, for the sake of being polite.

"I can't tell yet. Hey, what about that skinny door, on the far side of the staircase?"

It should've been easy for Denise to say, "Oh, it's just the attic. No big deal." Instead, she froze.

He crinkled both his lips and eyebrows. "What? Did you see something? Did I say something wrong?"

"No. It's just the door to the attic — on the other side, there's a little corridor with some stairs."

"Have you been up there?"

She sniffed with derision. "No. It's too gross. Nothing but bugs and dust and the corpses of rats or possums or raccoons."

"If you've never been there, how would you know?"

She cooked up a fib on the fly. "My mom and Mike checked it out. They said I shouldn't go up there, because it isn't safe. They're going to pay someone to clean it out, and get rid of all the nasty stuff."

Terry's eyes narrowed down to tiny, skeptical slits. He leaned out into the hall. "Hey, Mrs. Cooper!" he called at the top of his lungs. "Is it okay if me and Denise go see what's up in the attic?"

A reply wafted up from downstairs. "Knock yourselves out. Be careful, though. Okay? It's not super safe. Holler if you need help!"

"Yes ma'am!"

It was Denise's turn to dole out the ol' squint-eye. "Terry?"

"Uh-huh?"

"You're a jerk."

"Yeah, but I'm a jerk who's going upstairs. Are you coming with me, or are you chicken?"

"That is a logical fallacy, because those are *not* my only two options," she insisted, but all the same, she followed him out.

He went directly to the too-tall, too-narrow door and yanked it open.

She waited for a cloud of dust and doom and terrible smells to roll out into the hallway, but it didn't. Not this time. This time, she saw nothing but grimy stairs, and smelled nothing but mildew and staleness.

"I don't see what the big deal is," he fussed.

"Me either," she countered. "I can't imagine why you want to go up there."

"Does this light work?" He flipped the switch on the wall, back and forth, and on the third try a light bulb somewhere in the distant beyond fizzled to life. It didn't do much to brighten the stairwell, but Terry was determined to take it as encouragement. (As far as Denise could tell, he took *everything* as encouragement.) He thrust his recorder ahead, and before he climbed onto the first step, he asked, "Are there any spirits in this house?"

Without waiting for an answer he started up the stairs — leaving Denise to trail behind him. Hey, at least he was going first.

She let him take a pretty big lead — *not* because she was chicken, but because she didn't want his butt jiggling around in her face. She also didn't want him falling down backwards and taking her out like a bowling pin. The stairs were narrow and steep, and they were only meant for one person at a time.

She didn't know much about Terry yet, but she was pretty darn sure he didn't have her gymnastics background.

When Terry was near enough to the top that she couldn't see his feet anymore, Denise took a deep breath and brought up the rear. She stretched out her arms and put one hand on each wall, using it to support herself as she climbed.

Up she went, counting the steps . . . one, two, three . . . and listening to Terry articulate his questions with the speed and precision of a kindergarten teacher explaining vowels to five-year-olds. "Can you tell me your name?" Four . . . five . . . six . . . "Did you die in this house?" Seven . . . eight . . . nine. "Man, I wish I had the money for an EMF meter."

Denise passed the struggling light bulb and reached the top of the stairs. It should've been a relief; it should've come with a sense of accomplishment. But it only came with a muggy, hot cloud of mold-speckled air. "What's an EMF meter?" she asked him.

"It's a tool that measures electromagnetic activity. Sometimes you can detect spikes, when there are spirits present." Then, more to himself than to her, he added, "While I'm wishing for toys, I'd love a laser thermometer too. That's a —"

"I can figure that one out on my own, thanks."

The afternoon sun was orange and sharp through the attic's two round windows. Denise shielded her eyes from the dying westward glow, and Terry waved about in an odd little dance. At first she thought he'd walked through a spiderweb, but it turned out he was only fishing for the string to a light bulb that hung from the center of the tallest vault in the ceiling.

He finally caught the string and pulled it. The bulb clicked on.

The attic was a lumpy and angular space, unfinished and unfit for habitation by man or beast. A scaffold of roof supports crisscrossed above, supporting sheets of plywood — some of which were new, but most of which were a dark, swollen brown that said they'd been soaked down one time too many. The house had five gables, and all five were evident in the swoops and peaks of this impressive overhead space. In some spots, it was easy to stand upright — and you couldn't touch the ceiling, not even if you jumped — but in others, you'd have to crawl.

The floor was not so much a floor as another layer of more plywood, dropped across the ceiling beams of the next level down. It creaked and bent with every step they took.

The air smelled gray and green, sharp and soupy. The attic was at least thirty degrees warmer and much, much moister than Denise's room. She was already sweating through her clothes when she said, "Well, here you go. This is all there is to see. Let's go, please? You could steam rice up here, I swear to God."

He ignored her. "Are we alone in this attic?" he asked the empty space.

As her eyes adjusted to the uneven light, Denise stared around, noting the four chimneys that shot from the floor and went up past the ceiling. Their mortar was crumbled, and their bricks were sagging. A good sneeze would send them scattering, and if it did, maybe the roof would come down too.

She didn't like the thought.

She also didn't like the squishiness of the plywood under her sandals, or the grimy feeling on every inch of her skin, even between her toes. She didn't like the fluffy, rotten look of the insulation between the gaps where the plywood didn't reach. It was a gross shade of yellow, eaten up with what looked like soot or mold. And she *really* didn't like the old hatchet she saw lying under one of the tiny attic windows.

"Um . . . Terry?" She pointed at it.

"So?"

"There's an ax. In the attic."

He gave her a look that said he thought she was an idiot. "How do you think all those people got up on the roofs, when the Storm came? They didn't *all* climb out a window and swim."

"They hacked their way out? Why would so many people have axes in their attics?"

"It wasn't exactly the first hurricane the city ever saw, or the first flooding. Naw." He shook his head. "People learn. They remember. And then they put an ax up in the attic, for next time the water comes around."

She shuddered, feeling worse about the fact that the old bit of hardware wasn't a potential murder weapon. Somehow, its true purpose was even more horrible. "Look, man. It's probably not healthy up here," she warned. "Come on, let's go back downstairs."

Terry ignored her, and asked the attic, "Can you tell us your name?"

A faint puff, just the barest whiff of roses drifted up Denise's nostrils. She flinched, tensed, and looked around — but saw nothing. No footprints. No ghosts. Just Terry, holding up his recorder like the Statue of Liberty's torch.

He fired a hard look at her. "Did you hear that? I heard something, over there, behind you."

"Oh God, do *not* try to creep me out. I will *not* appreciate it."

He stumbled past her, his foot sticking in a seam between two pieces of plywood. He yanked it out and went to the nearest chimney column — the largest of the four. It was almost twice the size of the rest; Denise couldn't be certain which fireplace it served, but she thought it must go down to the big one in the parlor.

He asked, "Do you have a flashlight?"

"Sure," she told him. "Let me just pull one out of my butt."

"I don't want your butt-light, and I don't think . . ." He peered into a corner full of shadows. "I don't think I need it. I see something. There's something back here."

"Please tell me it's not alive. Please tell me it's never *been* alive."

"Not since it was a tree."

She came up behind him, and looked over his shoulder. "What? Oh," she said, intensely thankful to see something so harmless and ordinary stuffed behind the bricks. "It looks like . . . a book?"

He reached in slowly, in case of bugs or bats or anything else that might bite, and pulled out a rectangular brown shape wrapped in layers and layers of crinkly plastic-looking stuff. He unwound the film to reveal a package that was heavier than it appeared.

Something with a multitude of legs scuttled out from between the wrappings, and Terry shrieked. He dropped the book. It landed with a thud, and stirred up a mighty puff of dust that left both kids coughing and wiping at their eyes. When the debris cleared, they could see that the book was wrapped in a final layer that once might've been a garbage bag, or a grocery bag.

They crouched beside it, unwilling to touch anything until they were certain that all resident insects were gone.

Denise extended a finger and picked at the sack until the book slipped loose — a thick, dirty volume, tied up with two loops of twine.

She rubbed a place where she figured a title ought to be, but turned up nothing but a gritty film. Then she tugged at the strings. They came undone easily, and fell aside.

"It's a photo album, or . . . or something." Terry poked at the spine, but it wasn't really a spine. The album wasn't a properly bound book, but a collection of pages that were held together with three rusty metal rings.

Denise slipped her thumb under the front cover and flipped it open.

The topmost page was faded, and the edges were crinkled with age — but the text and illustrations were as bold as if it'd been printed there yesterday.

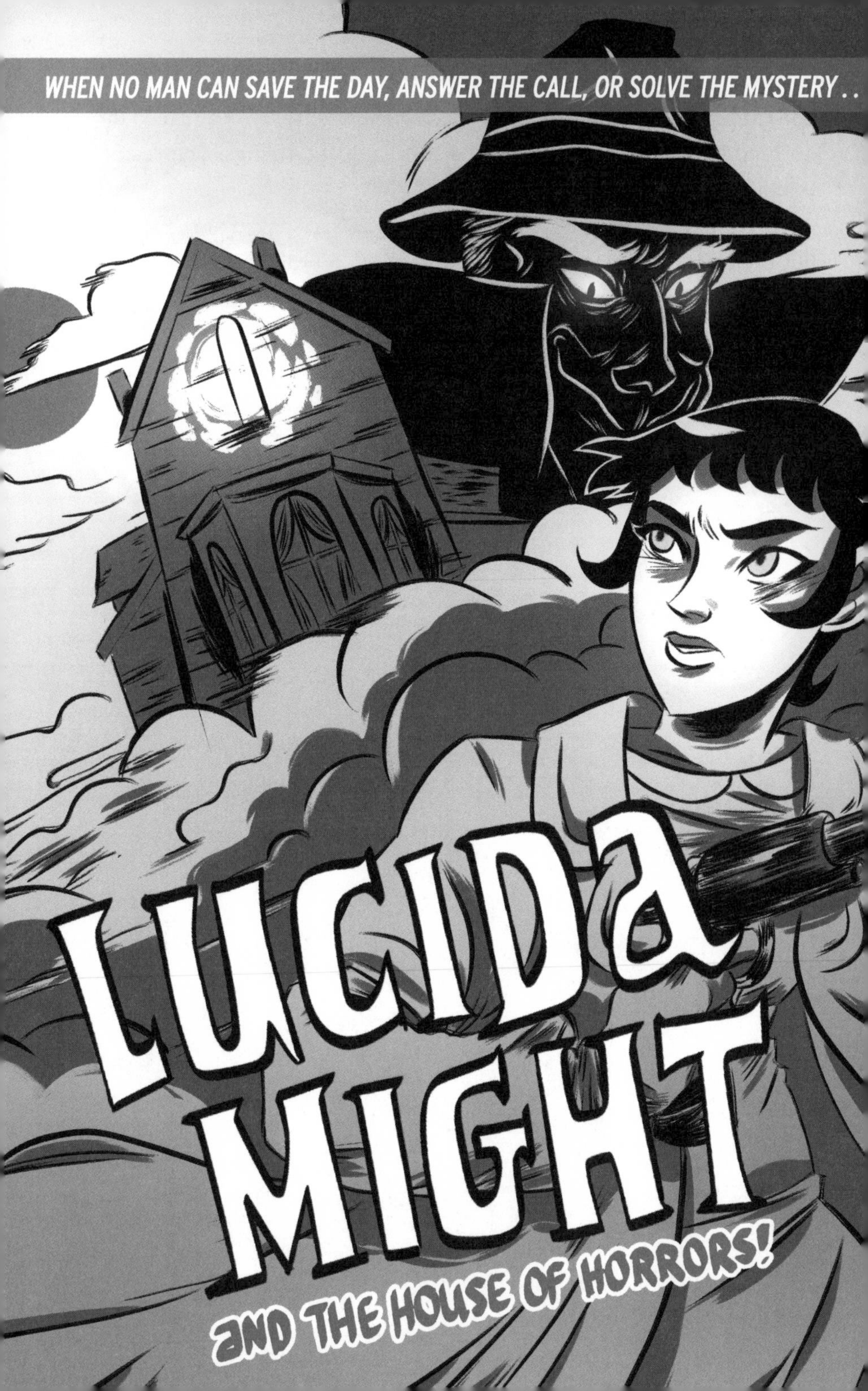
WHEN NO MAN CAN SAVE THE DAY, ANSWER THE CALL, OR SOLVE THE MYSTERY . .
LUCIDA MIGHT
AND THE HOUSE OF HORRORS!

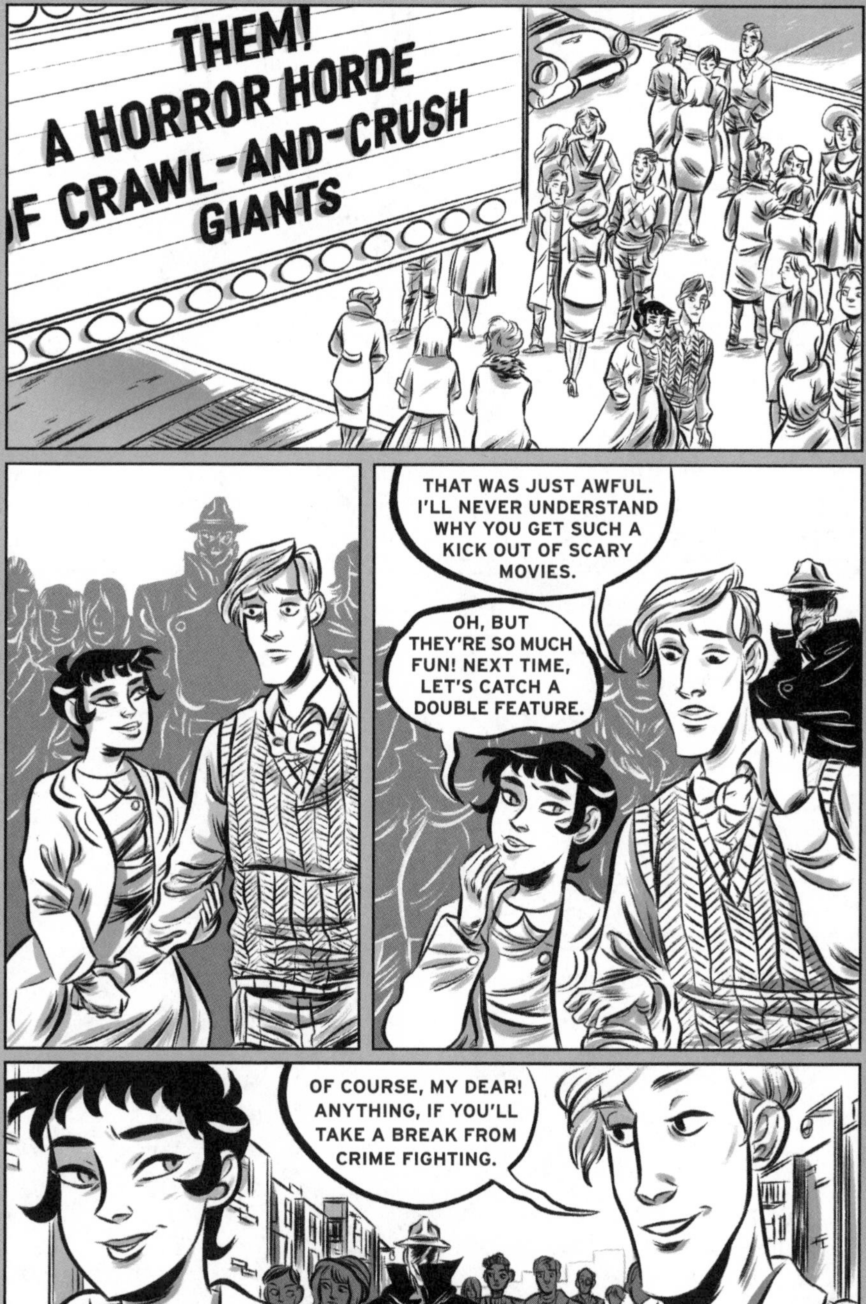
THEM!
A HORROR HORDE
OF CRAWL-AND-CRUSH
GIANTS
THAT WAS JUST AWFUL. I'LL NEVER UNDERSTAND WHY YOU GET SUCH A KICK OUT OF SCARY MOVIES.
OH, BUT THEY'RE SO MUCH FUN! NEXT TIME, LET'S CATCH A DOUBLE FEATURE.
OF COURSE, MY DEAR! ANYTHING, IF YOU'LL TAKE A BREAK FROM CRIME FIGHTING.

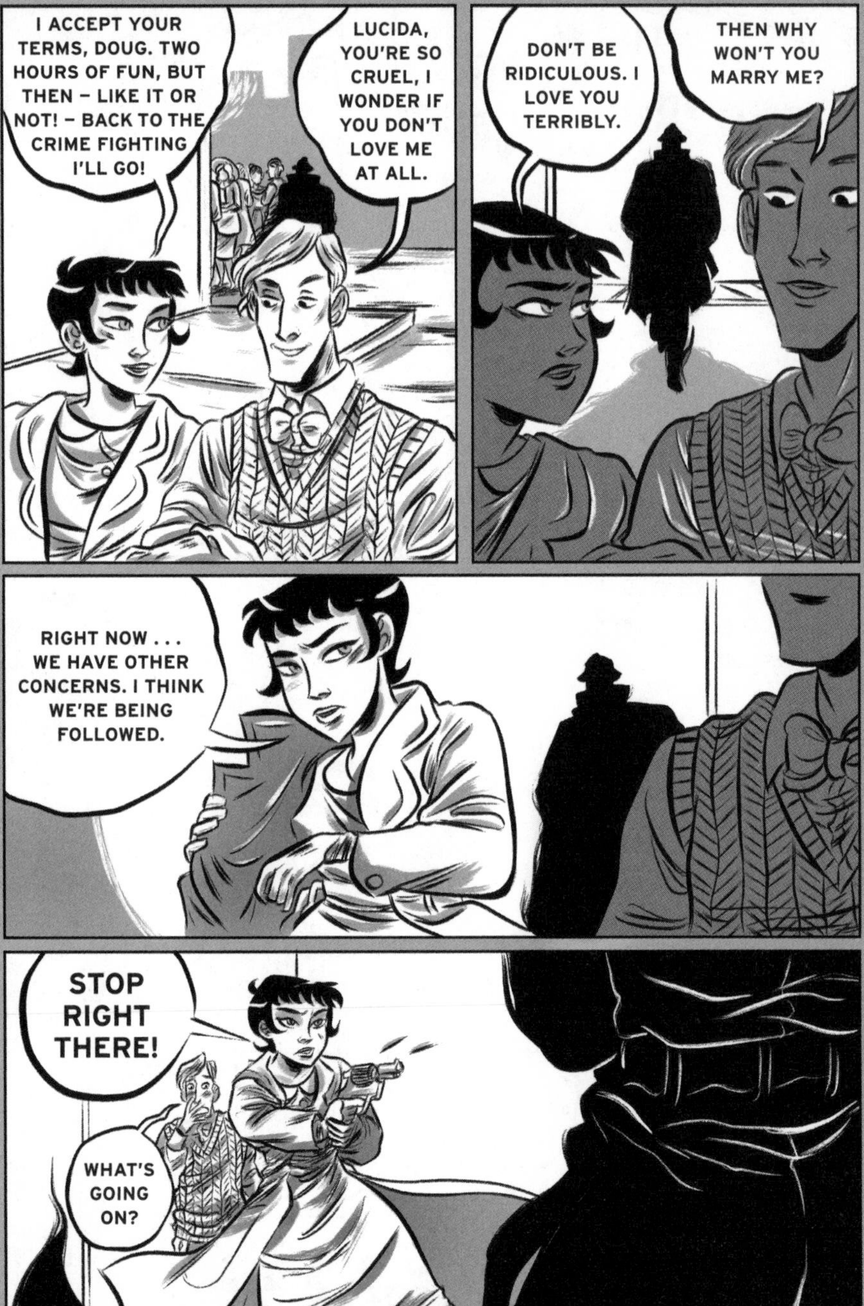
I ACCEPT YOUR TERMS, DOUG. TWO HOURS OF FUN, BUT THEN – LIKE IT OR NOT! – BACK TO THE CRIME FIGHTING I'LL GO!
LUCIDA, YOU'RE SO CRUEL, I WONDER IF YOU DON'T LOVE ME AT ALL.
DON'T BE RIDICULOUS. I LOVE YOU TERRIBLY.
THEN WHY WON'T YOU MARRY ME?
RIGHT NOW . . . WE HAVE OTHER CONCERNS. I THINK WE'RE BEING FOLLOWED.
STOP RIGHT THERE!
WHAT'S GOING ON?

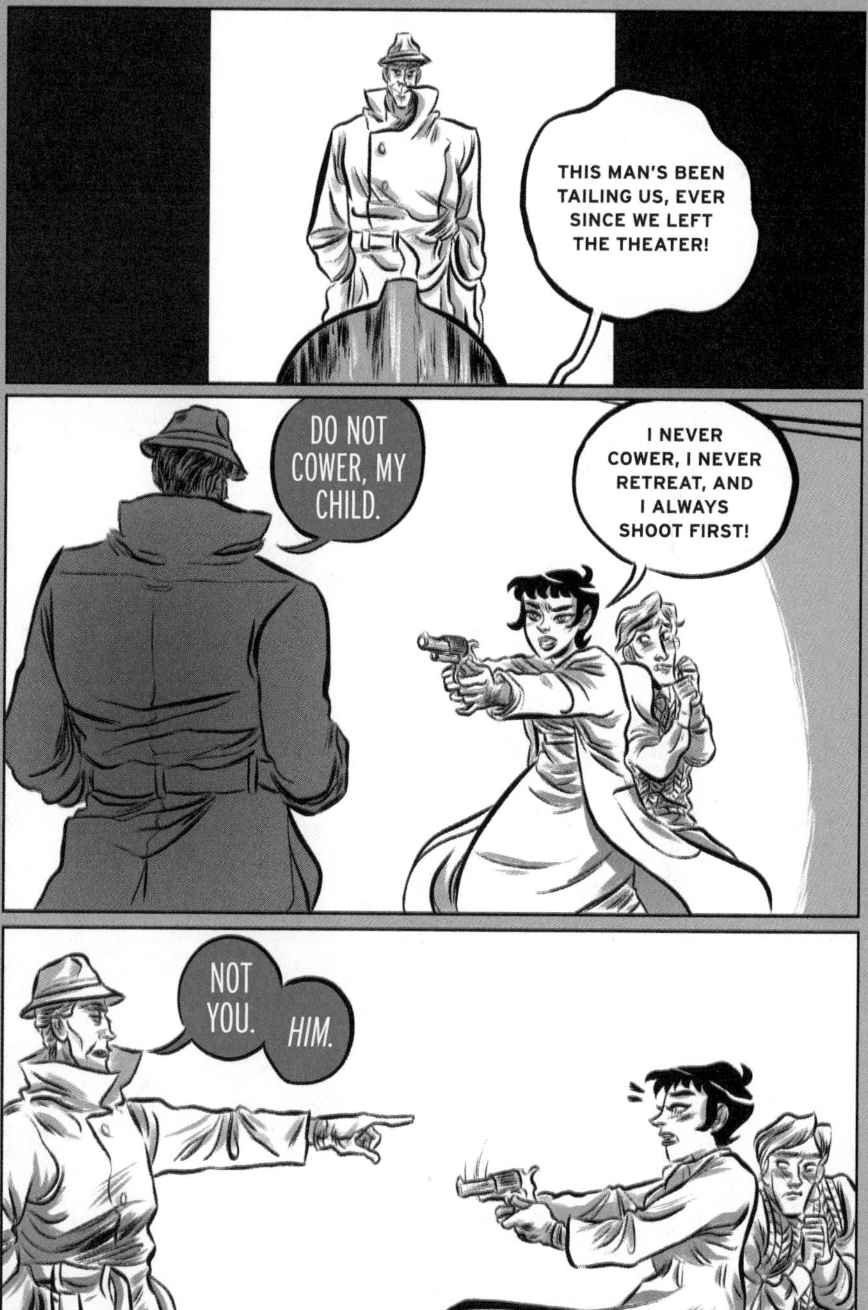
THIS MAN'S BEEN TAILING US, EVER SINCE WE LEFT THE THEATER!
DO NOT COWER, MY CHILD.
I NEVER COWER, I NEVER RETREAT, AND I ALWAYS SHOOT FIRST!
NOT YOU.
*HIM.*

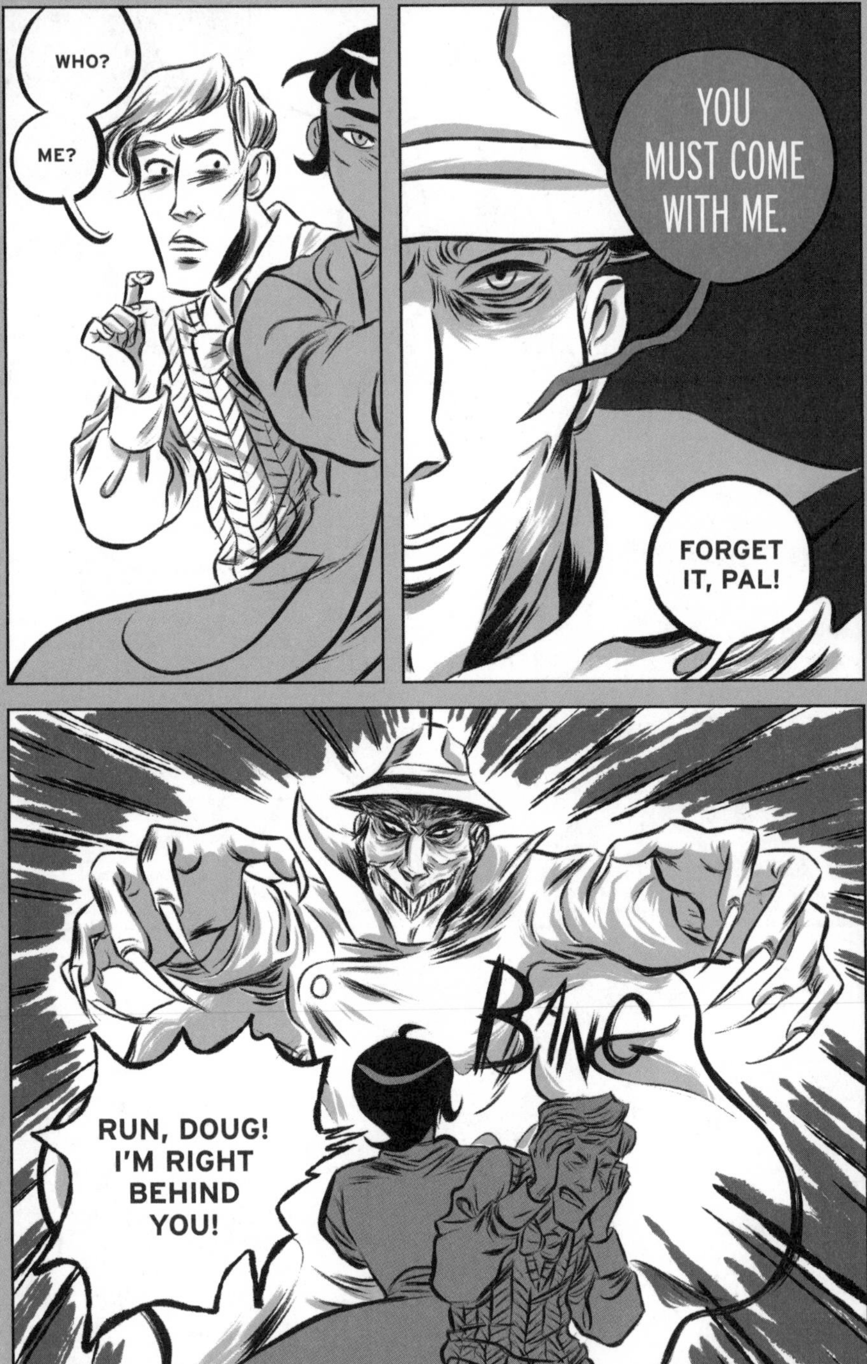
WHO?
ME?
YOU MUST COME WITH ME.
FORGET IT, PAL!
BANG
RUN, DOUG! I'M RIGHT BEHIND YOU!

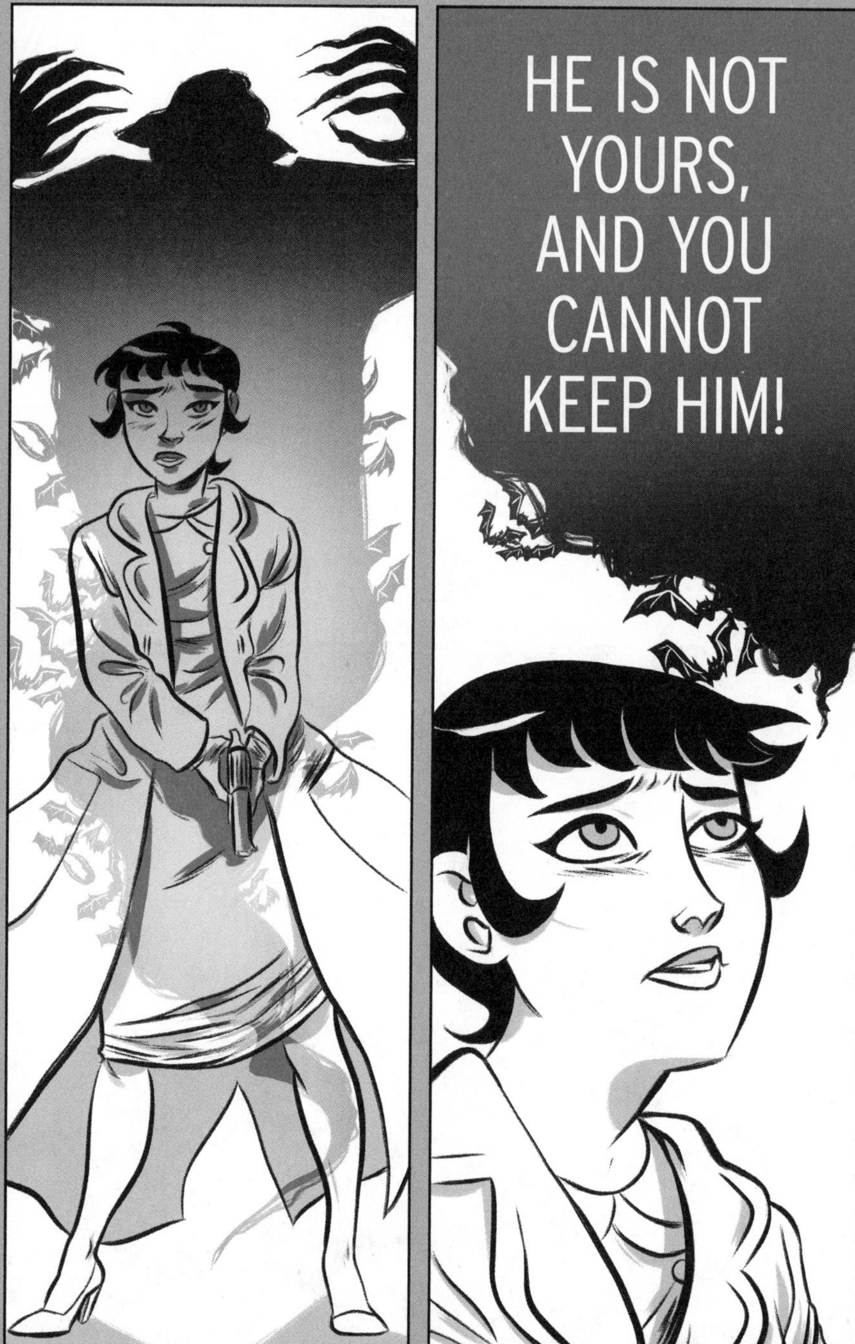
HE IS NOT YOURS, AND YOU CANNOT KEEP HIM!

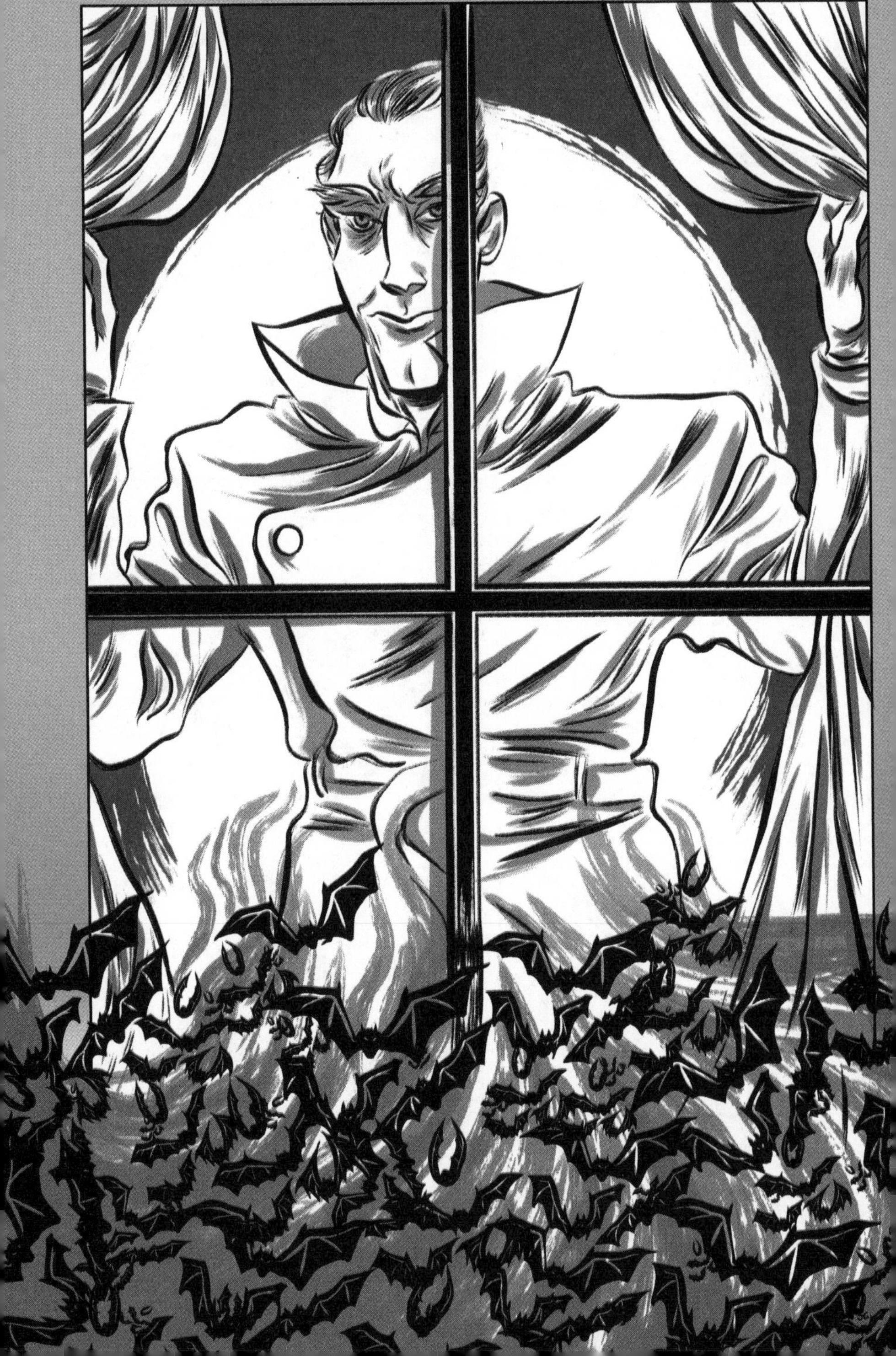

# CHAPTER FIVE

"What. In the hell. Is this?" Terry asked, pausing between the words like he might need an inhaler.

"It's . . . a comic book. Not a real published one, I mean . . ." Denise fiddled with the pages, pushing them forward and backward. "The art doesn't look printed. It looks like . . ." She held it up to her face, breathing in old paper and mildew. "It looks like it's drawn right onto these pages. I'm pretty sure."

Terry leaned past her and flipped back to the title page. "Here it is: J. Vaughn. It's right there. That's who wrote this, and . . . there's nothing about an artist, so I guess he drew it too. I've never heard of Lucida Might."

"Me either." A plump bead of sweat rolled down off her nose and splatted right on the sheet, beneath the *V* in "Vaughn."

"Gross."

"Well, it's hot up here. And it's dark too," she added, glancing toward one of the windows and seeing the last seam of sunset slipping through the glass. "Let's take this downstairs and get a better look at it."

"And maybe clean it up a little."

"Totally." She reached up to the light bulb string, and yanked it until the bulb turned off.

Back downstairs in Denise's bedroom, beneath the ceiling fan light, she pulled a couple of socks and a pajama top out of her dirty clothes pile. Terry made a face about it, but she told him, "They're cleaner than the book, aren't they?"

"They're clothes."

"They're not *underpants*. Get a grip." She tossed him the pajama top, and shoved the socks one over each hand, like gloves. "Now hold up the book while I wipe it down."

With a little patience and a whole lot of "ew" noises from Terry, they got the peculiar album as clean as it was going to get. When they were finished, it looked like it'd only been stuck in a box for twenty years — rather than stuffed in an attic for a hundred.

"It *can't* have been up there for a hundred years," Denise argued when Terry suggested it. "They didn't even *have* comics a hundred years ago."

"Are you sure?"

Upon reflection, she wasn't sure at all. She didn't know much about comics beyond the holy trinity of Batman, Superman, and Wonder Woman — plus whoever Marvel was building up for a summer block-buster. And if she was honest with herself, or with Terry either, she'd only read a small handful of *actual* comic books, mostly at the library. Her knowledge of comics came almost exclusively from TV and movies.

She cleaned up her objection. "I don't *think* they had comics a hundred years ago, but even if they did, they wouldn't look like this. Look at the clothes Lucida and Doug are wearing. Look at the movie theater behind them, and the cars on the street. This isn't *that* old."

Terry squinted down at the page with the shadowy man, evaporating into bats and spiders. "I bet you're right. This wouldn't survive a hundred years up there. Not even wrapped in plastic. Not even sealed in Tupperware."

From downstairs, a loud shout rose up — followed by an even louder, "*Yikes!*"

Denise and Terry sat upright. "Mom?" Denise called out, but when no one answered, she scrambled to her feet. Terry followed suit, leaving the book on the floor behind them.

Denise was out in the hall, and at the top of the stairs in a heartbeat. "Mom, are you okay?"

"Fine," came the answer, but it came from Mike. "She's fine."

"Yeah, I'm fine," Sally groused, as the kids rumbled down the steps and into the living room. "It's that stupid . . ." She gestured at the nearest window. "The window. I was going to clean out all the old paint and rethread the rope, so we could open and close it again." She cradled her right hand in her left, and hissed and breathed and stomped around to take the edge off the pain. "Stupid old single-panes. Stupid old ropes."

Mike took her injured hand and checked it out himself. "It's not that bad. Nothing broken, all right? You'll just have a great big bruise, in the morning."

Sally reclaimed her hand and squeezed it some more, wringing out the dull throb of an injury that was already starting to swell.

"Windows like this, they're on a rope-and-pulley system," Mike explained. "Half of ours are painted shut, and the other half are missing their ropes and weights. But this one." He indicated the problem child in question. "We wrestled it open and the line snapped, and the window dropped shut on your mom. It could've been a lot worse — nothing broken, nothing bent. Only a bruise," he said again, in case saying so could make it true.

"All the work it took, all the paint stripping and sanding just to get it open . . . I never would've thought it could fall shut so fast," Sally mused, still massaging her right hand with the left. "It was strange. It shouldn't have happened."

"Those old nails must've been holding it up and they . . . rusted out, or . . . something," Mike said, gesturing at a few loose, round-headed nails rolling around on the ground. "We'll have to be more careful, that's all."

Denise let out a long, tense sigh, and sat down on the fireplace's brick-lined bottom. "We're going to need better health insurance."

Terry checked his phone. "And I'm going to need to get home. Dad won't be back for a while, but I should get supper started."

Sally knitted her brows in his general direction. "Seriously?"

"I'm an excellent cook," Terry said proudly. "He's pretty tired when he gets off work, so . . . I try to have something ready for him."

He was politely excusing himself, so Denise helped him out. "I'll get your bag. You left it in my room." A moment later she returned, with his backpack, which felt like it was full of rocks. "Here you go. I'll um . . . I'll catch you later."

"Let me know what you find out about that comic. Here, actually . . ." He reached into his bag and pulled a pencil stub that was only an inch or two long, with an eraser nub that was chewed down to nothing. He spied a napkin on the dining room table, and he wrote on it. "Here's my phone number. Give me yours."

She tore the napkin in half and obliged him. "Okay, here you go."

"What comic?" Mike wanted to know.

"It's . . . kind of weird. I'll tell you later."

Denise really *did* mean to tell Mike later, but later, it was time to sit around with Sally and an ice pack, and time for him to fret over his wife like she was a baby bunny. He forgot all about the passing reference to comics, and Denise forgot to fill him in.

Later, it was alone time upstairs in her bedroom with her phone.

She had no other Internet access, not yet, and maybe not for a long time. Getting the power working and the plumbing un-leaky was more important than getting Wi-Fi set up. Mike could leech Wi-Fi from a coffeehouse when it was time for him to go back to work, that's what he said — and Denise could do the same. She had a laughably old laptop and a printer for schoolwork, both of them propped up on a couple of milk crates beside her closet, gathering dust at the moment. But for connection to the outside world that wasn't reliant on borrowed Wi-Fi . . . all she had was this out-of-date iPhone that her mom had found on Craigslist. It'd been her sixteenth birthday present.

It was better than nothing.

Denise sat cross-legged on her bed, phone held longwise between her fingers. She used her thumbnail to turn off the sound so she wouldn't hear the text clicks, and went searching for "lucida might and the house of horrors" or anything related to "j. vaughn."

Down the Internet rabbit hole she went, and an hour later she'd learned a great deal about Lucida Might and her enigmatic creator.

For starters, he was allegedly "one of the great golden age masters of comics," according to Wikipedia. The article had been edited a handful of times, as a couple of guys had gone arguing back and forth over whether he was now "largely forgotten" or merely "little known," because apparently some people cared a lot about that kind of thing; but the meat of the page appeared to be generally agreed upon.

JOSEPH P. VAUGHN (born circa 1910? — d. sometime in March, 1955) was an American author and artist, widely considered to have been one of the great golden age masters of comics. Best known for the *Lucida Might* comics.

#### BIOGRAPHY

Little is known about Vaughn's personal life, including his exact date of birth. According to some sources, he was a talented finish carpenter who took up the visual arts in the wake of a back injury, and found success in the precode publishing industry. He was active from the late 1930s through the mid-1950s, when the **Comics Code Authority** regulations effectively ended his career. The remains of his estate were represented by Marty Robbins at **All Hands Literary Agency** up through 1996, when the agency folded.

## CAREER

Although Vaughn produced over a dozen short-run comics during his prolific career, he is best known for creating *Lucida Might*. In the *Lucida Might* stories, the titular girl hero has many adventures—often in order to rescue her boyfriend, the hapless Doug Finch. With her wits and her fast-talking, fast-shooting skills, she fights everything from mummies in an Egyptian tomb[1] and Eastern Bloc terrorists with nuclear aspirations[2] to mafia dons[3] and corrupt police departments[4].

Vaughn was a regular guest of science fiction and comic book conventions around the country, although these events were not (at that time) as large and media-centric as they have become in more recent years. By all reports, he was an enthusiastic panelist who enjoyed talking about his best-known heroine to fan audiences.[5]

## LUCIDA MIGHT

The comic's tagline, progressive for its time, was "When no man can save the day . . . when no man can answer the call . . . when no man can solve the mystery—Lucida *Might!*" Sometimes described as noir or pulp, the Lucida Might comics were marketed alongside such staples as **Weird Worlds**, **Detective Comics**, and **Amazing Stories**. Initially published by the now-defunct **Future Age** press, Lucida Might was in print for thirteen years. It was syndicated nationally in dozens of newspapers, and collected into countless digests. It even spawned a short-lived television show (**Lucida Might: Girl Adventurer**—1951-1952). But when the **Comics Code Authority** seized control of the industry in 1954, Vaughn disappeared—leaving behind a vast pop culture legacy and many unanswered questions.

## COMICS CODE AFTERMATH

Some said Vaughn quit writing because of the CCA's strict regulations, which effectively prohibited not only gore and violence, but people of color and women in nontraditional roles. Therefore, Lucida Might's feisty, rule-breaking heroine was no longer welcome on newsstands or in comic shops. [Needs citation] Her rueful refrain of, "Doug won't save himself!" did not align with the new standards.

## ARCHIVE

Some of Joe Vaughn's papers are archived at Tulane University, in New Orleans, where he lived and died. The special collections library lists a collection that includes letters, drafts of comics both published and unpublished, and limited edition digests.

The article continued, mostly with a list of known Lucida Might comics and a bunch of footnotes, but Denise didn't see any mention of a "House of Horrors" on the list. The closest thing to a vampire comic was one where Lucida fights a "monstrous cave beast" . . . and the cave beast in question was only vaguely batlike. There was no *Lucida Might vs. Dracula* on the list, or anything like that, either.

Not that the list was guaranteed to be all-inclusive.

Denise'd had enough teachers yelling at her about citing Wikipedia to think for one hot minute that it was the end-all and be-all of research, but she always considered it a safe place to start — and it *did* mention the archives at Tulane.

She left the list and scrolled back up, to the last biographical bit.

## CIRCUMSTANCES OF DEATH

In 1955 Joe Vaughn was found dead in New Orleans. He'd fallen down a set of attic stairs and broken his neck. Police

investigation suggested that the home's owner had gone missing
sometime before, and although Vaughn was found on March 5,
he might have been dead for several days by then. The home's
owner was never found.

A terrible sensation filled the pit of her stomach. The math was
just terrible: Terry said somebody famous had died here, and Joe
Vaughn had died in a house in New Orleans. What were the odds
that it was *this* house, where she'd found *his* manuscript? Better
than zero.

She looked toward her bedroom door, but couldn't see too far
into the hall; she didn't get a peek at the attic door, too tall and too
thin, with its stairs inside that only a gymnast could navigate in
one piece.

"I guess Joe wasn't much of a gymnast," she said out loud, trying to
make it sound ironic, or funny, or anything but completely horrified.
Was there a spot on the hall carpet runner? A man-shaped stain that
never quite went away?

Dead for several days, the article said. Lying there in the Louisiana
heat. Even in March, it would've almost certainly been warm.

She could imagine the smell, even though she didn't want to. Or
was it her imagination at all? She'd smelled the perfume before, and
something foul from the attic corridor . . . was that the stink of death,
left too long in a place that was too warm, and too wet?

Denise shuddered. "It might not be true," she whispered. "He might
not've died *here*, in the Agony House." But she didn't believe herself, not
even a little bit.

Denise's phone's battery was deceptively low; it had a bad habit of
saying she had more time remaining than it was prepared to give
her. It was getting late anyway, so she plugged it in to the socket

beside her closet and went downstairs to tell Mike and Sally good night.

She found them sacked out together on the couch, Sally's hand cradled by a melted ice pack that used to be a bag of frozen corn.

"Cute," she whispered with a smile, and she left them where they were.

Mike had taken a few weeks off from his job with the digital map management company, and therefore, he wouldn't get up in the morning until he good and felt like it. His boss had offered him a month without pestering him for contract work, as a wedding present.

*Must be nice,* she thought. Sally had never had any time off in her life, not that Denise knew of. Man, having a gainfully employed stepdad was a whole new world. Even if he was minimally, contractually employed.

She crawled into bed and kicked the thin velour blanket down to the foot — then whipped the cotton sheet open like a sail. It settled down slow across her body starting at her feet, catching the peaks and valleys of her knees, ribs, belly, and toes. Last of all, it draped over her boobs, then she took the top hem and tucked it up under her chin. She blinked over at the tiny lamp that was sitting on a box beside the bed, since she didn't have a nightstand. It didn't make much light. She might as well leave it on.

Not that she was afraid of the dark. And not that she needed to see anything, but she gazed around the room anyway, secure in her cotton sheet cocoon.

The fan above the bed spun just too fast for her to watch an individual blade go full circle, and the cracks in the walls and on the ceiling looked just like they always had. They did not seem to wobble into weird stick figure pictures when she stared too long. Along the floor at the far end of the room, something crawled . . . but it was probably a palmetto bug, and nothing more sinister than that.

The peculiar manuscript was sitting on the floor where she and Terry had left it. Its cover was open, revealing that title page and the big black letters that'd gone watery from old age and damp.

"Lucida Might and the House of Horrors," Denise breathed.

Her eyes drooped shut. In the end, she dreamed of spiders and bats, and shadowy men, and old ladies in musty perfume.

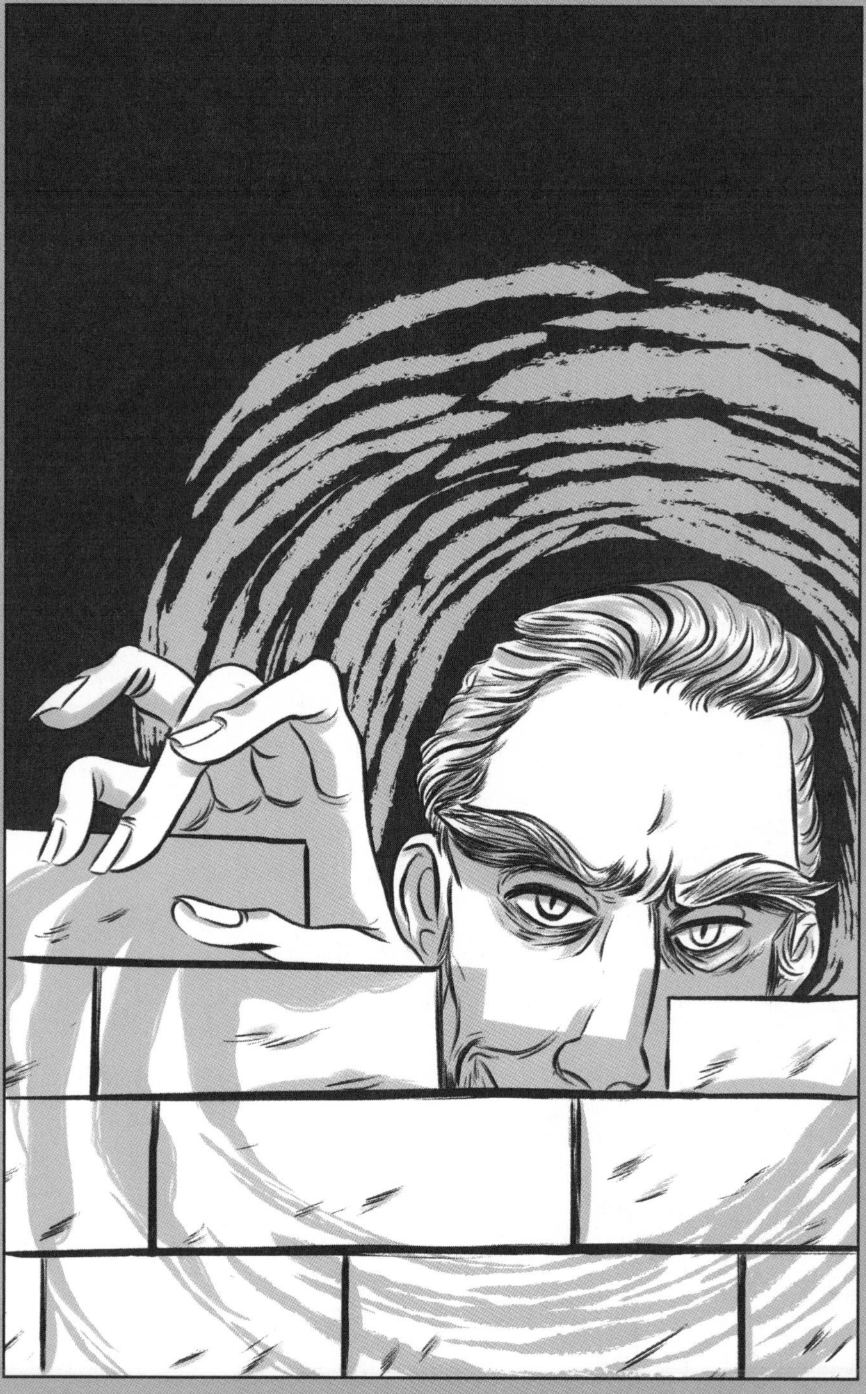

# CHAPTER SIX

Denise's bedroom was sparkling. Or not exactly sparkling . . . but low-key respectable.

It was the next day and sure, the closet didn't have a door and she had no furniture that wasn't a box, and she still had a mattress and box spring on the floor for a bed, but it was tidy *and* now it was scrubbed. She'd even taken soapy rags to all the baseboards. Sometimes it felt like she was just redistributing spiderwebs, but hey. Effort had been made, and the room felt like it was properly *hers*.

The bathroom felt like it was nobody's yet. Denise had smashed out the weird shelves behind the tub with the sledgehammer — and she'd done it to her mother's wild cheers, and a great sense of satisfaction. She'd never gone out of her way to break anything before, and it felt good. She knew she was helping the house, in the long run, and it was nice to have a good outlet for her frustration.

Wallpaper was good for frustration too. Good for creating it, anyway. Now that the shelves were down, the wallpaper was supposed to come down too — but that was easier said than done.

Denise shoved the scraper along the wall and dragged it up and down. The paper she slowly, laboriously peeled was once red with white pinstripes. Now it was a feeble shade of mauve, with pale lines running up and down — disappearing into the wainscoting. It came loose a single scrap at a time, slowly and none too steadily. It was the kind of job that could eat your whole life, if you let it.

She knew she'd lost track of time when Sally came upstairs to ask, "Pizza?"

"Yes?" Denise pushed her hair out of her face.

"I'm too tired to cook. It takes too much going up and down the stairs for another damn lasagna." The microwave was plugged in upstairs, in the wasps' bedroom, which was a decidedly inconvenient location when you wanted to cook a meal. That cursed room had one of only three-prong outlets in the house that worked, and the refrigerator was using the other one. If you tried to make it share, it'd throw a tantrum and flip the breakers. They'd learned this the hard way.

Rather than point out that her mother had been wrong about the kitchen mostly working, Denise caved to convenience. "Yeah, I'd eat some pizza. Hook it up."

"Usual toppings?"

"Y'all two fight it out. I don't really care."

Thirty minutes later, there was a knock at the door. Denise dropped the scraper beside the pile of old wallpaper scraps and headed down the stairs, where Mike was trying to figure out where he'd seen the delivery guy before.

"Swear to God, I've seen you someplace." He looked up and winked when Denise hit the bottom stair. "Maybe Denise can refresh my memory."

Lo and behold, it was one of the only two people in the neighborhood she'd actually met. "Norman?"

"Oh, hey. Wait, *this* is your place?" He looked back and forth between Sally, Mike, and Denise. He settled on Denise. "Holy cow, I am *not* stalking you. I had no idea."

She laughed and almost blushed, but didn't quite. "I believe you. I think."

"I've just got your large pizza, that's all." He pushed it forward to Mike, who put it on the table.

Mike felt for his wallet, realized it was missing from his pocket, and held up a finger. "Let me get some cash; hang on." Then he turned away. With a short, shuffling hop, he limped off towards the master.

"Hey, Mike," Denise called after him. "What's wrong with your leg?"

He stopped short, and leaned against the doorframe. "It's not my leg. It's my foot."

"Fine. What's wrong with your foot?"

Her mother jumped in. "A brick fell on it. He was lucky, really. It could've hit his head."

"Never fear, though. The brick is fine. My foot broke its fall."

"That's why we call you Mike. It's Greek for 'graceful,'" Denise joked. "Next time you get a case of the dropsies, stay away from the power tools, why don't you."

Sally sighed. "I told him not to work in sandals. They make steel-toed boots for a reason."

"Maybe he should go to a doctor?" she tried.

"Trust me, I'll live. Contrary to all the evidence so far, the house isn't actually trying to kill us. I don't think . . ."

Norman took this opportunity to clear his throat. It was the kind of throat-clearing that's asking for an audience. "Um, sir?"

"Call me Mike, son."

"All right, if you want. I was just going to say . . . you guys have a lot of work to do, here. It's gonna feel like even *more* work, if you've got a bum foot."

"It's not *that* bummy," Mike protested.

"But if you want to take it easy, or easier . . . I could help out. I work for cheap, and I know my way around power tools. Pete's my uncle."

"Pete?" Sally asked.

"The hardware store. It's called Pete's," Denise filled her in. "But you've already got a job . . ." She gestured at the pizza box.

"I've got a couple of jobs. I also do cleanup in the cafeteria at Tulane, a few days a week. School's out, and I've got to hustle. I'll take minimum wage. How about eight bucks an hour?" He looked around the demolition in progress, no doubt realizing they couldn't afford any more than that.

Denise felt embarrassed by the house, but encouraged by the idea of having Norman around. He was all right, and her social life wasn't exactly on fire. "It'll take me another week to bring down the second floor wallpaper all by myself," she hinted. "Oh, hey — Norman, are you afraid of wasps?"

"Wasps?"

"We've got a wasp nest. Or a beehive, or something. In one of the bedrooms." She set aside her embarrassment in the name of practicality. He wasn't blind; he could see for himself that the place was a dump. Why not bring him all the way up to speed on the situation? "So far, nobody's bothered to knock it down. We just leave the door shut, unless we need to microwave something."

He opened his mouth slowly and closed it again, like he was about to ask about the microwave, but then he didn't. "I might charge a little extra for the beehive."

"That settles it," Sally declared for everyone. "When are you available, between your other two gigs?"

He thought about it. "Tuesday and Thursday, from noon until suppertime. Then I've got to get home to my mom."

Soon it was agreed that they'd see him from noon to four o'clock, twice a week.

"Let me leave you my number," he said, pulling a coupon out of his pocket and using the pen he kept on hand for credit card signatures. While he scribbled across the back, he said, "Call me if you need to. If you change your mind, or anything." Then Norman took Mike's cash and said, "Good-bye, Coopers. I'll see you Tuesday. Unless . . ." He looked at Denise. "Do you ever go down to the po'boy place, a couple blocks past Pete's? They've got Wi-Fi and the beignets are cheap. That's where everyone kind of . . . kicks around, when school's out. It's called 'Crispy's.' It's got AC."

"That's . . . good to know. Thanks. Maybe I'll see you there."

After he left, Denise cocked her thumb awkwardly back up the stairs and said, "Sooooo . . . Trish finally messaged me. I need to text her back. I could use a break from the wallpaper, anyway. I'll take my pizza upstairs with me."

"Shouldn't you start studying those prep books, for your ACT and SAT?" Sally said. It sounded like a question, but it wasn't. "You're still taking both of them. The real versions, not the 'pre' versions."

"I'm sure I'll do great on the real thing. *Anyway,*" Denise stressed. "At this time, I'm going upstairs to text until my fingers fall off. When I'm done, if I still have the energy, I'll open those stupid books to see how much studying I really need to do."

"All of it. You need to do it all, whatever it takes."

"*Mom.* I know. Have a little faith. Please?"

Sally tensed up tight, squeezing the back of her chair and loudly not saying anything she'd said a thousand times before. Unspoken keywords included: "scholarships," "amazing opportunity," "exorbitant college costs," "broke-ass family," "so much potential," and "don't screw this up."

But all she said in her outside voice was, "I have all the faith in the world. And you only have another year to go. Then you're free to go have a first day of college somewhere else, on someone else's dime, and I will be the proudest mom on earth. I know it's hard now, but—"

"*Mom.* I'll be fine. I'm tired, and I have some trashy food, and I have my phone and books. Holler if you need me," she concluded.

It wasn't quite a masterful exit, but it worked well enough. She picked up her backpack and messenger bag, grabbed a couple slices and some napkins, and lugged everything up the stairs to keep her word about the texting and the studying.

She had to.

# CHAPTER SEVEN

The next day, Denise decided she could use some Wi-Fi. Her beat-up, secondhand laptop was slower than Christmas, but it had an antenna — and it was easier to type on the keyboard than on her phone. She had some more questions for the Internet, mostly about the writer named Joe Vaughn.

Sally was stuck on the phone with the plumbers, so Denise asked Mike if he'd give her a ride to the po'boy place. "I've got the directions on my phone. It's not very far past Pete's."

"What you're saying is, you could easily walk there."

"But it's *hot* . . ." she whined. "Come on. It'll only take you a minute."

"As opposed to the *five* minutes it'd take you by foot. We gotta get you a bicycle or something." But he reached for his keys. "Come on, now. I'll tell Sally where you're off to when she finally pries that phone off her ear."

Crispy's looked like a chain restaurant — which was to say, it wasn't very sketchy, and once Mike saw it, he felt a little better about dropping her off there for an hour or two of nonmanual labor. "Call or text when you want a pickup, okay?"

"I will," she promised. She heaved herself out of the car, slung her messenger bag around her chest, and stepped into the parking lot — then shut the door with her butt.

Mike waved and drove off.

Denise stood there, looking up at the big light-up sign. She'd never heard of Crispy's before, but the place was bright and shiny, with a sign on the door that said WI-FI FOR PAYING CUSTOMERS ONLY. She had three dollars in her pocket, plus the change from her soda the other day. Mike hadn't asked for it back, so she'd kept it.

She might not be able to afford a po'boy, but she could get a drink and some fries or something. They'd let her use the Internet for that much, right?

The glass door chimed when she pushed it open and came inside. There were a dozen other customers. Many of them were about her own age, but none of them were Norman or Terry, so she didn't know anyone. She went to the register and ordered a Coke and some beignets, because those sounded better than fries right that moment and you could get an order for ninety-nine cents. When she got her food, she picked a seat and tried not to feel weird about being the only white person who wasn't working behind the counter.

She opened her laptop. It would only last for ninety minutes without the cord, but she didn't see a place to plug it in. She pulled up a browser window, and started to type.

Before she could check the first round of results for Joe Vaughn that weren't on Wikipedia, several girls sidled into the table right behind her.

One of them started talking, loud enough and pointed enough that Denise knew it was intended for her ears. She ignored it until the girl got more direct about it. "Hey. Hey, you. I heard somebody bought the old nail house on Argonne. Was that you?"

Denise looked up from the laptop and turned around to make eye contact with a black girl about her own age, lean and tall, with short, natural hair. "Nail house?" she asked her. "What's a nail house?"

"A house that sticks up, like a nail on a board. And there's . . ." She sat back. "There's nothing else on the block. Just the one house. A nail house, get it?"

She must be meeting more of the neighbors. "Yeah, that's us. My mom and stepdad bought it."

"Aw, man . . ." A guy sitting alone at the next table over turned to look at her. "The Argonne place? I know that house. You're lucky."

"Lucky?"

"*Everybody* knows that house," said the girl who'd originally asked the question. "And now you've bought it, and I guess you're gonna fix it up."

"My mom wants to make it a bed-and-breakfast. Like . . . a little hotel, kind of."

The girl rolled her eyes. "I know what a bed-and-breakfast is, and now I know you're a carpetbagger. You gonna wind up at Rudy Lombard this fall, or what? I know y'all usually get homeschool, or you go someplace private."

Denise swiveled on the seat to face the girl head-on. She wasn't alone, and Denise was, but that didn't stop her from responding. "Excuse me? How am I gonna *carpetbag* out of Houston?"

"You can carpetbag from anyplace," the girl said offhandedly, like it was something everybody knew. "Y'all come in from Florida, from California, New York. Wherever. It's always the same: You kick people out of their houses, and make them so much better, nobody here can afford them." She returned her attention to her lunch, and to her friends. "I seen plenty of her kind, coming and going. They look better going."

Denise closed her laptop. "Come on, now. The house my mom bought was abandoned — we didn't take it from anybody. And for real: Do I *look* like money to you?"

"Hell no, you don't," offered the guy who'd almost been nice, a minute before. Maybe he was still being nice. It was hard to tell.

Most of the girls at the other table still had their backs to her, but she told them anyway: "I got a laptop that's old enough to go to preschool, and a bedroom without a bed, for Chrissake. We didn't come here to flip. We came back *home*."

"Back?" Another girl drew up her knees and stretched out one leg, taking up two seats beside her. "How come you left in the first place?"

"The Storm chased us to Texas. Couldn't afford to come back, not until now."

"Yeah, you sound like Texas."

"Well, that's where I been."

"But now you're back? In a house?" asked the guy.

Denise didn't quite shrug, and didn't quite roll her eyes. But she kind of did both. "If it makes you feel any better, the nail house is a total craphole."

The first girl was unconvinced. "Maybe you started out here, and maybe you didn't — I don't always know a liar when I see one — but I *know* when I see another damn gentrifier." She gestured with a spoon, and announced to the restaurant at large, "My aunt and cousins lost their place to people like this. My grandma did too. Landlords sell out fast; they take that flipper money and *run*. Then new folks push out folks who belong here, and let in folks who don't."

"I told you, I was *born* here."

"In St. Roch?"

"No . . ." She hesitated. "We were out in St. Bernard, I think. I was real little. But my daddy *died* in this city." She played her only ace, wondering if it'd matter. "The Storm took him, and my grandma too. That's why we couldn't come back any sooner."

"Should I feel sorry for you?" the long-legged girl with two chairs underneath her asked.

"I didn't say you should. I was just explaining." Denise heard mumbling all around her, and behind her. She mumbled too. "I didn't hardly know them, anyhow." This was pointless. She swiveled her legs back over the seat, and returned to her food. "Forget it. Y'all don't want me here, and I don't want to be here — so there's something we agree on. But look, I only got a little bit of time before my battery dies. Leave me alone, or keep giving me grief, I don't care. I've got headphones."

They were only earbuds, turned gray from being bounced around in her messenger bag for a couple of years, but she pulled them out and plugged them in. She opened the laptop again and pretended to give the screen her full and undivided attention.

Slowly, the curious onlookers who had started watching turned back to their tables.

"Come on, Dominique," the guy said, just loud enough for Denise to hear him around the earbuds. "You and Val don't have to be like that."

"She can take it," Dominique said. Then she turned and to another girl sitting at the table, she asked, "Why aren't you eating?"

"Fries are ninety-nine cents, and all I've got's a dollar."

"What's tax? Anybody got a dime? Something like that?" she asked the room. "Come on, get her a handful of pennies or something. Between us, we've got it." All around the restaurant, hands fished in pockets, scaring up change. "Y'all need one of them jars, where you can take a penny and leave a penny," she hollered at the front counter. The guy at the register shrugged.

So Dominique wasn't always awful to everybody, mostly just gentrifiers. Didn't Terry say he had a friend with that name? Maybe this was her. Denise sighed down at her computer, and pulled up Google.

It was much easier to search around on the computer's big keyboard than on her phone's tiny one. She found several links she'd missed the first time, two of which were about Joe's reaction to the CCA. She'd seen mention of it on the Wikipedia page, but didn't really understand what it was about. An article written by someone at the Comic Book Legal Defense Fund looked like a promising place to start. Besides, she needed to get used to reading things by lawyers — if she ever planned to become one.

But the article was also really, really long. She might have skimmed, even though she very much wanted to hear what it had to say.

She felt a little out of her depth, so she kept clicking around and picked up the gist.

Apparently, the Comics Code Authority happened when the government wanted to start censoring comics for being too obscene. To avoid being squashed by federal regulation, the industry formed the CCA to regulate itself. People who wrote and drew comics agreed to submit them to the CCA, and the CCA would decide if they were clean enough to be published.

Lots of people had lots of opinions about that. Lots of people thought it was really stupid and bad.

For one thing, the new code meant that you couldn't write stories about vampires or werewolves anymore — and for another, there were lots of regulations about *how* you could tell stories, and who could be in them. Denise got the very distinct impression from some of the code's wording that stories about kick-ass girl detectives and boyfriends who needed rescuing would have been a no-go. Something about the whole "value of the home and sanctity of marriage" lines, along with all the bits about "honorable behavior" and respect for the order of society.

Yeah, she could read between the lines.

A bunch of comic book producers went out of business when the CCA went into effect. People left the industry, or were pushed out of it.

Denise tried to understand why it'd ever happened in the first place. Supposedly, librarians and teachers and cops were burning comics and banning them, because of all the filthy and gruesome content, so that must've been part of it. Maybe the CCA was trying to save the industry from itself, but it sure sounded to Denise like the comics code did more harm than good.

After an hour, her screen started to flicker. She was never going to make it to ninety minutes, not today. The laptop beast was cranky, so she texted Mike for a rescue.

*Could you come get me? Laptop is dying.*

She packed everything back up, finished her beignets, and refilled her soda. By then, the girls who'd bothered her had left. The guy who had halfway tried to stay out of the fray studiously avoided eye contact.

And Mike was pulling into the parking lot.

He was singing along to some weird bro-country song on the radio — she could tell before she was even close enough to hear it. His head was back, and his eyes were closed, and it was like he couldn't care less that anybody could see him.

Denise grabbed the door handle and let herself inside to a wave of crooning about barefoot girls and pickup trucks. "Jeez, Mike. You know these windows aren't tinted, right?"

"Yes, madam, I *do*," he said with all due solemnity. Then he turned down the radio before she had a chance to demand it, or do it herself. "Not that it's ever stopped me once. And how was your time with proper Internet?"

She shrugged. "It was cool."

"Make any new friends?" he asked, a note of optimism rounding out the question.

"God, no. I only had time to make a couple of enemies."

He hesitated, not sure how serious she might be. "Are you being funny?"

"Just calling it like I see it."

"All right, fine. Today you're the strong, silent type. But when we get home, I have a surprise for you — and I damn well want to hear a squeal of joy."

"Temper your expectations," she warned. "I'm not much of a joyful squealer."

"Not usually, I know. But give me a chance."

She gave him a curious side-eye. "Mike? What did you do?"

"You'll see!"

Denise hoped she wouldn't have to disappoint him. "Okay, I guess I will. So how about your foot? Is it getting better, or should you *really* go find a doc-in-a-box?"

"Much better." He wiggled it around on the gas pedal for emphasis, and the car surged forward.

She rustled up a weak laugh. "Very nice. I'm glad you're so improved that you feel comfortable risking our lives."

"Oh, there's nobody out here — and we're almost home. Hell, kid . . . you're almost home when you're sitting on the restaurant's stoop. I was serious about that bicycle."

"You want me to ride a bike in this heat? Through this neighborhood?"

"The heat, I'll give you. But don't crap on the neighborhood. Don't be one of those white kids who's weird about being around black kids."

"I'm not. I'm trying not to, and . . . that's not what I meant. I've . . . I've got black friends in Houston. Kim's black." She knew it sounded dumb even before it left her mouth, but there it was. "But that's not the problem, I don't think. Well, I don't know, maybe that's part of it. The point is, I don't have any new friends."

He glanced back at Crispy's and continued, "Well, you've met Norman, and he seems like an all right guy. You've met that Terry kid too. That's two friends you'll have at Rudy Lombard, in a couple of months. It's a start."

She sighed and nodded. "I think 'friends' is a little premature, but yeah. At least I'll know *somebody*." As Mike pulled into the two ruts that worked for a driveway at the Agony House, Denise changed the subject. "Hey, what's Mom doing? Did she sort things out with the plumber?"

"Yeah, but now she's meeting with an electrician about the knob-and-tube wiring. There's no sense in throwing up drywall and new fixtures if we're only going to have to yank it all down again. Tomorrow the plumber's coming by, and then we'll know how expensive that's going to be too."

"Mike?"

"Yeah?

It took her a few seconds to figure out the question she really meant to ask. Then she asked it, like she hoped and prayed he'd tell her the truth. "Mike, are we going to be okay?"

He put the car in park, set the brake, and turned off the engine. "The loan is supposed to cover repairs because we're contributing to the community and opening a new business; but I'm not going to lie to you — the money will barely get this house up to code, and that's if we all pitch in for labor. Sally and me, we knew when we bought it that the house was . . . you know . . ."

"A craphole?"

"Fine, it's a craphole. But the sheer *scope* of the crapholeyness is bigger than we thought, and it's going to get expensive. Electrical and plumbing . . . I can repair that stuff in a pinch, but I can't replace their entire systems. We *have* to suck it up and hire some professionals."

"So you're saying . . ."

"I'm saying, the next few weeks are going to be noisy and they're going to be tight, but we'll make it." It was already getting warm in the car without the engine and AC running, so Mike opened his door and stepped out onto the gravel driveway. "Don't be surprised if you find some random dudes hanging around when you get home."

She followed his lead, and shut the car door behind herself. "In my room?"

"In every room. But we'll give you a heads-up so you can hide the bodies, or whatever, before work gets started in your space."

"Thanks. I appreciate it. So . . . where's this joyful squeal-worthy surprise I've been promised?"

"Inside!" He led the way, meeting Sally at the door. She gave him a kiss, and he asked, "Where's the electrician?"

"He'll be back on Thursday, with people and equipment."

"And the estimate was . . . ?"

She lowered her voice, like Denise couldn't hear her anyway. "Don't worry, we can swing it." Then, louder, she said, "Get inside, young lady. Mike picked up a surprise for you."

"Should I be afraid?" she asked, stepping past her mother and into the foyer. "I don't see anything . . . ?"

"Upstairs," Mike told her. "Go check out Fort Denise."

It probably wasn't a trick, but it probably wasn't the grand event that Sally and Mike implied. Or so Denise assumed . . . until she reached her bedroom and heard the steady hum of something that wasn't the rickety ceiling fan. She put her hand through the doorway, and a trickle of ice-cold air weaved between her fingers.

"Shut. *Up.*" In the window that opened the easiest — maybe the only window that opened at all — an AC unit was mounted and running, chugging away and leaving a faint fog of chill around its vents. "Y'all got me a window unit?"

Behind her, Sally and Mike reached the top of the stairs. "It's all yours, baby! It's secondhand — pulled out of a house that was getting central heat and air installed, but it still works fine and it didn't hardly cost a thing. Mike saw it beside the road and gave a guy ten bucks for it."

"Aw, don't tell her that."

"I don't care where you found it, or what it cost. I seriously *don't.*" Into the room Denise strolled, hands out, eyes closed, doing a little twirlie in the empty space that was now as frosty as a fridge. "This . . . is the greatest of gifts," she said dreamily. "I might sleep tonight. I might not wake up with my hair melted to the pillow."

Sally joined her in the room, flexing her elbows and airing out the damp patches under her arms. "Now I want to be clear," she warned. "This thing costs a lot of money to run, so I don't want to find it cranked up to eleven, day in and day out. This is for evenings —"

Mike jumped in. "And for daytime breaks, when us manual laborers need some decent climate control."

She quit twirling happily, and flashed him an honest smile. "Thanks, Pops. This was a real score."

Mike cheesed back, from ear to ear.

Supper was all right too. Sally had gone grocery shopping after all, and she'd been cooking a big home-style tray of frozen manicotti upstairs in Wasp Central because the oven still didn't work worth a damn — or that's how she put it. At Denise's invitation, everyone took their plates upstairs, and sat on the floor of her room with a chilled two-liter of Coke to pass around, campfire-style. Especially if the food was hot, it helped if the room was cool.

Sally took a swig of soda, and wiped the mouth off with her sleeve. "I bet dorm life will look something like this," she advised. "I hope you get lucky, and get good roommates."

"Trish will be a great roommate."

Her mom ignored that declaration. "Those college applications, honey — you need to fill them out and send them off, sooner rather than later, so I hope you're doing some research *now*." Her mom had paid her way through two years of college before running out of money. There had never been any scholarships or grants. Just loans that piled up until she cried uncle and dropped out.

"I'll figure it out later." Denise sighed, and accepted the Coke when it came her way. "Let me deal with one problem at a time, please."

Mike asked, "Have you given any thought to anyplace other than Houston?" Then he scooped a forkful of ricotta into his mouth.

She knew what they wanted to hear. They wanted her to pick Tulane, even though a school like that would be on the lower end of the offers she might (emphasis on *might*) get — part of her tuition, and none of the living expenses. The university was right there in the city, though. Close enough to home that she wouldn't even need to live in the dorm. She could live here, where renovations would be ongoing forever, and ever, and ever. She could spend the next five years studying to the sound of power tools and the smell of dead stuff in the attic.

Or, she could go back to Texas and become a Cougar on a full ride (hopefully), and share a room with Trish and maybe even Kim.

"I'm still thinking about it," she said diplomatically. "Just give me some breathing room. Let's get this house livable, and then I'll worry about whether or not I want to live somewhere else. First things first. Right?"

Sally nodded reluctantly. "First things first."

"You trust me?"

"It's the world I don't trust. Or luck, or fate, or what have you." For a moment, Sally looked like she'd love to have something stronger than a Coke in hand. "We've been close to good before, haven't we? But things fall apart, last minute. Things go to hell."

"Mike, you gonna let her talk about you like that?"

He shrugged, undaunted and unteased. "She's only saying, she doesn't want you to struggle."

"Not like I did. Not like *we* did, when you were little. You can do better, that's all."

When supper was finished, they carried all the plates and cutlery back downstairs, and Denise grabbed a tumbler full of ice to finish off the last of the soda. "I'm going back upstairs to the civilized part of the house, okay? I've got some messages to reply to."

No one argued, and before she took the stairs, Denise saw Sally pull a box of wine out from the fridge. *Good for her*, she thought. *Have at, you crazy kids. You've earned it.*

It wasn't late — it wasn't even dark — but she turned on the lamp and settled in with her headphones and her cell phone. The phone was blessedly full of text messages . . . even a couple from Annie, who she hadn't been super-close with. She responded politely and briefly.

After exchanging a few tired texts with Trish, she reached into her pocket and pulled out a pizza coupon that had a different phone number written on it. She thought about using it.

But she was getting sleepy, and she chickened out.

# CHAPTER EIGHT

The next day, Denise spent half the morning poking around links related to Joe Vaughn when she should've been working on the hallway wallpaper with the scraper. She hadn't read any further on the comic book, but she couldn't shake the thought of Joe Vaughn, dead comic writer, lying on the floor just outside her bedroom — so she spent some time combing that all-too-brief web listing for clues that might suggest that somehow, he'd lived or died someplace else.

After all, there were too many loose ends to call it a done deal. For one thing, all she knew about the house where Joe died . . . was that it didn't belong to him. That's all the Internet had told her so far. It was in New Orleans, and it wasn't his.

If the Agony House was really his, then he couldn't have died here. That said, if he never lived here, why was his old manuscript stashed in the attic? This house could've belonged to anybody — a fan, a friend . . . She considered the perfume and the humming.

"A lady friend?" she mused.

At any rate, there were holes in her horrified suspicions, and she clung to them. She had more questions than she had answers, and maybe she wouldn't like the answers when she got them — but she had to keep looking.

She settled on the All Hands Literary Agency as a possible source of info. She googled the company eight ways from Sunday, along with the name "Marty Robbins," and mostly turned up unrelated garbage. Here and there, she caught his name or the agency's name in reference to an old trade paperback deal. But she found nothing any newer than the mid-1990s.

Then she idly clicked back four or five pages in the search results, and a related name turned up: Eugenie Robbins, a partner at a firm called the Kessler and Robbins Literary Agency.

It couldn't be a coincidence. Could it?

Another few clicks revealed that Eugenie Robbins was accepting new clients, and was particularly interested in science fiction, fantasy, and romance. She accepted queries by email. She expected to see the first three chapters and a synopsis of any book you wanted to show her.

She probably didn't expect a message from someone like Denise Farber, but that didn't stop Denise from pounding out a quick letter with her thumbs.

> Hello Ms. Robbins,
>
> My name is Denise Farber, and I'm hoping that you're some relation to an agent named Marty Robbins. Marty Robbins used to represent a man named Joe Vaughn who wrote comic books a long time ago, and I think he might have died in my house. My parents bought this place in New Orleans (a neighborhood called St. Roch, if that helps) and I found a manuscript hidden in the attic. It's not a printed comic book, but more like a script for one. It's called Lucida Might and the House of Horrors.

She paused, and scrambled off her bed to where the comic was still sitting. She flipped it open and carefully snapped some pictures of the first few pages. Then she went back to the email and attached the pictures to it.

> Anyway, I've included some shots so you can see what I mean. Can you write me back, and tell me if you know Marty Robbins? Do you know where Joe died? Whose house was

it? Why would he leave this manuscript hidden upstairs in mine?

Also, do you know if this comic was ever published? It would be cool if I could see it all finished.

Thank you for your time, and I look forward to hearing from you.

It was a formal sign-off, but she'd read it someplace and liked the sound of it. Very professional. Very confident. It totally stuck the landing.

She hit SEND and her phone immediately chimed in response. It was Terry, texting to say he was on his way over. Not asking if he could come over . . . just giving her a heads-up.

"Typical," she sighed, even though he'd never done it before. She had a feeling that he did it all the time. Give him an inch, and he'd take a mile. Well, he already had an inch, and there was no stopping him now.

From downstairs, her mom called out: "Honey, we're going to grab breakfast. Shall we bring you the usual?"

"Yeah, that's fine!" she called back.

But just before they could leave, Denise heard Terry arrive. Her mom greeted him at the door with a question, "Oh! Hello, Terry — are you here to help Denise scrape wallpaper?"

He floundered, and said something like, "Um . . . whatever she needs me for, I guess!" and scurried up the steps with Mrs. Cooper following behind him. "Hey Denise," he greeted her, then moved aside for Sally to lean into the bedroom.

She scanned the scene for signs of productivity. "I see a lot of ratty wallpaper on the walls up here, and not on the floor."

"I'm *working* on it," Denise said with an eye-roll. "I'm just taking a break. It's hot, okay? It's miserable in every single room except this one. I'll get back to the bathroom in a little bit."

"I hope we don't regret getting you that AC unit."

"You won't, Mom." And after she'd left, Denise admitted under her breath, "Not until the power bill comes."

"Have you *actually* scraped any wallpaper today?" Terry asked, looking around her room. She hadn't started in there yet. Or out in the hallway, where she kept picturing a corpse lying, decomposing, leaking body-juices down into the floor.

"No, but I've thought about it real hard. What brings you over today? You want to read the comic some more? Because I'm pretty sure my mom would frown upon such leisure activities, when there's so much wallpaper intact."

"I would love to read more of the comic, but that's not actually why I'm here." Then he asked if he could show her something.

"Sure, hit me."

He whipped his backpack around his shoulder, unzipped it, and pulled out his voice recorder. He sat down on the edge of her bed, and motioned for her to come closer. "I'm going to turn this up real loud, okay? You have to listen hard. It's kind of tricky to hear, but I've got the good stuff all queued up."

She humored him by leaning forward and cocking one ear toward the handheld device. "All right. Go for it."

He pressed PLAY. At first, Denise heard only full-volume static blasting from the tiny speaker. It was loud and rough, a noise so big that it took up the whole room. She listened because she was supposed to, not because she thought there was anything to hear — but then, very softly, she caught something else buried within it — a whisper of rushed words, harsh and low.

I keep what's mine.

She jerked her head away from the recorder like it might bite her. "Is that . . . was that . . . ?"

He beamed from ear to ear. "It was a *ghost*."

She shook her head, not really believing him, but not arguing with him, either. "How do I know you even recorded that here? You could've done it at home, when nobody was looking. You could've . . . you could've gotten your dad to say it."

His broad smile went sly, like something was funny. He pressed PLAY again, and Denise's own voice blew out of the speaker, louder than life — since he hadn't turned down the volume. "You're wasting your time," she heard herself say. "This is completely stupid."

"I think I got this one out in the hallway, right in front of the attic door." He didn't turn down the volume, but he rewound the tape to play that first bit again. "What does it sound like he's saying, to you? To me, it sounds like "I want more time.""

"Don't play that again —" she started to command him, but he'd already hit the button and the gravelly, angry-sounding words rushed out again.

I keep what's mine.

It scared her, because she knew good and well that it wasn't Terry or his dad, and it didn't sound like anybody she'd ever heard speak. It didn't sound like anybody who was alive. Before she could stop Terry, he played the damn thing once more.

I keep what's mine.

She snatched the recorder out of his hand. "It's not *time*," she said, clutching it to her chest. Her heart banged against her hand. "I think . . ." She tried to compose herself. Slow breaths. Stay cool. "I think he's saying '*mine*.'"

He wiggled his fingers at the recorder. "Give it back. Let me play it again."

"I don't *want* you to play it again!"

Terry grabbed for it anyway, and got just enough of a grip to wrench it back into his own grasp. "It's not awful — it's evidence of the afterlife!"

She held up her hands, not surrendering, but calling for a halt to all this nonsense. "Maybe you used an old tape, and some other recording bled through . . . or my parents had the radio on downstairs and we didn't notice, or somebody was outside the window, or out on the street. Anybody could've said that, Terry. It doesn't have to be a ghost."

"But it *was*, and you know it. If you thought it was anything else, you wouldn't be so scared right now."

"I'm not scared!" she yelled at him.

"Do you always holler when you're not scared?"

She quieted her voice. "It's not a ghost, it's just somebody, somewhere, saying 'I keep what's mine.' I think that's what it says."

He considered this. "Hmm. Maybe." He whirled away from her, rewound the tape against her wishes, and hit PLAY even as she danced around him in a circle, trying to take the recorder away again.

I keep what's mine.

"Yeah, I think that's it. 'I keep what's mine.'"

"Put that thing away. I don't ever want to hear that voice again. It's gross, and weird, and it sounds mean."

"No, not yet," he protested. "I got several other pieces too, when I was walking around the house, asking questions. I want you to hear them."

"Oh God, no . . ."

"They're not all from that same guy, I promise! I got one that sounded like it came from a lady."

She could've chosen that moment to tell him about the humming and the perfume, and the tiny footprints that came and went.

But she didn't. "Jesus, Terry. How many people do you think died in this house?"

"I don't know. It's really old. Probably lots of people haunt it. At least two, I know that much for sure. The mean guy, and the nice lady."

Denise clenched her fists, and unclenched them again. "I've had enough of this, and enough of your stupid recorder."

"That doesn't mean your house is any less haunted."

"Stop talking like that!"

"Maybe I'll ask your mom . . ." Terry ignored her like he always did, except that he paused to look around. He went to the window and asked, "Hey, where are your parents going?"

The blue Kia was sliding out of the parking pad and reversing into the street. "They've gone to pick up breakfast," she told him. "The electrical breakers are off, down on the first floor — so we can't use the kitchen."

"What are *you* going to eat?"

"They're bringing something back for me."

"Do your parents believe in ghosts?"

"I don't know."

"I bet they do, and I bet they'll find this interesting." He had his stubborn face on. She wanted to smack it clean off. "I bet they'd be interested in hearing from Mean Guy and Nice Lady."

"You're completely wrong."

"Why are you being such a jerk about this? Most people would be excited to find proof of ghosts."

"You're wrong about that too. God, Terry. It's like you don't know anybody in real life."

The stubborn face hardened. "I know lots of people. *Lots* of people like ghosts."

Denise folded her arms and opened her mouth to evict him, but he changed his approach, going from demanding to pleading.

"Come on, don't you at least want to *hear* the lady? If you're going to be scared of the man, you should at least—"

"I'm *not* scared."

"— Fine, but wouldn't it be great to know that there's someone nice, looking out for you?"

She frowned. "Looking out for me?"

"Just let me play you the other messages. Come *on*."

Denise sighed with great, unhappy drama. She could either force Terry to leave, or listen to him play a couple of clips from his voice recorder. It'd probably be faster and easier to let him play the voices and *then* kick him out.

She relented. "Okay, *fine*. Play them, and then get lost before Mom and Mike get back."

"Great!" He sat back down and waved her over, and she reluctantly obeyed, sitting cross-legged, to match her crossed arms.

"Let's get this over with."

He was way ahead of her, thumbing his way toward something else on the little cassette. "Okay, but listen to this, and listen close. She's quieter than the mean guy." The tape queued up. Terry's thumb squished the button, and static poured out again. Then a whisper, a woman's voice that was low and soft, but firm.

. . . you lousy greaser . . .

Denise laughed, then clapped her hands over her mouth to catch it, and hide it—but it was too late.

"See?" Terry pressed. "This lady ghost has moxie!"

"What the hell is *moxie*?"

"Attitude," he informed her. "I looked it up online. I found a whole list of old-fashioned slang when I looked up what a 'greaser' was."

"Is that what she says?" She reached for the recorder again. This time, he let her take it. She rewound, and listened again. Just three words, clear as day: . . . you lousy greaser.

Terry explained, "A 'greaser' is basically a loser. One of those guys who wears too much hair stuff and thinks he's hot, but he's really just stupid-looking. It's just one of those words they used to use, sixty or seventy years ago."

"Like 'moxie.'"

"Uh-huh. Your nice lady ghost talks like a character from an old detective movie. Here, I've got another one." He reclaimed the device, urged the tape along, and pulled up his next find.

. . . mine . . .

That was the only word she could make out. But the tape kept rolling, and the woman's voice said: . . . never yours. When they find me . . .

. . . they won't . . .

"Wow," she said. She didn't mean to be impressed. She meant to toss Terry out, and eagerly await her glorious fast-food breakfast. "It's like they're arguing about something."

Her phone picked that moment to ring, startling the crap out of her. She flailed wildly and pulled it out of her back pocket, where she wasn't quite sitting on it. It was Mike. "Mike! Where are you, man? I need me some breakfast burritos, stat!"

"The McDonald's was closed — something about a plumbing problem."

Her mom called from the background. "So how about chicken biscuits instead?"

Denise sighed into the phone. "Chicken biscuits sound fine."

Terry swallowed wetly. He didn't say anything—not with his mouth. His eyes, on the other hand . . . he might've been one of those sad-faced dogs in a humane society commercial.

She closed her eyes and slumped down against the mattress, her butt settling on the floor. Surrendering to the inevitable she said, "Mike?"

"Yuh-huh?"

"Any chance you could pick up a couple of extras? Terry's still here, and I was going to send him home, but . . ."

"Two more biscuits, added to the order. Yes ma'am."

When the call was over, Denise put her phone on the table. "Happy now?" she asked Terry, who was vibrating in his seat.

"I completely forgive you for being a jerk about the ghost recordings."

She almost objected, but shrugged instead. "Fine. I was a jerk about those. You're right, and they're kind of cool. Did you catch anything else?"

"So you believe me now?"

"I believe . . ." She hesitated, hard. "I definitely believe there's something strange about this house."

"Close enough. And no, that's all I found—and I listened to this tape backwards and forwards, with the speakers at top volume, for hours, man. *Hours.*"

"Do you think the mean guy is Joe Vaughn?" she asked. "I mean, I kind of hope not. He wrote a comic about a kick-ass girl detective. I'd rather not think he's a jerk."

"Or a lousy greaser."

"Or that, either."

"Have you finished reading the comic yet?" Terry asked, with a greedy gleam in his eyes.

"No, I've been busy."

"Can I read it?"

"You can't take it home with you, if that's what you're asking. It's mine."

"No it isn't."

She unfolded her legs and stretched them out, then put her feet on the floor. "We found it in my house, and possession is nine-tenths of the law."

"Who told you that?"

"Lawyers," she informed him. It was generally true. Lawyers probably wrote the books about passing the bar exam. "It's mine, but you can read it if you want. While it's here. With me."

"It might belong to somebody else, though."

"Like who?"

"Like . . . if Joe Vaughn is our ghost, and he's dead . . . he might have kids who aren't."

She drummed her fingers on the table beside her phone, considering the implications of this. The *Lucida Might* manuscript might be worth some money to the right person, and she could definitely use some money. Maybe somebody would give her a finder's fee. Even the best scholarships couldn't cover everything. "You know what we should do?"

"What?" Terry asked, but it probably didn't matter. He sounded like he was game for anything.

"We should put it on the Internet. Not all of it," she added quickly. "Just some teaser pages, to see if anybody knows anything about it. Maybe someone will come forward. Maybe we can give it back. Or sell it."

"Do I get a finder's fee?" he asked immediately, because apparently they were more alike than Denise wanted to think.

"How about a couple of chicken biscuits?"

"For a down payment," he suggested shrewdly.

"All right, we'll talk about it later — if anybody actually, you know, recognizes the thing . . . much less wants it badly enough to buy it. Come on," she said, smacking him on the arm. She rose from the chair and collected her phone. "Let's open that bad boy up. I need to take some pictures."

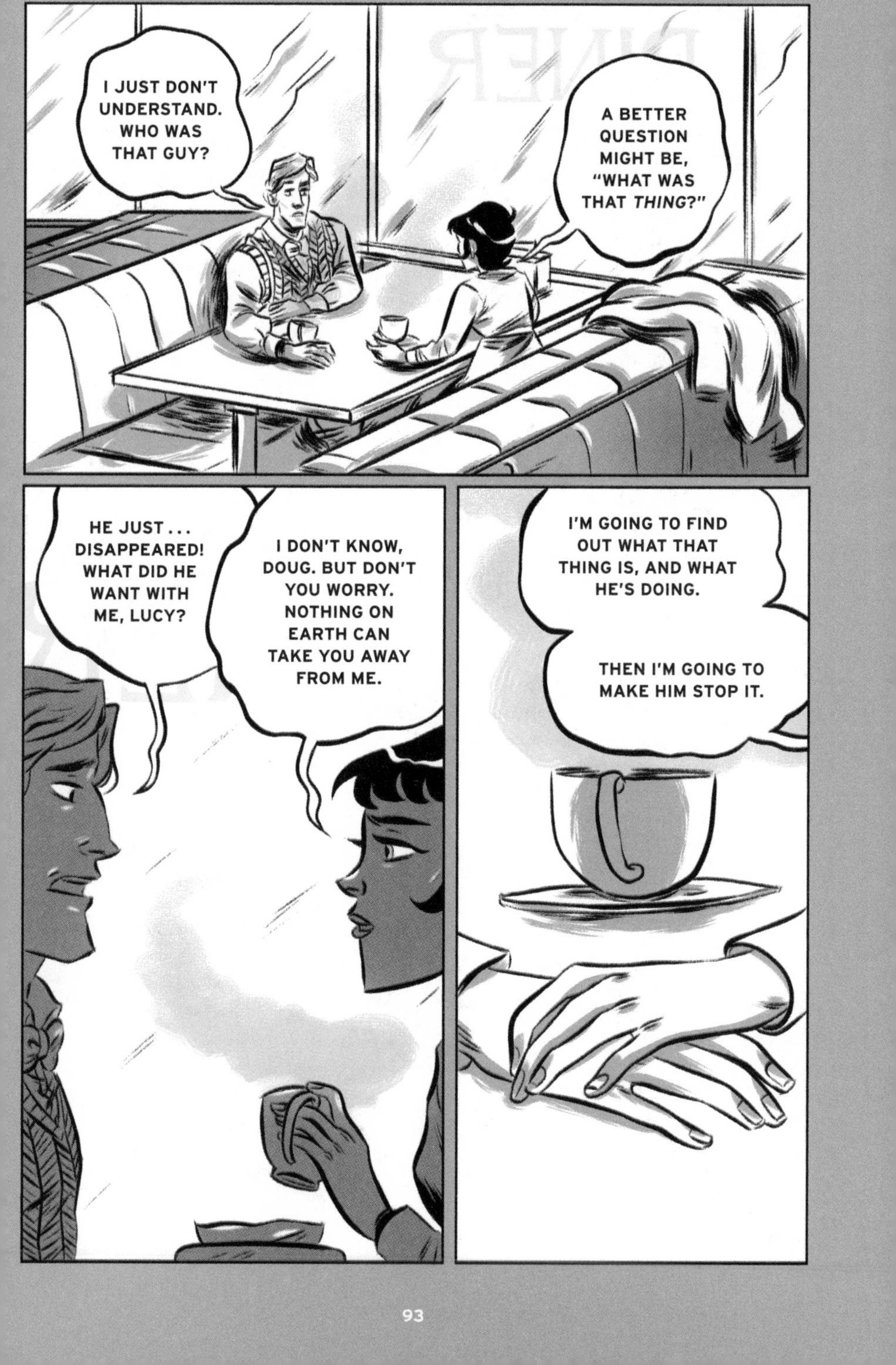
I JUST DON'T UNDERSTAND. WHO WAS THAT GUY?
A BETTER QUESTION MIGHT BE, "WHAT WAS THAT *THING*?"
HE JUST . . . DISAPPEARED! WHAT DID HE WANT WITH ME, LUCY?
I DON'T KNOW, DOUG. BUT DON'T YOU WORRY. NOTHING ON EARTH CAN TAKE YOU AWAY FROM ME.
I'M GOING TO FIND OUT WHAT THAT THING IS, AND WHAT HE'S DOING.
THEN I'M GOING TO MAKE HIM STOP IT.

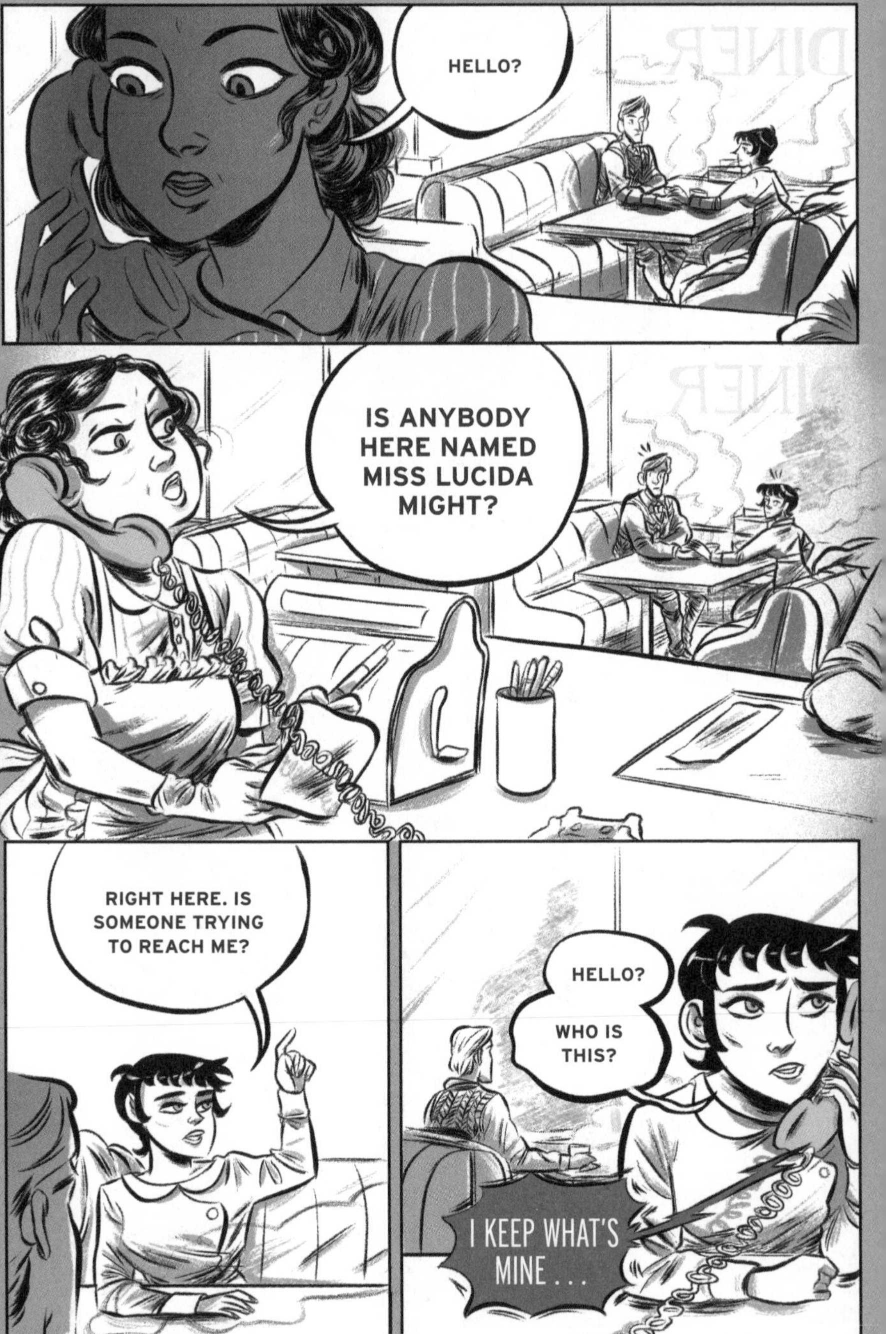
HELLO?
IS ANYBODY HERE NAMED MISS LUCIDA MIGHT?
RIGHT HERE. IS SOMEONE TRYING TO REACH ME?
HELLO?
WHO IS THIS?
I KEEP WHAT'S MINE . . .

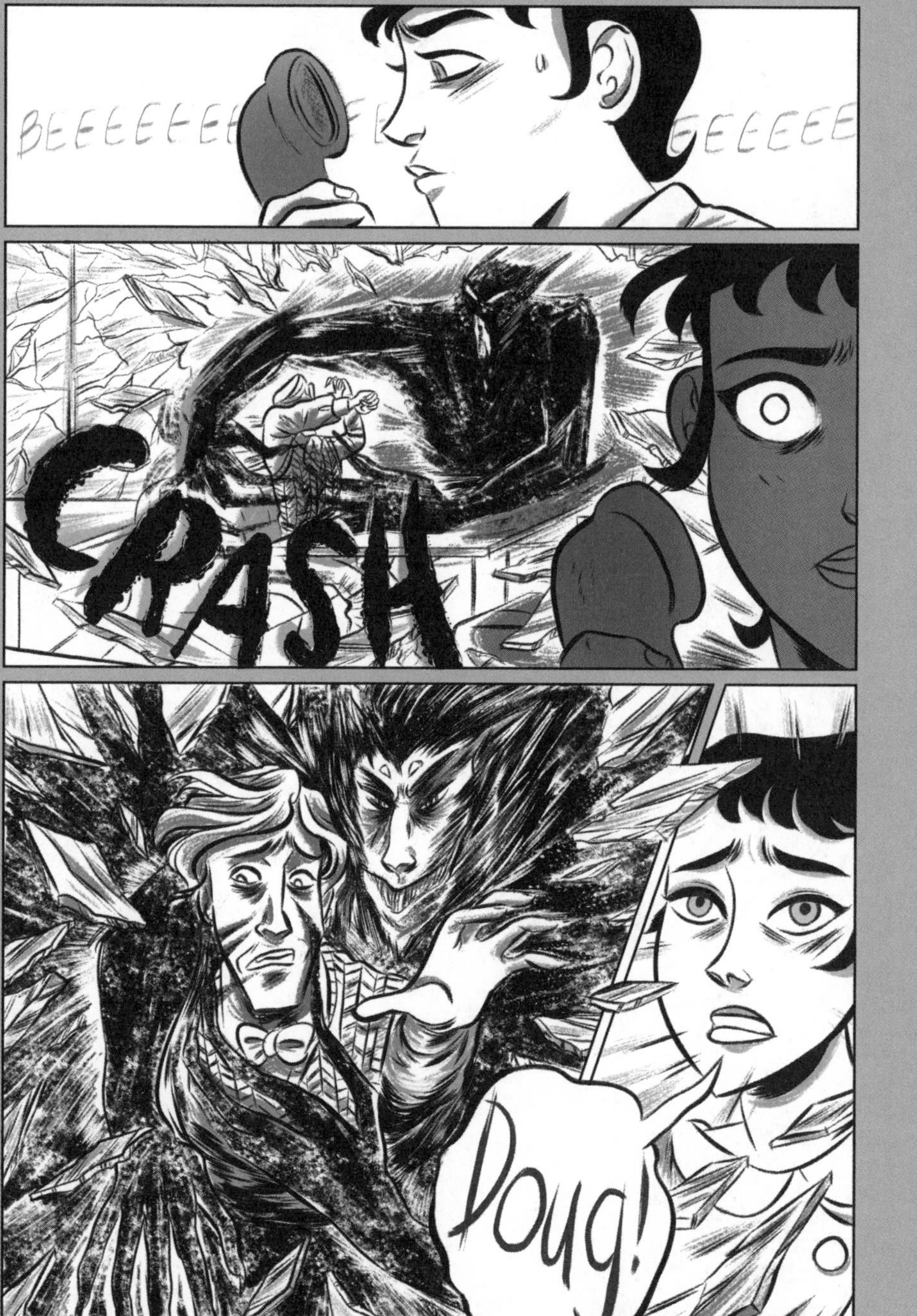
BEEEEEEEEEEEEEEEE
CRASH
Doug!

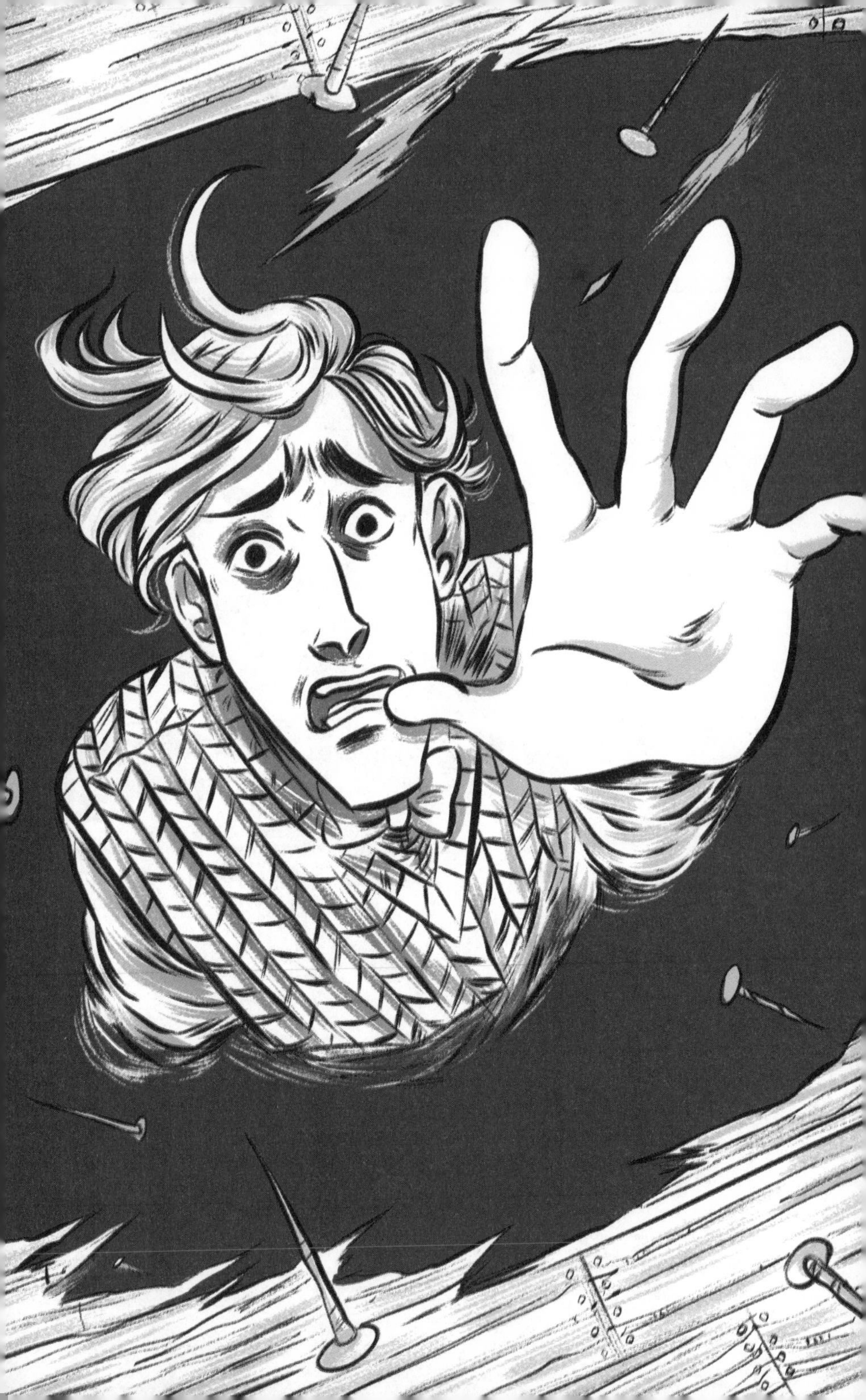

"'I keep what's mine' . . . that *can't* be a coincidence!" Terry declared triumphantly.

Denise was flustered. She tapped at the word balloon and rubbed it with her fingers like she could erase it. *"Anything* can be a coincidence."

"It's probably not, though. And I hate to tell you this, but I'm kind of getting into it," Terry informed Denise.

"Why would you hate to tell me that?"

"Because now I'm going to be over here all the time, until I'm finished reading it." He reached for the corner, to turn the page — but she smacked his hand away. "Your hands are dirty."

"Then *you* do it."

"Fine."

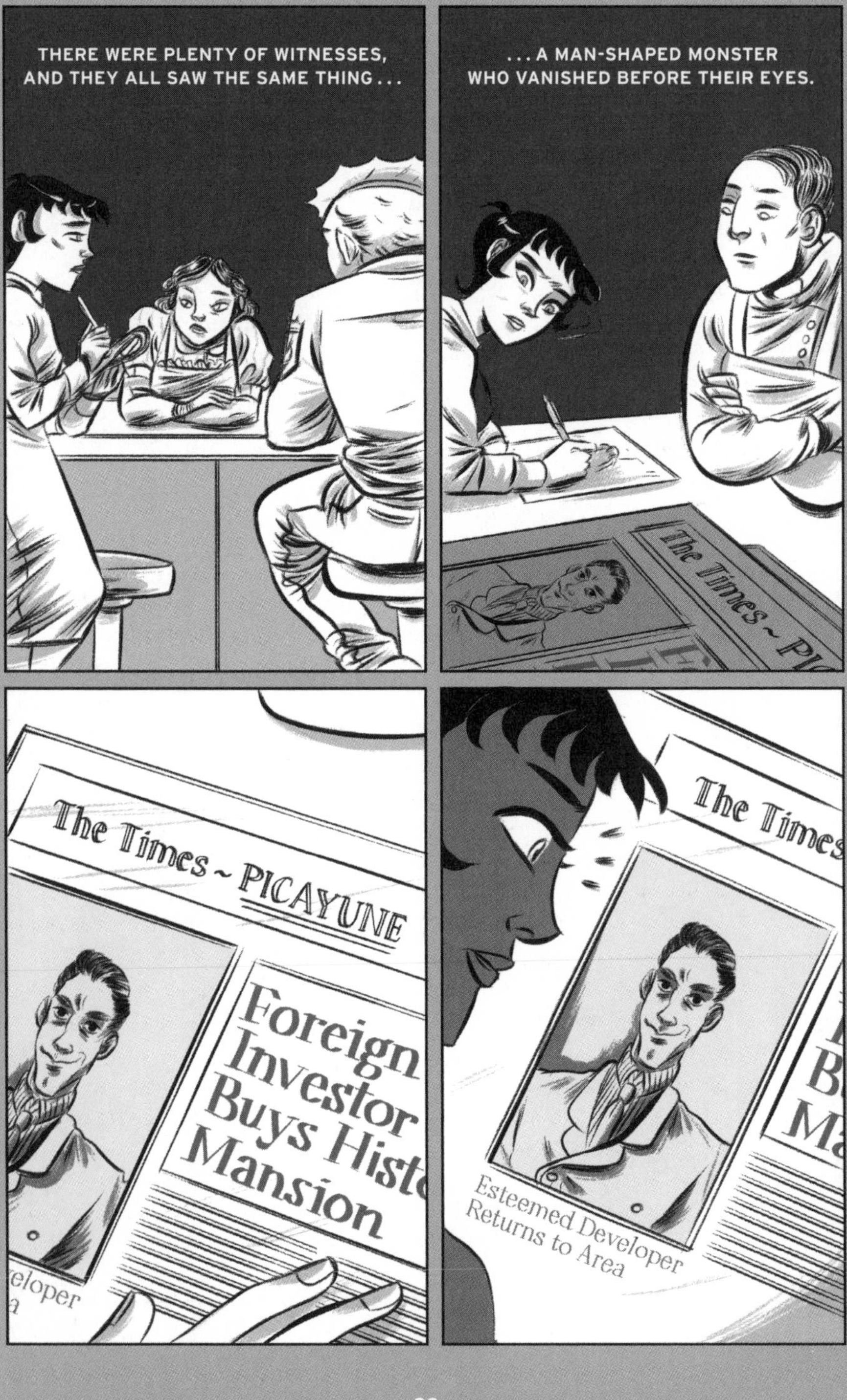
THERE WERE PLENTY OF WITNESSES, AND THEY ALL SAW THE SAME THING . . .
. . . A MAN-SHAPED MONSTER WHO VANISHED BEFORE THEIR EYES.
The Times ~ PICAYUNE
Foreign Investor
Mansion
The Times
Esteemed Developer Returns to Area

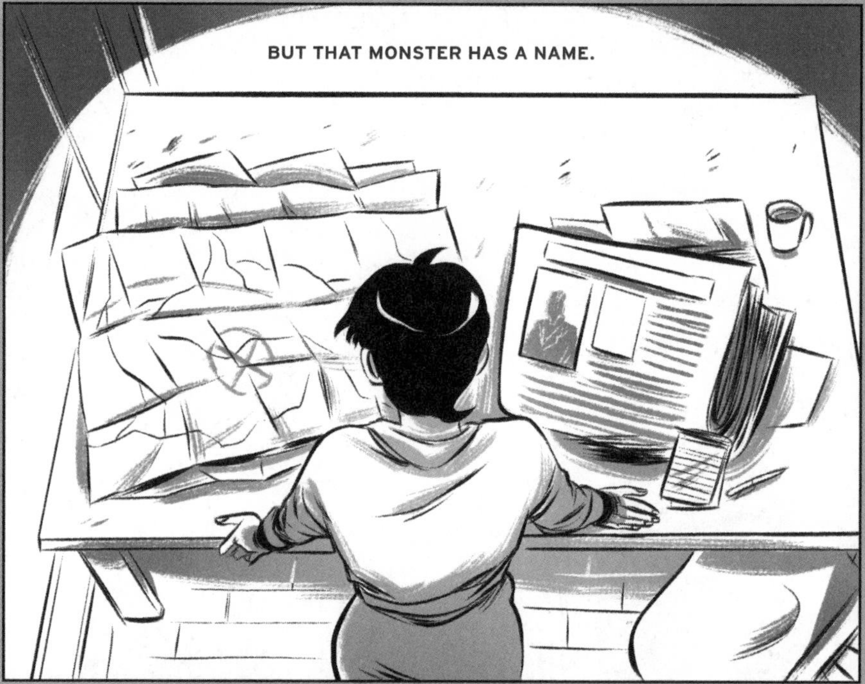
BUT THAT MONSTER HAS A NAME.

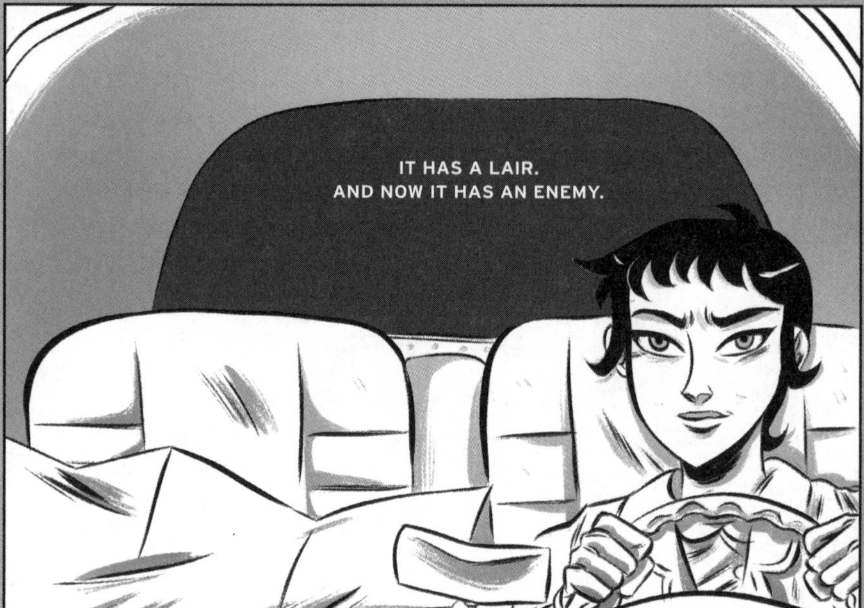
IT HAS A LAIR.
AND NOW IT HAS AN ENEMY.

DOUG FINCH HAS BEEN TAKEN HOSTAGE BY NONE OTHER THAN **DESMOND RUTLEDGE**, A SHADOWY FIGURE WHOSE PECULIAR ABODE AND SUSPICIOUS BEHAVIORS HAVE BEEN THE SUBJECT OF MEDIA SPECULATION.

AND **LUCIDA MIGHT** IS GOING TO GET HIM BACK.

# CHAPTER NINE

Denise and Terry sat stunned, the manuscript splayed out on the floor before them, open to the page with the big panel about the big house. Denise slowly dropped a finger down onto the artwork, feeling the faint press of pen strokes on the paper. "Are you seeing this?" she asked aloud. "This is . . . this is *obviously* my house, isn't it?"

"Obviously," he echoed with a nod. "Back before it got . . . before it was . . . back when it was, um, newer."

"Back before it was a dump. You can say that, if you want. I give you permission."

"Okay, back before it was a dump."

"I wonder if there are any pictures of this house, from all the way back then. At the library, or someplace."

"Have you tried the Internet?" Terry suggested helpfully.

"Not yet. It only just occurred to me to look. Hang on." She'd stopped taking photos of the manuscript several pages back, because she was getting caught up in the story — but now she retrieved her phone and called up a browser. She plugged in 312 Argonne Street, and found a bunch of real estate listings, property tax records, assessments, and other pointless things she didn't care about. Next, she tried an image search, and got a little closer to the mark.

"Is that it? Let me see . . ."

"Hang on, Terry. Jeez." She dragged her thumbs around the screen, enlarging a promising black-and-white shot of a Victorian neighborhood that could've been St. Roch. "Is . . . is this it? Do you think? It's kind of grainy; I can't tell."

He squinted at the screen. "Maybe. See if you can find a better picture."

"This is the clearest one I can find. Everything else is just . . . some neighborhood pics, from some survey. Looks like the 1930s? Something about a streetcar line." The caption was fuzzy, and hard to read. "I'd be better off with a real photo and a magnifying glass."

"Or a laptop screen. You need more pixels."

"We don't have any Internet in the house, so it's this or nothing. Unless you want to go down to the po'boy place."

"Crispy's? I don't have any money."

"Me neither."

Outside, the sound of tires on gravel said that the battered blue Kia had returned, bearing her mom, Mike, and extra chicken biscuits for her self-invited guest. Both of them heard it. Terry sat upright like Jesus called his name, and scrambled to his feet.

"That's them," Denise said without even looking out the window. Terry was already halfway into the hallway.

"Wait up, man. You're not allowed to eat my parents' food without me." She hauled herself to her feet and followed along behind him, catching up at the top of the stairs. She could hear them outside, talking and laughing. Well, Sally was groaning — but Mike was laughing. He had no doubt shared some truly terrible joke, and Denise was blessed to have missed it.

She grinned anyway, and took the stair rail, pushing past Terry — then tripped down the steps in a hasty, greedy fashion. Terry was hot on her heels, showing more speed than she would've expected from him, but hey. Biscuits.

Up the front porch steps the food-bringers clomped, and down into the living room the kids descended. They would meet in the middle, at the dining room. There would be biscuits stuffed with fried chicken, and fast-food hash brown patties, and at least a fistful of ketchup packets, because Mike had learned the hard way that when Denise said "a fistful" she meant "preferably more than that, so use both hands when you raid the bin."

Except they didn't come inside. They didn't open the door with their elbows and knees, their arms full of bags.

Denise heard a crash instead — on the other side of the door, out on the porch. Immediately, she thought of the comic up in her room — but that was crazy, wasn't it?

Through the door's sidelights, Denise saw white paper bags go flying, and one of Mike's arms go flailing, and she heard her mother shriek in time with the sound of shattering wood.

Mike yelped in pain, then shouted, "It's okay, I'm okay!"

But when Denise whipped the front door open, her stepdad was chest-deep in splintered beams and jagged edges. He'd stepped right through the porch floor. It'd eaten him whole. He was still holding one bag, but he set it down beside himself and gasped. "I'm fine. No, no." He waved Sally's hand away. "I'm fine, look. I'm freaked out, that's all."

"Um . . . Mike?" Denise gazed in horror at the front of his shirt, just inside the hole.

He looked down and saw the streak of red oozing through the tee. He touched the wet spot and winced, but nodded. "It's a scratch. No big deal."

"You're bleeding!" Sally cried, only a little late to the party.

"It's just a scratch!" he repeated. "My leg's a little scraped up too, but that's the worst of it." He put his hands on the edge and tried to pull himself up, but succeeded mostly in pulling down more wood. He withdrew his hands, and looked around for something more solid.

Terry leaped into action. "Here," he offered, picking up a couple of pieces of plywood and dragging them over. "Use this."

"Not a bad idea," Mike agreed, reaching for it. "Put it down over here, and someone give me a hand, hold it steady. I don't know what I'm standing in, but it's squishing through my shoes."

"And you're bleeding," his wife reminded him.

"I'm more worried about the shoes." He might've been kidding, or he might've only been trying to make her feel better.

If that was the idea, it didn't work. Sally scooted to the edge of the plywood and sat on it, then urged Denise and Terry to get Mike's arms. Between them, and with a little cooperation, they got him up and out, and onto sturdier turf. He flopped down and panted, staring up at the underside of the flaking blue porch roof while the stain on his shirt spread ominously.

Sally yanked up the shirt and paused. "It's . . . it's not that bad, you're not going to die."

"Nope," he agreed, still catching his breath.

"But you need stitches."

He looked down, scrunching up his chin against his throat. "Oh yeah. I guess I do." He sounded more disappointed than traumatized. He swore, then apologized for his language when he remembered he was using it in front of somebody else's kid. Terry shrugged it off with a look on his face that said he'd heard far worse.

"What happened?" Denise wanted to know, as she stared down into the dark, wet, dirty hole.

Mike sat up, and used the hem of his shirt to dab at a scrape on his chest. "The floor is old. I am heavy. You do the math."

"We need to get you to an urgent care, and knit you back together. And maybe shoot you up for tetanus," Sally fussed, still patting him down for any further tears, scrapes, breaks, or bruises.

"I know, I know." He struggled to his feet, and checked out his left leg while he was at it.

Denise asked, "Did you cut up that one too?"

He shook his head. "Not cut up — just bruised up. Might be a little raw, in a place or two."

Sally directed her attention to Denise and Terry. "You two, stay here — and stay off this porch! I'm going to get him help, at the first place I can find on my phone."

"I'm going to tell the doctors you beat me up, because I dropped the chicken biscuits," Mike teased.

"I'm going to beat you up for real if you don't get your ass into the car." She hoisted him up and positioned herself under his armpit, for support. He didn't really seem to need it. He was only a little wobbly. "You kids, you heard me? Stay off this porch."

"Yes ma'am," Terry assured her.

"Good. Don't touch anything. Don't *do* anything," she ordered. "I'll be back as soon as I can."

"I'm not dying. You're overreacting," Mike protested, as she ushered him toward the car.

"Our house just tried to kill you." Sally stuffed him into the passenger's side, and opened the driver's door. One last time, she pointed her finger at Denise and Terry — who still stood in front of the open door. "Get inside, and stay inside. We'll be back." She closed herself inside the car, flung the gearshift into reverse, and peeled out of the gravel drive, back into the street.

"Oh God," Denise whispered.

"That was *crazy*," Terry agreed.

He looked around, and spotted the scattered, still-sealed bags of breakfast food. Slowly, carefully, he reached for the nearest sack and collected it under his arm. He wasn't exactly being sneaky, but you could see it from there.

"Terry . . . what are you doing?"

"The food's getting cold."

"You want to eat? At a time like this?"

He grabbed another crinkly bag and adjusted the top, rolling it up tighter. "You heard your stepdad: He's fine. He'll get some stitches and call it a day. We can't let this perfectly good food go to waste."

She was hungry enough that she kind of agreed with him — but she agreed with her mother, more. "I think Mom's right. This house is trying to kill us."

He hesitated, then collected bag number three. "I hope not. I mean, it wouldn't be the house, but maybe the ghosts . . . ?"

"Oh, knock it off," she said grouchily. She turned to go back inside. "It's an old building that creaks, and moans, and shakes, and falls apart — every chance it gets! It's not a conspiracy."

He bobbed his head toward the hole in the floor. "*That* didn't just fall apart. Look, would you? Look over there, and over there . . ."

At first, she didn't know what he was talking about. She didn't see anything except broken boards, loose nails, and the ragged edges of the plywood. They'd collected the plywood because they were going to use it to cover the floor holes inside, so the workmen could walk around without falling through the floor, like Mike had done.

"What are you talking about?" she asked.

He nudged the nails with his foot. "These nails. They're all over the place, like someone pulled them out. The mean guy really does want to kill you! Or kill *somebody* . . ."

She tiptoed to the edge, and craned her neck over the side. He was right, but she couldn't bring herself to agree out loud. She backed away from the edge, and returned to the doorway. It felt safer there, though maybe it shouldn't have. She didn't know what to say, or how to undermine the fact that yes — someone must've done it, no matter what she said to herself, or Terry. "They must've been like that already."

"That's not true, and you know it. The ghost did it. I bet you anything."

# CHAPTER TEN

Denise headed inside, and paused in the foyer to let Terry catch up. He was the one bringing the food, and like it or not, she was starving. She thought about telling him to beat it, and leave her alone with the biscuits. She didn't want to hear his theories about ghosts, or bad mythical somebodies, or yanked-out nails. But she wasn't quite that mean, not even when she was quivering from low blood sugar and the leftover fright from seeing Mike halfway buried in the front porch, like it'd tried to eat him.

Terry swung inside behind her, balancing the bags with less skill than Mike had done; but everything made it to the dining room table, and Denise went to the kitchen to grab some paper towels because there were never enough napkins. She pulled the bottle of ketchup out of the fridge while she was at it, in case Mike had failed her on that front.

She threw the ketchup onto the table so hard that the bottle fell over, and her hands fluttered as she tossed the paper towels down too. She grabbed for the nearest bag, and unrolled the top to take a big sniff. The aroma of fried batter and salted potatoes wafted up and out.

Terry opened the next bag. He shoved his face in, and frowned. "There's nothing in this bag but ketchup packets."

"Really?" Denise asked, suddenly cheerful. She swiped the bag and dumped the packets onto the table. They tumbled out, along with two sleeves of hash browns. "Naw, see. You're a liar."

"It's *mostly* ketchup. Who even needs that much?"

"I do. If Mike was here, I'd give him a big hug. I never should've doubted him."

The third bag held everything else of note, and soon the table was covered with food for them, and food set aside for the adults upon their return. Mike and Sally could reheat theirs in the microwave upstairs when they got back.

They *would* be back, and everything *would* be fine.

Denise believed it with all her heart. But she ate her chicken biscuit with a mouth that was a little dry, and with an imagination running wild. What if Mike was hurt worse than it looked, and he didn't want to say so in front of her? What if he had some weird internal injuries — what if he was dying and no one noticed? They had health insurance, but it was bare-minimum stuff; Sally said it was just liability coverage on their bodies. What if he wound up in the hospital and it cost thousands and thousands of dollars, and they couldn't afford to do any more work on the house?

What if they had to keep living in it, just like it was?

What if they lost it, and had nowhere to live at all?

"You okay?" Terry asked.

Around a mouthful of food, she said, "What?"

"You're eating weird. You stopped chewing, like, a minute ago."

She swallowed, barely working the big lump down. She looked around for a soda, or a glass of water or something, and saw none. She also saw no reason to answer his question. "I need a Coke. You want one?" She shoved her chair back and went to the fridge without waiting for an answer.

"Sure."

The fridge was still kind of cool, even though the breaker was off. She pulled out two sodas and returned, rolling one past the wads of discarded wrappers and into Terry's hand. They cracked their respective cans at the same time.

The soda barely helped anything at all, but it did wash down the lump.

Terry took a sip and said, "Seriously, though: Are you okay?"

"I'm fine."

"You don't act fine."

"I'm worried about my stepdad."

"Is that all?" he asked, honest curiosity on his face. "You're not worried about the ghosts?"

"Say 'ghost' one more time, and I will throw you headfirst out the damn door."

Carefully, he corrected himself. "You're not worried about any-thing *else*?"

"*No.*"

Terry seemed to understand that he was on dangerous ground. "Do you . . . do you want to read some more of the comic? Might take your mind off the porch, and your stepdad."

"You mean the comic that's obviously about my house, which isn't creepy at *all*?"

He took a second or two to answer. "Yeah, that one."

Denise sighed. They had both finished eating, and they didn't have a TV or anything. "Fine, let's do it."

Terry hopped up out of his seat. "Right on!"

"You are *way* more invested in this comic than I am."

"No, I'm not. I'm just willing to admit that it's hella-cool. I don't know why you're pretending it isn't. Somebody famous used to live here."

"Joe Vaughn didn't live here. Some lady did. I think . . ." She looked over her shoulder, back up the stairs. "Terry, I think Joe Vaughn *died* here." It was the first time she'd said it out loud to anybody, and it felt gross. But it also felt a little good, to have it out in the open.

"You do?"

"Look, the Internet doesn't know that much about what happened to him — just that he was found dead at the bottom of some attic stairs, in a house that didn't belong to him. It belonged to some lady. She disappeared before he died."

"Maybe she's the lady ghost! The one with moxie."

Denise couldn't rule it out. "That's my guess. Except . . ." She started back up the stairs.

The stair rail rattled when Terry grabbed it too, and came along behind her. "Except what?"

"Except, if Joe died here . . . why was his manuscript up in the attic of somebody else's house? Did the lady steal it? Was she . . ." Denise wracked her brain. "Some kind of deranged fan? She could've been a stalker, maybe."

"Or a girlfriend."

"Also possible. Maybe Joe gave it to her. Maybe it was a gift, and she hid it in the attic to protect it."

Terry shrugged. "We can ask the ghosts, next time we try a little EVP. Hey, did you post those sample pages yet?"

"No. Haven't really had the time, man."

"*Somebody* will know *something*."

"But *somebody* might not be surfing the internet. Somebody might be dead and gone."

"Or just dead."

She stopped at the top of the stairs, and rubbed her eyes, and glanced at the attic door without meaning to. "Yeah. Probably just dead."

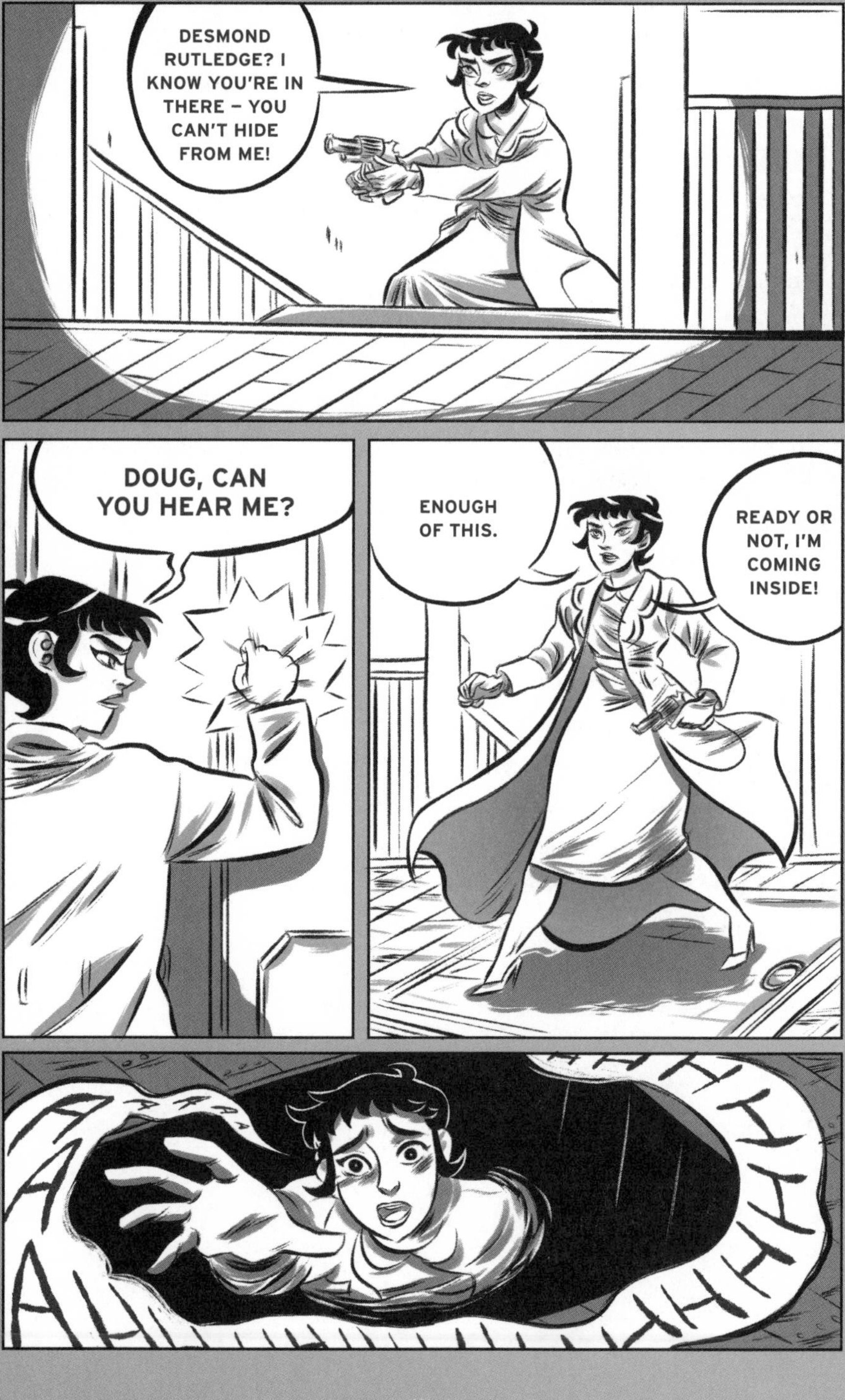
DESMOND RUTLEDGE? I KNOW YOU'RE IN THERE – YOU CAN'T HIDE FROM ME!
DOUG, CAN YOU HEAR ME?
ENOUGH OF THIS.
READY OR NOT, I'M COMING INSIDE!
AAAAA
AAAAHHHHHHHHHHHHHHH

Denise sat up and smacked the book shut.

"What?" Terry asked, trying to grab it back. "Come on, man! It's getting good!"

"It's getting even creepier!" she squeaked. Exasperated, she climbed to her feet and carried the book away from Terry's greedy little mitts. "Come on, my stepdad fell down through the porch — just like Lucida and Doug did!"

Terry shook his head, motioning for her to give the book back. He gave her such an earnest, hopeful look that she had a hard time refusing him. Reluctantly, she passed it back. He opened it to the last page they'd seen, and pointed at the drawing. "No, it's not the same. Lucida Might went through a trapdoor. Your stepdad went through . . . well, he made his own hole."

"Or somebody else did, you said it yourself!"

"I say a lot of things."

Denise almost wanted to cry. "I don't understand why the house — or anybody in it — would want to hurt us."

"Me, either . . . and it's pretty weird that Doug, Lucida, *and* your stepdad got eaten up by a hole in the porch."

"Dammit, Terry." Gently, she took the book back from him. She looked briefly at its blank cover, and squeezed it against her chest. "This is extremely weird and creepy, that's all I know for sure."

"I am all about the weird and creepy!"

She almost smiled at him, but just then she caught a whiff of something sweet. Not candy-sweet, but flower-sweet. Not roses, or not *just* roses. Some other flower, with a sharp note of alcohol on top.

Her nostrils flared, and Terry perked up too. "I smell something. Do you?"

It wouldn't do any good to deny it. She said, "I think it's perfume."

"More like cologne."

"But for ladies, not for dudes."

He agreed with a nod, then looked around Denise's bedroom. "Is it yours?"

"No, it's not mine." She put the book down on her bed, which still hadn't been assembled yet—but she was totally going to get to it, one of these days. So really, she left the book on top of a mattress and box spring.

"Then where's it coming from?"

Denise swallowed, and crossed her arms under her boobs. "The hallway."

"Is there a ghost in the hallway?"

She gave up, and crossed her arms over her stomach. "You're the expert. You tell *me*."

Terry scrambled out the door like a cartoon character. He got two steps away before he remembered his equipment was in his bag, and his bag was on the floor—so he skidded back, unzipped the bag, and whipped out his recorder. He tossed the bag aside and made it all the way to the hall this time, brandishing the recorder like a torch. "Are there any spirits present with us today?" he asked with ridiculous speed and gravity. He sounded like somebody making hasty legal disclaimers at the end of a drug commercial. "Would you like to communicate with the living? Is there a message you'd like to pass along?"

Denise followed out the door more slowly. The perfume smell grew stronger, and she heard a soft, melodious hum. She looked down at the carpet to see if there were any footprints this time—but Terry was in the way, blocking her view. She couldn't see the carpet runner or the attic door.

She froze in the entrance to her bedroom and let him keep walking, holding up the recorder and staring off into space.

"Do you hear anything?" he asked Denise, not the spirit world. "I hear someone singing, but not quite."

Denise whispered, "It's someone humming. I heard it once before, but it doesn't sound the same. This sounds like . . . like a man, I think. I don't like this. It feels like a trick."

"It's going downstairs!" Without a second thought, he adjusted course to follow the unearthly music that wasn't quite music, because they couldn't quite hear it. They could only sense that it was there, somewhere at the edge of their hearing.

"Terry, don't. Be careful."

"Don't be careful. Great advice. I'll take it." He descended the stairs in quick staccato footsteps, and Denise wasn't sure if he was joking or if he'd actually misheard her.

She went down after him. She *had* to. It was her house and these were her ghosts. These were her stairs, and that was her room full of ladders and extension cords at the bottom; those were her boxes of fasteners and bins of tools; that was her stair rail's graceful swirl at the bottom, stuck through with rusty nails, just waiting for someone to grab on and bleed.

The nails on the porch, scattered like jacks.

Nails in the rail, pounded through so the points stuck out, and stuck up.

"Terry! Nails!"

He wasn't paying a lick of attention. He was too wrapped up in the chase, following his nose like a cartoon bird on a cereal box.

She tumbled down the stairs after him, trying to head him off. Her feet tripped over one another, but she stayed upright and she pushed past him as he reached down for support. The nails were plenty big enough and dangerous enough that Denise and Terry should've noticed them on the way upstairs, shouldn't they? She should've seen them before. Someone should've pointed them out, and removed them. Mike would've done it. Sally would've done it. Denise would've done it, if she'd seen them.

No, those nails had never been there before. Someone had put them there, quietly and deliberately. Unnaturally.

"Denise, I'm losing the trail . . ."

She swore at him, and bodychecked him out of the way before he could low-five the mystery pincushion. He spun around with confusion, smacking face-first against the wall and ricocheting back at Denise in the narrow, sharply angled space. It wasn't graceful. It wasn't fun. But Terry didn't get hurt, so . . . mission accomplished.

Denise put up one hand to catch him. She put back one hand to catch herself.

She felt the nail before she saw it, and before she felt it go clean through the web between her thumb and first finger. The violence was finished before she could announce it with a shriek, and a fling of her wrist that sent a thin spurt of blood across Terry's face, up the wall, and across the rickety steps themselves.

Staggering backward, down, off the steps and into the living area where the parlor had holes in the floors and there wasn't any air-conditioning to speak of, Denise clutched her hand to her chest and squeezed at the dirty, bleeding puncture.

Terry leaped to her aid, or at least he leaped to her personal space. "What happened? What are you doing? Why did you push me?"

She held up her hand and let it bleed in front of him, answering enough questions that he turned white. "Oh. My. God." He wiped a smudge of blood off his forehead, looked at the smear on the back of his wrist, and went even paler.

Her eyes scanned the scenery and spied the napkins on the dining room table. She darted over there and seized a fistful, pinching them against the wound. She breathed in and out through her mouth, making whooshing noises all the way—breathing like she was having a baby, because that was supposed to make pain easier to take. "I have to stop the bleeding. I have to keep it from getting infected. I need a first aid kit."

"Do you have one?"

"Under the kitchen sink." She flapped her other hand to show him the general direction she meant, and he went to retrieve it. A dribble of blood oozed down her wrist and trickled down her forearm.

He produced the kit quickly and cracked open the white plastic case.

Denise said, "I need some antibacterial ointment, and some alcohol." She winced as she said the word, knowing how bad it was likely to hurt. "And a couple of Band-Aids."

"I don't know if a couple of Band-Aids are going to cut it."

She left him for the kitchen sink. She put the bloody fast-food napkins beside it, ran the water until it was a little cool, and forced herself to wash her unwanted piercing with some soap. It wasn't really bleeding that bad, all things considered. It was only a little stab, and that was a good thing too. The nail had gone straight through, palm to back, and it didn't hit anything bony.

"It's only a flesh wound," she decided.

"We should call your parents."

She smacked the lever to turn off the water, retrieved the least bloody and most uncrumpled napkins, and applied pressure to the injury. "Absolutely not."

"But you're bleeding."

"Not very bad."

"You screamed."

She rolled her eyes. "It surprised me. It hurts, but that's okay," she assured him, and herself too. "A lot of things hurt. It's not the end of the world. They've got enough problems without me falling onto sharp things."

"No, but it's a rusty nail," he argued. "When was the last time you had a tetanus shot?"

She honestly couldn't remember. She was too rattled. She knew she'd gotten one at some point. It might've been a couple of years ago, or it might've been a lot longer. "It had to be . . . somewhat recently?

Don't you have to have your shots up to date, before you can go to school?"

"You should get another one, just to be safe. Call your mom, and ask her." He held up the antibiotic ointment and a small bottle of peroxide, which would work as well as alcohol in a pinch. "Please?"

Denise didn't respond other than to nod at the kitchen sink, where he put the supplies. She wadded up all but a couple of napkins, thrust them inside one of the empty takeout bags to hide their bloody nature, and stuffed them deep into the trash can beside the fridge. She wrestled one-handed with the peroxide until Terry took it away from her and pushed the childproof cap loose. He offered to do the honors, so she let him — cleaning the wound and treating it and wrapping it up with the biggest Band-Aid that was left in the mostly empty box.

"Look, I won't tell your parents," he said finally. "But people get hurt less every day, and it turns into a big deal because they didn't take care of themselves," he insisted. "Don't be that guy."

"I've never been that guy."

"Yeah, well. Don't start now."

Outside, they heard a car's engine come low and slow up to the house. Wheels turned and ground on gravel. "Hurry up!" Denise urged, using her free right hand to scoop up the bits of leftover bandage packaging, the ointment, and the first aid kit itself.

While Terry performed the last of his doctoring, she used one hand to cram everything back inside the plastic case and toss the garbage into the trash. When he was finished, she stashed everything where it belonged, running back and forth between the dining room table and the kitchen sink, and the stairway rail — where she used the last of the napkins to swab down the visible blood and wipe down the nails.

But whoever had pulled up to the house was only turning around. The car was large and green, and it didn't stay — it only backed up and headed the other direction.

"Oh thank God," she breathed, watching it leave through the parlor window. "There's still time."

Terry was washing his hands at the sink. Over his shoulder he called out, "Time for what?"

Denise looked around for the tool bins, and selected a sturdy hammer with an oversized head. She quietly thanked God, or heaven, or friendly ghosts, that she'd only hurt her left hand, and the right was still strong enough to pry nails out of the stair rail before they could hurt anyone else. Or before anyone else could see them.

"Like I said, I'm going to fix this mess that Joe made." She tested the hammer's weight in her hand.

"You think it's really him?"

"Yeah, I do. Because of all the nails. There were nails rolling around when the window shut on my mom, and nails on the porch when Mike fell through, and now there are nails on the stair rail." She didn't smell flowers anymore, and there wasn't any more blood on the staircase. Of course, there weren't any more napkins, either, and Mike would probably notice. She'd say she spilled something, and used them to clean it up. It was practically true. She would tell him it was ketchup. He'd believe her.

"What's Joe got to do with nails, though?"

It was a reach, but her gut was giving her the green light so she aired her hunch out loud. "He used to be a carpenter; that's what Wikipedia said. Maybe he thinks he still is one."

Terry nodded thoughtfully, and dried his hands on the dish towel hanging from the stove handle. "Maybe. Or maybe he's just a jerk who likes to play with sharp things. Either way, I'm going to help clean this up."

Denise appreciated the help, but she wasn't sure she should accept it. She half thought about sending him home for his own good. After all, she had a comic book upstairs that was basically a portent of doom; every time she read it, something bad happened.

That was crazy, right? Too crazy to be true, for sure.

She kept her mouth shut while she levered the hammer's head up and down, dragging the nails up and out of the bannister and handing them to Terry, one after another.

Until it was just full of holes.

# CHAPTER ELEVEN

Denise hid her injured hand in her pocket. When no one was looking, she changed the Band-Aids and squeezed more ointment onto the ragged, round holes that were red and angry-looking, but were they more red and angry-looking than the day before? She couldn't tell. She looked up "blood poisoning" online, because Terry had said she might get it. But no matter how hard she checked, she didn't see any pink lines creeping out from the hole, creeping up her arm and toward her heart.

She was slightly less certain about the symptoms of tetanus. She knew there were shots for that one and she'd probably had one in the recent past; but sometimes people called tetanus "lockjaw," and that sounded much more disturbing. She opened and closed her mouth as wide as she could, over and over again — testing to see if anything was seizing up, or getting stiff.

She really didn't want to show it to anybody, despite Terry's insistence that she get some proper medical attention. And of course, he had a suggestion. Terry *always* had a suggestion.

According to him, the high school's nurse moonlighted at a CVS clinic during the summer. Her name was Ms. Radlein, and when she wasn't patching up kids at Rudy Lombard High, she was doling out vaccinations and advice in the pharmaceutical section of the nearest drugstore.

By all reports, she was a popular and reasonable woman, and she had been known to be discreet. "Anyway, she's a friend of my dad's," he'd finished. He'd given her directions to the bus that would take her there, and then he finally gave up trying to make her go — telling her to do whatever she wanted, but not to come crawling to him when she dropped dead.

Denise wasn't too keen on the idea of dropping dead.

She also wasn't keen on the idea of her mom and Mike finding out about this, so she sucked it up, and first thing in the morning she took the bus to the drugstore. It was less than two miles away, but she was glad for the sticky cool air of the bus, because outside it was far, far worse. She'd had to wait until Sally was across town, arguing with the bank about when the next disbursement of the loan would be coming down the pike — and Mike was sleeping in, doped a little on painkillers and worn out from his traumatic experience.

Denise left a note, just in case. It was a vague note. It promised little, except that she was alive and she intended to return. If she was lucky, she'd be back in time to wad it up and throw it into the trash — and no one would ever read it.

The drugstore was on a block with a strip mall that was brand-new, but half-empty. In addition to the CVS it held a cash-for-gold place, a cell phone shop, and a laundromat. The other three slots were vacant, but a sign promised a chain pizza joint: COMING SOON!

Denise got off the bus and stood in a freshly paved parking lot with jet-black asphalt that felt like the surface of the sun, even through her flip-flops. She checked her hand for fresh swelling or streaks, took a deep breath, and pushed the glass door to let herself inside.

The AC was as new as everything else; it hit her in the face so hard and so fast that it dried out her eyes. She blinked until they worked right again, checked the signs above the aisles, and headed to the back right corner of the store — where the drugs were doled out and the nurse allegedly lurked, ready to stab people with needles. Or whatever.

She arrived at the small lobby area in front of the pharmacists' window, where everything smelled sterile and new. It was quiet back there too. No one was waiting for a prescription, and the people in the white lab coats were all busy in the shelves, setting up medicine for absent customers.

Around the fake wall that didn't even reach to the ceiling, she could hear a woman's voice explaining something calmly. A moment later, out stepped the girl whose name Denise was pretty sure was Dominique. She was stuffing something into her backpack, and when she realized that she'd been spotted, her eyes flashed. She zipped up her bag.

She wouldn't even look up as she fled.

The nurse followed behind her. She was tall, thin, and white — with short silver hair and a gray pantsuit under an unbuttoned lab coat. She checked around, and saw that Denise was standing there, alone and shifty-looking. "Do you need tampons too?" she asked. "I know it gets tricky when school's not in session, so I keep a stash. Are you new here? Did Dom or one of the other girls send you?"

"No ma'am. That's not . . . what I need." She suddenly felt very self-conscious. "And yes ma'am, I'm new. I didn't mean to . . . I wasn't try-ing to . . . I can get my own tampons, thanks. We're not rich, but we're not that bad off. Yet," she added.

"All right then, what can I do for you?"

She had a funny accent, one Denise couldn't quite place. It almost sounded like a northern city accent, but she suspected that it wasn't. She shifted her weight from foot to foot, feeling more awkward than if she really *had* come to collect some tampons.

Denise pulled her hand out from under her backpack, where she'd gotten used to hiding it. "I . . . I hurt myself, at home. I can't tell if it's getting infected . . . ? I don't know." She peeled off the bandage and waved her hand a little, shaking off the sting.

The woman, whose name tag confirmed that she was "Nurse Radlein," assumed an expression of cautious concern. She took Denise's hand and turned it over, checking the entry and exit punctures. "How did this happen?"

"Rusty nail. My mom and stepdad are fixing up an old house. It's a craphole," Denise said, preemptively. It was becoming a defensive habit. "I wasn't paying attention. Nobody's fault but my own," she added. That part was defensive too.

"The nail went right through, didn't it?"

"Yeah. I've been trying to keep it clean, but . . . I don't know. Am I going to get blood poisoning, or something?"

"When was your last tetanus shot?"

"I'm not sure."

Nurse Radlein released her hand, and withdrew toward the nook around the wall—motioning for Denise to follow her. "It can't have been *too* long ago. You have to provide vaccination records before enrolling in school. You're not homeschooled, are you?"

"No ma'am. Public school, but I've been in Texas." She stood there uncertainly, squeezing her hurt hand with her unhurt hand and wondering if this was really such a good idea.

Nurse Radlein glanced up, and then waved her closer. "All right, well. Go ahead and sit down."

The nurse sat on the edge of her desk, motioning for Denise's hand again. When she had it in her grasp once more for an up close and personal inspection, she said, "This isn't bad at all, and I don't see any signs of infection. You've done a good job taking care of it. When did it happen?"

"Yesterday."

"Then I wouldn't worry too much, because it's looking good. But in case it's been a few years since your tetanus booster, you might want to get another one, just in case. It can't hurt, and might help."

Denise shook her head. "Naw, I can't do that."

"Why not?"

"Because my parents . . . um . . . they don't know about this. I didn't want to worry them. We don't have much money, and my stepdad already had to go to the urgent care place."

"You've got money enough to fix a house. Money enough for tampons over the summer, apparently."

"I didn't . . . I wasn't being all *judgy* about that." Denise's eyes narrowed. "Look, we barely had money enough to buy that house, even though it's practically condemned. I know there's kids who are broker than us, but we aren't flush."

"I didn't say you were. All I meant was —"

"We've got every last dime tied up in this awful old place, and it'll probably fall down anyway, before we can prop it up good. Don't act like tampons and tetanus shots are the same thing. Just 'cause I can swing one doesn't mean I can have both."

"I *understand* that," the nurse insisted. "But I can help you with free tampons, and not a free tetanus shot. That's what I'm trying to tell you: Your resources may be limited, but you've got more to work with than some people — and I can help you juggle them more wisely."

Denise gave the nurse a long, hard look. She wasn't sure if she believed her or not. Finally, she sighed. "Forget it. I appreciate the offer, but I can't take you up on it. I *can't* tell my parents. It's not just the money . . . it's the house. And whoever's still in it." She slung her bag around, and turned to leave. "I'm sorry. I shouldn't have come here. I need help, but you're right. I don't need it that bad."

"That's not the message I was trying to convey. Here, at least let me bandage you back up . . ."

"I've got my own Band-Aids." She wrapped her hand back up again as best as she could while on the run, and fled the makeshift office just like Dominique had, embarrassed for different reasons — reasons she couldn't quite put into words. She squeezed out around the fake wall, into the soft mumbling echoes of the drugstore with its rows of greeting cards, housewares, vitamins, and shampoo.

She hustled away from the pharmacy toward the front door. Around the first corner she went, her flip-flops squeaking on the floor, one after the other, going so fast that by the time she rounded the last aisle past the makeup counter, she was almost running.

That's why it hurt, when she plowed into Dominique.

The other girl wasn't coming from the other direction; she wasn't moving at all. She stopped Denise cold, with the force of just standing there.

Denise bounced back—partly by reflex, partly by physics. "Sorry," she said fast, and she meant it. "I didn't mean to. I'm sorry about that—I didn't see you."

"I know."

"Were you . . . were you waiting for me? You're . . . you're Dominique, right? From Crispy's?"

"Yeah, that's me. What were you doing in there? Were you asking for stuff? Stuff you could buy your own damn self?"

"No," she told her. "I swear, I wasn't. I wouldn't take advantage."

"You know Miss Ginny buys it for us. Out of her own pocket, sometimes—especially over the summer when we can't just go to her office in the school."

"Nurse Radlein . . . is Miss Ginny?"

"To *us*, not you."

Dominique took a step forward, and Denise took a step back—stopping against a L'Oreal display that she couldn't afford to mess up. She held up both of her hands, showing the bandage. "I went to the nurse for help, all right?"

Dominique looked at the half-bandaged covering there, and saw a spreading red dot. "Oh, crap. What happened?" she asked, like she honestly wanted to know.

Denise closed her hand and felt it growing damp. The puncture wound was bleeding again, a sharp little stigmata that just wouldn't close all the way. "I got hurt, all right? I can't tell my parents. I thought I needed a tetanus shot."

"Why won't you tell your parents? Go to your doctor, or something."

"We don't *have* a doctor! We don't have money, either. *God*," she said, using the hem of her tee to apply pressure. The shirt was black, and it wouldn't show. "All we have is a craphole of a house and a ghost that's trying to kill us."

The door's greeting bell rang louder than a gunshot, and a cop strolled inside, taking off his sunglasses and tucking them into his pocket. He was white, with hair that was almost white too, in a crew cut that said he meant business — probably all the time, whether he was in uniform or not. He gave the girls a side-glance.

They straightened up and fake-smiled for all they were worth. Dominique batted her eyelashes and said brightly to Denise, "Look, they have that new mascara. Is this the kind you wanted?"

Denise had been watched by enough security guards in enough makeup aisles to know how this worked. "Oh yeah, that's it. Do they have anything except that blue-black? That stuff looks like crap on me; my hair's too light for it. The dark brown looks better."

Dom flipped through the offerings, pretending to look. "I see brownish black. Is that close enough?"

"Might be. Let me see . . ."

After a few seconds of suspicious observation, the cop gave them a nod of his head, the kind that said he was going to walk away, but he was still watching them. Then he lost interest and headed somewhere else in the store.

Dominique was rattled.

Denise was rattled too, but not quite the same way. "I hope he didn't think we were stealing."

Dom leaned in and whispered: "Don't even say that, not so loud. You don't want him coming back, do you? *Jeez*."

"No, I really don't," she mumbled back.

Dominique had already turned away. She pushed her way past the glass door, and was gone.

Denise thought about going after her, but she saw the bus pulling around the corner, so she went to the stop instead, feeling a little lost. She looked for Dominique but didn't see her, and she gave up when the bus drew up to a halt and the doors split open.

Inside, she gave the driver her transfer and took a seat right behind him—where she fiddled with the dirty little bandage and used her next to last fresh Band-Aid. It didn't want to stick. Her skin was too messy from dried blood, or too damp with the blood that hadn't dried yet.

She tucked her hand into her shirt and tried not to look as gross as she felt.

Back home, she tossed the note she'd left behind, because Mike was still snoring in the bedroom and her mom's car was nowhere to be seen.

Then she washed her hands and very, very carefully applied her final sticky bandage.

When she was as first-aided up as she was going to get, she sat down at the dining room table with a Coke and poked idly at her phone.

As it turned out, her old school friends in Texas were mostly talking about some kid from her class who'd died in a car wreck. It was no one she'd known very well. He'd been a face in the hall, and she might've recognized him on sight, or then again, she might not. It was a surprise, but not a catastrophe. It happened a million miles away, to someone she barely recognized.

But jeez, everybody back at her old school was in crazy mourning, at least online. She shot Trish a text asking about it, hoping for details.

*What kind of car wreck?* She asked. *Was it his fault, or somebody else?*

Trish responded immediately, and briefly. **Nobody knows yet. Rumor has it he ran a stop sign or something. Will let you know if I hear anything for sure.**

*Didn't know him very well but it's sad,* Denise added.

**He was a friend of Kierons. You should reach out, say something nice to your dear old ex.**

*No.* She shook her head as she texted. It'd be more trouble than it was worth.

Then Trish said something about getting ready to catch a matinee, and turning off her phone, so Denise started to close hers too, but then her email pinged to say she had something new. She tapped the icon with her thumb, and frowned with confusion, then smiled.

Hello Miss Farber, my name is Eugenie Robbins. My father was Marty Robbins, and yes, a long time ago he was Joe Vaughn's literary agent. As you may have learned by now, Joe disappeared decades ago. (And I regret to say that my father is now deceased.)

I was very excited to see the images you sent! I'm not familiar with that particular Lucida Might story, but Joe wrote so many of them. It doesn't mean that *Lucida Might and the House of Horrors* was never published.

Your message mentioned that you live in New Orleans, and you're afraid that you live in the house where Joe died. I suppose you might? I don't know exactly where he was found, but I will try to look up an address for you. All I remember, off the top of my head, is that the house belonged to an older woman, and no one really knew why Joe was in her house.

I'd love to see the whole manuscript—if you have the time or interest in scanning it for me. Joe's comics are all out of print, and no one remembers the TV show anymore, but a lost manuscript might revive interest in his backlist. As far as I know, Joe had no heirs or near relatives; at least, no one ever came forward to claim his estate.

I'm not saying that you're sitting on a gold mine by any

means, but there might be some money to be made—you never know. I'd be happy to talk about representing the project for you or your parents, if you're interested in shopping it around. My agency manages my father's surviving clients (or their estates), and in all honesty, the thought of handling one of Dad's authors (even indirectly, after all this time) makes me very, very happy.

It's funny, my dad used to say that Joe sometimes hid "Easter eggs" in his stories, little pieces of autobiography, here and there. Does the house in the comic look anything like yours? That would be fascinating, wouldn't it? Maybe that's why he was there. Maybe he used it as an art reference. He must've known the lady who owned it.

Think about it. Let me know. Feel free to be in touch, and by all means, enjoy the reading!

At the bottom of the email, she'd included her office address and phone number.

"Huh," Denise said out loud.

A grumble of gravel suggested that her mother's car was pulling up beside the house.

She closed her phone and tucked it into her back pocket.

Around noon, Norman showed up for his new side gig with a large pizza. "Unclaimed at work," he explained, deploying the box to the middle of the dining room table with a casual flip of his wrist.

"I love this guy!" a freshly awakened Mike declared with honest enthusiasm. "What are the toppings?"

"They're *free* toppings," Denise guessed. "The best toppings of all."

Sally came down the stairs, shaking her head all the way. "No, no, no. Don't be silly. Thank you, Norman — that was very thoughtful, but of course I want to pay you for it. You didn't have to bring lunch."

"No way, Mrs. Cooper. I got it for free, so you get it for free. My only condition is that I get a piece. I'd ask for two, but I had one at work already."

They gathered around, pulled up chairs, and split up the free pizza.

When it was successfully reduced to crumbs, Mike slowly helped clean up, moving stiffly. He'd come home with stitches and an order to stay off his feet, but he wasn't paying much attention to that order. He was still doing all the same stuff as before — just slower, and more carefully.

Norman leaned over and asked Denise quietly, "His foot's still not any better?"

"It's not his foot anymore," she whispered back. "He fell through the porch and got hurt."

"Holy crap. This place ought to come with hazard pay . . ."

On her way to the kitchen, Sally said, "Norman, today we're going to pull down the rotted trim in the extra bedrooms upstairs, and prep for painting. There's still some wallpaper that needs to come down, and probably some plaster in need of patching."

"You name it — just point me at the supplies!"

She disappeared into the kitchen to grab some paper towels, and Denise's phone buzzed on the table.

"Anything interesting?" Norman asked.

"Maybe?" She wasn't sure if she should tell him about Lucida Might, but then again, she couldn't see why not. "See, the other day I found this manuscript, up in the attic. It's a comic book," she explained. And then she told the rest as fast as possible, concluding, "Supposedly this guy's papers are archived out at Tulane. Didn't you say you work there, sometimes, during the week? At the cafeteria? Maybe you could show me where the library is. I've never been there before."

"Yeah, sure. I can do that. It's only a couple of buses and a little walking. Can I see the comic book, if I take you out there?"

"Sure."

"Cool. Then what are you doing this weekend?"

"Not a thing."

He bobbed his head from left to right. "We can do it on Saturday. Meet you at the bus stop outside the school?"

"Sounds awesome. What time?"

"How about eleven? We can change buses down by the market — and pick up some lunch or something, if you want."

Oh, yes. She definitely wanted.

# CHAPTER TWELVE

**How are ur ghosts? Still ghosty?**

Denise grinned down at the text. She'd only told Trish the bare basics of the spook situation. *Still ghosty, but quiet ATM. Mike is doing better, I think. Not quite so grunty and stiff.*

**That's good. I hope nobody else gets hurt. By ghosts or whatever.**

She could only agree. *Me too.*

**So what about school next year? UR still coming back, rite?**

*Planning on it. Got a good roommate waiting back in Texas.*

Trish replied, **Awwww. You mean me? You had BETTER mean me.**

*Always you, yes — you big dork :)*

Eventually, after a slow-growing headache from staring at her ancient phone, Denise gave up and decided to hoof it down to Crispy's. She badgered Sally to pick her up when summoned via text, and her mom agreed — just to get rid of her, Denise was pretty sure.

She brought two bucks because that's all she could scare up. It was only enough to get a drink and a small order of fries, but that was okay. She wasn't really hungry for anything except Internet.

She generally avoided the smattering of other kids who were hanging out in the dining area — all of whom were doing pretty much the same thing she was. One or two had phones, a couple had laptops open. One guy kept jiggling his power cord's connection, and Denise knew that feeling. If she didn't have hers positioned at just the perfect angle, it'd pop out easy as pie.

When she'd collected her food on a tray and picked a seat against the wall, she turned on her phone — but the only new message was a late closing volley from Trish, who declared herself QUEEN OF THE DORKS and don't u forget it

The door chimed, and someone came in. Someone hung out in Denise's peripheral vision, hovering. It was Dominique, acting like she wanted to say something.

"Hey," Denise said. "What's up?"

"Nothing," the other girl said back, but she worked her way a little closer. "Except, I was gonna say sorry about the CVS thing. I didn't know you were hurt, and then you played along later, and I appreciated it. So . . . are we cool?"

"Sure. We're cool." She wasn't sure how to ask what prompted the apology, but she wanted to know so she stumbled around the subject. "You um . . . you mean about the cop?"

"Oh, that guy's a jerk. He harasses us all summer — but I was standing next to you, in the white privilege zone," she said with a grin. "Anyway, my grandma will kill me if I get banned from the drugstore, for stealing or mouthing off, or anything else. She sends me down there all the time, running her errands and buying her smokes."

"But you weren't stealing."

"No, but that might not've stopped him, if he'd been in the wrong mood. Or if I'd been by myself. Or . . . I don't know." Dominique looked relieved and kind of embarrassed. "Anyway, that's all. I just wanted to say that."

"I'm just glad you're not mad."

"No, I'm not mad. See you around." Dominique melted back into the lobby to join somebody else she knew, and then Denise was on her own again.

Until Terry arrived.

He strolled into the joint and made a beeline for her. He didn't go to the counter to buy anything, but parked himself into the swivel chair across the table from where Denise had — once upon a time — had every intention of getting some sweet, sweet Internet-and-AC time.

He asked, "How's your hand?"

She held it up and waved it around. "It bleeds a little, sometimes, but the nurse said it looked fine. Hey, I was gonna ask you: Do you have any extra Band-Aids lying around at your house? I'm running out, and I still haven't told Mom or Mike what happened."

"All we have is one first aid kit. My dad stocks it from work, when he can. We don't have any extras, not Band-Aids or anything else. Sorry."

"No, I understand. I um . . . I shouldn't have asked."

"The nurse didn't give you any?"

"The nurse and I disagreed over whether or not I should tell my parents about the whole thing. She says they should take me to get a tetanus shot, just to be on the safe side. I said we couldn't do it, not after Mike's accident."

Terry nodded knowingly. He politely refrained from saying, 'I told you so.' "How'd your stepdad turn out, anyway?"

"They gave him a bunch of stitches, and he has some pretty bad bruises. He's taking it easy for a few days so he doesn't bust any of the sutures. Mom's waiting on him hand and foot, and telling him not to get used to it. If I'm lucky, she'll come and give me a ride home when I text her."

"If she doesn't, I'll walk back with you."

"Thanks, man. If she does, I'll get her to give you a lift home too. If you want."

He smiled, and his cheeks were as round as apples. "You're awesome. So . . . have you read any more of the comic?" he asked, his voice dripping with the hint.

"Nope. I stuffed it under my bed."

"You have a bed now? Not just the mattress on the floor?"

"I quit waiting for Mike to assemble it, and put it together myself." A smidge of pride seeped into the declaration. "It took me half the afternoon, but I did it."

He stopped hinting. "Go you. So . . . if you want, I could come over and we could read it together. If you want."

She relented. It was easier than fighting him. "I'm sure it's fine." Her phone buzzed. It was Sally, saying she'd have to walk home on her own after all. "Great. Mom says she's not going to pick me up. So it's foot-power for both of us. What the hell. Let's go."

Terry predicted that the trip wouldn't take them ten minutes, and he was right. They arrived at the Agony House before anybody'd sweated through their clothes too badly, and they found the place empty.

Sally had left a note on the dining room table.

*The power's on, so you can run your AC. Electricians are done for now. Plumbers are barely started, but they should be gone by the time you read this. They'll be back tomorrow. Sorry I'm not home, and sorry you had to walk. I trust you survived the journey. I'll be back soon. Mike blew out a couple of stitches, so I'm running him back to the doctor for a patch-up.*

"Great," Denise declared, with great sarcasm. "Now I *definitely* can't tell them I need a tetanus shot."

"Maybe they won't charge him, if it's only a couple of stitches. Since they already got paid to do it once."

She ignored his optimism, knowing it was useless. "I don't think it works that way. I swear . . . by the time we're done with this house, that doctor will be able to buy himself a yacht. Maybe I should change my major and go to med school. I could use a yacht."

"You don't have a major yet. You're still in high school." Then he paused and frowned. "Right?"

"I'll be a senior this year: Rudy Lombard, or bust. And I *will* have a major, pretty soon."

He dropped his bag on the table, beside hers. "What will it be?"

"Law," she said. "I'm going to be a lawyer."

"Everybody hates lawyers."

"I know. That's why I'm going to be one." She explained, "Me and Mom, when it was just the two of us . . . we got screwed over a bunch. Our landlords were always cheap bastards, or crooked bastards. They'd take our money and let the place go to hell, or refuse to give us our deposits back, so we couldn't move to a better place. First and last month's rent is hard to pull together when you can't get your deposit back."

"Tell me about it."

"They always had some BS reason for it, and they always would send us letters from their attorneys, kicking us out or saying we owed more money than we ever agreed to. It was a racket," she declared, echoing something her mom had said years before. "There was one lawyer who tried to bleed us dry, when my mom got served for driving without insurance — and another lawyer who charged us a bunch of money when Mom got hit at a stoplight. Some dumb girl was texting, and plowed right into her. It tore up Mom's shoulder and neck real bad, but all the money we got from the girl's insurance went to the lawyer's fees. Mom needed physical therapy for months. We could only afford it for a couple of weeks."

Terry scrunched up his face, like he wasn't entirely sure where she was going with this. "So . . . if you can't beat 'em, join 'em?"

"Exactly! If we'd had a lawyer . . . if we could've afforded a *real* one . . . things would've been different for us. Once I'm a lawyer, I'll make sure that kind of BS doesn't happen again. Not to my mom, or me, or anybody else who needs help but can't pay through the nose to get it."

"You'll be a lawyer for free?"

"Not for everybody—only for the broke folks. Or that's the plan. Now come on, I'll drag out the comic since it's just you and me."

"You promise you won't get creeped out again, and slam it shut?"

"Yeah, I promise. Let's see what this ghost has in store for us next. Forewarned is forearmed, right?"

"I have no idea. I don't even know what that *means.*"

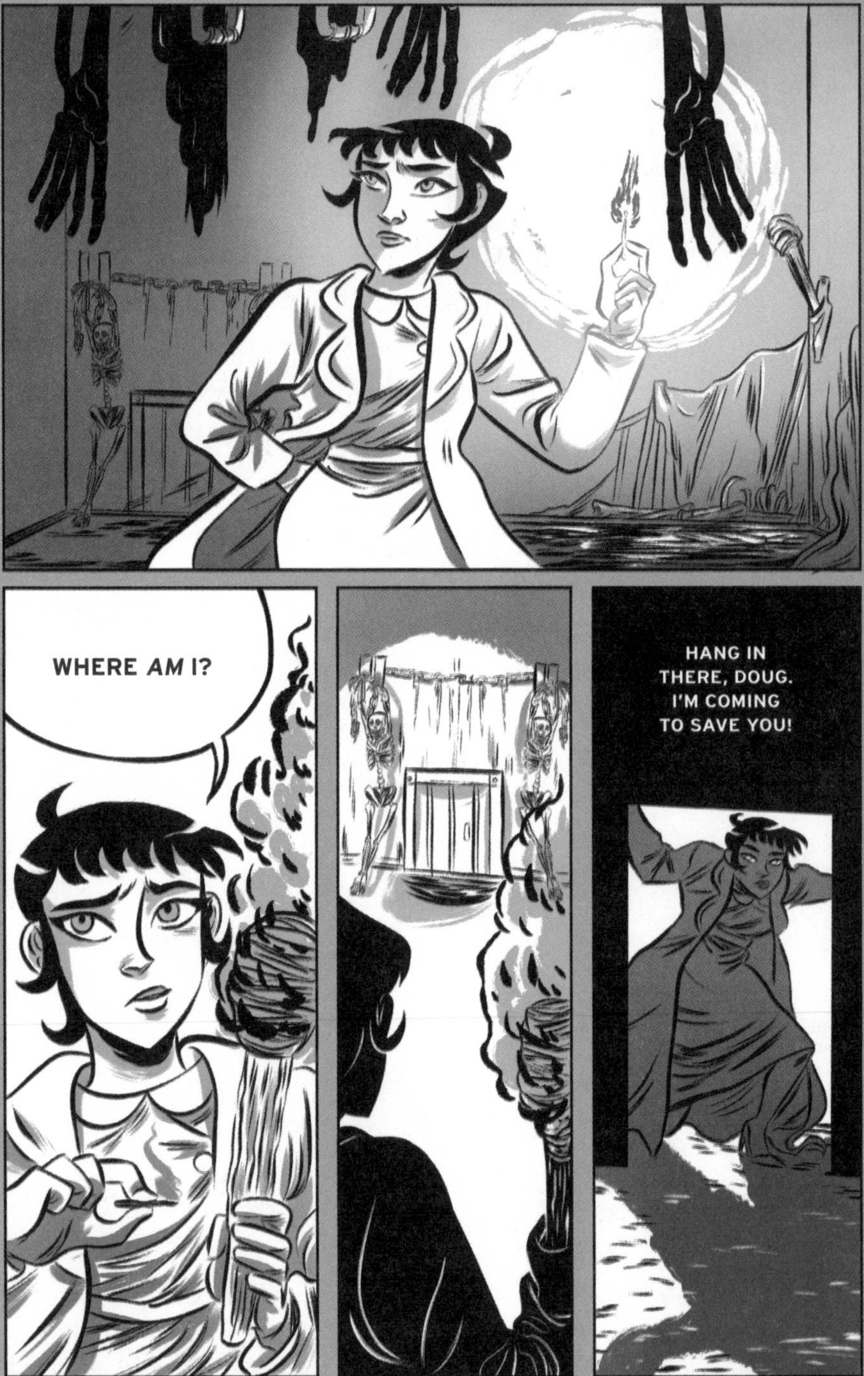
WHERE *AM* I?
HANG IN THERE, DOUG. I'M COMING TO SAVE YOU!

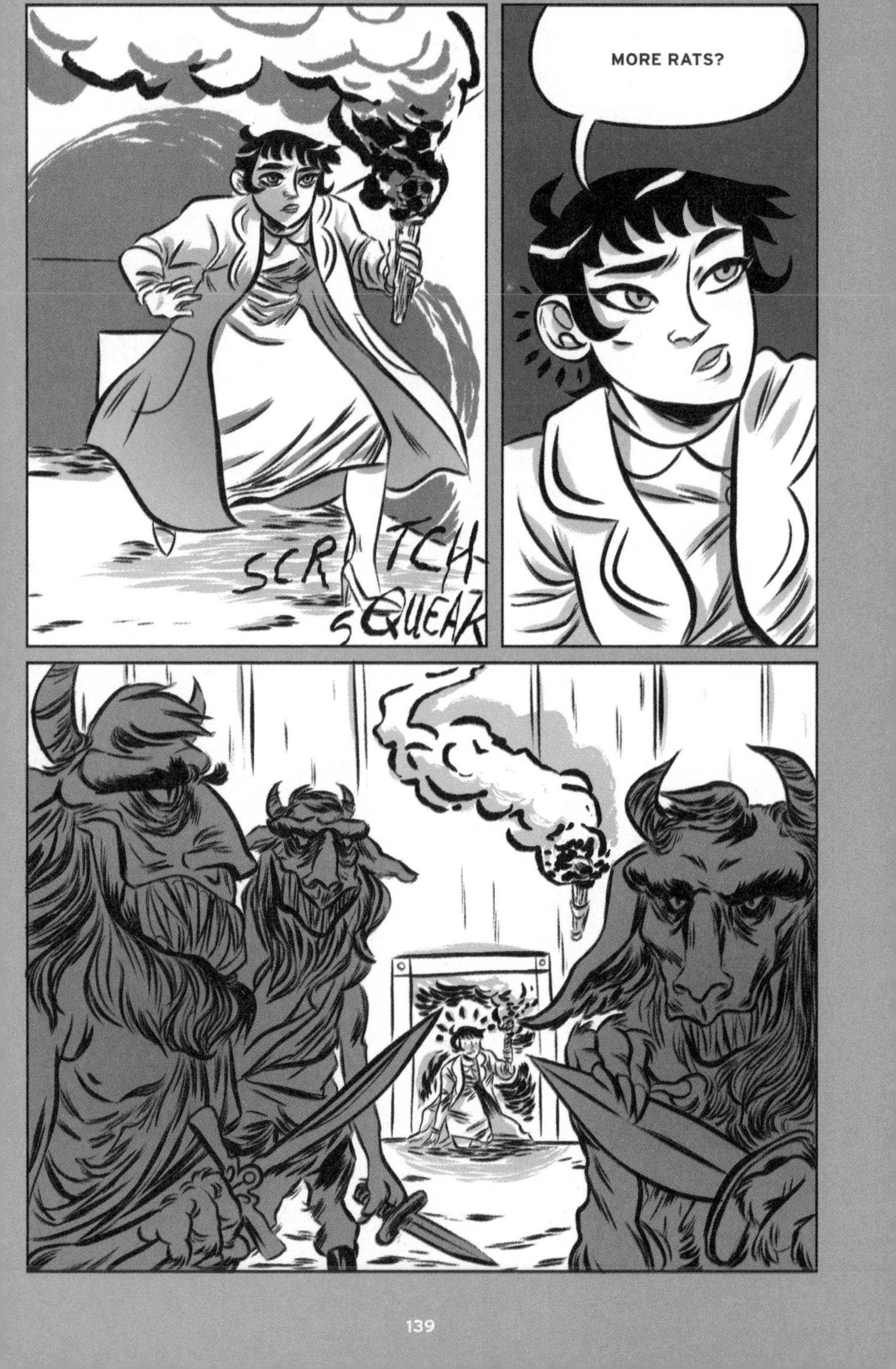
SCR TCH
SQUEAK
MORE RATS?

Terry leaned back against Denise's bed, and let out a little laugh.

"What's so funny?" she asked him.

He pointed at the open manuscript. "See? The comic isn't predicting what's going to happen. Unless you seriously think you've got goblins, in addition to rats and spiders. And ghosts."

"So far, we have absolutely zero goblins. No rats, either. I think? I haven't seen any. Plenty of spiders, though."

He nodded gravely. "Oh, you definitely have rats. *Everybody* has rats, around here. But it'd be worse if we were any closer to the river."

"Please do not tell me these things."

"I'm only trying to help."

"Stop. Stop trying to help," she urged. "Forget what I said about being forewarned. What I don't know won't hurt me."

"Oh my God, you are *so* wrong."

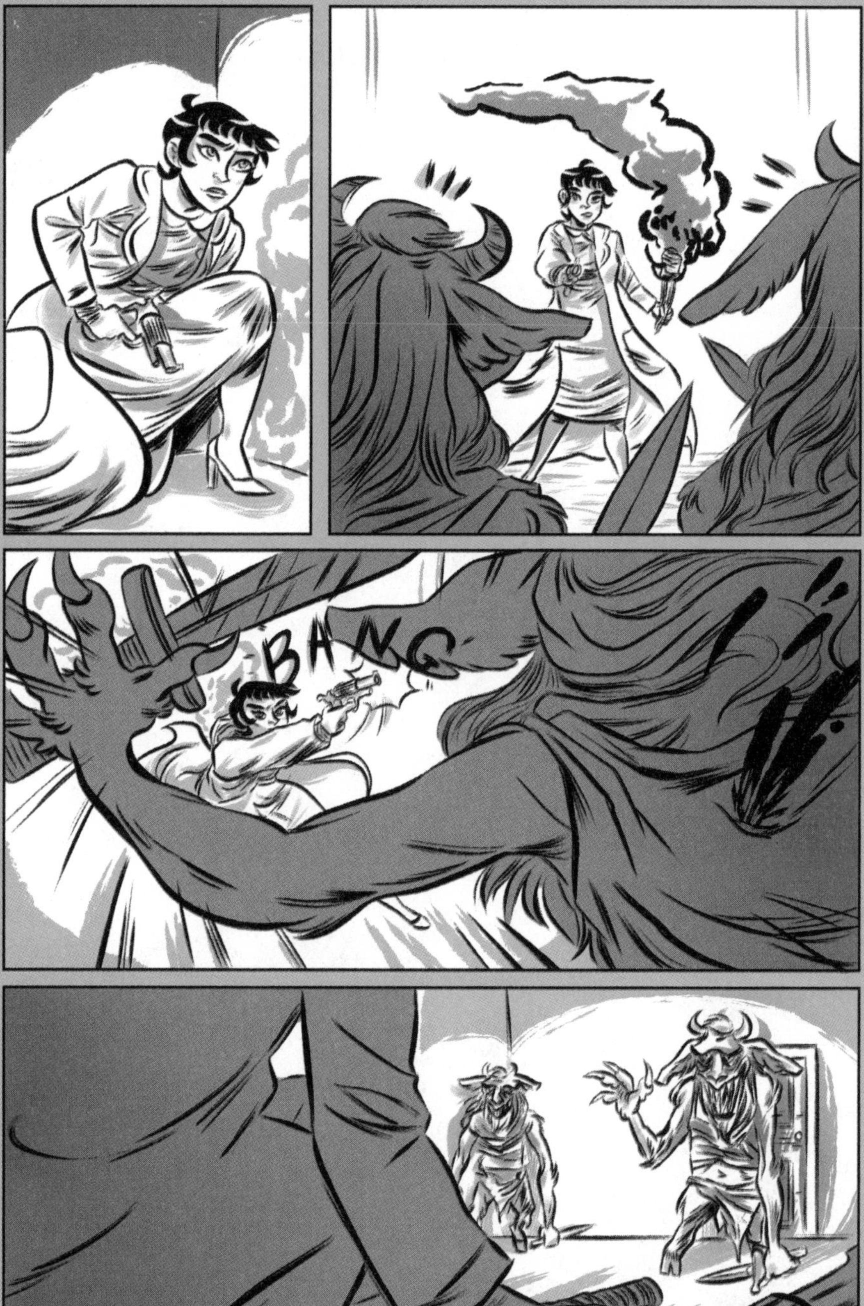
BANG

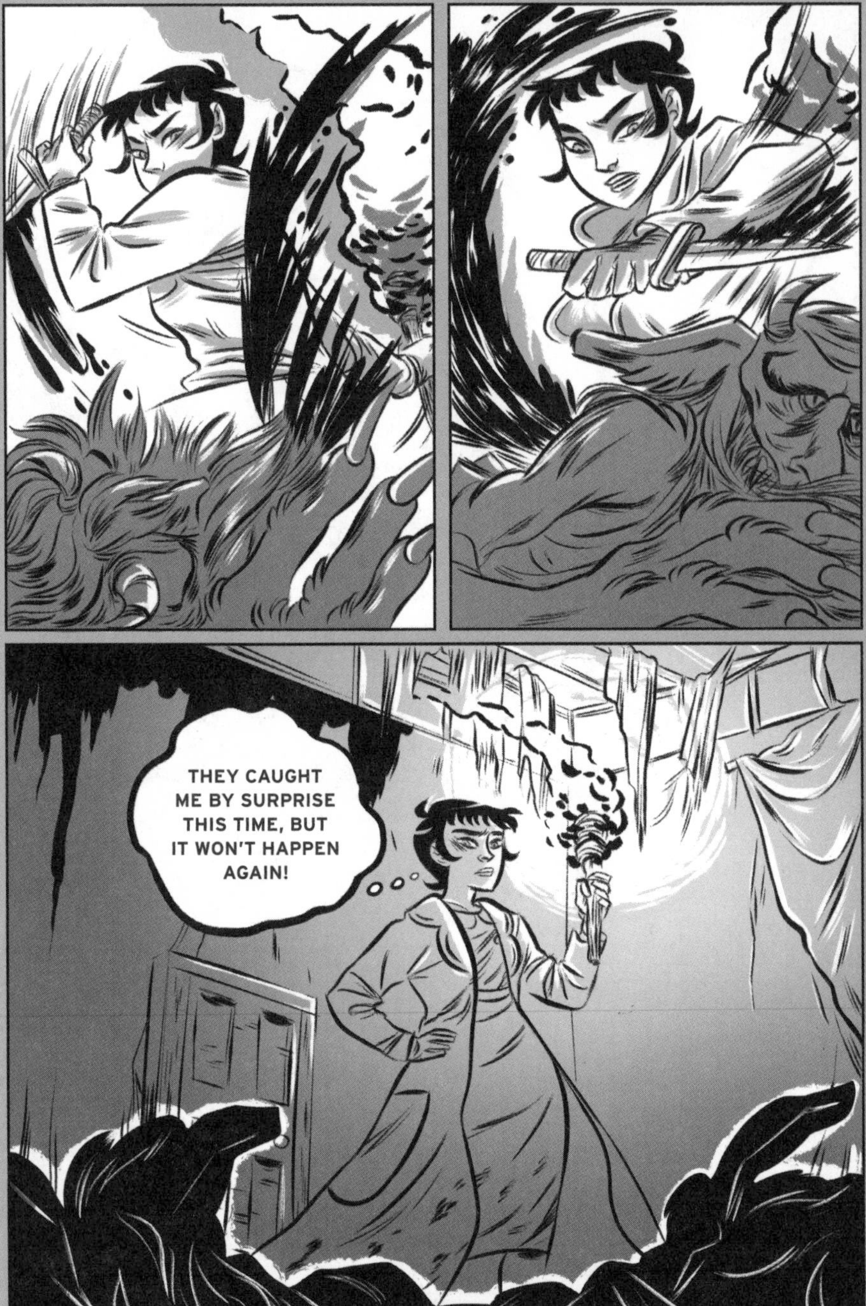
THEY CAUGHT ME BY SURPRISE THIS TIME, BUT IT WON'T HAPPEN AGAIN!

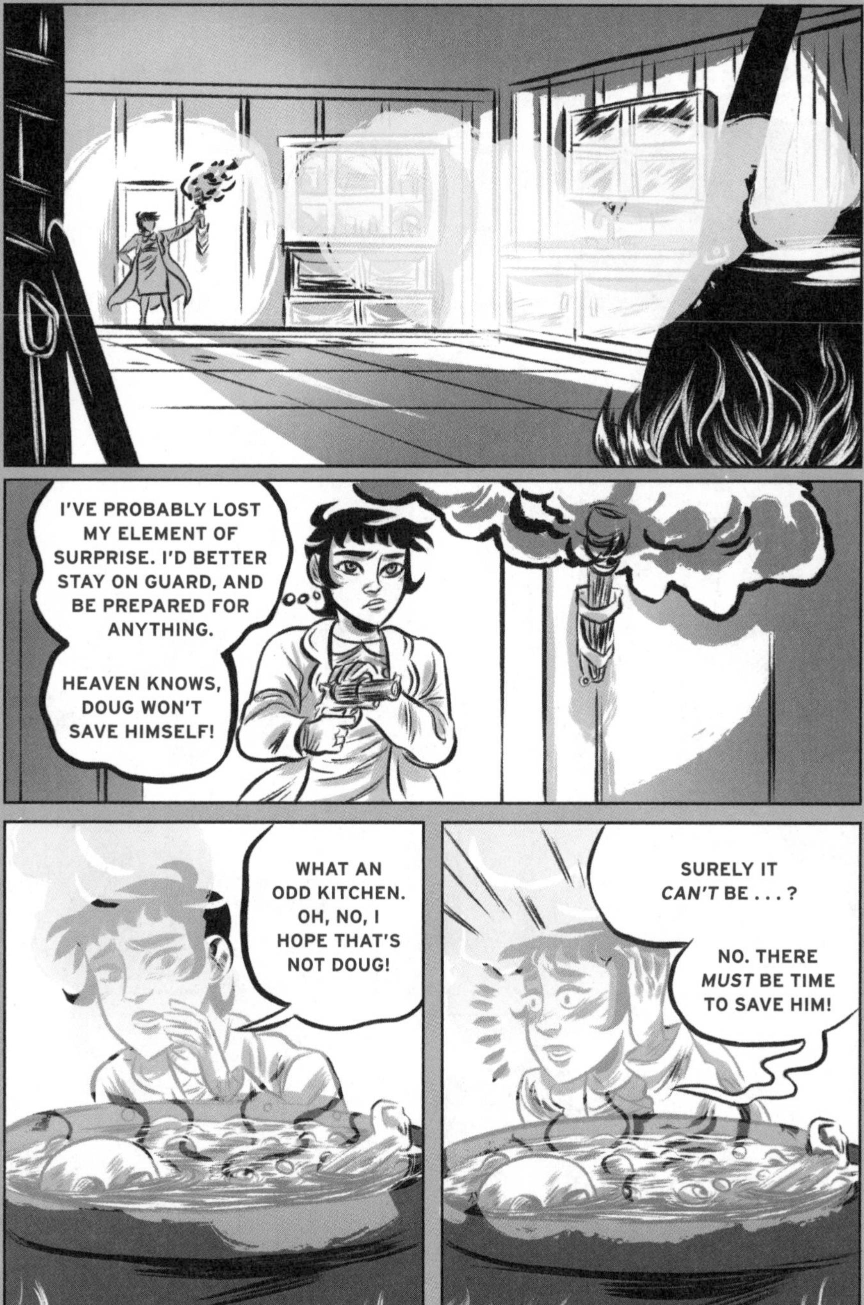
I'VE PROBABLY LOST MY ELEMENT OF SURPRISE. I'D BETTER STAY ON GUARD, AND BE PREPARED FOR ANYTHING.
HEAVEN KNOWS, DOUG WON'T SAVE HIMSELF!
WHAT AN ODD KITCHEN. OH, NO, I HOPE THAT'S NOT DOUG!
SURELY IT *CAN'T* BE . . . ?
NO. THERE *MUST* BE TIME TO SAVE HIM!

UUGGGGGGGHHHHH

DOUG?

DOUG, IS THAT YOU?

Denise smacked her hands triumphantly on her knees. "That is *totally* our kitchen, in that scene right there. Look, it's the same layout, with the sink under the window, and the door's in the same place, and the walls look similar."

Terry's eyes went wide. "You have a fireplace in your kitchen? Holy crap. I've got to see this . . ."

She stopped him before he could leap up from the floor and dart down the stairs. "No, dummy. We don't have a fireplace, or a cauldron full of boiling bones, either. But the window is in the same place, and I bet there used to be a fireplace where the cauldron is. For cooking or whatever."

"I only barely saw your kitchen for a minute the other day. I'll take your word for it."

She touched the panel with the table and chairs. "The dining room is pretty much the same too, though it's tough to tell."

As if on cue, tires ground into the grass and gravel beside the house.

"It sounds like they're home." She went to her bedroom window. She stood in the full blast of the AC, enjoying the chill for another few seconds before turning the dial down to "low." If Sally thought she'd been blasting it ever since she got home from Crispy's, Denise would never hear the end of it. She watched her mom get out of the driver's side quickly, then run around to the passenger's side and open the door for Mike. He climbed out carefully, one arm clutching his chest, and let Sally lead him up to the house.

"I'd better go see how he's doing." She turned to find Terry on his feet, the comic in his hand.

He set it on her bed. "I'm sure he's good."

"Me too, but I want to hear it from him."

Together they headed downstairs, greeting Mike and Sally at the door.

"Hey there, Terry," Mike said with a lopsided grin. "Nice to see you again."

"Thank you, sir. Nice to be back."

Denise looked him up and down. "You blew out some stitches, huh?"

Sally rolled her eyes. "I told him to lay off the handyman stuff, but he didn't listen. My beautiful dumbass thought he'd take a crowbar to the wainscoting in the dining room, and it was more than the sutures could take."

"I just wanted to pull it off before the electricians reach it tomorrow. It's in good shape," he insisted. "We can put it back up later. They'll just tear it loose or cut right through it. We should try to save it."

"*I* should try to save it," his wife corrected him. "Or we can ask Norman to take care of it tomorrow. *You* should go lie down."

"I can't. I'm too hungry."

Sally shook her head. "Aw, dammit. We were going to run past Wendy's, and I forgot."

"We could order pizza . . ." Denise suggested. The mention of Norman had made her think of it.

"Pizza," her mom agreed wearily. "I don't have the energy for anything else. Terry, are you sticking around?"

Politely, he demurred. "I don't have to, ma'am. Y'all already fed me once. I should probably go home and make something for myself."

"And your dad?" Denise asked.

"He's doing a double shift. He won't be home until after I'm in bed."

Mike waved away the boy's protests. "Then that settles it. You're not eating home alone, not while we've got pizza on the way. Sally, hand me your phone." He shot Denise a wink. "Maybe Norman is working the delivery routes again, eh?"

She rolled her eyes and said, "Come on, Terry. Let's go upstairs."

Once in Denise's room, they settled in with Lucida Might again — but as they opened the manuscript, Denise changed her mind and picked up her phone to check her messages.

"Do you have to do that right *now*?" Terry complained.

"Settle down, you addict. I was just going to show you this email I got, from an agent. Her dad used to represent Joe Vaughn. She wrote me back."

"Who wrote you back?" Denise and Terry jumped. They looked up and saw Sally standing in the doorway. "Sorry, I didn't mean to startle you. I just came up to say the pizzas will be here in another twenty minutes."

Denise's stomach growled in response. "Good," she said, and opened the email before her screen went dark.

"Is it something important?" Sally asked. "Is it about a scholarship?"

"*Mom* . . . no, stop it. It's something else." To Terry, she said, "She wants me to get in touch with her."

"*Who* wants you to get in touch?" Her mom came inside, and tried to get a look at the phone.

Denise held it out of her reach. "This lady, okay?"

"Some stranger on the Internet?"

"Yes. No, I mean. It's not like that."

"And since when are you into comic books?" she asked, suddenly noticing the open manuscript lying on the floor between Denise's and Terry's folded knees.

"Since I found this one in the attic. It's not a real comic book, exactly. It's a manuscript for one, but I don't know if anybody ever published it." She looked back down at the email. "Don't make fun of it. It might be valuable."

Sally was unconvinced. "Yeah, I bet."

"This lady in New York wants to look at it. Her dad was the writer's agent, a long time ago. She thinks this might be a lost manuscript. Someone might buy it, or pay us money to publish it."

"That's fine, but I don't want you making phone calls to any internet randos. And if the comic book is valuable, don't let that lady see it without paying you first."

"I don't think that's how it works, Mom . . ."

"What's this?" Mike appeared in the doorway. "We have something valuable in this house? You can't be serious."

"It's just some old comic book." Sally gently smacked him on the arm. "Don't get too excited about it. Dee says she found it in the attic, so it's probably just a waterlogged mess, anyway."

"No, it's not," she insisted. "It was wrapped up real good, in plastic."

"If you say so, dear." Sally squeezed out the door past Mike. "I'll be downstairs, scaring up enough dollar bills to tip the pizza guy."

"Check my wallet. I think I have a couple of ones." Mike told her. Then he asked Denise, "Can I see it? I like comic books."

She shrugged, and pushed it forward. "It's called *Lucida Might and the House of Horrors.*"

"Lucida Might . . . that rings a bell." Gingerly, he sat down cross-legged across from Denise and Terry, and turned the manuscript around so he could look at it upright. He flipped back to the beginning, leaving one set of fingers sandwiched in the pages where they'd left off reading. "Joe Vaughn," he read from the cover page. "Yeah, I've heard of him."

"You have?" Denise asked.

"He had a TV show, years and years ago. If this is one of his manuscripts . . . I wonder when he wrote it? Hell, I wonder what it was doing in our attic . . ." he added, shuffling quickly through the early pages, taking in the artwork.

She cleared her throat. "Um . . . I don't want to freak you out or anything, but I think he died here. In this house." She told him all about her Internet research, and her suspicions. "And on top of that, I think he's still haunting the place."

"Really? You think we have a ghost?"

"I think we have *two* ghosts," she confessed. She looked at Terry, who gave her an encouraging nod. "I think they're probably Joe, and the old woman who used to own the house. She disappeared before he died, and nobody knows what he was doing here. But this agent I talked to online—she said that maybe Joe was using the house for an art reference. I mean, the house in this comic sure *looks* like our house."

Terry had her back. "No way it's a coincidence!"

Mike made some more murmurs that said he was thinking, as he checked the thing page by page. "Ghosts, eh? I didn't know you believed in ghosts."

"I didn't, either. Wait, do *you?*"

He shrugged, still gazing down at the pages. "I've never seen much evidence for them, or against them."

"Terry has," she said, before he could volunteer the information. "He takes recordings. It's crazy, but he's picked up some really strange voices."

Mike looked up and eyed Terry. "Is that so?"

"I'd be happy to play them for you, sir! I didn't bring my recorder today, but next time . . ."

"Next time, then. And stop calling me 'sir,' would you? It's just Mike," he smiled. "If I've got two ghosts on the premises, I'd like to know more about them."

Denise watched her stepfather warily. "You're being awfully cool about this whole 'haunted house' thing, Mike."

The look he gave her in return was guarded. "Let's just say I've seen and heard some weird things myself, since we got here. And leave it at that."

"What about Mom?" she asked. "Has *she* seen or heard anything unusual?"

He shook his head. "If so, she hasn't mentioned it. If this house *is* infested with ghosts, I say we keep it to ourselves for now. Your mom has enough on her plate. Don't give her one more thing to worry about, please? I can worry for the both of us."

Denise wanted to tell him not to worry, that it wasn't a big deal — the ghosts were friendly! Probably! But she didn't think it was strictly true anymore. If he could worry for Sally, then Denise could worry for Mike. They could share the worry load, and maybe everybody wouldn't be scared to death all the time.

Was that how it worked?

Denise said, "Ghosts aside, I want to let this agent see the manuscript. I don't expect free money or anything, not that it wouldn't be awesome to have some. Do you think . . ." she began, almost shyly. "Mike, do you think it would be okay, if I talked to her?"

Downstairs, there was a knock on the front door.

Mike gave her a grin. "If it were me, I'd call her in a heartbeat. But this is your book. You found it, so you decide what to do with it. If you want to, go ahead and call the lady up. See what she has to say." They all heard Sally greeting the pizza guy, who turned out to be a pizza girl. No surprise visit from Norman, oh well. "But do it tomorrow. For now, let's eat."

After pizza, Denise went back upstairs to the meat locker (as she'd begun to almost lovingly think of her nice, cool bedroom) and she banged out a quick response to Eugenie Robbins's email. She didn't want to call because she hated talking on the phone, but she wanted to reach out — and an email was a good compromise.

> Thanks so much for getting back to me. I really appreciate your time, and your interest in representing the comic book for publication. If you're sure that no one else owns the rights, I guess there's no good reason not to try and sell it. I am off to college next year, and then to law school. I could definitely

use the money — any money at all. I hear the textbooks are
expensive.

    I can take more pictures and show you the pages, or
maybe if you're in New Orleans anytime soon, you can come
see the book for yourself.


She almost included her address, but restrained herself. One thing
at a time, just in case this lady wasn't who she said she was. She closed
out the email and hit SEND, and then sat back, wondering if anything
would come of it.

She knew the hard way that maybe-money was no better than
no-money-at-all.

It was even worse, if you got your hopes up.

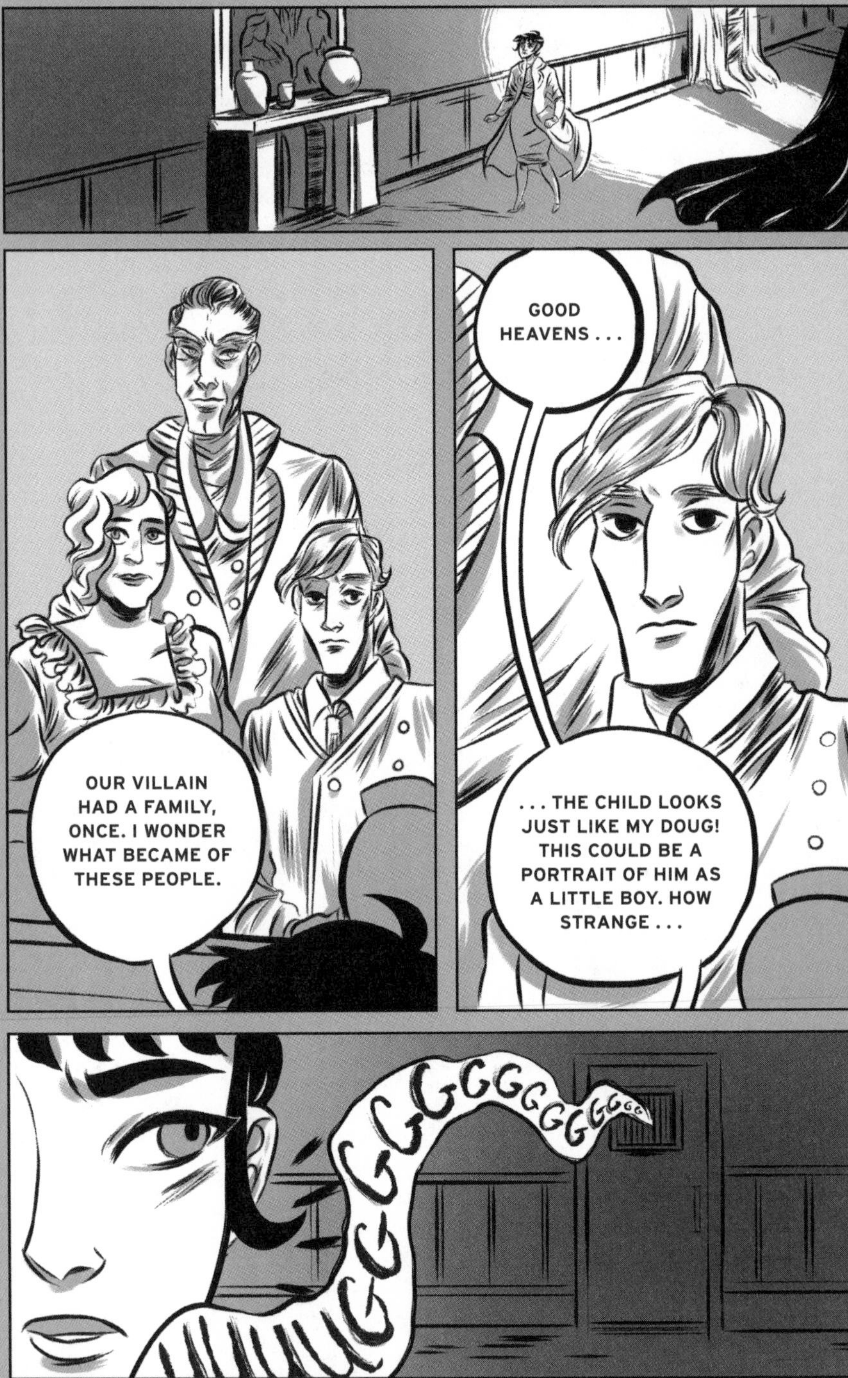
OUR VILLAIN HAD A FAMILY, ONCE. I WONDER WHAT BECAME OF THESE PEOPLE.
GOOD HEAVENS . . .
. . . THE CHILD LOOKS JUST LIKE MY DOUG! THIS COULD BE A PORTRAIT OF HIM AS A LITTLE BOY. HOW STRANGE . . .
GGGGGGGGGGGGG

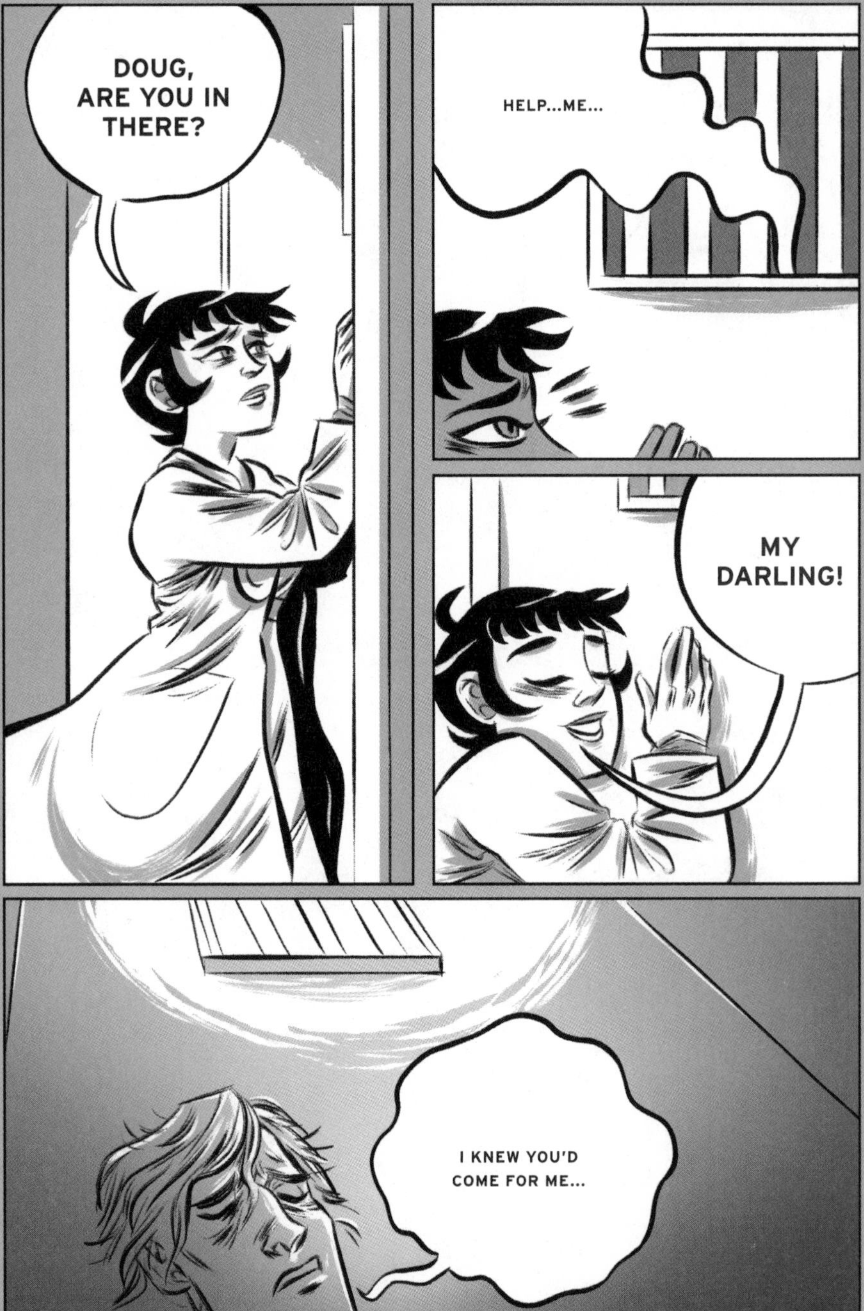
DOUG, ARE YOU IN THERE?
HELP...ME...
MY DARLING!
I KNEW YOU'D COME FOR ME...

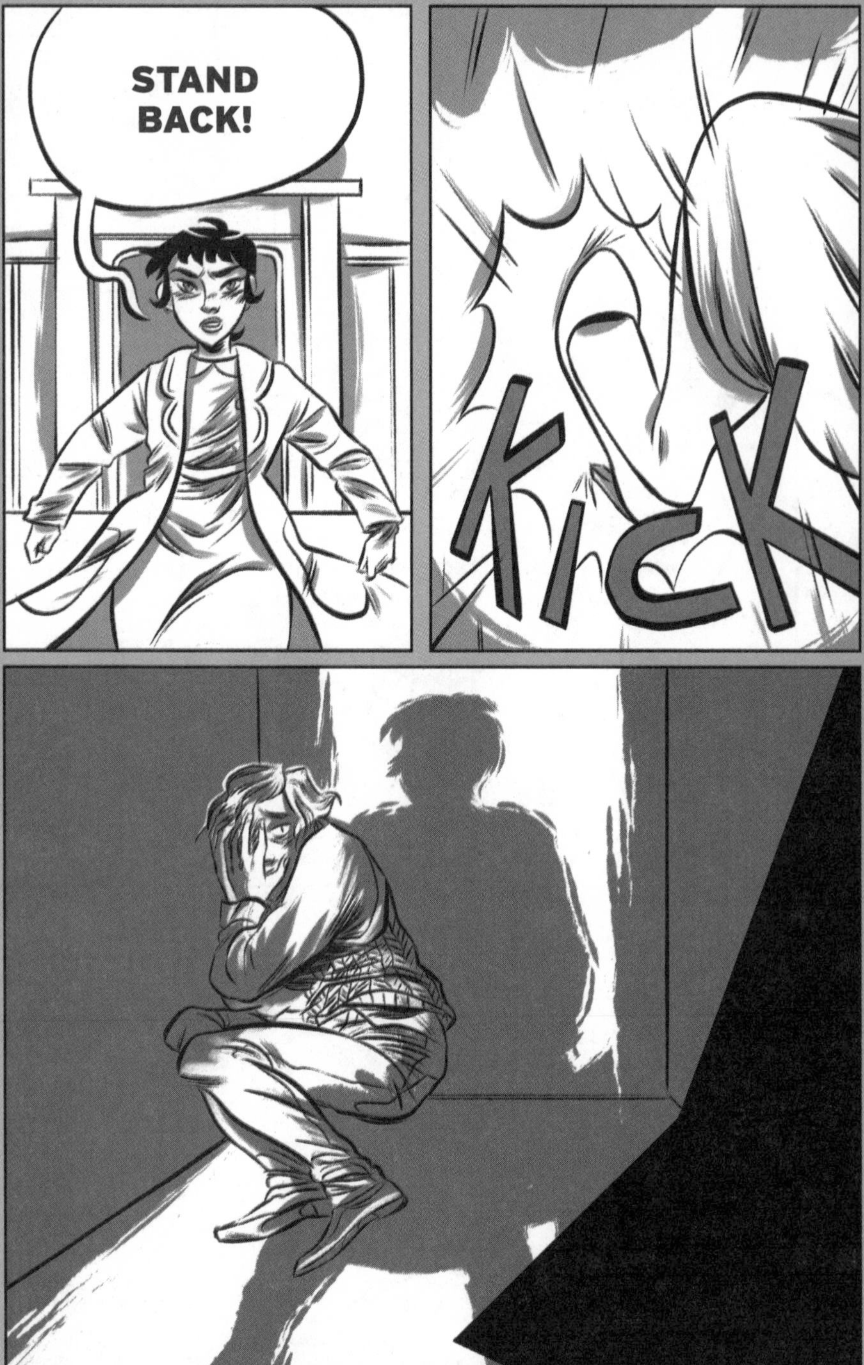
STAND BACK!
KICK

# CHAPTER THIRTEEN

Mike paused, and poked his finger at the image of Doug. "Wait, who's this guy?"

Denise said, "He's Lucida's useless boyfriend. You should just read this from the beginning."

"I will, one of these days. This is crazy, how you just found it . . . I've never seen anything like it."

They were sitting together on the floor, their backs braced against the foot of her bed. Terry had gone home after pizza, and Sally was entirely disinterested in anything comic book related, so it was just Denise and Mike. The book was open with one flap on her leg, and the other on his.

"I've never seen anything like it, either. Nobody has, apparently."

"Hey, I've been meaning to ask you," he said, nodding his head at her hand. "What happened? What's with the Band-Aids?"

Denise tried to play it off. "I got into a knife fight with a pirate."

"And that's all the damage you took? Well played. But come on, kiddo. What gives?"

"It's no big deal." She tried to say it cool, like this was obviously nothing to get excited about. "I poked myself with a screw, while I was putting my bed frame together."

"Will you let me take a look?"

"These are my last Band-Aids. I'll show you after I take a shower, but for what it's worth, I showed a nurse, and she said it was fine."

He gave her a long, hard look. "Okay," he said. And he let it go.

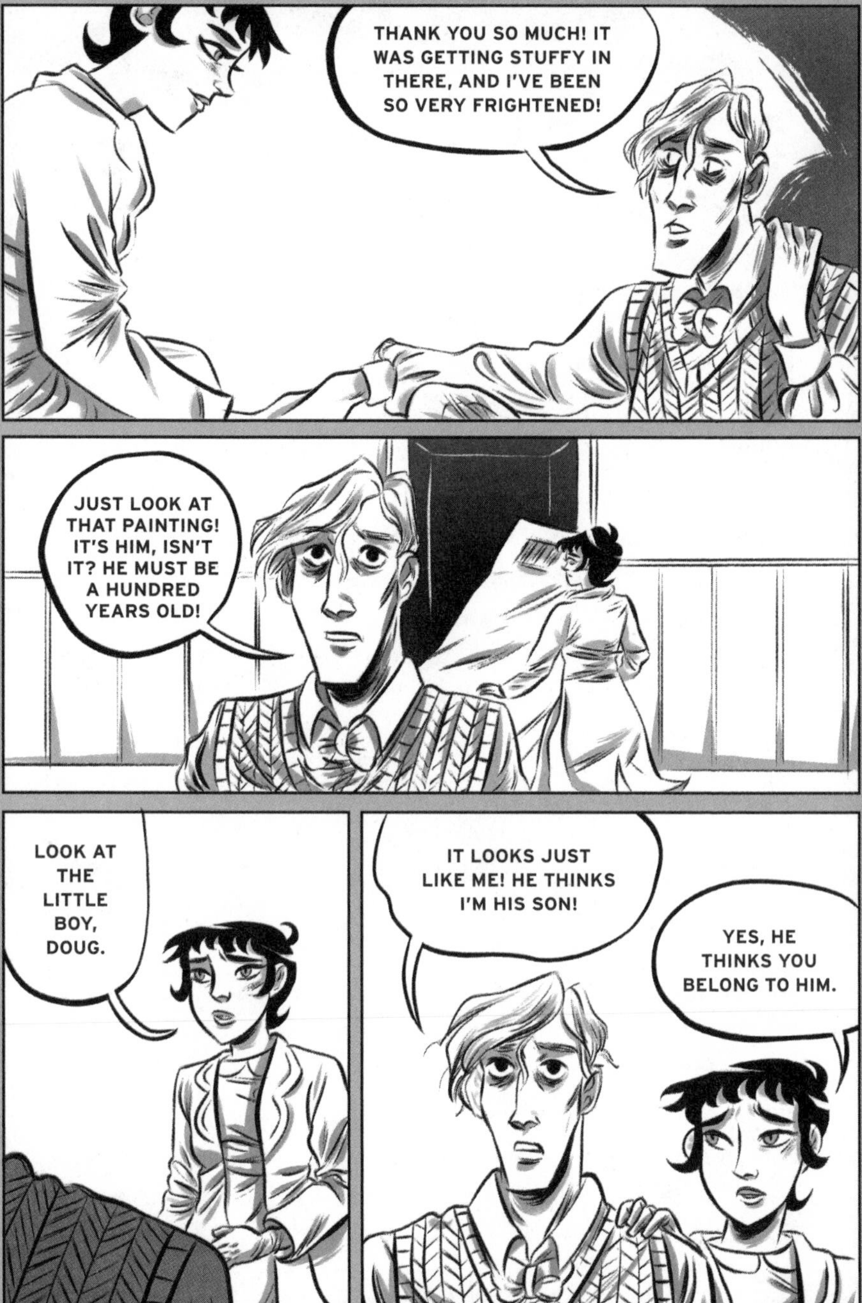
THANK YOU SO MUCH! IT WAS GETTING STUFFY IN THERE, AND I'VE BEEN SO VERY FRIGHTENED!
JUST LOOK AT THAT PAINTING! IT'S HIM, ISN'T IT? HE MUST BE A HUNDRED YEARS OLD!
LOOK AT THE LITTLE BOY, DOUG.
IT LOOKS JUST LIKE ME! HE THINKS I'M HIS SON!
YES, HE THINKS YOU BELONG TO HIM.

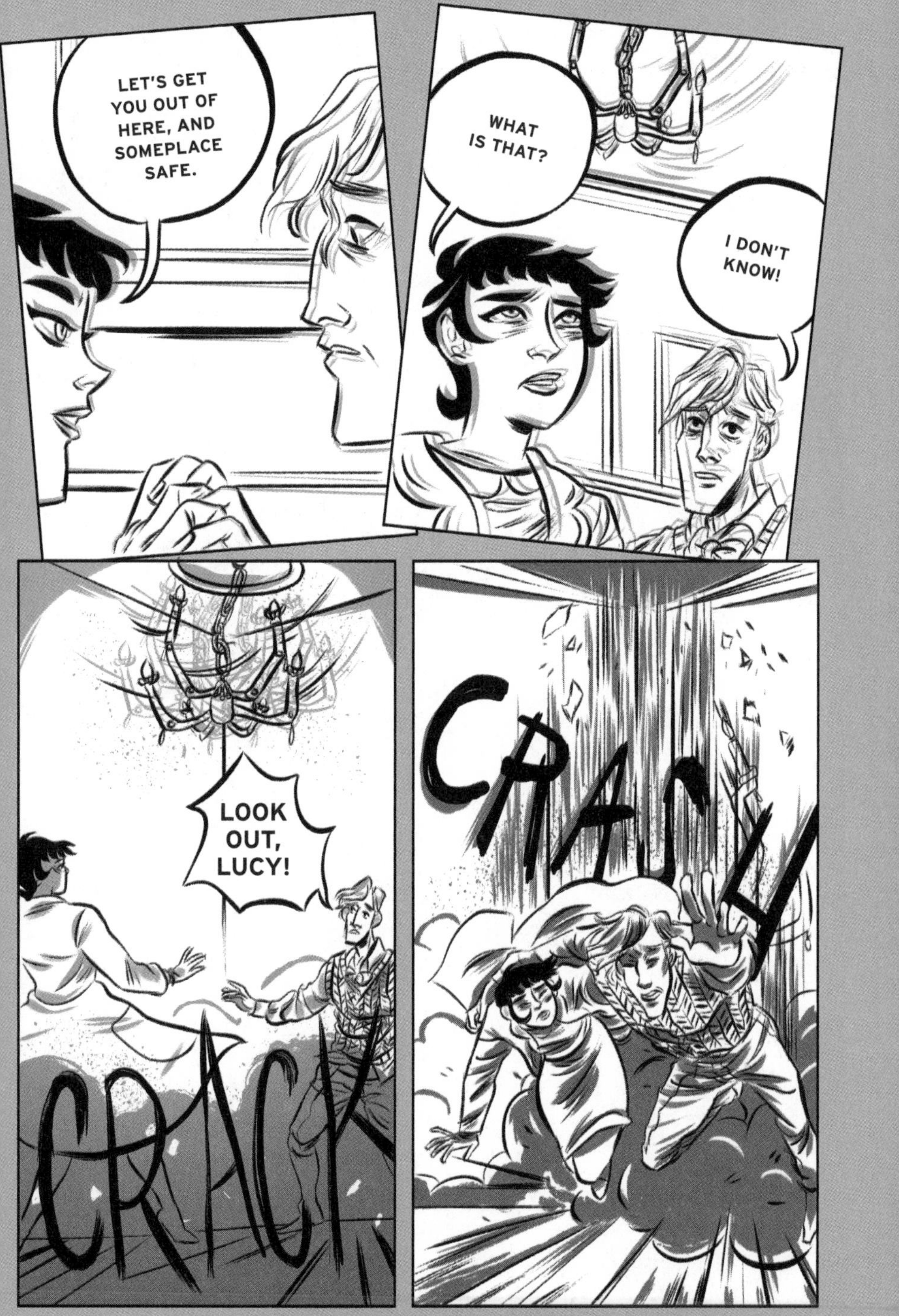
LET'S GET YOU OUT OF HERE, AND SOMEPLACE SAFE.
WHAT IS THAT?
I DON'T KNOW!
LOOK OUT, LUCY!
CRACK
CRASH

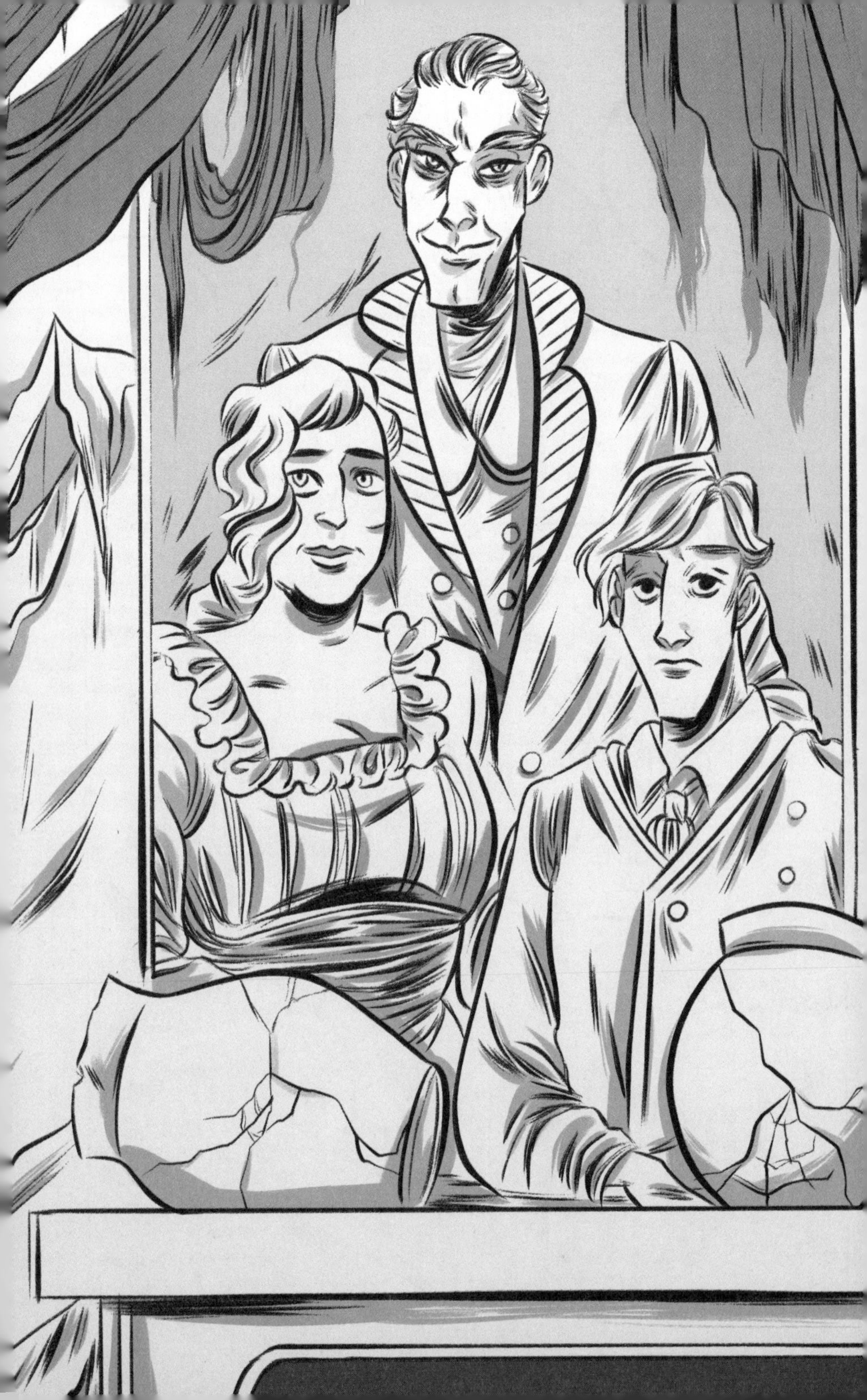

Mike lifted his head and looked around. "Wait . . . do you hear that?"

Beneath their feet, they could feel a rumble. They could *hear* a rumble. Denise smelled grave dirt and sulfur with a dash of mold. "Where's Mom?" she asked frantically. Before he could answer, she yelled out, "Mom?" and scrambled out of the bedroom ahead of Mike, who was still moving a little slowly.

She was halfway down the stairs when she heard two things at the same time: her mother shouting, "Jesus!" and what remained of the ceiling collapsing into the parlor.

"Mom?"

"Sally?" Mike cried from the top of the stairs.

Denise was already at the bottom. Dust filled the room and dirtied up her eyes — some of it was powder like drywall, and some of it was brown and fluffy. She could hardly see. Everything smelled awful, and she wasn't sure where her mother was. "Mom?"

"Over here." Sally coughed and waved, like she could banish the filthy air with the back of her hand. "I'm fine. It missed me. Mostly. I think." She sounded creaky and uncertain, but she was definitely alive. The ceiling was on the floor, and a big jagged beam leaned down from above, its bottom end jammed through a rug at Sally's feet.

Sally made for one of the windows, wading through several inches of poop-colored fluff, and forced open the only two windows that worked. The air cleared a little. The stuff on the floor waved and swirled, like the grossest, driest snow anybody ever saw.

"What *is* this stuff?" Denise asked, wanting to run to her mom, and not wanting to step in any of that garbage.

Mike came down the steps behind her, covering his mouth and nose with the bottom of his shirt. "Insulation. Maybe . . . vermiculite? Or rock wool? Whatever it is, don't touch it. Don't breathe it, if you can possibly help it. We should get out of here."

Denise followed Mike's lead, pulling up her collar so she wasn't flashing her bra at anybody. "Oh my God, yes. As fast as possible."

"Why?" Sally demanded, even though she was wiping at her eyes and coughing.

"Best case scenario, there's mold and bug crap in this stuff. Worst case scenario, it's asbestos," Mike said unhappily. "In a house this old, the odds are too good to risk it. Everybody, to the bathrooms and wash up — then go pack an overnight bag. We're getting a hotel."

"With *what* money?" Sally asked, loudly, and with a shrill undertone of despair. "We can barely pay the electricians and the plumbers and I just bought pizza for the neighbor kid . . . and now this?" She stood in the wreckage of the parlor, where all the holes in the floor were covered by drifts of brown muck. More quietly, and with more exhaustion than sorrow she added, "I'm all tapped out, and we can't get the next portion of the loan disbursed until the pipes and the wires pass code."

"I've got some space on a credit card," Mike told her softly. "I'll find us a Motel 6 or something. Let's not panic just yet. The electricians already told me that there wasn't any asbestos in the walls, so there might not be any in . . . in whatever this brown stuff from the ceiling turns out to be, either. I'll go to Pete's hardware and get a test kit tomorrow, and then we'll know for sure."

"They make kits to test for asbestos?" Denise asked.

"Yes, they do," he confirmed. "And we'll spend one night in a hotel, as a precaution. Tomorrow, we'll know if we need to borrow more money, or if we just need to use the Shop-Vac. We'll figure it out. Now go on, get out of here. Both of you," he extended the gentle command to his wife, as well. "Nobody needs to be breathing this junk. Let me get my phone, and I'll find us a place to crash."

Denise didn't like how tired he sounded, and how hard he was trying to sound strong and positive; but somebody needed to keep cool, and her mom was wound up so tight you could bounce a quarter off her. "Mom?" she said. "Be careful, don't forget there's a hole in the —"

"I know there are holes in the floor," she snapped. "I'll find my way to the bedroom without breaking an ankle, don't worry." With that, she waded through the dry, dirty debris and off to her bedroom.

Denise looked up at Mike, who was still standing on the stairs a little bit above her. She wasn't sure what she wanted him to say, or do. He was already saying and doing everything he could. She really, *really* appreciated it, and she hoped that the look in her eyes got that message across, because she was too close to tears to say anything out loud.

"Go on," he said. "I'll take care of your mom."

She whispered, "Okay. Thanks." He stood aside to let her pass.

Up in her room, she was all alone but she felt like she was being watched and it drove her crazy. She wanted to check under the bed, and in the closet that still didn't have a door.

She didn't check. She grabbed her messenger bag, and picked up the old duffel she'd thrown on the floor in a corner. She selected a black tee from the shirt box, a pair of long shorts from the bottoms box, and to hell with it — a pair of flip-flops from that pile of shoes by the door. She had enough makeup in her purse to fake it for tomorrow. A fresh pair of underwear and her toothbrush topped off her whirl-wind of packing, and that was it. Even a Motel 6 would have some soap, right?

She was ready to go. Her duffel was slung over one shoulder, and the messenger bag weighed down her other one. *Lucida Might and the House of Horrors* was lying facedown on the floor at the foot of her bed, right where she'd tossed it when the ceiling caved in downstairs.

Just like the ceiling in the story.

She didn't want to touch that book. But. She couldn't leave it lying there, not like that — all rumpled and upside down. Not if someone was going to pay money for it, and that lady in New York wanted to read it, so . . . she couldn't just walk away from it.

She picked it up off the floor, and smoothed the pages back down.

She closed it, and before she could change her mind, she stuffed it into her bag and zipped the whole thing shut.

The voice on Terry's recorder had said, "I keep what's mine." Was the ghost talking about the book? What would happen if she took it out of the house? Would the terrible coincidences follow her, even to a hotel?

Out in the hall, the dust from downstairs had wafted and settled on the floor, the doorknobs, and the handrail leading to the stairs. It wasn't the grime that made her throat go dry, and it wasn't the musty smell. It was the footprints leading to her room: broad, flat, square-toed imprints, made by a large man's dress shoe.

The footprints went in. They didn't come out.

Denise fled to the top of the staircase and took the steps down to the living room as fast as she could.

But she stopped near the bottom, because she heard her mother talking softly. She didn't mean to overhear her, but when someone talks softly, you have to listen hard to hear them. So you *do* listen hard, even when you're not supposed to.

"I don't know *what* I heard. All I know is what I *think* I heard, and I don't know what to make of it."

"Well then, what do you *think* you heard?" Mike asked, using his best sympathetic ear voice.

"I thought I heard a woman, and I know I *smelled* a woman."

"I'm sorry, say that again? One more time?"

Sally took a deep breath. "I heard a woman say, 'Get out of the way!' and I felt something shove me. Something . . . somebody . . . I got *pushed*, Mike. Right out of the way, like some kind of dang guardian angel was watching out for me, or something."

"And you smelled this guardian angel?"

"Yeah, she smelled like . . . like perfume. Roses and lilies. Old lady perfume."

"Your guardian angel is a pushy old lady. Got it."

"Sweetheart . . ." Sally was tired and exasperated. "I don't know. All I'm saying is, something moved me, and if it hadn't? That big support beam would've cracked me right in the head."

"You swear you aren't hurt?"

She cleared her throat. "No, I'm fine. It just scared the bejeezus out of me, is all. You know, if there's asbestos up there —"

"No, don't go down that road. Not yet. Don't borrow trouble. We'll find out tomorrow, for sure."

Denise didn't like to eavesdrop . . . or at least, she didn't like to *look* like she'd been eavesdropping, so she slowly descended the last handful of stairs. She cleared her throat to get their attention, and cautiously poked her head around the wall at the bottom.

"Mom? I don't think you have a guardian angel. I think we have a ghost."

"A ghost?" Sally narrowed her eyes. "Is that what we've come to, making up ghosts?"

Denise hopped off the bottom stair and into the living room, where she sheepishly stood in the wreckage of the ceiling. "Are ghosts any crazier than angels? Look, there are two dead people still hanging around this house," she explained. "I'm basically sure of it."

Sally looked at Mike, who hemmed, hawed, and said, "Sweetheart, hear her out. I've heard some weird things too."

"Both of you? You both think we've got ghosts? Were either of you planning to tell me about them?"

"I'm telling you now, okay?" Denise said, trying to head Mike off at the pass. She could take the damage on this one. She didn't mind. "Don't be mad at him; it's not his fault. I told him not to say anything," she fibbed.

"She's been doing research," Mike said, trying to lend a hand. "Tell her what you learned, kiddo."

Quickly, before Sally could spend any time getting mad about feeling left out, Denise said, "One of our ghosts was a guy named Joe

Vaughn, who died here back in the 1950s. He's a jerk, but there's another ghost — a lady. I don't know her name, but she's nice. I bet she's the one who pushed you. And I bet Joe's the one who brought down the ceiling."

Sally held very still and did not argue, but her eyes flickered between her daughter and her husband and the gaping chasm above their heads. "I *knew* something funny was going on," she finally said. "I keep smelling perfume, and finding stray nails lying around the house — in places they shouldn't be, places where they could hurt somebody."

Denise was both delighted and appalled to hear that her mother had discovered more nails. "Joe was a carpenter, supposedly," she said. Now that she thought about it, Desmond Rutledge was a developer. That was kind of the same thing, wasn't it?

"And a jerk," her mother confirmed.

Denise bobbed her head. "A total jerk. So you believe me?" She didn't mention her own encounter with the nails. Give her mom one new thing to worry about at a time, that was her thinking.

"More or less," Sally said, not quite ready to commit to having confidence in the afterlife.

But it was good enough for her daughter, who smiled feebly. She said, "Well you two, I'm all packed up. It's getting late. Mike, did you find us a hotel?"

Mike reached around the corner and collected a duffel bag. "Yeah, but it's a couple miles away. You're right, we'd better get going."

The hotel was more like ten miles away, and it wasn't a Motel 6 — but a mom-and-pop place with a neon sign that was half burned out, advertising GLF SD OTL rather than GULF SIDE HOTEL. They parked between a Dumpster and an old ice machine that looked like a great place to hide a dead body.

The room itself was clean enough, but nothing matched — not even the soap and shampoo samples. Still, when Denise checked all the sheets for bedbugs, she didn't find anything. She took one of the beds, and

Mike and Sally took the other. By the time everyone was settled in, it was after eleven o'clock.

The lights went out, but Denise couldn't sleep.

Over the roar of the old AC unit, she heard the honks of boat horns and the rumble of car engines on the busy street nearby. Flashes of headlights peeked around the curtains, and the hissing hum of the neon sign buzzed, fizzled, and turned the room orange when it flickered.

She reached over the side of the bed for her bag, and pulled out *Lucida Might and the House of Horrors*. She also retrieved her phone. As quietly as possible, she pulled everything under the covers, and drew the blanket over her head. One thing she'd give the GLF SD OTL — the AC was powerful enough to keep her chilly, even with the blankets all tented up.

She called up the flashlight app, and turned it on.

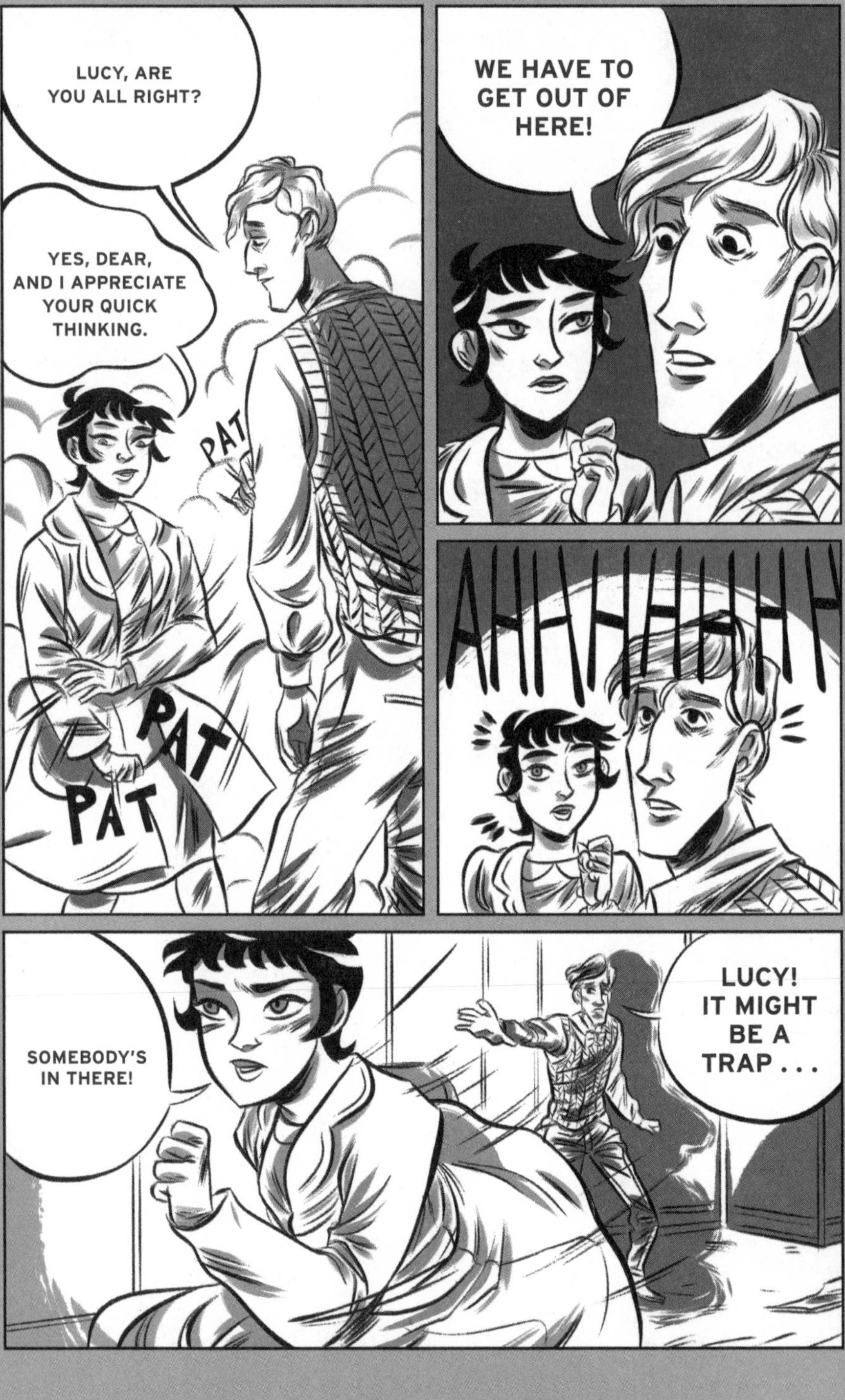
LUCY, ARE YOU ALL RIGHT?
YES, DEAR, AND I APPRECIATE YOUR QUICK THINKING.
PAT
PAT
PAT
WE HAVE TO GET OUT OF HERE!
SOMEBODY'S IN THERE!
LUCY! IT MIGHT BE A TRAP . . .

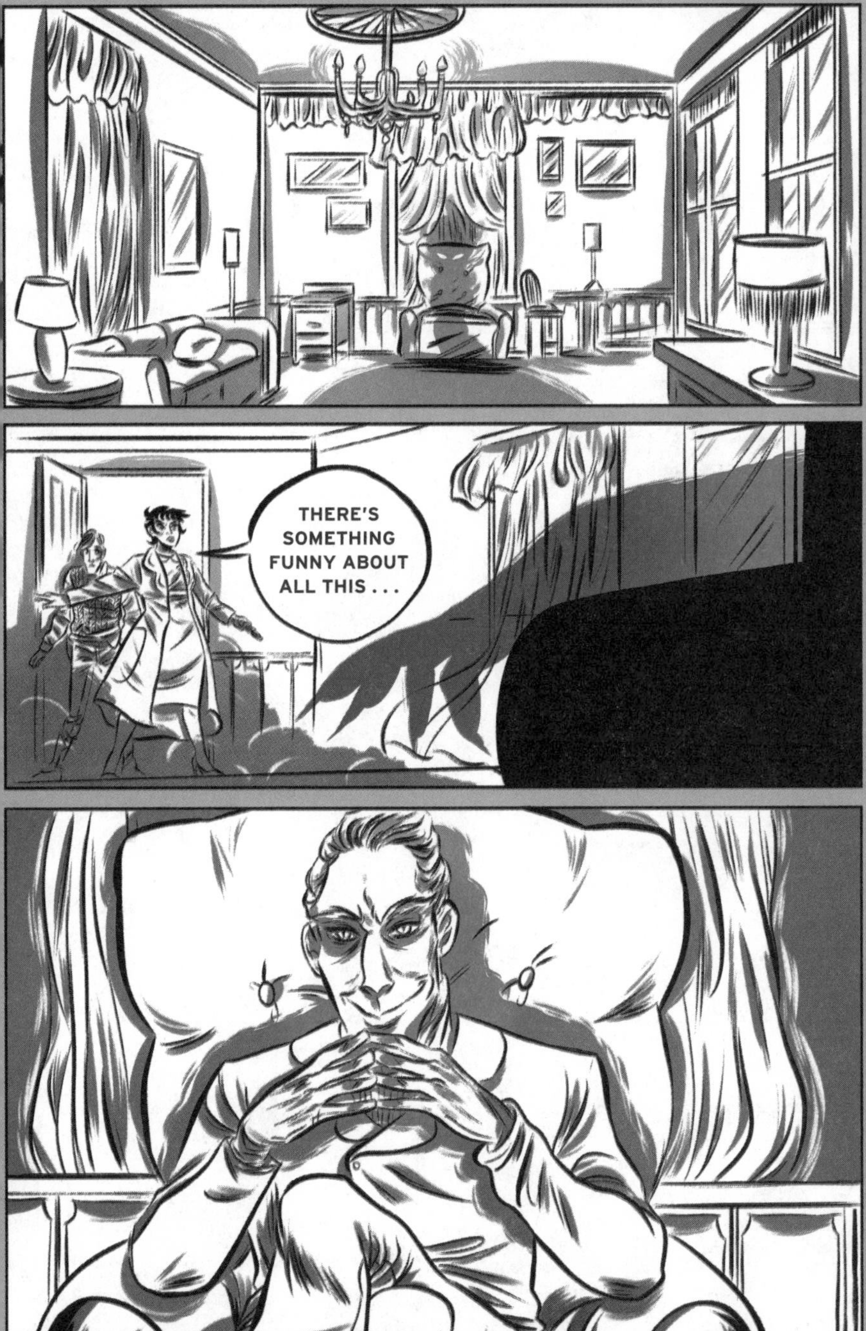
THERE'S SOMETHING FUNNY ABOUT ALL THIS . . .

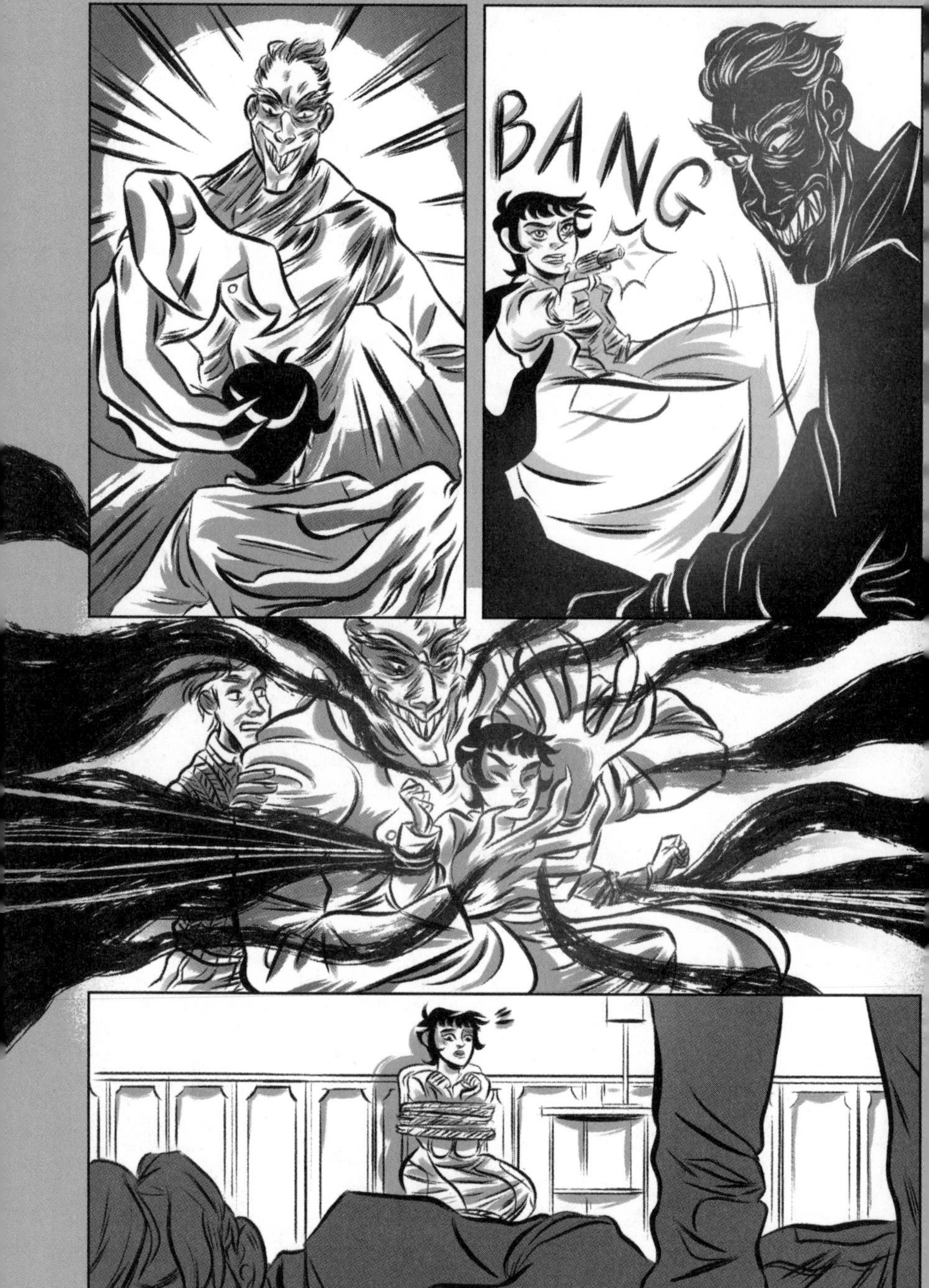
BANG

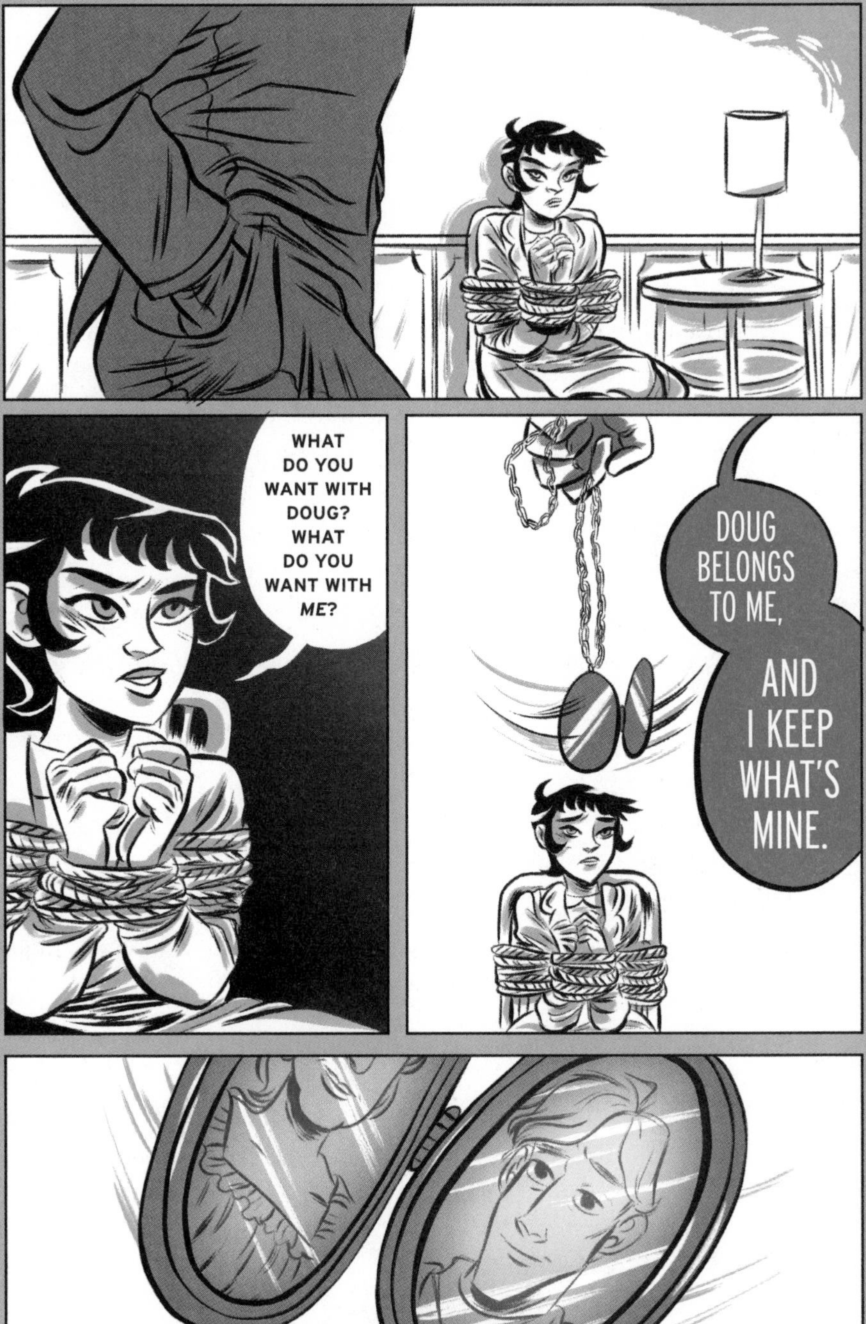
WHAT DO YOU WANT WITH DOUG? WHAT DO YOU WANT WITH *ME*?
DOUG BELONGS TO ME,
AND I KEEP WHAT'S MINE.

Denise's reading was interrupted by a text message from Trish, saying good night and that she hoped that the ghosts didn't bite — a message accompanied by the traditional ghost emoji with its tongue hanging out.

Denise didn't reply to that one. Not even with a lazy thumbs-up.

Her phone battery was running low, so she closed out the flashlight app — then found the outlet beside her bed and plugged it in. She pushed Lucida Might onto the nightstand, and fluffed her pillow, trying to make it feel less like a flat feather rock. When it was as comfy as it was going to get, she dropped her head down, and closed her eyes.

On the next bed over, Mike was snoring softly and Sally wasn't making any noise at all, so she was probably awake. She probably knew that Denise had been up too late, reading under the covers. She must not have cared. For all the trouble her family was taking to keep worries off her plate, she still had too many other things to worry about.

Denise's brain itched. It was hard to sleep when the AC unit rattled and howled a few feet away, and the neon light fizzled through the curtains. It was difficult to nod off when the bed was lumpy and the sheets smelled not so faintly of bleach.

She thought about Lucida Might. It was better than thinking about this miserable hotel room, or the Agony House, or tetanus shots that should've happened — but didn't. And as she finally drifted off to sleep, she considered how weird it was, how the villain talked about Doug like he was an object, and not a person.

But that was silly, wasn't it?

Unless Joe Vaughn wasn't really talking about a character named Doug. Maybe he was talking about something else. As Denise finally, restlessly drifted off to sleep, she couldn't help but wonder *what*.

# CHAPTER FOURTEEN

The hotel alarm clock went off at oh-God-thirty and Denise shot awake in a panic, wondering where she was. She sat up in a tumble of sleep-pressed hair and dried drool, flailed around for her phone, found her phone, realized her phone wasn't making the alarm noise, and then slammed her hands up and down along the nightstand, trying to find the source of the buzzing horror.

Mike found it first. He rolled over and slapped it silent.

Only then could Denise stop freaking out, and take a moment to remember what was going on, and why she was in a hotel, and how come the alarm had gone off and it was still so early.

Was it early? It felt early.

"Oh yeah," she mumbled. Her brain gradually came back online.

Groggily, Denise groaned and stumbled into the bathroom, where she skipped a shower because to hell with it, that's why. She was only going to the po'boy place to kill time with the Internet over breakfast; she wasn't glamming up for a beauty pageant.

That's what they agreed to, over arguments on who was brushing whose teeth first.

"I don't know how long the test takes, and you seem to like it there," Mike said. "I'll give you five bucks and you can get some breakfast. Let's get this cleared up as soon as possible, so we can go back to work on the house, cleaning up that mess."

Crispy's did breakfast, mostly biscuit-related or beignet-related, often with eggs thrown into the mix. Mike's five bucks felt like all the money in the world at that hour — Denise could even get one of the small combo meals with that much. Did she want coffee? She needed coffee. But she'd rather have Coke, so that's what she ordered.

She took her tray to the table which was becoming "hers," if possession was, indeed, nine-tenths of the law. A couple of kids who recognized her as a regular tossed her a head-nod when she sat down. She gave them a bob back, and pulled out her laptop. She plugged in her phone to let it charge, and felt very sorry for herself — and for everyone else who was up this early in the middle of summer.

Norman was up early.

He appeared with a loaded-down tray, boasting two big bacon-egg-and-cheese biscuits and hash browns too. Smoothly he slid into the bench beside her, dropping a messenger bag on the floor. He pushed it under the table with his foot. "Hey there. Fancy meeting you here."

"Hey there, yourself. What are you doing here at this hour?"

"At this hour? It's not that early," he argued. "Sun's up and everything. I've already been down at the river, taking pictures. You ever see the sun rise over the delta?"

"I have not. And I have no desire to, either."

"Your loss."

"Sunset, maybe," she said. "You ever take pictures of sunsets?"

He nodded. "Used to. But I think the sunrises are prettier, and I'm usually not working a pizza shift through those."

"Fair enough," she told him.

They settled in to eat, fussing about old houses and joking about crappy working conditions. Norman asked about her hand, and Denise was evasive. He asked what she was doing there so early, and she told him about the mess with the ceiling and the maybe-asbestos. "And that's not the worst of it. On top of everything, we have ghosts."

"Ghosts?"

"One bad, one good. If we're um . . ." She was pretty tired. "If me and Terry are reading the situation correctly. Terry, he's this kid . . ." she began to explain.

"I know Terry. *Everybody* knows Terry," he said with a grin.

"Why am I not surprised. But what I'm saying is, if you're gonna keep working in the house with us, you should *definitely* ask my stepdad for that hazard pay you were joking about."

"I ain't afraid of no ghost."

She chucked a packet of salt at his head. "You should be afraid of ours. One of them is a real jerk, and I think he's been setting up all these crazy little accidents. I think it's Joe Vaughn, the guy who wrote that comic book we found in the attic."

He plucked the packet out of his lap, where it'd fallen, and tossed it onto the table. "Dang, it sounds like you've had a crazy couple of days."

"And gross. You should see the floor of our living room and parlor."

"I've got some free time today, if they want to spring for the help. I can use the money, and I'm not afraid of gross stuff from the ceiling. Especially if there's hazard pay involved." He waggled an eyebrow.

"I'll mention it. But if it's asbestos, there's no way they'll ask you to help shovel it out. Hazard pay or not."

When they were mostly finished eating, Norman asked if she'd brought the comic book.

Denise nodded as she chewed her final bite, wiped her hands down like she needed them for surgery, then topped off with a smidge of hand sanitizer. She handed him her extra napkins and the tiny travel bottle of sanitizer. "I've got it right here, but your buttery hands can't touch it. Clean up, man."

"Do I need a fancy pair of white cotton gloves?"

"No, but I don't want butter on it. Or cheese," she added, pointing out an orange spot on the side of his hand. "Just ask Terry: I like to keep it clean."

He accommodated her with exaggerated caution. Clean hands achieved, he wadded up the napkin and tossed it on his tray—then pushed the whole thing out of the way. "Now can I see this majestic manuscript?"

Denise reached down and brought her bag up onto the bench. She dug down deep into the satchel and pulled out the book, then set it down on the table — edging her butt over so he could see it better.

"Dang . . ." he said with a touch of awe. "How did it survive up there?"

"It was wrapped up in a bunch of plastic. It's got some mildew on the corners, but mostly it's okay."

"That's a miracle."

"A *cool* miracle." She opened the cover and showed him the first few pages. "There's an agent in New York who's asked to see it. Her dad used to represent Joe, a long time ago."

They flipped through the pages together for a few minutes, when Denise's phone buzzed on the table beside her. "It's . . . look, it's my mom. Apparently I have to go back to the house. Or . . . I *get* to go back to the house? Sounds like there's no asbestos. Just filthy garbage . . . hooray."

"Are you sure you don't want me to come with you?"

"If you're not afraid of no ghosts, or no probably-not-asbestos . . . you're welcome to join me. All they did was run a test they bought at Pete's. Who knows how reliable it is. It's not like they hired a professional or anything."

Norman wasn't too worried about it. "Everybody has asbestos, around here. If it's not in the ceiling, it's in the walls, and if it's not in the walls, it's under the floor. You're lucky if it's under the floor. Usually those are just tiles. You can break those up, and pull them out yourself."

She didn't ask him why people didn't get the rest of it removed. She already knew why.

Asbestos, old wiring, rusty lead plumbing . . . if it wasn't going to kill you right that second, you went ahead and lived with it — just like she and Sally had quietly lived with it, in one of their crappier apartments back in the day. Asbestos and mold had lurked all over the place, but the mom-and-daughter duo knew they wouldn't be there long. They could ignore it for six months at a time.

You add up enough six-month stretches, and eventually you've got years and years of pretending it isn't there, and figuring that if it was gonna hurt you, it would've done it by now. After a while, you forget it was ever there. You forget you were ever worried about it.

But Denise and Sally and Mike couldn't forget about this one, this time. This time, everything had to be up to code.

Denise and Norman tossed their garbage and started walking, but they didn't get very far before Dominique joined them. There wasn't much room on the sidewalk, so Denise and Norman stopped.

Terry came running up behind them. "Hey Denise, Norman. Hi Dominique," he said, covering all his bases.

Dominique smiled at him. "Hey there, Tee. You doing good?"

"Yeah, just walking home. Or to the nail house, to see if Denise was there." He flipped a thumb at her. "But I saw y'all walking, so . . ."

"So come on, and walk with us." To Denise she said, "Terry told me all about your ghost."

"I gave her the rundown," he said modestly. "Hope you don't mind."

"Nah. It's no secret, I guess. Everybody knows that somebody famous died there."

The rest of the way to Argonne Street, Denise gave Dom a few more details on Joe and his afterlife — with Terry chiming in when he felt the need to elaborate. Dominique didn't look like she understood the need for laser thermometers, voice recorders, or EMF readers any better than Denise did . . . but she was game to listen, and she made appropriately impressed noises at all the right times to keep him happy.

Norman, on the other hand, got nerdy about it. "You got a recorder? With real EVPs? I love that stuff on TV."

"I'll play them for you, later! Oh wait, Denise!" he interrupted himself. "You were having electrical work done on the house, right?"

"I'm not sure if they're finished yet or not. Every time I think somebody's done with something, it turns out I'm wrong."

"If you ever get a chance, ask an electrician for an EMF reader. Maybe they'll let you keep one overnight."

"I wouldn't know what to do with one."

"*I* would!"

"Got it: You want me to borrow an expensive piece of equipment so that you can come to my house and play with it."

He beamed at Dominique. "See? I told you she was kind of smart. She's going to be a lawyer."

Norman said, "Sweet! You and me will have to stay in touch. You never know when you'll need a good lawyer."

"Why? You planning to go committing any crimes?"

"Like you've got to break any laws, in order to need a lawyer."

Denise nodded approvingly. "I knew I liked you. You *get* it."

Dominique laughed a little. "Yeah, my cousin here — he's all right."

"Yeah, he is." Then she said, "You um . . . you want to come see the house? It's kind of gross and full of grumpy spirits, but if you wanted to see inside . . . ?"

"You had me at gross, and lost me at spirits. I don't do ghosts, man. I leave that stuff to Terry. It freaks me out. But thanks for the invitation, and I'll take you up on it one of these days . . . in broad daylight, with all the lights on. Hey, this is where I turn to my street, so I'll catch you later."

"Your cousin?" she asked Norman.

"Second or third, if you want to get technical," he said. "I was going to head over to your place after breakfast, Dom, but do me a favor, would you? Tell Grandma I went to work in the nail house early. Tell her about the ceiling, and that they're cleaning up. Tell her they need a hand."

"You real sure? She was hoping you'd swap out her old AC unit today."

"Oh yeah, I forgot about that." He gave Denise a pained look.

"Don't worry about it," Denise told him. "My parents would probably die of embarrassment, if you saw the place right now. It's pretty bad."

"I've seen worse, but whatever makes you happy." He gave her a smile followed by a little salute, and walked off with Dom.

Terry waved good-bye, and Denise threw them a head-nod that was supposed to look cool, but probably looked like a spasm.

Terry left her at the next block, because ghosts or none . . . he had no great desire to wade through the ceiling garbage. Not even for Lucida Might. Denise didn't blame him.

It was only one more block to the house, so she walked it in summer heat that was absolutely choking. "Sunscreen. I need sunscreen," she muttered to herself, feeling the back of her neck turning pink. "Better yet, a parasol."

Her sunglasses had a crack on the right lens, but they were cheap and she hadn't expected much from them in the first place. She rubbed them on her shirt to clean them off, and mostly got them even sweatier. She gave up and stuffed them into her bag, just in time to step into the shade of the rickety porch with its weird baby blue underside that her mom called "haint blue," though Denise didn't know what that meant. Something about good luck, or keeping bad spirits out.

It obviously didn't work.

She glared at the house and said, "All right, Joe. Just so you know . . . if it comes down to you or us . . . *you're* the one who's outta here."

Nothing in the house responded, so she stomped up the first two stairs . . . and tiptoed up the next two, remembering what had happened to Mike. In the porch floor the hole was still there, wide and ragged, but covered with plywood and a handwritten warning sign that said HOLE IN FLOOR. In case anybody came to the house and didn't know already.

The door was only sort of locked, with a dead bolt that was set — but a broken sidelight through which any idiot could just stick her hand and unlock it. The sidelight was supposed to be fixed by now, but so were a lot of other things.

Denise used her key, anyway.

This time, the note on the dining room table said that Sally and Mike were at the bank, signing off on some paperwork that would release more of the mortgage money. Apparently the plumbing was officially good to go.

One of the electricians was still present, packing up his bag. He was a short white guy, round faced and blond. He had a crack at the back of his shorts that Denise tried not to stare at. "Oh, hi there," he said when he realized she was present. "Don't mind me, I'm just wrapping up."

"How's it going?" she asked.

"Got a late start, after your parents cleaned up most of the ceiling insulation, but we're getting there. These old houses, man. They'll eat you alive, won't they?"

She wasn't sure if that was a joke or if she was supposed to laugh, so she just gave him a weird look until he cleared his throat and continued.

"I've got the new circuit boxes coming tomorrow, and then I'll be ready to finish the rest — probably within a couple of days. I know it seems like it's taking forever, but we'll be done soon. Listen, I'm gonna leave this stuff here, rather than haul it all to the truck, okay? I'll be back first thing in the morning."

Denise silently thanked God that Terry wasn't there to explode like a fistful of nerdy confetti. "Go for it. No one will bother them." She had gotten an idea. She stood still and listened as he drove away.

Denise didn't want to steal any of his tools, but maybe she'd borrow one. She realized she didn't have the faintest idea what an EMF reader looked like, so she pulled out her phone to google them.

"Okay," Denise said to herself. "I can find that."

It was red, with a little window on top and a needle that moved back and forth. Now she just needed to know how to use it. For a second she thought about calling Terry. Then she thought no, this was *her* house. She could do a little ghost-hunting on her own.

How hard could it be?

She ran a quick search on how to use the EMF reader, but that got real complicated, real fast. So she narrowed the search to "using an EMF reader to look for ghosts" and turned up some helpful sites with terrible graphics. One had a cackling skeleton GIF that rocked back and forth. One had some bats that flew out of a window. It was all tacky Halloween stuff, circa 2003.

But the information looked legit.

She flipped a switch on the side, and the little yellow light behind the needle lit up. The needle bobbed back and forth along a scale of "mG," with a range from zero to fifty. It settled around the left-hand side, barely registering 1 mG, whatever an *mG* was supposed to stand for.

According to the most promising website she found on the fly, anything between 2 and 7 (without an obvious electrical source) might indicate a paranormal presence. Appliances ought to read much higher, from maybe 10 to 30 mG. You were supposed to take test readings around your TV, microwave, and maybe your electrical outlets.

She turned in a circle, and the thin blue needle bobbed across the red scale, lifting off the "1" position and wobbling. There was no TV to check, and Denise didn't know how long it would be before her parents got home, so she didn't bother testing for a baseline.

She just dove in.

"All right, spirits." She cleared her throat. The meter's needle didn't move, so she moved instead, slowly circling the dining room. "I know there are two of you. Joe Vaughn, I think you died here. Are you the one who's been trying to hurt us?"

She didn't know why she was talking out loud. It wasn't like she was holding a voice recorder, but what else was she going to do?

"Come *on*, Joe," she added under her breath. "Talk to me. Why do you want to chase us out of the house? Or if *you* don't want to talk . . . um . . . lady ghost? Are you there? I think you helped my mom yesterday. I think you're trying to protect us. Was this your house?"

The needle twitched.

She thought maybe it twitched when she was facing the parlor, but she wasn't sure — so she went that direction and got another twitch in the hallway. A big spike, up to about 8, then it settled down around 7. She turned to the living room, and the needle dropped again. Another turn, and there was another bump — one that stabilized around 11 — when she stood in the parlor doorway.

"Got it. It's like . . . playing hot and cold."

It had to be. There weren't any electronic devices anywhere in the parlor — not even power tools, switched off. All of those were stashed around the living room and the back of the kitchen.

"Seven is supposed to be high . . ." she said to herself. "Eleven has to be even better, right? Even more . . . electromagneticky?"

One careful foot at a time, she crept into the parlor and swung the EMF reader slowly one way, then slowly the next. A couple of lights blipped, and the needle jerked — all the way up to 16.

"Is that . . . good? Is there someone here with me?" She wasn't shaking, not exactly, but it was hard to hold the meter steady when her hands were so sweaty and she was looking up and down, back and forth between the room at large and the device she was holding. "If there's anybody here, please be a nice old lady. The kind who wears flowery perfume, and doesn't try to scare anybody. Please don't be a mean man. Joe . . . you weren't mean, were you? You wrote a cool comic, about a cool girl detective. Maybe I'm talking to somebody else."

Her voice wasn't exactly shaking, but it didn't sound steady, either. Not even to her.

"Hello?"

She thought she smelled flowers. Expensive soap, or a funeral bouquet.

"Hello, is someone there?"

She followed the scent, and she followed the bouncing EMF needle. It shook and leaned, farther and farther to the right, as Denise grew closer and closer to the fireplace. An alert buzzer went off, and Denise leaped like she'd been snakebit. She dropped the reader and let it lie where it fell, its needle straining to burst through the little window.

It wanted her to look in the fireplace.

The fireplace was not quite a ruin. Its mantel was intact, if dusty, and the tiles that surrounded it were a pretty shade of turquoise blue, mottled with gold. Across the opening where a fire ought to go, a cast-iron cap was fixed. Mike had told her it was called a "summer cap," and they used to put them over the fireplace when it wasn't being used — to keep birds and mice from coming down the chimney. It was decorated with a fleur-de-lis and some scrollwork, and it looked a little bit thin and rusty.

If she touched it, it might crumble to dust.

She touched it anyway. It didn't crumble, but it creaked a little. There was a knob in the center, and one on the bottom. They were handles, or so she figured out real quick when she gripped them. She crouched, lifted with her legs, and wiggled the cap loose, then pulled it away. It smacked down hard on the floor — it was a lot heavier than it looked.

She let it lie down flat. It rocked back and forth, and stopped with a groan.

Inside the fireplace there was darkness and soot, swirling in soft, black poofs — disturbed by the cap's removal. When the soot settled, she saw naked bricks with crumbling mortar. She smelled flowers. She heard a whisper, coming from somewhere up inside.

Denise fumbled for her phone. She pulled it out and found the flashlight app, then turned the phone upside down. She slipped it inside the recess, and shined it around. More brick. A large chunk of fallen stone or something, up above. It dangled down into view, almost.

Keep looking.

Her head shot up so fast, she clocked it on the underside of the mantel. Not hard enough to see stars, but hard enough to make her eyes water. She rubbed at the back of her head with her free hand. She asked aloud, "Is somebody here . . . ?"

Then she saw it: around the fallen chunk of brick, or stone, or whatever it was. Something hung there, just on the other side of it. There was a little hole, big enough for a hand. A lady's hand. Denise's hand. She held her breath and reached inside, trying not to touch anything. Still touching everything. It all felt like gravel and dead bugs and sand and dust. It felt like paper.

Paper? Kind of.

She wrapped her fingers around something brittle and pulled it out. It was waxed paper, and it was wrapped around something, secured with an old rubber band. She tried to unstretch the rubber band but it snapped off and fell to pieces.

She tucked her phone under her armpit, unfolded the waxed paper, and found a small cache of folded, yellowed letters.

The first one had brown stains all along the seams, where mildew had worked its way past the butcher paper that'd been used to protect it. She straightened it out between her palms.

I really wish you would reconsider. The CCA won't last forever (I don't believe it CAN), and you told me you weren't finished yet—you said you had a dozen more LM stories, bubbling on your back burner. You're just going to drop it like this? Let it all go up in smoke, because some pencil-pusher made some rules you don't like? You're bigger than that. LM is bigger than that! People still love her, and want to read more. You're cutting off your nose, to spite your face. You can fight the power from the inside.

Maybe we should talk about licensing. LM can live on, maybe in film—maybe a cartoon, wouldn't that be something? So the TV show didn't pan out, big deal! TV shows fail all the time, and that doesn't mean they weren't great, or that nobody loved them. It just means Hollywood is a crapshoot, even worse than comics.

You could try something different. You could take LM a new direction, maybe get her and DF married off at long last, and that would take the edge off the CCA complaints. You could even make the little putz the hero once in a while. It wouldn't be the end of the world, and it wouldn't be the end of Lucida Might.

Please, talk to me. Call me, for God's sake. Stop avoiding me. Stop avoiding this.

It was signed "Marty."

"Marty." Marty Robbins, the agent. There was a second letter, hidden behind the pages of the first. It was falling apart, but Denise put the pieces back into place and smoothed them out flat on the floor, so she could read it. It looked like Joe's reply.

I wish I could say I believed you. about the CCA — but we both know how the world works. and we know they're here to stay. at least for the foreseeable future. By the time that foul organization follows the dodo into the great beyond. it'll be too late for me. It's already too late for Lucida Might.

I appreciate that you're trying to save my bacon. and save your own while you're at it. but I wish I could make you understand: To change the dynamic between Doug and Lucida is to change the heart of the story. I never wanted to tell the story of a weak boy becoming strong. There are plenty of those stories already. I wanted to tell the tale of a woman. strong already — but accepting of (and even loving toward) a partner who can't keep up. Apparently that's as baffling and obscene as the gory undead.

You're not wrong. and there's a story to be wrung from a partnership's shift in power dynamic. but that's never been the intent of Lucida Might. Lucida Might must be a challenge to the usual. not a capitulation toward some loathsome standard. But the loathsome standard is law of the land. and I'm already so beaten down by the nasty business between you-know-who and I (which I fear has not yet found its end. God help us). and I simply lack the stamina to struggle onward and fight both him and the CCA on top of everything else.

I'm getting old. and life is short. Marty. It's just too damn short.

Denise sat on the floor and put the pages in order, one letter and then the other, side by side. She read them over and over again, while the faint whiff of flowers faded from her nose. The soft whispers of soot and ghosts from the fireplace retreated, and there was only a residue of black grime that coated the mantel, the tiles, and the old pages themselves.

Word by word. Line by line.

If this wasn't Joe's house . . . then why were these letters stashed in the fireplace? Was the mystery lady keeping them to blackmail Joe? Denise considered the possibility. Maybe she'd stolen the manuscript too; maybe there was something incriminating written inside. If so, Denise hadn't found it yet. She didn't see anything incriminating in these letters, either — nothing she couldn't have gathered from her limited Internet research.

Joe was unhappy, so Joe was quitting. Marty didn't want him to quit. Joe was quitting anyway.

Then what about the lady? Who was she? What was her role in this weird vintage drama?

Denise didn't know, and she had no idea how to find out.

# CHAPTER FIFTEEN

Come Saturday, Denise told Sally and Mike that she was going to visit Tulane, and they didn't quite believe her. "I thought you were hell-bent for Houston," Mike said.

Sally hushed him. "Stop it. If she wants to go visit Tulane, then by all means let her go forth and research. How are you getting there? Are you going by yourself?"

"What prompted this?" her stepdad added, more suspicious of her motivations than eager to see her off.

She answered her mother first. "I'm taking the bus, so can I have a few bucks for fare and lunch? And no, I'm not going by myself. I'm going with Norman. His mom works there, and he said he could show me around."

"But *why* are you going there?" Mike pressed.

"Because I want to look at their library," she said truthfully. "I read something that said they have some archives of Joe Vaughn's stuff."

"The comic book guy?" Sally asked. "Our resident dirtbag ghost?"

"Yeah. If he died outside my bedroom door . . . then I want to know more about him. Maybe I'll find out why he's such a jerk."

Sally was looking at Denise through narrowed eyes. "All right," she relented. "Fine. You can go, as long as you promise to answer your phone if I call — and you swear you'll be home by dark."

"We could always drive you two," Mike suggested.

"Oh, for crying out loud," said Denise. "I ought to learn the bus system anyway, right? I'll just . . . I'm meeting him at the stop near the school. If we get stuck or lost somewhere, I'll call one of y'all to pick us up."

Mike relented, and Sally told her to take a few bucks out of her purse and to have a good time. Denise went straight for Sally's purse before she could change her mind, and pulled out an overstuffed wallet that was mostly full of baby pictures, shopping lists, receipts, discount cards from assorted stores, a pen that didn't work very well, half-sucked cough drops wrapped back up and saved, reminder cards for various appointments that were at least a year old, and Band-Aids.

So that's where all the extras went. She pocketed a couple of those too. On principle.

Inside this wallet that was roughly as fat as a sandwich, she also found about three dollars in change and eleven one-dollar bills.

She pulled out all the quarters, and took six of the ones. She hoped it wasn't too much, and Sally wouldn't regret giving her permission to raid her bag, but she didn't want to look too broke if they got lunch at the market. After bus fare, five bucks ought to be enough to get at least a pastry and a soda. She could always say she was on a diet.

"Thanks, Mom!" she shouted on her way out the door.

Her messenger bag was slung across her chest, and her flip-flops slapped up and down as she ran down the front steps.

It was hot as hell outside. Maybe as hot as literal hell, for all Denise knew. She wasn't halfway to the bus stop in front of the school before she started wilting and wishing she'd remembered the sunscreen — but it was too late for that, and she wasn't sure that they even had any. Six ones and some change wouldn't buy any. Not even a sample size from a drugstore, if she planned to buy lunch too.

She wiped her forehead, and swabbed at the back of her neck with the rolled-up sleeve of her button-up. It was mostly white with a hint of black plaid, and very soft, and although the extra layer trapped a little heat, the cotton kept the worst of the sun off her shoulders. Her hair was tied up and back in a ponytail because there wasn't anything else you could do with it, in that humidity.

The bus stop near the school had a rickety-looking shelter over it, covered with graffiti both scrawled onto and scratched into every inch. It also had Norman, who grinned when he saw her. "Hey!" he called out, and he stood up. "You made it!"

She smiled back, and wiped a line of sweat off one cheek. "When does the bus come?"

"Another five minutes, if it's running on time. On the weekends they're pretty reliable, but during the week, they're crowded and kind of iffy. Did you ride the bus much in Houston?"

"All the time." She took a seat on the bench beside him. "For about a year, we were in this place where the school bus ran really late in the afternoon — like, if I took the school bus home, I wouldn't get back until after dark, so I took the city bus instead. It usually got me home before the sun went down."

He nodded. "Right on."

"I had to change buses downtown, at the main depot. Sometimes, I'd skip the last bus and walk down to the library instead. I'd call my mom and tell her I'd missed it. Then she'd have to drive out and pick me up."

"I bet she loved that."

"Totally. But there was this creeper who took that second bus, and sometimes I just didn't feel like dealing with it, you know? The driver never did anything to stop him." She wasn't sure why she was telling him that part, but it was true.

"Did your mom believe you?"

"Yeah, but she was working ten-hour days at this hotel restaurant, and when she was done, she wanted to go home — not drive all the way downtown to collect my sorry butt. I tried not to do it too often."

He nodded again, and stared straight ahead. He had a pair of sunglasses perched on top of his hair. He pulled them down onto the bridge of his nose. "Creepers gonna creep. Dom got a guy kicked out of school for like, a week, for being a creeper on the school bus last year."

"Oh, that's right, she's your cousin."

"We have a grandma and a great-grandpa in common. Or we did, but grandpa died in the Storm."

Denise nodded, and shifted her legs so that her shorts covered most of the bench underneath her. It was as hot as everything else, and she didn't need the chicken-fried thighs. "My grandma did too. And my dad. We didn't lose anybody else, though."

"I'm sorry about your dad and grandma."

"I'm sorry about your great-grandpa."

The bus picked that moment to come around the corner, so they both stood up. The big, rumbling vehicle stopped, the doors opened, and a thin drool of cool, damp air rolled down the steps. "After you," Norman generously offered.

"Thanks." She asked for a transfer, and went back to the first seat that was empty enough for two.

Norman joined her, settling down beside her.

The bus pulled forward. They both lurched, then settled back.

He asked, "So what did you mean? When you said you didn't lose anybody else?"

"Oh, you know how it goes." She shrugged. "When the water hit, everybody went in a million different directions. My aunt and uncle ended up in Atlanta, and my mom's cousins went to Minnesota. Mom's half sister went to Chattanooga. We don't see very much of any of them, not anymore. We're Facebook friends with everybody, but . . . nobody's home for the holidays, if you know what I mean."

"I know how it goes. I've got two uncles who are still in Fort Worth. They just . . . never made it back."

"We've got a couple of cousins who came back, but I don't know them real well. And one of my aunties got us the real estate agent, and helped find the house."

"How's it working out? Living in that big old house?"

"You say that like it's fancy or something." She smiled without showing her teeth, and without meaning it. "You know good and well it's just a big craphole."

"But y'all own it. It's *your* craphole."

"Sort of. My mom got some kind of historic business mortgage for it, because of the bed-and-breakfast. But if people keep getting hurt, I don't know." She waved her still-bandaged hand. "Everything feels so dirty, all the time."

"Sounds typical to me," he said with a knowing bob of his head. "Mom and me live in a duplex that used to be a single house. She goes crazy trying to keep it clean, but there's mold in the walls, so it always feels kind of dirty and wet."

It was Denise's turn to nod. The mold remediation in the Agony House was technically finished, but she was still pretty sure there was more mold lurking around somewhere. She could always smell it in the bathroom, no matter how much bleach she used.

Before long, Norman pulled the string to signal he wanted the next stop. "The market's right up here. Have you been to it yet?"

"No. I haven't really been anyplace."

"You're gonna love it."

When she stepped off the bus, back into the heat, she was prepared to believe him. The sidewalks around the market were bustling with shoppers, and the outdoor seating was all occupied, despite the late morning warmth. A few trees and a handful of umbrellas offered shade around the tall, long building that looked freshly restored from top to bottom.

It made Denise think of an old train depot, with all its windows and two stories' worth of height. The front entrance on St. Claude Avenue added to that feeling when she followed Norman through big double doors, into the market proper.

Inside, the lovely high ceiling was supported by a row of painted white columns, with vendors on either side of a central dining hub. All around, Denise heard tourists chattering about the seafood, and locals asking what was new, and sellers announcing the daily specials. Coffee grinders and juice machines hummed and ground and blended in the background. Kids ran back and forth between the front and rear, trailing balloons, or beads, or paper streamers and laughing their heads off, begging for a visit to the booth with all the sweets. She swiveled her head around, taking it all in. She almost lost Norman, but his back was moving ahead of her, ducking and weaving around the kids, the tables, the shoppers, the tourists with their too-big bags and goofy sunglasses. She followed him farther into the center.

The air was still too warm, but it was too warm everywhere and all the terrific collection of smells stirred and stewed. She got a whiff of coffee from over here, and a sharp note of the salty catch of the day from over there. Chocolate too — and the fluffy light sweetness of meringue. A quick gust of spiced rum, not that she was supposed to know what that smelled like, but it was one of Mike's favorites.

Norman stopped in the middle, between two white tables with black metal chairs. "Well, what do you think?"

"It's pretty great," she said. What she didn't say, was that she hoped she could find something she could afford to eat.

Almost as if he'd heard her thoughts, he said, "There's some pricey stuff here, but there's also a lot of stuff you can get on the cheap. What do you like?" he asked, gesturing around at the vendors of po'boys, and seafood, and candies, and booze.

"What do um . . . what do you like? I've never been here before. What's good?"

"Everything. I usually go to the Haitian guys, down over there," he pointed. "Good island food, if you're into that kind of thing. They've got . . ." He squinted around. "Tex-Mex too. Over there. You came from Houston, right?"

"I moved *back* here from Houston."

"That's what I meant."

He pointed out a counter that offered all kinds of promising and familiar food. "You can get street tacos pretty cheap. And chips and salsa, that kind of stuff. The guac is good too. Then you've got, juice and salads, crepes, and have you ever had Vietnamese food?"

"Nah, never. Maybe the Tex-Mex?"

"Okay, sounds good. I'll meet you back here . . ." he waved his arms around to indicate the general vicinity of these particular tables, ". . . in a few minutes."

She ended up getting two street tacos, a side of guacamole, and a glass of water. It didn't look like a lot of food, but by the time she'd finished it, and Norman had killed off some crawfish étouffée that probably didn't come from the Haitian vendors, she actually felt pretty full and pretty awesome.

"Thanks for this," she said to him as they bused the contents of their table into the nearest trash can. "I'm really glad I got to see this place."

"Me too. You ought to get out more. Get to know the neighborhood beyond the golden fried food of Crispy's. Which is great, don't get me wrong. But you should see the rest of it sometime too. Don't hole up in the nail house, just because it's weird."

"What's weird?"

"Oh, come on," he said, ushering her back out the door and toward the bus stop.

She had a feeling she knew what he meant, but she didn't want to say it herself, so she let him do it. "What do you mean?"

"White girl, coming from Texas, moving to a black neighborhood. A mostly black neighborhood," he adjusted, probably thinking of Terry. "Then your parents go off and buy a big house — even if it's not the world's greatest house, it still looks like money coming in from outside. Nobody around here could afford to buy it at all, much less get the money to fix it up. Nobody but the gentrifiers."

"Please don't call me that."

"I didn't." He took a deep slurp through his straw, finishing up all his water and maybe sucking up a little bit of melted ice. Then he chucked the cup into a trash can beside the bus stop. "But that's what happens around here. People come in from someplace else, they buy up crapholes and turn them into mansions. Everybody used to think it was funny. We used to joke about them."

"How come?"

"Oh, they'd take one house on a block and fix it up real nice, and then it was the *only* nice house on the block. They'd try to sell it for ten times what any other house would go for . . . and it'd sit for a while, nobody living in it. Finally, maybe they'd get a renter. Usually some white family, on a mission to save the city from itself, coming in after the Storm like they're gonna make a difference. Then maybe those renters buy a place, and maybe they bring some friends. Pretty soon, you've got a little block like an island, like a fortress. Bunch of people who see a couple of black guys waiting at a bus stop and call the police, like we're casing their houses or something."

Denise blushed. "But it's good if they're fixing the old houses, making the neighborhood nice again, right?"

"Good for somebody," he said, and stood up to announce that the bus was pulling up. "Not for everybody. I mean, look at this market, right? It was just about demolished, and now they've fixed it back up again. Now it's fancier than it ever was before the storm, and that's pretty cool—but now a lot of the locals can't afford the food."

Denise handed the driver her transfer and went to go sit down. Norman joined her.

"You know we're not like that. You know I'm not."

"I know you don't mean to be, but you might turn out to be. Your momma turns that place into a bed-and-breakfast, who's gonna come pay to stay there? More tourists who want to gawk at what the Storm left behind, and more white knights."

"I hope not." But the more she thought about it, the more worried she was that he could be right. And she didn't have any idea what to do about it, so she asked. "What should we do, then? How should we make the nail house part of the neighborhood?"

He thought about it a minute, and said, "Hire people *from* the neighborhood to work on it, and work *in* it when it's finished — and pay them what they're worth. That'd be a start."

"Well, they hired *you*." She didn't know if they were hiring neighborhood professionals for the pricey stuff, but she resolved to bring it up to her mom and Mike later on.

"That's true! And I'm worth every penny."

The number 90 bus headed uptown, to a stop in "Carrolton," or that's what she thought she heard over the intercom. The next one was for the university, and that's where she and Norman got off.

They climbed down off the steps at the bus's back exit and stepped into a sidewalk beside a bright, clean campus. Rows of bicycles were locked up on long metal racks outside each building, and everything looked very new.

Denise said, "Wow, this place is nice!"

"It doesn't all look like this. Don't get me wrong, the rest of it ain't bad," he added, "but some parts are nicer than others. Come on, I'll take you to the library."

"Do you want to stop by and see your mom, first?"

"She's off today."

Denise felt stupid. "I forgot it was Saturday."

"Sometimes she works on Saturdays. A lot of students live in the dorms and stuff, and school runs year-round. They've gotta eat every day, right?"

Okay, well. She didn't feel quite so stupid. "I guess that's true. Where does she work again?"

"Bruff Commons, at the dining area there. That's where I work too, when I'm off from the pizza place. I clear tables and empty trash, and sweep up. Here, we're going around this way." He pointed at a sidewalk, and led the way. "To the Howard-Tilton Memorial Library."

He said that last bit with a fancy flair that it seemed to require. "I've only been inside it a handful of times. I don't have a library card or anything, because I'm not a student. My mom gets some perks for working here, though. She wants me to enroll when I graduate. If I can get in, and if I can get enough student loans, but I don't know, man. It's a lot of money, and my grades are good, but . . . it's just, it's like. It's *so* much money. I keep my eyes open for art and photography scholarships and stuff, on the off chance anybody wants to help foot the bill — but so far, I haven't had any luck."

"My mom wants me to come here too," she confessed.

"It's a real good school."

She said, "I know, but like you said . . . it's a lot of money. I was thinking I'd go back to Houston when I graduate. I got friends there. I know my way around. School's cheaper too. I can probably still get in-state tuition."

"Sure, but you're making friends here too, and I'm showing you around. Maybe this place will grow on you."

"You saying we're friends?"

"Yup. Me and Terry, we're your friends. Dominique too. If you give her a minute. It's not the whole city, but it's a start."

She wasn't so sure about Dom. "I don't think your cousin actually likes me very much."

"She doesn't like anyone much, but she thinks you're okay. You should take it. It's worth something, when she decides she's on your team."

Around another corner, and the library came into view. It was three stories tall and made of concrete. It looked like it came right out of the 1980s. Inside, it smelled like every other library Denise had ever seen: like old books, strong air-conditioning, carpet cleaner, and a dash of mildew.

"What are we looking for exactly?" Norman asked.

"The special collections librarian."

He frowned. "Do they have one of those?"

"Wikipedia says they do."

They asked at the big central desk and got sent to a different desk, on the third floor.

The plaque on the special collections librarian's desk said he was Casey Pines. His name may have sounded like a nursing home, but he was a slender, handsome black man who was probably in his thirties. He had cute little glasses and a shiny shaved head.

"Excuse me, Mr. Pines?" Denise began.

"Yes, can I help you?"

She introduced herself and Norman, who waved awkwardly, and told Mr. Pines about Joe Vaughn and the comic manuscript in the attic. "I saw online that you have an archive of his papers."

Mr. Pines snapped to his feet with a broad smile of enthusiasm. "First, I must tell you not to take everything the Internet says at face value, because it's my job to warn you — but on this occasion, it's at least part right! Yes, yes, yes. Let me take you to the stacks, and I'll show you what we've got."

They followed him into a very quiet section of the library with half a dozen shelves that went all the way to the ceiling, and a wall that was stocked with boxes that looked like they belonged in a law office. Each one had a faux wood grain printed on it, and a white label with catalog numbers and letters scrawled in black Sharpie.

"This is the special collections?" she asked.

Mr. Pines said, "Some of it. We have more important things on lockdown — this is mostly local history of a more recent, less valuable variety. Come in to this room here, if you would please, and I'll bring you the box of Joe's archives."

She peeked through the door. It looked like a perfectly normal conference room. "Are his papers valuable?"

"All of our archives are valuable in some respect or another. Are Joe's papers worth money? I'm not sure. But he's dead, isn't he?" He didn't wait for a response. "Signatures of dead people can be worth money, and so can old comics."

"We don't need to see the comics. We're mostly interested in any articles about him, or letters, or that kind of thing," Denise said.

The librarian nodded. "I'll see what I can do."

Denise and Norman took chairs at the table, side by side, and fidgeted while Mr. Pines disappeared and rummaged someplace in the special collections stacks. Or boxes, or file cabinets, or wherever they kept that kind of thing.

She was a little disappointed when the librarian didn't return with a box at all, but a manila folder.

He placed it on the table in front of her. "Except for the comics . . . this is all we've got, I'm afraid. It's not much to go on, but if I recall correctly, Joe Vaughn was a rather private man — and not much is known about him. I think he used to be a woodworker, or something?"

"A carpenter, that's what I read," she told him.

"It may or may not be true." He shrugged. "Frankly, I'd be surprised if that was even his real name."

Norman cocked his head, looking more closely at an old copy of a Lucida Might comic that had tagged along with the material in the folder. "This is definitely the same artwork as the one you've got," he said to Denise.

Mr. Pines took a seat at the end of the table, and collected the pieces that Denise and Norman put aside. "I would leave you to this," he explained, "but without a student ID . . . I'm not really supposed to bring you back here at all, you understand. Please forgive me if I hover."

"Sure, sure," Norman replied without looking at him. He was engrossed in the folder's contents. "What are we looking for, exactly?" he asked Denise.

She sighed down at the folder. "I'm hoping I'll know it when I see it. Wait, what's this?" She pulled out a thin, brittle piece of paper the color of sand.

You've been a hell of an agent, Marty, and you've always done right by me. I owe you, and I owe you big. We've had a great run, and yes —I have more *lucida* Might in me...but not as much as I'd thought. It deserves a wrap-up, a send-off, a final chapter, doesn't it? Well, I've written one, and I've drawn it up.

I don't think I can ever publish it. It's a shame it'll never see the light of day, but I feel better for having done it. You might call it a confession, of sorts. Everyone feels better after confessing, right?

At any rate, I've written my manifesto. Maybe I'll box it up, and stuff it in a safe deposit somewhere. Maybe I'll burn it. (I probably won't, but with my mental state these days, I can make no promises.) Maybe I'll just hide it so no one can take it away from me. You-know-who would take it away, if I gave him half a chance. He enjoys playing the part, and the money that's come with it all this time, but all good things must come to an end.

Thank you, Marty. Forgive me, Marty. But my life has become a house of horrors, and my time in the business is over.

Mr. Pines cocked his head. "I don't get it."

"Check out that last line." Denise flipped the page over. There was nothing on the back. "He says his life has become a house of horrors. That's what my comic is called."

"Really? That's amazing!" Mr. Pines looked genuinely tickled. "Well, if you ever think of donating it someplace, I do hope you'll think of us!"

"Absolutely!" she fibbed.

Norman took the letter gently from her hands, and scanned it for himself. "He talks like he's having trouble with somebody."

"Yeah, that's the second time I've seen him make a reference to somebody he just calls 'you-know-who.' I wonder who it is? Wait, here's another letter. Or part of the same one . . . ? No, I don't think so." She pulled out another page. The paper was a different color, and it began mid-sentence.

*what will happen. Things are coming to a head here. and Marty. I don't know what to do. I'm afraid. I don't know what he'll do. He's taken the news so badly.*

"This doesn't feel right," Denise protested. "None of it feels right."

"Where's the rest of it?" asked Mr. Pines.

But there wasn't any rest of it. Just the single fragment. Apart from a few more comics, there wasn't much else: an envelope addressed to Marty Robbins in New York City, an award notice from some comic industry group, and a royalty statement that made it sound like Joe Vaughn didn't really earn much money at all.

"Those are 1950s dollars," the librarian noted. "It's more money than it sounds like, and this is only for the newspaper syndication, if I understand the statement correctly. It doesn't include the comic sales, or the cash from the TV show."

"Oh. Well, I guess that's everything in here. It's not a lot to go on, but thank you, Mr. Pines. I've learned a lot."

"I'm always happy to help young researchers find their way around the shelves," he said modestly. "Perhaps you two will come back as students, and I can give you the official tour!"

Denise and Norman walked back to the bus stop and discussed their theories all the way home, but neither one of them knew what to make of any of it. By the time they were back at the stop in front of the school, they were both stumped and silent.

They stepped out of the bus and the doors closed behind them.

"Thanks for everything, Norman. I really appreciated it."

"It was fun. Right?"

"It *was* fun." She smiled tiredly. "Seriously, thanks for getting me out of the house. I'll see you soon."

Later that night after supper, she sat on her bed, in her room with the water stains on the ceiling. The air-conditioning ran loud and cold, and she knew she ought to get up and turn it down, but she didn't. Instead, she texted Trish the latest on the ghost situation, and Trish sounded one-hundred-percent down to hear about it. And have opinions about it.

**POLTERGEISTS did I spell that right**

Denise grinned. *I think so? I don't think Joe's a poltergeist. Just a jerk.*

**what's the line between a pissed off ghost and a poltergeist tho**

*Throwing things? Hurting people?* Well, if that was the case, maybe she was wrong. Maybe Joe was a poltergeist after all.

**why is this guy such a jerk**

*I do not know. But I'm trying to find out.*

**Let me at im. I'll defend you. Send him packing.**

She laughed. *Don't say that. What if you chase him off, and he follows me back to Texas next year? You want a poltergeist in the dorm room?*

**Yes. WE can sell tickets. Write our memoirs and people willmake movies about us. We will be zillionaires with the help of your jerk ghost.**

She laughed again, and said, *You've got a point.*

**Ive still got a roommate too. Right?**

Denise stared down at her phone. *Um, YEAH. What have I told you that would make you think different? I want out of here. Someplace where nobody died on the floor.*

Terry picked that moment to crash the party. His text alert popped up over Trish's message: **Any new ghost sightings to report? Or ghost smellings? Hearings?**

She switched over to his message real quick. *My dude, I would tell you if there was anything spooky going on. You're probably the FIRST person I would tell.*

Then Trish asked: **Is there a gross stain?**

Back to Trish. *No.* She said it without even glancing out the door. If there'd ever been a stain, it was gone now. She'd checked a hundred times already. *And no, I don't want to stay in NOLA. I want to go home, and room with you and your rich-ass self. We will have a swank dorm room, right?*

Trish didn't really need to live in the dorm, but her parents had some money and she had some demands. She had been promised a dorm room, so long as she had a parentally approved roommate. Denise — with her test scores and willingness to tutor — was parentally approved.

Terry was back. **First person? Rlly?**

*Yes*, she told him. *First person, I swear. Feel all special and stuff.*

Trish returned to the conversation, fantasizing about their future dorm room. **Itll be the swankest of all time, you no it. I still want to see this haunted house of yours. And this comic book. You won't keep itall to urself would you?**

Terry was ecstatic. Denise could practically hear it through his next text. **I do! Feel special! You shuld sleep with a recorder, or camera. Do you have a camera? How about your phone?**

She replied, *Phone would probably go into standby if I just left the camera or recorder running.* Wouldn't it? She thought so. *Evenif I left it plugged in.*

Then quickly, back to Trish: *You are welcome here, of cours — but wait until we don't have holes in all the floors. I have an AC unit in my bedroom, so you know it is POSH up in here.*

Trish liked this idea. **Count me in!**

Terry had thoughts about batteries. **Maybe we could find a motion-detecting camera on ebay. Wouldn't use that much power.**

**Yeah,** she said. *I'll keep my eyes open when I'm finished rolling them. That stuff's expensive.*

**I dare to dream!** she concluded.

By then, it was getting late, and everyone was ready to call it a night. But not Denise. She was awake, and she had some battery life left, so she pulled up the Internet on her phone.

She went back to Wikipedia and started clicking around through the sources cited at the bottom of Joe Vaughn's entry. That's when she learned that the *Times-Picayune* had an archive, and although it wasn't online, someone had been kind enough to post a JPEG of the story about Vaughn's death. This someone was an earnest nerd, somebody with a Tumblr that was dedicated to the real-life people behind pre-CCA comic books.

"Truly, all information is contained within the Internet," she murmured to herself. That's what one of her old history teachers used to say. He said that the *real* trick was knowing how to find it.

She scanned the photo, struggling a little because it wasn't very big and the text was kind of fuzzy. But she got the gist easily enough. Joe Vaughn, local artist and author, had fallen down a flight of stairs and broken his neck. He was found in a house belonging to a lady named Vera Westbrook. Miss Westbrook had been missing for several days.

"Vera Westbrook! Nice to finally have a name to go with the perfume and the footprints." And nice to have a new lead. How had she not stumbled on this before? "Whatever happened to you, Vera?"

As far as the Internet could tell, nobody knew.

Vera Westbrook had disappeared off the face of the earth. The article with Vaughn's death by misadventure was the next to last mention of her that ever appeared in print. Her final appearance came in a city auction a few months later, when her house and everything inside it was put up for sale.

Vera Westbrook. It *sounded* like an old lady name. An old lady who wore roses and lilies to church every Sunday. An old lady with tiny pointed shoes, and a lilting voice that hummed a strange tune, just barely audible.

"Did Joe know what happened to you, Vera?" she asked aloud. Vera didn't answer, and neither did anyone else. "Did *any*body?"

The Internet couldn't help her with that one, but Denise had an idea.

She was developing a theory.

# CHAPTER SIXTEEN

Denise spent Sunday morning trying to text Terry, but he never did respond, and when she texted Norman, he replied that he was stuck at his grandmother's for church and potluck, then vespers that evening — so he was no good to her, either. If she'd had her number, Dominique might have been game to chat. She knew about the ghosts now too.

But she didn't have her number, so it was just Denise and her parents. They braced themselves for a day of vacuuming out the last of the fluffy gray goo, and probably water damage, and maybe bugs, by donning the longest gloves and the tallest boots they had — plus some paper face masks that Mike had picked up at Pete's. Denise felt ridiculous, her hands and feet were sweating buckets, and she sounded like Darth Vader when she breathed, but she *did* feel sufficiently protected.

"From everything but the ghosts," she added, when Sally asked her opinion on the safety gear.

"Screw the ghosts," Sally replied. "This is our house now, and they can lump it."

Mike chuckled awkwardly. "Let's not say such things quite so loud, eh? They might be listening."

"Good," his wife declared.

"Yeah. Like Mom said, this is *our* house now. Besides, I don't care if Vera stays — she's all right. It's Joe we've got to worry about. He's the jerk."

"Who's Vera?" Sally asked. "Or is that what we're calling the old lady ghost, for no particular reason?"

"Vera Westbrook, that's her name. Or that's the name of the lady who owned this house, back when Joe died like a chump. I did a little more digging, and turned up her identity."

"Was she his girlfriend or something?" Mike wanted to know.

"I haven't a clue." Denise picked up a trash bag and shook it open. "And nobody knows what happened to her, either. She vanished before Joe died."

Sally shook her head. "This whole thing gets weirder by the day."

Mike plugged in the Shop-Vac and made sure it was set to "suck" instead of "blow." "As long as *one* of the ghosts isn't trying to kill us, I'll call it a win."

"But you're fine if the other one is a homicidal maniac," Denise said wryly.

"I'm not fine with it, but I'm saying it could be worse. They could both be out to get us."

They spent the rest of the morning vacuuming and bagging trash, picking up the last of the ratty brown insulation that had come from the ceiling, and wiping the residue off every available surface. They'd gotten the worst of it earlier, but today was the fine detail work, and it was going to be never-ending as far as Denise could tell.

The fluffy stuff in question was indeed vermiculite, according to some guy at Pete's who Mike had chatted up on the subject. Nothing to get excited about, but wear gloves when you pick it up. Wear masks when you mess with it. It'll get into your chest and make your lungs all itchy.

When all that was done, they moved on to the wainscoting and wallpaper, those two miserable projects.

Mike and Sally were happy and a little day-drunk, playing dorky 1990s songs from Mike's playlist again while they scraped wallpaper in the dining room by electric lantern light, since the fixture still wasn't working.

Denise needed a break. She declared this loudly and scraped

together enough change for a soda and a beignet, and promised to be back in an hour or two.

Then she hiked down to Crispy's with her laptop, planning to wait around until someone she knew showed up.

*Surely* someone she knew would show up. Eventually.

Yep. Church had let out, and everybody'd finished up lunch at home. Now the little restaurant was collecting the usual suspects, wanting Internet and some freedom. She recognized most of the kids her age, but didn't know them well enough to chat them up. She thought about asking to sit with them, but chickened out at the last minute and took her usual table against the wall.

Finally, Terry arrived. She grabbed him before he could even order any food, and dragged him over to her table. She leaned forward and said, "Guess what: I think I know the name of the old lady ghost."

"Really?"

"It's *Vera Westbrook*. The house belonged to her, and get this: She vanished, not long before Joe died. Nobody knows what happened to her, but I'm pretty sure she's dead, and she's the second ghost — the one without a hit list."

"Hey y'all two." Dominique brought a tray from the front counter and slipped it into the slot next to Terry like she was sliding into home plate. It held a clear cup for holding water, not soda, and a ninety-nine-cent order of beignets. "Any more news about the ghosts?"

They caught her up on the Vera Westbrook development, and Denise concluded, "I think Joe was having some kind of fight with Vera Westbrook too. He might've even killed her. It sounds like she doesn't like him much. Maybe when Terry comes back over with his recorder —"

"Not if, but when!" he declared happily.

". . . then maybe we can get Vera to tell us what happened to her. She's been helpful before; she might be helpful again."

"You let me know how that goes. I want to know," Dom told her firmly. "But I don't want to be there, when you find out. I just want the download when you're done, got it?"

Denise liked how Dom didn't argue with her, or tell her there was no such thing as ghosts, or act like this was stupid. "I will. I'll tell everybody. Maybe I'll write a big Tumblr post about it, and tell the whole world." Then she told her about the agent, Eugenie Robbins. "You never know. This lady might get me enough money for a decent laptop."

Norman joined them then, adding his tray to the assortment that now covered the entire table. He'd paid extra for a second corn dog, and brought a plastic Aquafina bottle from home, so she guessed the potluck hadn't filled him up. "Been refilling it here for a couple of weeks," he explained. "Hello, ladies and Terry."

Together, they discussed theories of ghosts, probabilities, and how to find further evidence until the restaurant manager started to give them the side-eye about hanging around for so long without buying anything else. Denise had already texted her mom and told her she'd walk back soon, and after she promised Norman that she'd update him tomorrow, he'd headed back in the direction of his own home. Dominique and Terry kept pace with her as she walked back to the Agony House.

"Hey, Denise, listen," Dominique began. "If you've got a minute today . . ." She trailed off.

"If I've got a minute, what?"

She cleared her throat, and hemmed, and hawed, and generally acted like she was very uncomfortable about what she needed to say. "See, my grandma wants to know if you'll come talk to her."

"What?"

Terry perked up. "Mrs. James? How's she doing?"

"She's good, Tee. Same as always. So . . . what do you say? I just live a couple of blocks away from you. Grandma wants to ask you about your place, that's all. She wants to talk about the nail house."

Denise shrugged. "Sure, I guess. Let me text my mom that I'm running late, so she doesn't worry." She pulled out her phone and fired off a text begging an extra twenty minutes to find her way home. She hit SEND and pocketed the phone again. "Let's do this."

Dominique's house was long and narrow, with a single story and tall front shutters on either side of the front door. The porch was close to the ground, just two short steps that sagged like the ones at Denise's place. There was even a haint-blue ceiling, like it was just something everybody around there had. The porch was clean, and so was the living room, where a couple of antique chairs flanked a couch that once had been a very fancy velvet, and now looked a little too lived-in to call fancy anymore.

Before they went inside, Dominique turned to Denise. "She's going to ask you about ghosts, I just know it. She loves all that spooky business. I don't know what's wrong with her."

"Spooky business is fun business!" Terry declared.

"Yeah, says you. Fun to hear about, that's all. I like for my dead people to stay good and dead."

"What's the fun in that?" he asked.

"The fun of not getting your butt scared off." Then she cleared her throat, and said loud enough to project all the way to the back door: "Grandma, I'm home — and I brought that girl from the nail house!"

A voice came from the kitchen. "Good, I'm glad to hear it." Mrs. James poked her head around the corner and said, "Give me just a second, if you would. Take a seat, and make yourself comfortable. Terry? You came along too? Nice to see you, son. Can I get either one of you a Coke?"

"No thank you, ma'am," said Terry.

"No thank you, ma'am," Denise echoed.

Everybody sat down, and a moment later their hostess joined them, wiping her hands on a dish towel. "I'm glad you were willing to come around, dear. Remind me your name?"

"Denise, ma'am. Denise Farber. Dominique said you wanted to talk about the house."

"That's right." She took the chair that faced them all the best, and folded her hands across her belly. She was a thickset woman with sharp eyes and a kind expression. She could've been forty or seventy. She just had one of those faces, where it was hard to tell. "Your folks picked up the old nail house, over there on Argonne."

"Yes ma'am."

"Well, I asked Dom to bring you here because I know your parents are doing all that work on the place, and I wondered if you'd . . . *found* anything."

The very picture of innocence — or possibly confusion — Denise asked, "Like . . . what?"

Mrs. James's eyes just about twinkled. "Like anything . . . or any*one* . . . hidden inside that place. My momma always said the house was abandoned because someone disappeared, and was never found. When I was a kid, we used to dare each other to go inside, looking for a body."

"I think my stepdad found a dead possum in the bathroom wall, but that's been the worst of it."

The older woman laughed gently, then looked a tad embarrassed about it. "I can't decide if that's good to know, or a little disappointing. There were so many stories, and we all wanted to get inside so *bad* — but we were all so scared. Just looking inside the windows was enough to make us squeal. You'd see lights in there, sometimes. People walking past the windows."

"Yikes . . ." Denise whispered.

"Just squatters or trespassers, I figure. It'd been boarded up for so long, before that last fellow bought it — the one just before y'all picked it up. He said he ran out of money, but I heard through the grapevine that the place spooked him too bad to keep working on it. Like something inside that house don't want anyone looking around too much. Like it doesn't want anyone to stay."

Terry opened his mouth, but Denise gave him a kick on the leg that wasn't particularly discreet — but effective. He closed his mouth again.

Denise cleared her throat. "I don't know why the last guy left the house like he did. It sure *looked* like somebody got started and ran out of money, so that's probably all it was. As for us, like I said — we found that dead possum."

Mrs. James nodded. "But your parents, they're remodeling, aren't they? Gonna open it up, like a little hotel? Haunted hotels in New Orleans are a dime a dozen, but people love 'em. You should play that up, if you ever get it off the ground."

Denise sighed hard. "God knows we're trying to get the place in order, but it's falling apart at the seams."

"It's not much to look at anymore, if you don't mind me saying — but it can't be that bad on the inside."

"Ma'am, the inside's no picnic. The other day, we had to spend a night in a hotel because the living room ceiling caved in. But there weren't any corpses up in there, either. Nothing that used to be alive except for a snakeskin or two."

"Well, you keep your eyes open. For years and years everybody talked like there was a body inside, someplace."

"Probably just because Joe died there," Terry said helpfully.

"Joe?" she asked with a very keen look on her face. "Joe who?"

"Joe Vaughn," Denise answered. She sure did wish that Terry could keep his mouth shut. "He was a comic book writer, back in the 1950s. He fell down the attic stairs and broke his neck, but I'm pretty sure they took his body away and buried it. It's definitely not at the foot of the stairs anymore, so . . ." Her voice faded out.

"Maybe that's it," Mrs. James agreed. "Neighborhood lore can get tangled up something awful, with little bits of truth and little bits of lies all mixed in together. You never know for sure what's real, and what somebody made up to scare a bunch of kids away from a danger-ous old house. Have you opened all the walls yet?"

"The plumbers and electricians did. It took a few days."

"*All* of the walls?" she pressed.

"All of 'em with wires or pipes inside, so that's . . . just about every-thing, right?"

"I suppose." She leaned back and looked at Denise hard, like she was trying to decide if she was telling the truth. "But you're saying there's nothing in that place? Not a single haunt or haint? Not even . . . a whiff of perfume? The fellow before you said he kept smelling roses and lilies," she said, and the twinkle in her eyes was now a gleam.

Denise held her breath. When the phone in her pocket buzzed and pinged, she let it out in an unladylike gasp. "I'm sorry," she sputtered. "It's my mom, I'm sorry. I really have to go. Thank you," she said as she stood. "Mrs. James, thank you for the hospitality, but I have to run. Terry, Dominique . . . I'll catch y'all two later."

When she got home to Argonne Street, she stood out front, like she did the very first time she saw the house. Mouth half-open, feeling glum, wondering if it could be saved. Or if it was even *worth* saving. But before she could drag herself up the porch, Sally opened the front door. "There you are. I was starting to wonder."

"I took a detour. I sent a text, didn't you get it?"

"It was a vague text." She stood aside to let Denise up the steps and around the hole on the porch, which still hadn't been fixed. "Come on inside, if you want something to eat."

Dinner was seafood, something that wasn't quite the fast-food junk they'd mostly eaten for days. Sally had picked it up from a po'boy place somewhere that wasn't Crispy's, but Denise didn't care. She'd never had a proper po'boy from Crispy's, anyway.

"Not that I'm complaining," Denise said as she pulled out a foil-wrapped sandwich the size of a baby's head. "But when are we going to have a working kitchen?"

"Soon," Sally said. "The electricians are almost done."

"I keep hearing that."

"So do we." Mike pulled off his face mask and drew up a chair.

Sally passed out napkins. "We're getting there. Gradually. We've got that next chunk of money approved, and it should hit our bank account this week . . . but it's supposed to go to the next round of work. Maybe we'll take a couple hundred bucks and scare up a stove with more than one burner mostly working, and an oven that doesn't spit fire. Maybe we'll even spring for one that was made in this century."

"I'd settle for last century, so long as it worked." Mike bit down on a full, golden bun and chomped through the fried shrimp stuffing.

Everyone ate in silence after that, because everyone knew they were eating all the money they'd set aside that wasn't for the house. Nobody needed to say it out loud.

After food, Denise excused herself and went upstairs, where she turned the AC unit up half a notch past the agreed-upon setting, and pulled out her phone.

Trish had sent her a row of ghost and skeleton emojis, so apparently she'd found a Halloween stash someplace.

Denise grinned and typed back. *Did I tell you I saw Tulane the other day? It's a pretty campus. Library is great.*

After a pause, a typing bubble appeared, and then her friend replied: ur not chickening out on me, are you? still coming home to be my roommate?

*Obvs. Just saying, is all.*

She put the phone away, not entirely sure of what, exactly, she was just saying. Even if she could, she didn't really want to stay in Louisiana, did she?

Forget it. She didn't want to think about it.

She was almost finished reading *Lucida Might and the House of Horrors*, so maybe that would distract her. Only a handful of pages remained. She might feel a little bad about finishing up without Terry, but she'd already read pretty far ahead of him, and she could always invite him over to let him finish on one of these afternoons when the house and its ghosts weren't actively trying to kill anyone.

She fished the manuscript out of her bag and settled into bed — sitting on top of the covers, propped up by all her pillows.

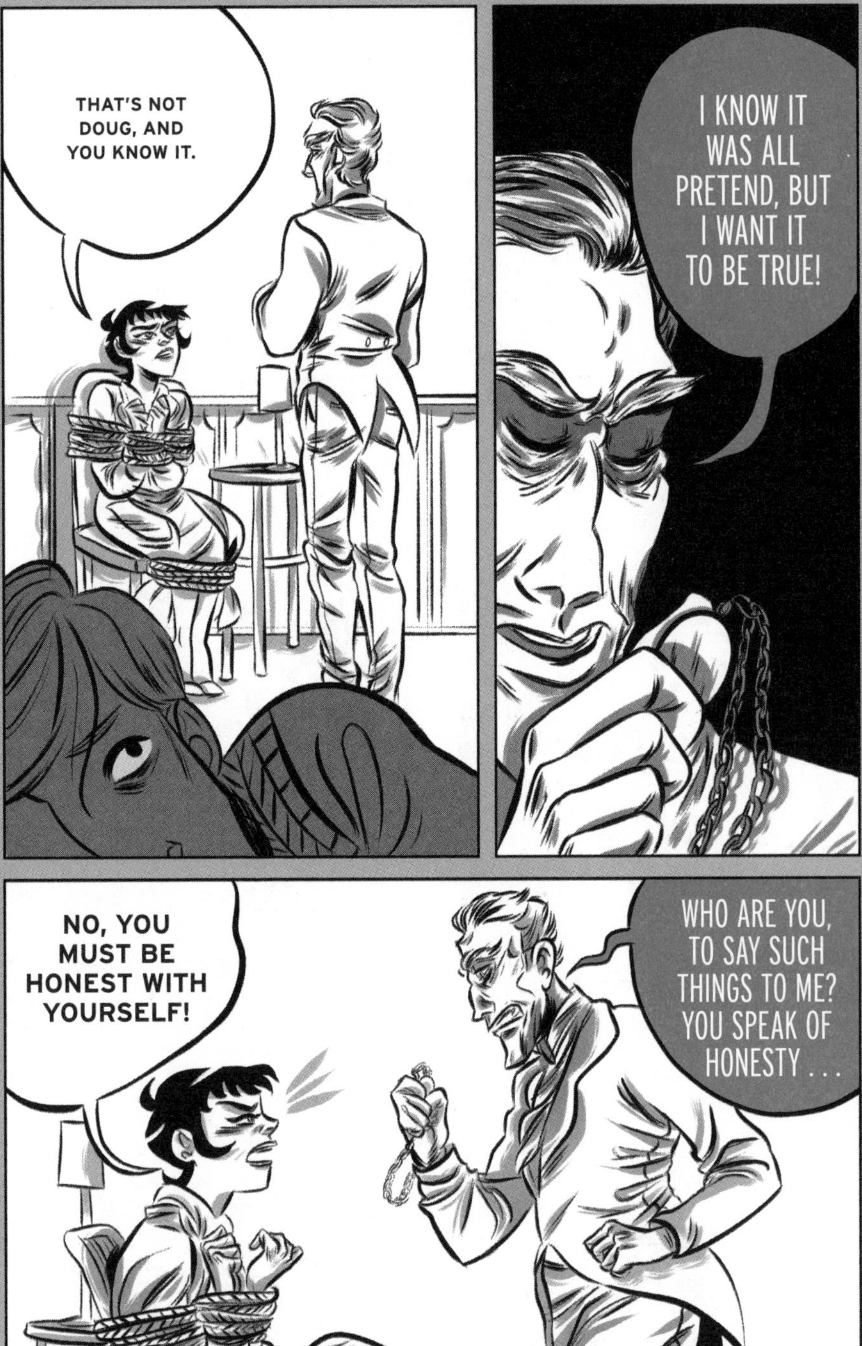
THAT'S NOT DOUG, AND YOU KNOW IT.
I KNOW IT WAS ALL PRETEND, BUT I WANT IT TO BE TRUE!
NO, YOU MUST BE HONEST WITH YOURSELF!
WHO ARE YOU, TO SAY SUCH THINGS TO ME? YOU SPEAK OF HONESTY . . .

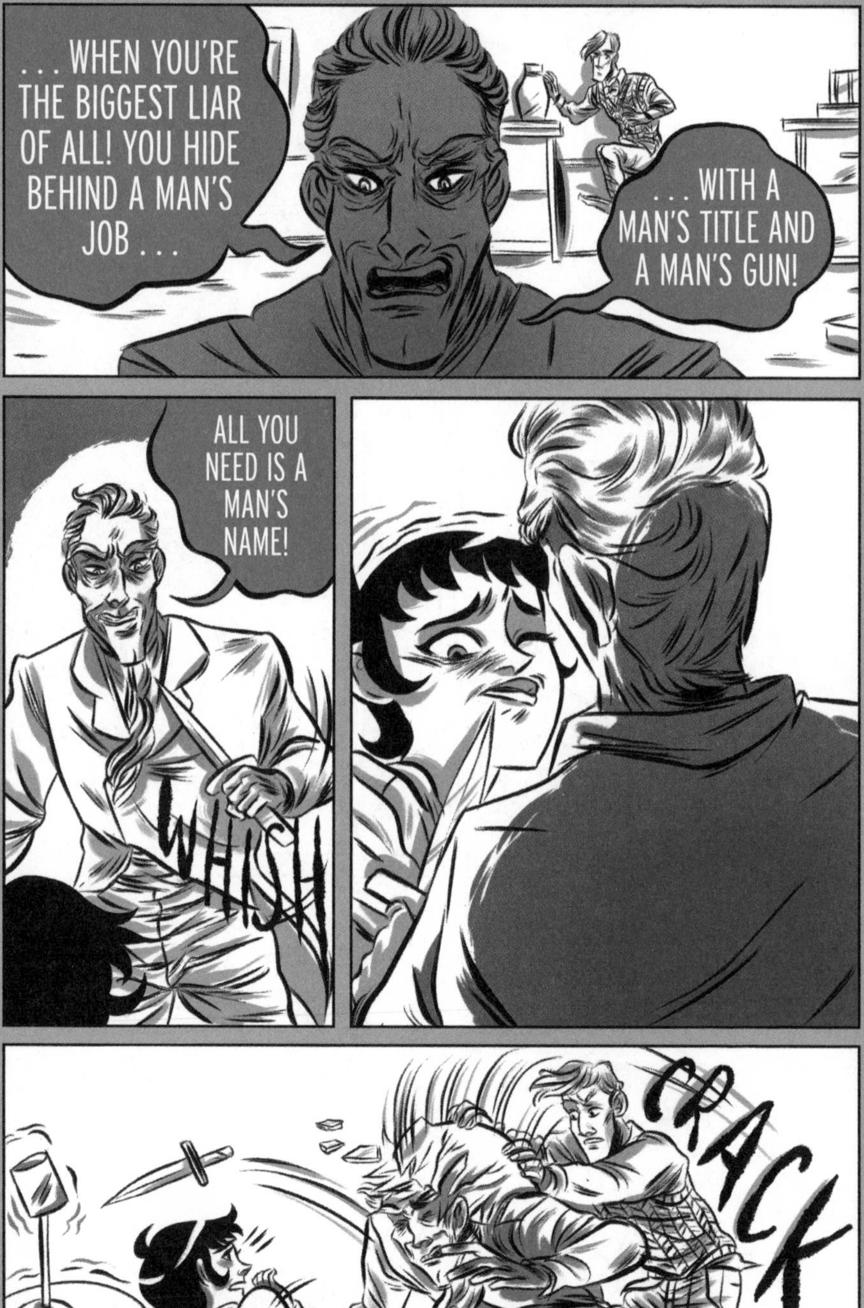
. . . WHEN YOU'RE THE BIGGEST LIAR OF ALL! YOU HIDE BEHIND A MAN'S JOB . . .
. . . WITH A MAN'S TITLE AND A MAN'S GUN!
ALL YOU NEED IS A MAN'S NAME!
WHISH
CRACK

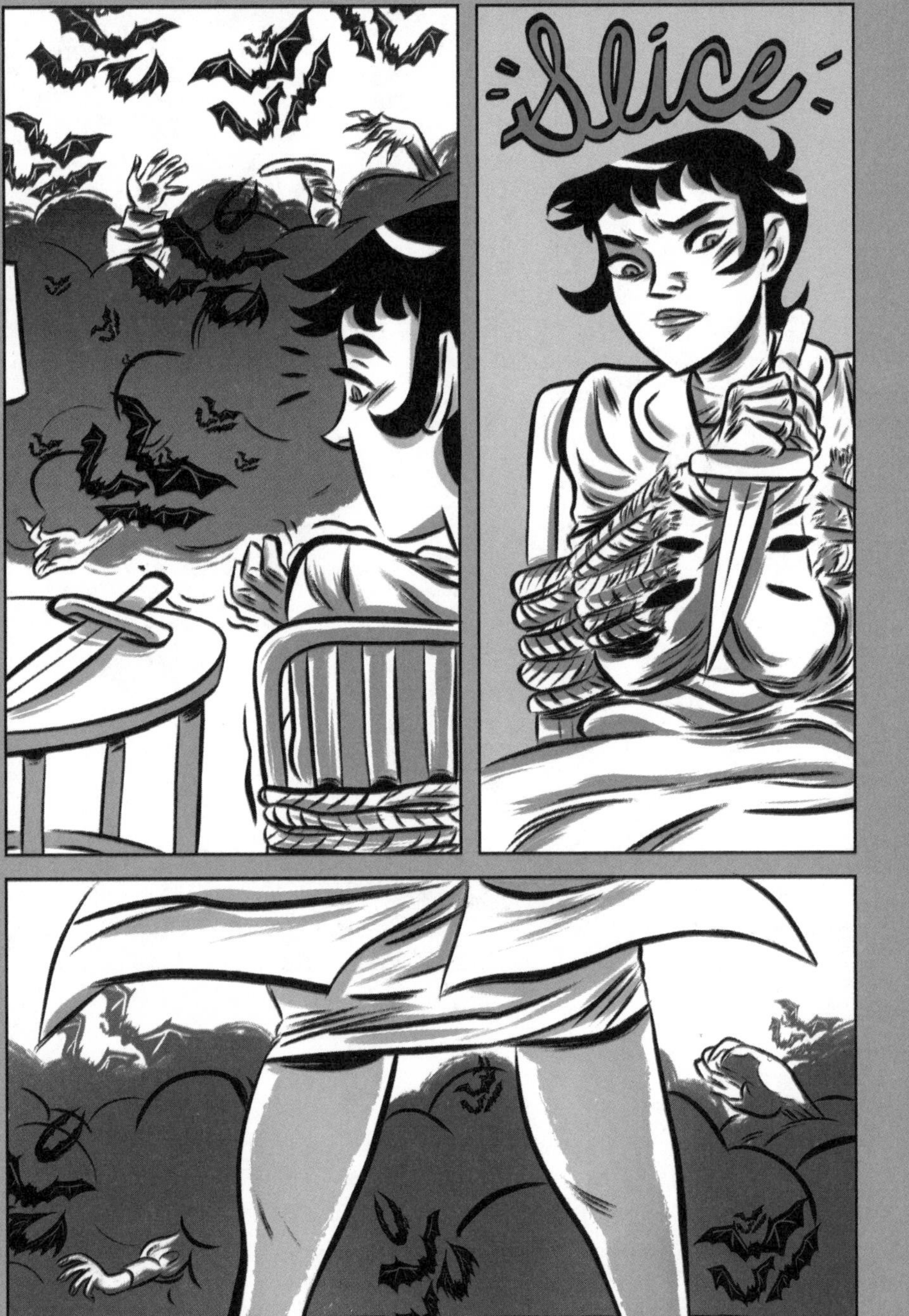
Slice

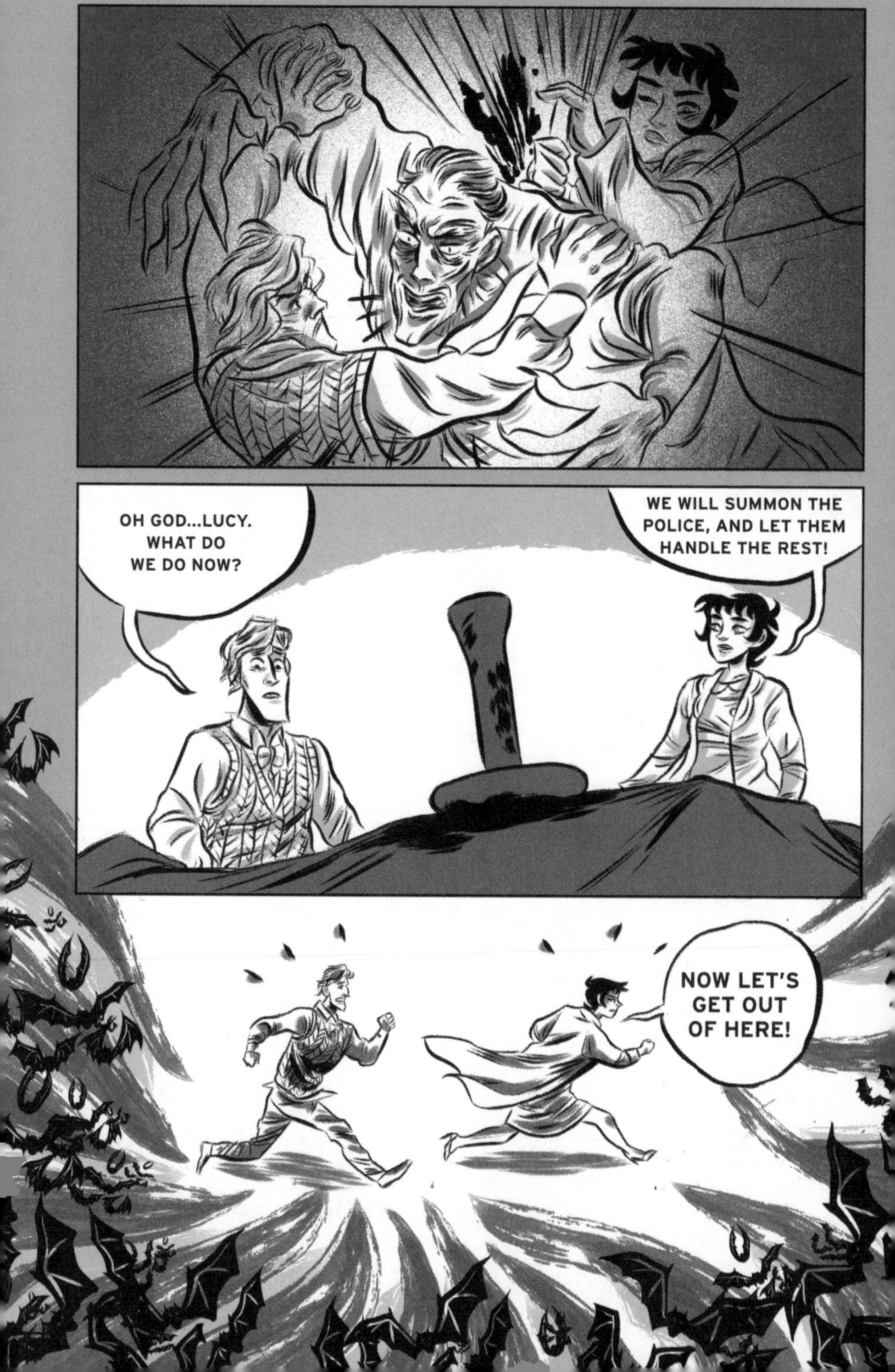
OH GOD...LUCY. WHAT DO WE DO NOW?
WE WILL SUMMON THE POLICE, AND LET THEM HANDLE THE REST!
NOW LET'S GET OUT OF HERE!

# CHAPTER SEVENTEEN

Denise looked up from the book. She smelled something.

Flowers. Roses and lilies.

She sniffed until she was sure; it was very faint, but it was definitely perfume. Soon, it would be dark outside, so she flipped on the bedside lamp that sat atop a box beside her. It wasn't dark yet, but the room was gold and dim, and she wanted every bit of light she could get.

The air didn't just smell funny, it *felt* funny. It felt like it was buzzing. Like music with nothing but the bass turned up, somewhere far away. Like the damp, brittle humming of the sky when there isn't any rain, but any minute, there will be lightning.

Denise closed *Lucida Might* and set it aside. She only had another couple of pages to read, and then she'd be done with it — but then again, that's what she'd thought when she'd picked it up half an hour ago.

She thought of the previous night, when she'd been reading about a ceiling collapse, and downstairs, that's just what had happened. She thought of Mike falling through the porch. Windows that fell shut and almost crushed hands. Nails that appeared in stair rails. Bricks that crashed onto feet.

Slowly, she reached for her phone. She pulled up Terry and composed a text. She wasn't sure who else to ping.

*Something weird is going on. I mean, EXTRA weird. Are you there?*

She wasn't sure what she expected him to say or do, but she needed to say something, to someone. Trish was too far away to do anything but worry; Norman might think she was crazy, and she didn't think she knew him well enough to pass off crazy as charming. Dom might be intrigued, but Denise had brain-farted and forgotten to ask for Dom's number, and anyway—Dom didn't want to get in the middle of any ghost drama, she'd made that clear. On the one hand, she wanted to respect her wishes, on the other, she would've just about killed to have her there . . . oh well. It was nobody's fault but her own.

She'd have to settle for Terry. He was most likely to understand, and he was adventurous enough to respond to her summons. She hit SEND.

Unhooking the phone from its cable, she slid out of bed and poked her toes through the slots of her flip-flops. She dragged her feet and the foam-bottomed shoes scraped across the rough boards.

The roses and lily scent faded, and something else took its place. The new smell was sour and dark.

"Mom?" Denise called out. She reached her bedroom door and hung on to it, looking down at the hall's carpet runner and checking for footprints. There weren't any. "Mike?"

Nobody answered.

The smell grew stronger. The air grew thicker, and Denise felt light-headed. She let go of the doorframe and stepped into the hall, then took the rail and stood near the top of the stairs.

"Mom? Mike?"

Nothing was going on. Nothing was weird. If there was a terrible smell, it was in her imagination — or else it was in the attic, where there were plenty of terrible smells to go around. Just a draft, that's all. Just a rush of air pushing down under the door, into the rest of the house. Just some ghost with a grudge, or a different ghost with a pleasant odor and gentle warnings.

She kind of wished she had Terry's recorder handy. She wondered if anything was trying to talk, and she just couldn't hear it. Surely *something* was trying to communicate.

Her phone was a solid lump in her shorts pocket. She pulled it out. Terry hadn't texted back, but the phone had a voice recorder feature buried in it somewhere.

Still standing on the stairs, she poked at the screen until she found what she was looking for. She pressed the icon to turn on the mic. She held it out like she'd seen Terry do, away from her body, away from the static noise of her clothes, her breathing, her heartbeat.

"Is there anybody here with me?" she whispered. "What do you want?"

The buzzing got louder, or it felt louder. She couldn't really hear it, so much as she could feel it moving on her skin. Under it.

A voice answered, "Denise?" but it was just her mom, calling from downstairs. "What are you doing up there?"

Denise came down the steps, half-dead from relief. "Nothing, why?"

Sally wasn't in the living room or dining room. Denise didn't know where she was, because she couldn't see her. "Then what's that strange noise? Are you playing music?"

Denise followed her mom's voice down to the parlor, and found Mike there too. They were both looking up at the light fixture, one of the last old pieces that remained. It was probably just glass and not crystal, but it would be real pretty when they got it cleaned up.

The light was probably not rocking back and forth, swaying like a pendulum. It was probably not keeping time to some odd humming that sounded more like a grumble than a song.

"You hear it too," Sally said with a gulp. "Don't you?"

"What the hell is going on?" Mike asked without taking his eyes off the fixture. Then he looked over at Denise, who hadn't answered her mom yet. "What are you doing with your phone?"

She quit holding it out like a torch, and dropped her arms to her sides. "I was looking for a good signal," she explained, in case they would think her EVP recording efforts were weird. They probably weren't working anyway, so she tucked the phone into her pocket and wandered back into the living room.

Sally wrinkled her nose. "What's that smell? *Please* tell me nothing is on fire. The electricians supposedly took care of the knob-and-tube a couple of days ago . . ."

"Mom, I don't think it's fire."

The light fixture rattled, its glass bits clinking together. The windows rattled too.

Denise backed out of the room, in case another section of the ceiling was going to drop. She left it just in time to see a dark, nebulous shape spill slowly toward them, slipping down the stairs. It took her breath away. She literally couldn't answer Mike, when he asked if New Orleans ever got earthquakes. Even if she knew, she couldn't have told him. She couldn't say a word. She opened her mouth, and nothing came out.

The dark shape didn't have much shape to it at first—it was a blob about the size of a person, and then it sprawled and spread. It poured along the floor in every direction, pooling around Denise's ankles and leaving them cold. She shivered, even though it must've been eighty-five degrees down there.

It could've been hotter than that, and it wouldn't have mattered. She froze anyway.

She watched the tall, ragged shape take form—assuming the shape of a tall, heavyset man with hunched shoulders, and long arms, and big hands. He didn't have much of a face, just a pair of eyes that were holes in the smoke, white and bright. He stayed put on the stairs, but the dark fog around his feet sprawled toward the parlor. What if it got Mike, or her mom? What would it do to them?

She unfroze herself. Scared beyond words, she tore her eyes away from the figment on the stairs and darted back to the parlor. "Mom, we have to get out of here!"

"You're right . . . that smell. It might be a gas leak, or poisonous fumes, or . . ." Sally stopped at the "or" because she'd just noticed the putrid swirl of darkness moving across the floor.

"Out," said Mike. "Everybody. Now. We can come back later, when we figure out what's going on."

Joe had other ideas.

The windows rattled harder, and the doors all shook, thundering in their frames. Outside, something huge clapped against the house. A second something followed it. Then a whole volley of bangs, one after the next.

It was the window shutters. Every last one of them slammed shut.

Glass broke, and sprayed inside. Sally shrieked, and when the power went out in a loud, grand poof of sparks, Denise screamed too.

She felt around in the dark—it was so *very* dark, with the windows all covered up, and the lights all turned off—but she found the parlor entrance and knew that the front door was just a few steps to the left. All she had to do was reach it, throw it open, and get the hell out.

Mike and Sally had the same idea. They were right behind her, pushing her even as they felt along the wall.

Denise found the doorknob. She grabbed it, twisted, and yanked. The door swung inward about a foot. "Everybody, come on!" she said, but it wasn't that easy. Hard and fast, the knob yanked itself out of her hand and the door shut itself again.

Mike pushed her aside. "Here, I've got it."

He didn't have it. He pulled until the knob popped off in his hands and a smattering of nails fell across the floor. He kicked them away and announced, "I'm going to break a window! Those shutters are rotted out—they're practically cardboard. We can kick right through them."

She sensed her stepfather moving past her. He was in a rush, looking for something big enough and solid enough to chuck right onto the front lawn. "Bash them in! Use the dining room chairs!" she suggested.

To her right, there was a clatter.

To her left, there was a knock on the door. Denise nearly jumped out of her skin.

Everything went quiet. Her mother breathed hard and fast, and her stepdad stood with the skeletal shadow of a chair in his hands.

"Hello? Is anybody home? It's me, Terry . . ."

Of *course* it was Terry. All it took was a text saying something weird was afoot, and it was like Denise had raised the Bat-Signal. She flung herself at the door, knocking back with both hands. "Terry, can you hear me?"

"Yeah, open the door."

"I can't! We're trapped in here!"

Sally joined her at the door. "And the power's gone out!" she added.

Denise almost told him to call the cops, and then she remembered her own phone. She whipped it out of her pocket. The microphone was still running, but she minimized the app and pulled up the call function. She entered 9-1-1, and hit SEND.

Nothing happened.

She tried it again.

"Denise?" Terry called.

She tried to sound calm when she told him through the door: "Terry, my phone isn't working. You have to go get help."

"You want me to call the police? What do I tell them?"

Sally answered, "Tell them we're stuck in our house!"

"Trapped," Denise corrected her. "Tell them we're trapped, and there's an intruder."

"There's an intruder?" Terry sounded suitably appalled.

"There's a *something*. Just make the call!" she yelled, trying not to think about the looming, lanky figure of Joe — who was surely stalking around them, even as she spoke. Just because she couldn't see him, that didn't mean he wasn't there.

"I'm calling, I'm calling . . ."

Then he was crashing. She heard the boards break and she knew, suddenly and with great horror, that he'd fallen down in the same hole that almost ate Mike. How could he have seen it? The porch light was out, just like everything else. "Terry!" she screamed, and she pounded on the door with her fist, and with the useless cell phone. It didn't matter if she broke it. "Terry, are you okay?!"

Mike swung the chair again and again, but could only break more glass. The shutters were holding. "I swear and be damned!"

Okay, so Denise couldn't make any calls. Could she turn on the flashlight app? Her screen had a big, fresh crack in it, but she found the light and called it up.

It was blinding for a few seconds. Her eyes adjusted, and she saw her mother squinting, holding her face away from the light. "Jesus, girl. That's bright, but good thinking. Mike, we're coming with a light."

"Light won't make a difference," he said. He huffed, puffed, hoisted the chair, and took another swing. This time Denise could watch him. This time, she saw the chair break against the rotted wood shutters that should've splintered into dust if you sneezed on them. His face was tight with fear and maybe pain. He was bleeding through his shirt.

"Honey, I think you've popped your stitches again . . ."

"I don't care!" He threw what was left of the broken chair at the wholly intact shutter, and leaned over, putting his hands on top of his legs and breathing too hard. "What is going on?" he asked the universe at large. "What do we do?"

Denise swung the light around the room, and could not tell which shadows were only shadows, and which ones were moving with slithering, nasty grace along the floors. Or the walls. The pattern on the paper seemed to move. She blinked, and wasn't sure that was it at all. "I think we're asking the wrong questions."

"What do the right questions sound like?" Sally's eyes tracked the mobile darkness. She watched it climb, crawl, and creep around the corners until it took the wobbly, loose shape of a tall man once again. Mike put his arm around her, in turn, and guided her toward the foyer. It was the middle of the first floor, and farthest from any corners.

"What would Terry do?" Denise said for starters. "God, I hope he's okay." She thought of Lucida Might, and how that fictional heroine had found a tunnel under Desmond Rutledge's porch. Terry knew about that scene. She crept back to the front door and peered around — it looked like Joe had faded back into the swirling black. Thank god. Maybe he couldn't take the shape for that long? She pressed her ear against the door. "Terry?" she called again, as loud as she could. She dropped to her knees, and called down to the floor, and to anything underneath it. "Terry, can you hear me?"

No response.

Mike was shaky all over when he asked, "Well? What *would* Terry do?"

"And why does it matter?" asked Sally.

Denise said, "Terry's got some funny ideas, but he gets results." She pulled out her phone, and tried to dial 9-1-1 again. It didn't work. She returned to the microphone and, yes, it was still recording. She held it up again, and asked in a slow, clear voice — like she was trying to explain math to a Saint Bernard: "What . . . do . . . you . . . want?"

She counted to ten, listening to the persistent rushing buzz that filled the house, and filled her ears, and made her forget that she'd ever been able to hear anything else. Then she replayed what she'd recorded. Her own words were too loud, because she kicked the volume all the way up.

"What do you want?" she heard herself ask.

Fizz, static, hum.

I keep what's mine.

Sally and Mike jumped, but Denise yelled at the darkness. "That's all you ever say! You have to be more specific! Tell me *what* you want!"

She heard something else, something below. Some rustling noise, and it might've been Terry, rallying from his fall. She prayed that it was Terry, and she didn't pray very often, so she wasn't sure she was doing it right. But she did it with all her heart, as she held up the phone and counted to ten. She held her breath, and played back the last few seconds.

Fizz, static, hum.

A different voice, this time — a woman, her words as soft as petals: Let me out so I can help.

"Who is that talking?" Sally demanded with a shrill note of hysteria. "Who's saying that? Is it Vera?"

Denise didn't answer. She tried again, counted to ten, and played back the clip.

Fizz, static, hum.

The man spoke this time: . . . bring this house down. Destroy everything . . .

"I heard that. I heard that loud and clear!" Mike's words quivered around the edges.

Denise rewound and pressed the button. She wanted to hear the woman again.

. . . Let me out, so I can help . . .

"This is the craziest damn thing I ever heard. Where's my phone?" asked Sally. "Yours don't work to call the cops, but mine might."

"Where'd you put it?" her husband wanted to know.

"In my purse. It's in our bedroom. Where's yours?"

Mike was so shaken, he wasn't sure. "I can't remember."

. . . let me out . . .

Something moved in the walls, or under the floor. Denise shined the phone-light all around, but she couldn't see anything except the swirling murk. "Please be Terry. Please don't be a rat, or something worse," she whispered to the scrambling noise. Then she called out, "Vera Westbrook!"

. . . so I can help . . .

Mike and Sally were retreating, clutching each other, fumbling toward the bedroom in search of Sally's purse.

"Vera, don't let him do this!" A whiff of perfume tickled her nose — a tiny tendril of sweetness that cut through the god-awful gloom and the stink of death that otherwise filled the house. Something about the soft smell of roses and lilies chased out some of the terror. Something about the thought of it, the hint of it, the clue of it . . . jogged something loose in Denise's head. Something about Eugenie Robbins, and Lucida Might.

Two snippets of text tumbled around in her skull, knocking against each other, making sparks.

*My dad used to say that Joe sometimes hid "Easter eggs" in his stories, little pieces of autobiography, here and there.*

"You're the biggest liar of all! You hide behind a man's job, with a man's title and a man's gun.

"All you need is a man's name."

Denise gasped.

Everything clicked together.

# CHAPTER EIGHTEEN

Something banged underneath the floor. Denise jumped, spun around, and almost dropped the phone — but held it fast and firm. Carefully, she kicked a response, like she was knocking "shave and a haircut."

"Terry? Is that you?"

A muffled, "It's me," made it up through the floorboards. "I'm okay. My phone's busted, but the screen still has a little light."

"Terry, oh my God — hang in there." She turned to look for Mike and Sally, but they must've made it to the bedroom to hunt for their phones. She could hear them rustling around, looking for Sally's purse in the dark. "Mike! Mom! Terry's under the floor! Get a saw — we can cut him out, and leave through the hole in the porch!"

The whole house shuddered at this announcement. Joe Vaughn was angry, but Vera was in there too; the roses and lilies stayed and rallied, faint but pure. Reassuring, but hardly strong enough to mount a challenge from wherever she was.

. . . find me . . .

. . . said the voice on the recorder.

. . . let me out, and I *will* help . . .

Mike came charging back in, Sally's phone aloft. "The phone's not working, but the light is fine." He demonstrated this by shining it right in Denise's face. "There's no Internet, either. No signal of any kind."

*. . . let me out . . .*

"We're in one heck of a dead zone." Denise let out a short, maniacal laugh. The house groaned, and something large, somewhere unseen, cracked with a noise as loud as a gunshot.

Sally was right behind Mike. "Terry's okay? Where is he?"

She tapped the floor with her foot. Terry said something loud, but unintelligible, confirming his continued survival and strange location. "He went under the house, just like Lucida Might did, in the comic."

"What's a Lucida Might?" Sally asked.

Mike said, "She's the girl detective from that comic Denise found in the attic."

"Me and Terry have been reading it together. Mike, come on — get him out of there. This house can't hold up much longer."

"There's no power. The Sawzall won't do us any good."

"Where's the pry bar?" Sally asked.

"Over there. Give it to me," he gestured with his free hand.

"No, I'll keep this. You take the sledge."

Denise got down on her hands and knees, and spoke into the floor. "We're coming for you, Terry. Get away from this spot — we're coming through the floor."

It was easier said than done. Mike and Sally reasserted Denise's warning to move away from the chosen demolition spot, then set to work prying, pulling, and slamming the sledge into the old wood floors that they'd thought about trying to save and refinish, just a week before.

Denise held back and aimed Sally's phone-light while they swung and pulled and swore. She tried not to shake, but it was hard. It was cold in there — as cold as she'd ever wanted the AC to make it — and the house wouldn't stop moving, moaning, and vibrating.

One-handed, she pulled out her own phone and loaded up the microphone again.

"Denise, *don't*." Her mother said, then jammed the pry bar between two boards and leaned her whole weight on it.

"But I can't hear them without it," she protested, and before Sally could say anything else, she called out to the house, and anything in it: "Vera, I don't know where you went!" Ten seconds passed. Fizz, static, hum.

And the woman came through, her soft voice answered with a southern white lady accent: I never left . . .

Everyone stopped. Even the house stopped. Mike and Sally stared at Denise's phone.

"Vera again," she explained weakly.

From under the floor they heard Terry ask, "What did she say?"

Denise flashed Mike and Sally a worried look. Her phone pinged. She looked down and saw that the microphone had been recording. She pressed the playback button and heard Vera again.

. . . house of horrors.

She couldn't tell if Mike or Sally had heard the message or not; it was faint, and hard to hear over the loud, angry sorrow of the house as it strained to hold itself together. She handed her mom's phone back to her, turned on her heel, and ran for the stairs with her own phone's light bobbing madly, showing the way. "Sometimes there are Easter eggs!"

She heard Mike ask, "What?" but didn't catch her mother's response. The sound of her footsteps stomping up the steps drowned it all out. The vivid white light rocked back and forth as she climbed, clinging to the rail with one hand, and trying to steady the phone with her other.

Her foot caught something small and rolling, and she almost lost her footing — but they were only nails, lying loose across the stairs. Then there were more, pounded into the step, ready to trip anybody coming or going.

"Dang it, Joe! You're such a jerk!" she said as she dodged them. "You and all these stupid nails . . ." *Nails are supposed to hold things together,* she thought. They weren't supposed to drive people away. Joe sure did have a lot of things backwards.

The hall at the top of the stairs was blacker than black, even when she thrust her phone forward. It was a knot of the shadows that wiggled and writhed. She put out her hand and could feel them, cold and clammy, like the air that spills out of a freezer unit. The shadows pushed back. She pushed forward. She pushed harder. She took a deep breath and closed her eyes. Her room was a straight shot to the right, and that's where *Lucida Might* was waiting—on her bed, where she'd been reading it, certain she was almost finished with it.

She held her breath. She closed her eyes.

She pushed through the sticky, slimy shadows and ran—both hands outstretched to catch herself, in case she fell.

Her legs collided with something soft. She stopped, knees knocking against the side of her mattress, and she almost sobbed because she'd made it. Her bedroom was dark, but only dark in the ordinary way. It smelled like roses and lilies, and her phone-light showed no twitching shadows. Only fresh cobwebs, and boxes of clothes, and an unmade bed with an old comic manuscript lying open across it.

"I think I've got it, Vera," she breathed.

She climbed onto the bed and flipped the book open. She couldn't be sure but the last few pages looked more quickly drawn. They'd been done in a hurry.

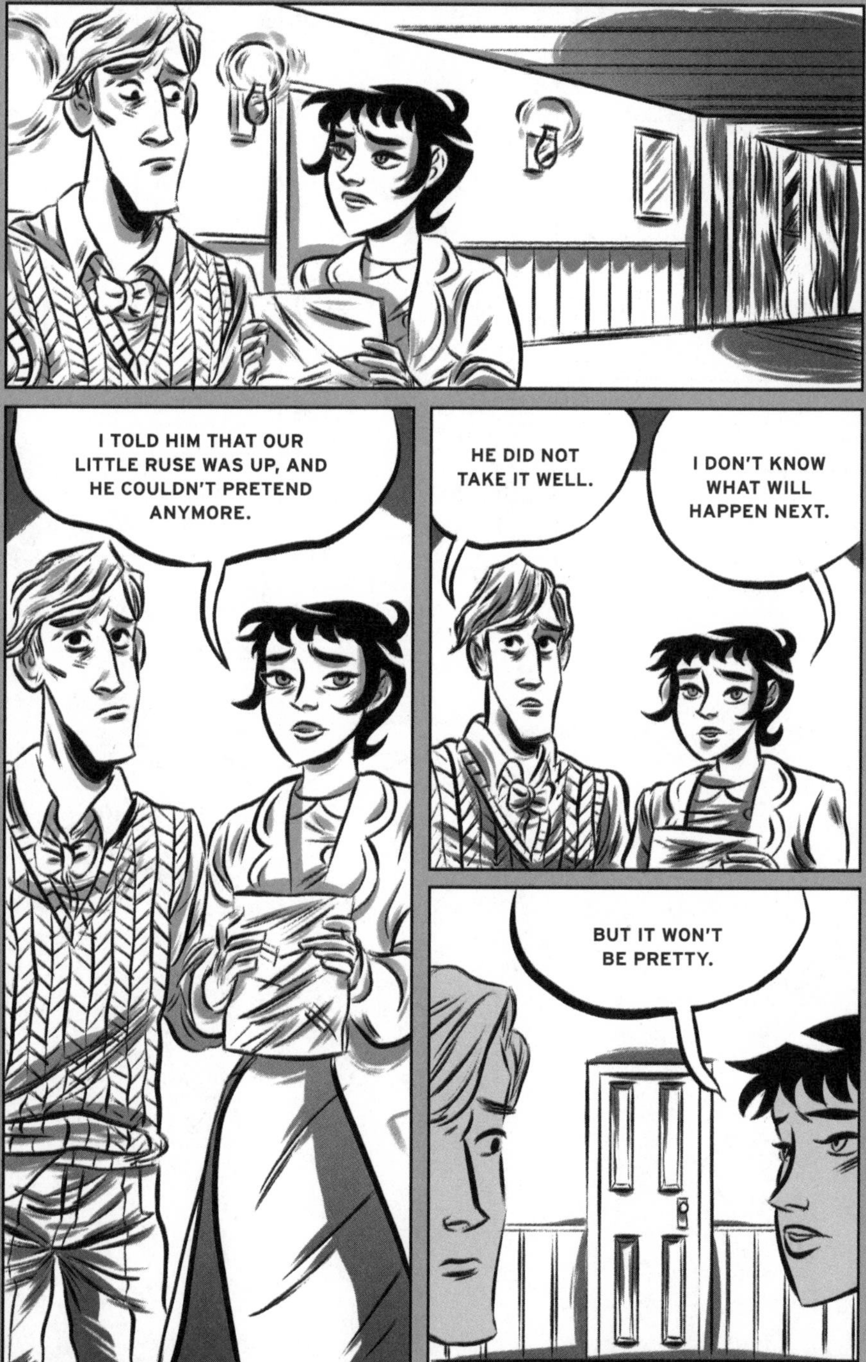
I TOLD HIM THAT OUR LITTLE RUSE WAS UP, AND HE COULDN'T PRETEND ANYMORE.
HE DID NOT TAKE IT WELL.
I DON'T KNOW WHAT WILL HAPPEN NEXT.
BUT IT WON'T BE PRETTY.

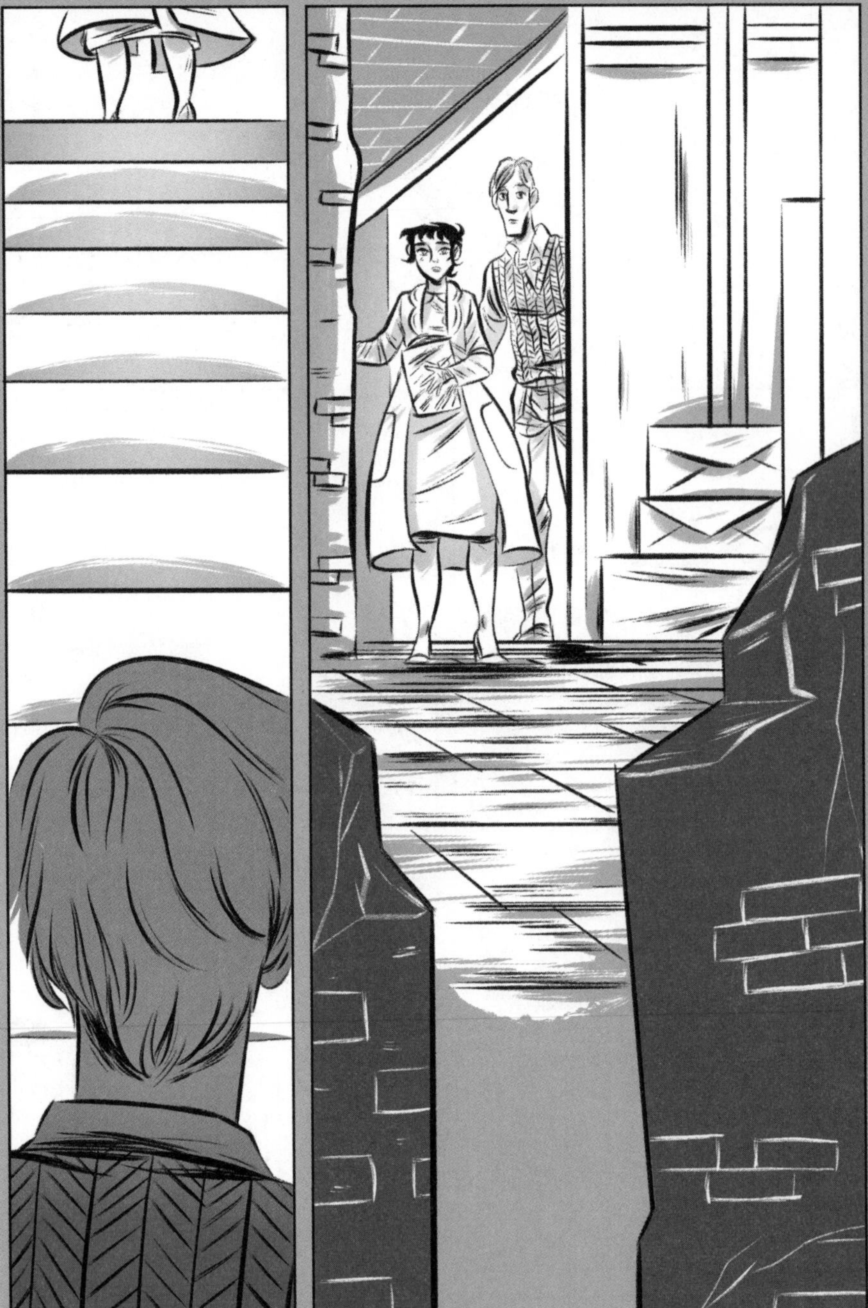

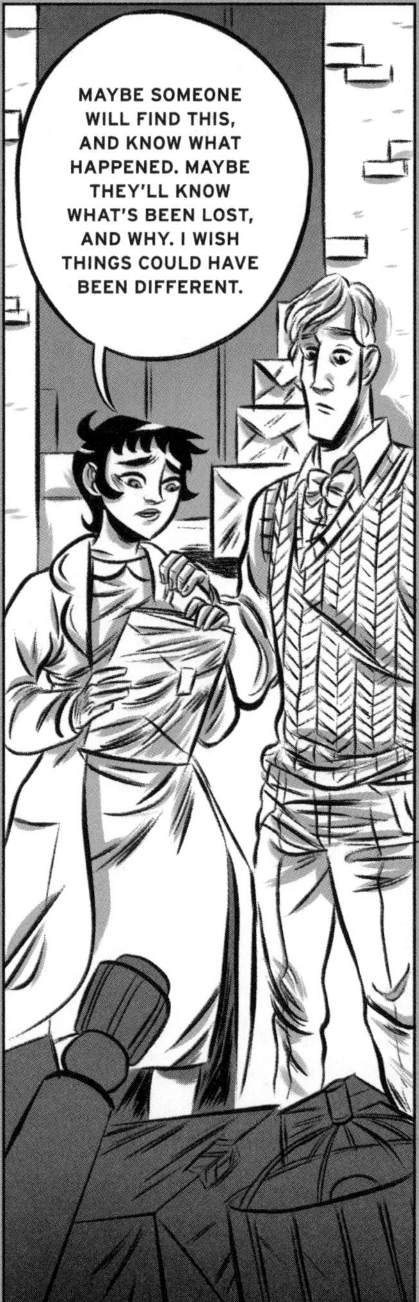
MAYBE SOMEONE WILL FIND THIS, AND KNOW WHAT HAPPENED. MAYBE THEY'LL KNOW WHAT'S BEEN LOST, AND WHY. I WISH THINGS COULD HAVE BEEN DIFFERENT.

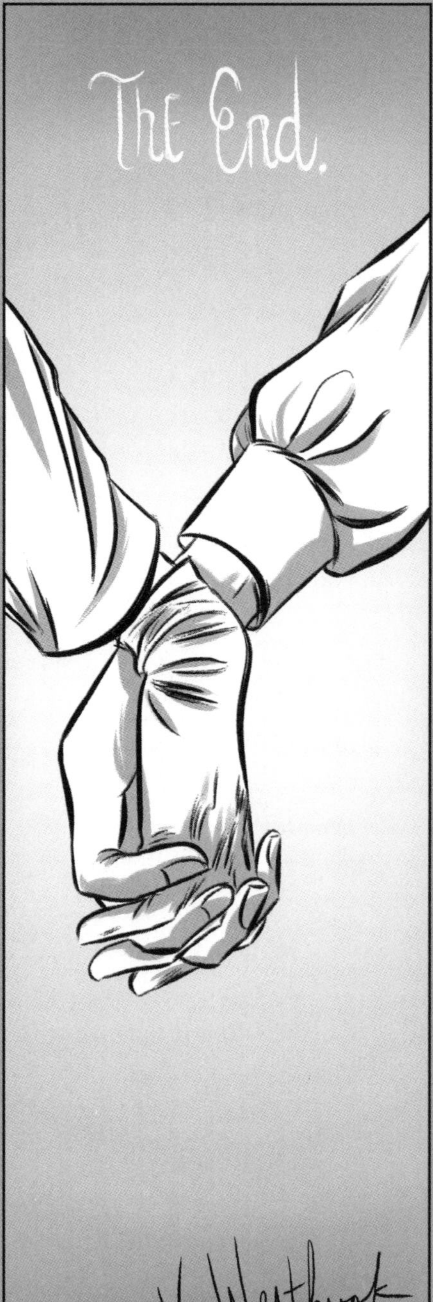
The End.
V. Westbrook

Denise slapped the book shut and the house shuddered, like she'd slapped it too. She tucked *Lucida Might* under her arm, and ran. The hallway felt like a fun house, dark and wobbly, rocking back and forth. She fell and caught herself on one hand. She didn't drop the book. By the time she was back on her feet and headed down the stairs, she could hear Terry loud and clear. He was saying, "Ow," a lot, and thanking Mike and Sally for getting him out of there.

"One more board ought to do it," Mike said. He swung the sledge down, got the end under the next plank, and pulled back, straining against the stubborn wood. It split and popped free of the nails, making a hole big enough for Terry to climb through.

With a little help from Sally, he hauled himself up over the edge and lay on the floor, panting. He was even whiter than usual — ghostly and blanched, from fright or blood loss. No, not blood loss. Denise ran her phone-light over him from top to bottom. She saw a lot of dirt, some bruises, and a couple of scrapes on the palms of his hands. "Dude." She leaned over him, and put her hands on his shoulders. "Get up. You're fine. I need your help."

"Give me a minute . . ."

"We may not have a minute!"

Mike nodded, and leaned on the sledge. "Pull yourself together, Terry. We're getting out of here. Sally, help me grab another couple of boards. I'm not a kid, and I won't fit through that hole."

"You want me to go back down there?" he squeaked.

Sally whacked at the hole with the pry bar. "Yes!"

"No!" Denise argued. "Terry, get up. I finished the book. I know what Vera's trying to tell us."

"What's going on in here?" he finally asked, like he'd only just noticed that the house was shaking itself apart, and there was no electricity, and the living room buzzed with that otherworldly hum. He sat up and looked around. "Is this the ghosts? Denise, are the ghosts doing this?"

"One of them is, and I think I know how to shut him up."

He asked, "How are you going to do that?"

"I'm gonna let him pick on somebody his own size. I mean . . . his own . . . level of deadness. Um. Just follow my lead." She shoved the book into his hands, so she could grab him by the wrist and hold her light at the same time. "Vera wants us to find her, and let her out. She wants to help."

With this, the swirling blackness that had filled the floor grew even colder; it felt like hands scrambling around her ankles. She squealed and turned around, looking for the shape of Joe and finding it in the doorway, twisting and forming, and reforming around those dead, empty eyes.

She smacked Terry on the shoulder and started running. "Come on!"

Over her parents' protests she fled back up the stairs, Terry hustling in her wake. He stumbled, but she helped him up and they both kept going. At the top of the steps, she turned a hard left and stopped at the attic door. "She's up there."

"You think Mrs. James is right? You think there's a body up there after all?"

"I'd bet money on it. I'd bet my whole *life* on it." She grabbed the knob and pulled. It stuck. She pulled harder, and she said out loud, "Or I'd bet somebody's life, anyway. Vera! If you can hear me up there, let us in!"

A small gust of air puffed out from under the door.

"Do you smell that?" Terry asked, wrinkling his nose, trying to figure out what he was sniffing.

"Yup. That's Vera. She's stuck up here." Denise took another crack at the knob and this time, it opened as smoothly as if that's what it always did, every time anybody tried it. Then she thundered up the narrow, dark steps, her phone's light waggling wildly. She caught herself on the wall, bouncing back and forth; she tried not to break the phone in her hand as she stayed upright by luck and force of will and some lingering memory of gymnastics tumbling, back in middle school.

She reached the top, just as the first curls of black mist tickled the bottom step behind her.

Terry reached it half a dozen seconds later, wheezing all the way. "We already . . . looked around . . . up here . . ." he said between deep, ragged breaths. "All we found . . . was the book."

"Give it here," she commanded. He forked it over. She flipped to the next to last page, with the drawing of the attic interior. "See?" She tapped it. "In *real* life, Vera Westbrook is the one who wrote the Lucida Might stories!"

"Then who was Joe Vaughn?"

"Some dude," she said. "I guess she didn't want to go to the conventions, or public appearances, or whatever. Maybe she had another job, and she didn't want people to know she was writing forbidden comics on the side. Who knows? The point is, Joe Vaughn didn't create any of this stuff. Vera did, and when she told him she was pulling the plug, I think he killed her. He wanted to keep the comic going, and take all the credit for it. Take all the money for it too."

"How do you know he hid her body up here?"

"Because they found *his* body at the bottom of the stairs. *Those* stairs." She pointed back at the stairwell. "He hid her in the attic, then he tripped and fell on the way back down."

"Evil *and* clumsy. Wow."

"Yeah, he was a real winner."

Frantically she looked from the page to the stuffy attic interior; she shined the light back and forth between them, and the vast, mostly empty room where four columns of brick rose up from the floor below, and went up past the roof overhead. Downstairs, these columns led to fireplaces. Above the roofline, they became chimneys.

Denise squinted down at the attic scene. "I think he stuffed her inside one of the chimneys."

"What!?"

She held the manuscript up, and shined her light on it. "It's obvious that she based the house of horrors on *this* house, right? Well, there are *four* chimneys here in real life, and only *three* in the comic book."

"So?"

"So, at the bottom of each chimney is a fireplace, right? We have one fireplace in the parlor, one in the living room, and there used to be one in the kitchen."

"Okay, then where's the fourth fireplace? I don't think I've ever seen it."

She held the light under her chin, and smiled like a maniac. "Terry . . . we don't *have* one."

He was swift on the uptake, she had to give him credit. He lit up like the Fourth of July, and immediately ran back to the narrow stairwell. He stumbled and tumbled down — yelling all the way, "Mr. Cooper, Mrs. Cooper — we need the sledgehammer!"

Then he said, "Oh God . . . oh wow . . ."

"Oh God what?" she hollered.

"This black stuff . . . it's everywhere . . ."

"Just get the sledgehammer!"

While he ran that quick errand, Denise pondered which tower of bricks wasn't original, and didn't match up to things downstairs. The house wailed and sighed on its foundation; the frame itself squeaked as the old timbers twisted and stretched. "I'm coming for you, Vera. I'll get you out of there, so you can save your house. So you can save *us* . . ."

She closed her eyes and pictured the house's layout.

The brick tower to the right, and a bit behind her . . . it would go straight down to the parlor. The extra wide one looked like it'd bottom out in the kitchen. The other two . . . it was harder to say. They were rather close together.

Either one might go down to the living room.

But when she ran her light over the bricks, they weren't the same at all. One column was made with red bricks, and one was built with brown bricks. The mortar was different too. Was one newer than the other? How was she supposed to tell?

Around her shoes, she felt a cold gust that coiled tight, and there were footsteps on the stairs. Big, heavy ones. Slow ones. Not Terry, and not Mike, and not her mom — she would've known their feet. This was somebody else. Something else.

"Joe," she whispered, and she kicked her feet like she could shake off the frigid squeeze. It didn't work. "Joe, knock it off." She shivered and shuddered. Her eyes darted from chimney to chimney. "Where are you, Vera? Help me. Help me, Vera . . ."

She didn't need the microphone, this time. The voice came soft as a sigh, in her left ear: This one, dear.

Terry came storming up the stairs, and from the sound of it, Mike and Sally were coming up behind him — but her friend was the one precariously waving a heavy sledgehammer like a victory flag. He traded Denise the hammer for the book.

She took her first swing at the indicated column as Mike and Sally arrived.

"What the hell are you doing?" her mother demanded.

It was too late to answer. Chunks of brick broke and flew, and when Denise swung again — then again — she opened a hole the size of her hand. A low, horrible gasp poured out of that hole, followed by a soft whistle and a tune that had become almost familiar.

Denise jumped back, and dropped the hammer to the floor.

The gasp kept coming, and it smelled like something worse than death. It smelled like hidden rot and funeral arrangements. It was sorrow and outrage, and loss and missed opportunities.

It was not only flowers, but *fire*.

It flowed like Denise had punctured a balloon, and not a chimney tower. It whistled as it came — soft at first, and then stronger, and stronger. It swept through the attic and around it, in some terrible small hurricane of fury, of burning lilies and scorched roses. It whispered fiercely, and something answered it. Terry held up his recorder and braced himself, planting his feet and narrowing his eyes against the weird maelstrom.

"What is this?" Mike hollered his question into the wind.

But Denise was too triumphant to answer. She pumped her fist and shouted, "Go get 'im, Vera!"

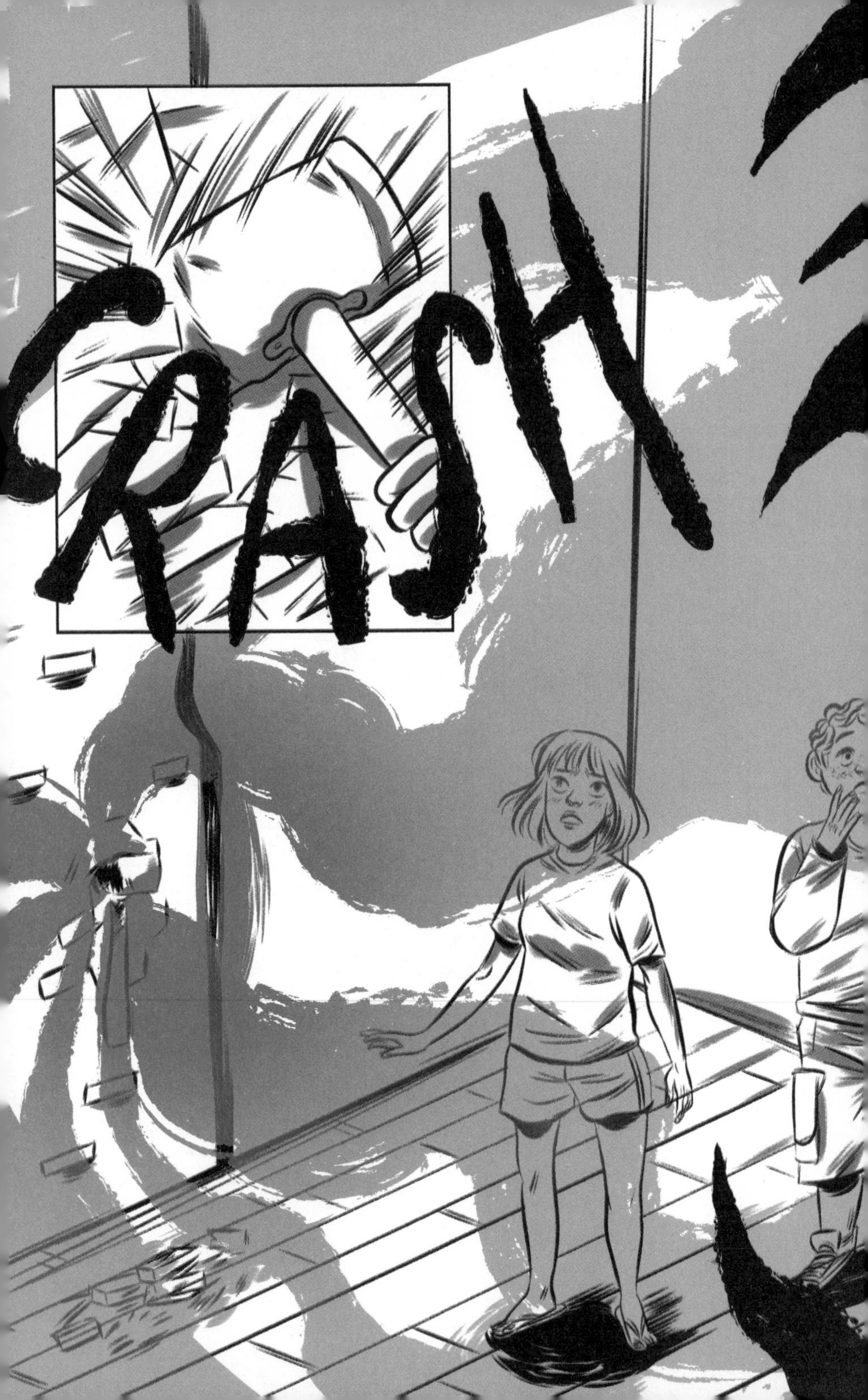
CRASH

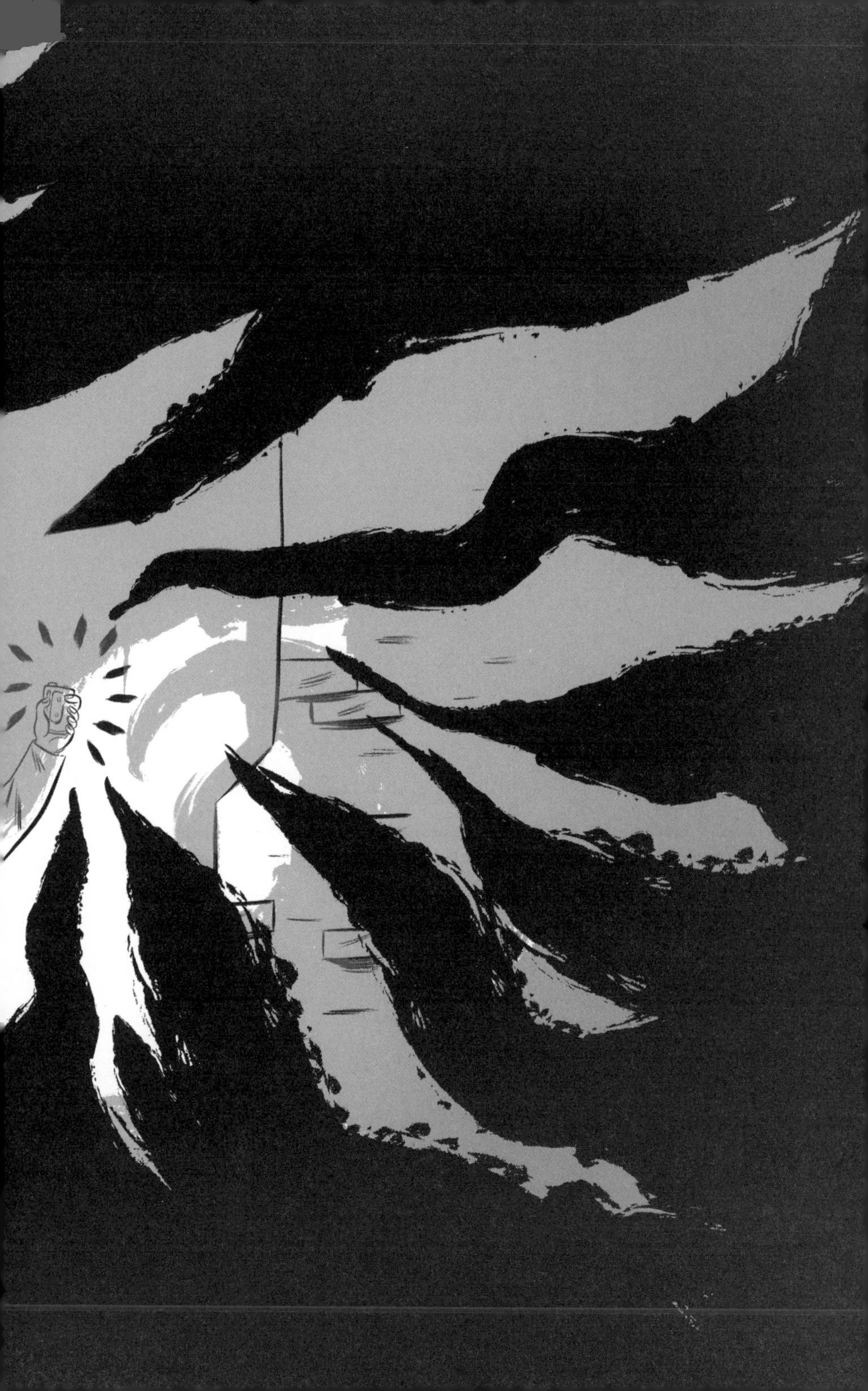

A thin, sour smell of rot and mildew threaded through the perfumed air — it writhed, and fought, and argued, and it was crushed. It was smothered. It was snuffed out with a pop of everybody's ears, and a groan from the floor and ceiling, and a creak and crack from the nearest small window that looked out over what was left of the Argonne block in St. Roch.

The house stopped shaking.

The dull hum faded, until it was so dull that no one could hear it anymore. The rush of air slowed, until it was only a whisper — and then it was only a secret. Only silence.

The house settled. It sighed. Then it was silent too.

Everyone stared at the hole in the chimney that wasn't a chimney at all — but a tomb. It was dark in there. Too dark to see anything at all, until Denise held up her hand all shaky, and shined the phone-light into the hole. She saw dust, and a deserted wasp nest. She saw the other side of dirty brown bricks.

She saw a faded pattern of crochet and buttons.

Like the kind you'd see on an old lady's sweater.

# CHAPTER NINETEEN

A small white car pulled up to the house. It hung out by the curb, engine idling, until the driver finally backed up and pulled around to park behind the first of two police cars. A woman got out, and shut the door behind herself. She stared at the key fob until she found the right button to lock the doors with an electronic beep.

"Who's that?" Terry asked. He took a bite of breakfast burrito and chewed. Sally had run to McDonald's, and once again, Terry was present for the fast-food feast. It was early. He was opportunistic. Nobody minded.

Norman had brought his own breakfast — a little baggie of beignets from Crispy's. He sat between Terry and Denise and got all powdery while the three of them watched the woman walk away from the car, looking back and forth between a piece of paper and the house. He said, "She doesn't look like a cop."

Denise swallowed a bit of biscuit and took a swig of orange juice from a paper cup. "She looks like she's lost."

It was a white woman in her forties, probably. She had short red hair and black-framed glasses. She was dressed for daytime in a laid-back office. Jeans and sandals, but nice jeans. Heeled sandals. She stepped sideways to go around the freshly reopened hole in the porch.

The kids couldn't see her through the dining room window anymore, but the woman didn't knock right away. Denise figured she was likely trying the doorbell, but it didn't work, so that wouldn't get her anywhere. It would be a few seconds before she realized her mistake.

Then the woman knocked, hesitantly at first. She knocked again, louder, more firmly. Like she had business there.

Mike called, "Denise, could you get that?" He and Sally were still talking to the one police officer in the living room, while the other one was upstairs taking pictures and looking for extra evidence in the attic.

"Yeah, I've got it."

Denise got up and opened the door. "Hello?"

"Hello," said the woman. She appeared almost surprised, but Denise didn't know why. "Um . . . is this 312 Argonne Street? I didn't see any numbers on the house, but . . ."

"This house is missing a lot of things. You've found the right place."

"Great! Okay. Great. So . . . is there any chance you're Denise?"

"There is a very, very good chance I'm Denise." She frowned, and cocked her head. "Do I know you?"

"Yes! Oh God, I hope this isn't weird. My husband said it was weird." She laughed nervously. "I'm Eugenie Robbins — we've been emailing a little bit? Back and forth? It looks like I've come at a bad time, though. I'm sorry. Is there any . . . um . . . are your parents home?"

"Yes, they're here. But they're talking to the cops. Did you *seriously* fly all the way from New York? Like . . . today?"

"I took a red-eye. There's a big independent booksellers' conference starting tomorrow, and I thought I'd see if I could squeak in early, and catch a word with you."

Denise stood aside, opening the door wider. "How did you find the house?"

"I went rummaging through Dad's old paperwork and found some correspondence between him and a police officer here in New Orleans. It all had to do with Joe's death — the cop included the address of the house where he was found, and asked if Dad knew who lived there. I don't know what my father told him, but I thought I might as well drop by, in case this was it."

Denise laughed. "Well, this is it. These are my friends, Terry and Norman," she added. "Terry was here for the whole show last night, just about. Norman just got wind of the excitement, and came over to see what was up."

"And to make sure everyone was okay!" he protested. "We all heard the ambulance and the cop cars . . ."

"Hi Norman, and hi Terry. It's nice to meet all of you. Wow . . . I can't believe I found this place. I can't believe it's still *standing.*" Eugenie Robbins talked fast, like her words were all in a race to get out of her mouth.

Denise led her inside. "You and me both, lady. Especially after last night."

"Yes, I mean . . . good heavens. Ambulances? Police? What happened here?"

Mike, Sally, and some cop whose name Denise hadn't caught all looked up when they came past the living room. Sally rose, in case this was a proper guest who needed proper hosting. Denise headed that off at the pass. "Mom, this is Eugenie Robbins. I told you about her. Her dad was Joe Vaughn's agent."

The cop looked from person to person, trying to decide what was going on, and if it was important. Finally, he asked, "Who's Joe Vaughn?"

Offhandedly, Denise replied, "She's the lady wrapped in the rug upstairs." To Eugenie, she added, "We found Vera Westbrook's body in the attic last night. This was her house, and she was the *real* Joe Vaughn. I mean, kind of."

"Maybe I need a word with *you,*" the cop said, a pen held aloft and a notepad in his hand.

"Sure thing. But first, I'm going to take her up to my room." She jerked her thumb toward Eugenie. "And show her my comic book."

Upstairs and down the hall to the right, Eugenie followed them. The whole way, her eyes scanned every inch of the place, taking in all the wonder and glory of the decrepit scenery — which now had a bonus layer of plaster dust and splinters on every surface . . . and a webbing of police tape across the attic door. "Good god . . ." she gasped, her mouth hanging open.

"Vera didn't do this," Denise clarified. "It was the other guy — the one who took credit for all her work. Vera wrote about him, in a roundabout way, in this book." It was lying on Denise's bed.

Eugenie sat down on the mattress beside it. "May I?"

"Go for it."

She flipped through the pages with great care, reading quickly and absorbing the art. She skimmed at a crazy speed, admiring everything as she went. Finally, she reached the last page, and scanned all the way down to the signature at the bottom.

"Oh, wow. *Wow.*"

"Vera drew the comic herself, and wrote it too. But for some reason, she didn't want the whole world to know about it. She let Joe Vaughn pretend he was her — I think she even paid him. He's the one who showed up for all her conferences and public appearances," Denise told her. "But Lucida Might *belonged* to Vera, and Joe got mad when she ended it. Your dad did his best to help. I found one of his letters hidden here, in the house. Let me get it."

She offered the old pages to Eugenie, who took them with reverence. "Dad always wanted to help," she whispered. "He must have known all along . . ."

"There's another letter or two at Tulane, in the library archives. I should've taken a picture to show you, but you get the idea from this, right?"

She nodded in response, her eyes never leaving the old letter.

Terry could hardly contain himself. He stood up and half paced, half bounced around the room. He said to Denise, "We'll have to go back to Mrs. James's place. She'll want to hear about the body in the attic because you *know* Dominique will tell her about it. It's going to be all over the neighborhood tomorrow."

"It'll be all over the neighborhood in another hour," Norman corrected him. "The neighborhood grapevine is faster than Wi-Fi."

Denise considered this. "I can't decide if that's awesome or terrible."

"A little of both?" Terry was still tickled pink. Literally. His round, freckled cheeks were flush with glee. "It's totally stranger than fiction. Stranger even than *Lucida Might*. But everyone will have to believe you! I was there — and my dad was there too."

His dad had been half of the responding EMT team, when they'd finally gotten the cell phones working again. Terry wasn't really hurt, but he was the one who'd called it in. His dad had freaked out and come right over, ambulance wailing and lights flashing.

Eugenie Robbins pulled out her phone and started taking photos of the last few pages. "My father would have loved this." She sighed, and held the book across her lap. "I'm positive that he never saw this manuscript. It definitely wasn't published; I learned that much from the material sent over."

"How?" Denise asked.

"Oh, there's an archivist in Texas — a guy named Jess Nevins — who's basically the king of the pop librarians. In his downtime, he compiles bibliographies of comics, pulps, and genre media. He had a complete listing of all the Lucida Might stuff that was ever published or otherwise produced, and he was very, very helpful." She paused and lifted her face. "Wait. What's that? Does anyone else smell it?"

Denise could smell it. One glance at Terry and Norman told her that they could too.

"Flowers . . ." Eugenie breathed.

"Roses and lilies," Denise agreed.

"Where's it coming from?"

Along with the flowers, came music — soft and vague, and then a little louder. Somehow it still sounded very far away, but very clear. Denise wondered about this odd little song . . . the one that Vera liked to sing when she wandered through the house leaving tiny, neat footprints in the dust. It was a cheerful, simple string of notes. They lifted and fell at the farthest edge of her hearing.

Eugenie looked around the room, trying to pinpoint the source. "Do you hear that? It sounds like . . . like someone singing."

Terry slowly reached for his bag, on the floor by the bed. He pulled out his battered recorder, pressed a button, and held it up.

"I know that song," Eugenie whispered.

Denise asked, "You do?"

She nodded, vigorously and with wonder. "Did you ever see the *Lucida Might* TV show? Anywhere online? It must be on YouTube somewhere." She hummed the notes herself, louder and for anyone to hear as clear as a bell. "You don't know that tune?"

Denise and Terry both shook their heads.

Eugenie's eyes were a little damp, but she was smiling anyway and squeezing the brittle paper between her fingers. "Oh, guys. The TV show. This was its theme song!"

Norman grinned from ear to ear. "I like this Vera lady. She's cool."

"She really saved our butts last night," Denise agreed.

Terry added, "I'm still not sure how, but she chased the other guy away and now . . ." He toyed with the recorder. "Now I think she's free and clear to hang around if she wants, or follow the light, or whatever."

"I hope she stays," Denise declared. "If we're going to have a bed-and-breakfast, it might as well be haunted by somebody famous. Maybe they'll put us on one of those ghost tour thingys."

Downstairs, there was another knock on the door.

It was Dominique, wild-eyed and fresh out of bed. She was still wearing a pajama top that said GIVE ME ALL THE ZZZZZZS with a pair of shorts and flip-flops when she came running up the stairs. At the top landing she paused, not knowing where to go, until Norman hollered, "In here, Dom. Everybody's in here."

She slid into the room and froze, looking back and forth between her cousin, Denise, Terry, and Eugenie. Rather than ask about the new lady, she said breathlessly, "The whole neighborhood wants to know what happened last night, and dammit . . ." she grin-scowled at Terry and Norman. "I thought I was going to find out first."

"My dad was the EMT who came to the scene!" Terry chirped.

"My mom was headed into work early, and saw the cop lights," Norman explained.

And Denise said, "We really did have poltergeists. Or . . . one poltergeist, and one badass old lady ghost who saved the day. We found her body upstairs, bricked up in a fake chimney."

"Oh my God!" Dominique looked back out into the hall and noticed the tape over the attic door. "Oh my God!" she said again and pointed. "Is that the attic, over there?"

Terry said, "Yep!", Norman nodded, and Denise said, "Yeah, but I wouldn't climb those stairs if I were you. They're a hazard. That's how the poltergeist died — he fell down them and broke his neck. His body was lying right . . . about . . . where you stepped when you got off the stairs," she teased.

The thought of it didn't bother her so much anymore, now that he was really gone. Gone-gone. All of him, even the nasty leftover parts that wanted to bring down the house and everyone in it.

It bothered Dom, though. "Well that is just plain gross." She clutched her own arms, then suddenly noticed the AC. She said with a smile that teased in return, "Hey, you've got your own unit! I thought you said this place was a craphole."

"I've got the only one in the house!" Denise said proudly. "Come on in, and have a seat on the bed if you want. The comic is a little scary, but not, like, corpses-in-the-attic scary. I'll turn up the air, if you won't tell my mom, and we'll get you all caught up."

Dominique agreed to this, and Eugenie Robbins made room on the mattress. Norman and Terry held back on the floor, and everyone enjoyed the dramatic reading and interpretive gestures that ensued.

By lunchtime, the agent had excused herself in favor of lunch and a nap before her convention began, and Terry's dad had picked him up and taken him home. Norman and Dom were getting ready to leave too, but Mrs. James showed up before they got the chance. She introduced herself to Sally and Mike, who invited her inside to sit in the living room while they rounded up the kids.

"We don't need rounding up," Dom announced as she descended the stairs. "We're all just hanging out in Denise's room. She's the one with the good AC. If y'all had any sense, you'd come up here, instead of asking us to come down there."

Norman and Denise followed behind her.

"Hi Mrs. James," Denise greeted her. "Nice to see you again."

"Nice to see you too, and to know that you were bluffing me about not having any bodies in the attic!" she said with something perilously close to glee.

"In my defense, I had no idea she was up there — not when I talked to you the other day."

"You knew there were ghosts, though. I know you did. It was all over your face, but you didn't want to say so." She accepted a soda that Sally brought around from the kitchen, and gave Denise a wink. "But that's all right. I'll forgive you."

Everybody piled inside and pulled up seats, even if those seats were just crates or wooden pallets. The living room seemed smaller that way. It also seemed warmer and safer. The fresh drywall looked like a promising start, rather than a work in progress. The newly plastered ceiling looked clean instead of plain. The capped-off wires that hung from the ceiling felt like a logical progression, not an unfinished chore.

The hole in the floor . . . well, it was still a hole in the floor, but somehow it looked less permanent.

"Mrs. James, you didn't have to come all this way to pick up Norman and Dominique," Mike said, once he understood the general relations. "I would've been happy to drive them home."

"That's sweet of you to offer, but I don't have a car and that's not what I'm here for. I just wanted to get the scoop!" She told them what she'd told Denise, about being a kid and daring her friends to sneak inside, years before. "And I wanted to see how the place was coming together," she admitted frankly. "Everyone is curious, you know. The house has been standing for so long, looking so sad. It's nice that a family has bought it, and good that you're working to bring it back."

Denise prepared herself for another conversation about gentrifiers — right here in her own house, in front of God and everybody. But Mrs. James stopped there and looked at Sally and Mike.

Sally mustered some excitement, even as they all knew they were sitting in a half-finished, half-rotten space that still had a long way to go. "Yes! That's the plan, eventually. My mother-in-law — she died in the Storm, but she was a wonderful cook and hostess, and she always wanted for us to buy one of these old places and fix it up. Well," she blushed a little. "She wanted that for me and my first husband, but he died in the Storm too."

"Sally, I am so sorry to hear that. You're in good company, though. I suppose this means you're coming *back* to town, not just coming in."

"That's right." She rehashed the old story about leaving, meeting Mike, and returning. "So here we are . . . just barely. This is all we could afford, but we're doing our best to bring it back to glory."

Mrs. James made some encouraging oohs and ahs, admiring the things that were original and the things that were halfway to being fixed. Then she said, "You know, there are plenty of professionals right here in the neighborhood. You can always talk to Pete and the boys down at the shop; they'll tell you who's good, and who's shady. It would be a nice thing, if you could keep the work and keep the money close to home."

"That's our goal," Mike told her, "And we're happy to pay fair, but we can't pay much. The bank is mighty stingy with the payouts, and we're stretched to the limit as it is."

"Oh, everyone here understands how tough it is. If you're willing to work with people, more often than not, they'll be willing to work with you. Oh!" She remembered something, and snapped her fingers. "Once you get things up and running, you should talk to Norman's mother. She's been in charge of the kitchen at Tulane for years, and they don't treat her with half the respect she deserves. Or half the money, either."

"That would be wonderful!" Sally exclaimed. "If she's interested, when we finally find our footing. We'll have to have her over for pizza or something," she said to him. "Or I'll just cook, if we ever get the kitchen in shape."

"You ought to throw a shrimp boil or something like that, it's a good way to meet the neighbors . . ." Dom hinted.

"So's church," her grandmother said back, but she didn't ask any questions, or make any assumptions. "Honestly, if you need resources, if you need recommendations, or extra hands . . . you send one of these two"—she waved at Dom and Norman,—"and I'll come around. I know everybody, and I enjoy putting people in touch with one another."

Norman agreed to be a messenger, and added, "When it comes to this neighborhood, if you want to do right—if you want to be part of the solution, not part of the problem—all you have to do is ask. Then, I mean, you have to listen."

Dominique agreed. "What happens after that is up to you, but the neighborhood is watching. And the neighborhood doesn't forget."

Sally looked a little embarrassed when she said, "We really do appreciate how kind everyone has been—and how helpful you've been, Norman. I know it seems like we've been keeping to ourselves, but the house has eaten up so much of our time and energy . . . we've had so many appointments, so many workers coming and going . . ."

Mike nodded along to what she was saying. "It must look like we're hanging out on our own private block, but I promise, that's not how we want it. Shoot," he said with a little half laugh. "After last night, we've got one hell of a conversation starter!"

Mrs. James laughed too. "That you do! So why don't you start with me? Tell me everything. I'm dying to hear all about it!"

When the last of the police had gone, and all the neighbors had returned to their corners of St. Roch, and the AC was buzzing a little too loud in Denise's room, she climbed into bed.

She didn't smell old lady perfume, but she didn't smell the primordial funk from the attic, either, and when she listened for ghosts, she didn't hear anything that worried her. Maybe there was a faint hum, an old TV theme song trailing through the halls. Maybe small, ladylike feet tripped up and down the stairs, bothering nobody — happy to roam the whole house once again.

Denise had a pretty strong feeling that Vera approved of their work. She also had a feeling that Joe Vaughn had left for good. Now that his secret was out and Vera's body had been found, he had nothing left to hide or protect.

"Vera," Denise said quietly as she snuggled under the covers and picked up her phone. "I hope you stay. I hope you haunt this place like crazy, and we get write-ups on ghost-hunting sites, and people pay us all kinds of money to spend the night in the attic. I hope you give everybody the scare of a lifetime, and I hope it makes you laugh."

She called up Trish's last text message.

"I hope you like us, and you won't try to chase us away. I hope you loved this house and this neighborhood . . ." She turned the phone sideways, for easier typing. "As much as my mom and Mike do."

Then she took a deep breath, and let it out slow. She stared at the glowing screen until it dimmed a little, in an effort to save battery life. She tapped it, and brought it back to full brightness.

*Today has been really nuts, and if you're up, I could tell you about it.*

No response, and no typing bubble to suggest that one was immediately forthcoming. Well, you couldn't catch Trish at the phone all the time, Denise supposed. She was thinking about calling it a night, when someone else pinged her phone.

It was Norman. **How you doing? You okay tonight?**

Aw, how sweet. She answered him: *Everybody's good. It's been quiet. Maybe it'll stay quiet.*

Then she realized someone else was looped in on the message. A bubble with Terry's name on it replied, **Maybe it won't!**

Such an optimist. A third bubble appeared, but it just had a number — and Denise didn't recognize it. She was about to ask who it was, when the bubble expanded to say, **This is Dom. Norman gave me ur number.**

*Cool*, Denise replied. Then she sent a little hand-waving emoji.

Dom sent a hand wave back.

Denise was about to continue their chat, when Trish finally replied. **TELL ME ALL ABOUT UR NIGHT. Especially if there were ghostsin it.**

She switched back to Trish. *DUH of course there were ghosts. Maybe when you hear how crazy haunted this house is you'll REALLY want to come see it. What I'm thinking is*

She accidentally sent the text mid-composition, and started again.

*Is I could show you around. I def want you for a roommate next year, don't worry, but maybe you could humor my parents. Sometime before school gets too crazy*

She couldn't believe she was saying this, but.

*You could come visit, and check out Tulane.*

Trish asked, **How far is your house fromTULane?**

Dom was back. **Terry played me some of the ghost voices. That's messed up!**

Denise smiled, and responded: *Extremely messed up! You want to come over and try next time? See if we can get Vera to say hello?*

I'll come too, Norman promised. Me and Terry. WE'll get the whole scooby gang together.

She liked the idea, and she told them so. *It's on!* Then she switched back to answer Trish's question, *Tulane's just a bus ride away. No big deal. You could be my roommate in my house, easy as a dorm. Room would be bigger. Got my own AC unit too. Or you could have your own room.*

Not the one with the wasps tho, rite

She forgot she'd mentioned it, during one of their midday chats. *Not unless you want them. I would save them for you, if you do.*

Terry again. There are other haunted houses in the neighborhood.

Denise asked, *Do people live in them?*

Some of them. We could start a ghost hunting club. We could ask for permission.

Dom wasn't so sure. Let me start slow. I like this old lady ghost, let me just talk to her first. She seems nice.

*No one will give us permission to hunt ghosts in their house*, Denise protested.

Norman disagreed. Terry's good at asking for stuff. You let him hunt ghosts in YOUR house.

*Well he was very persistent.*

Terry added, I don't take no for an answer!

"Truer words were never spoken," Denise muttered. "Or texted. Whatever."

Trish said, I've never been to NOLA.

*No time like the present. Or like, kind of soon*, Denise said. *U might like it. If you don't, oh well. But I want you to see it.*

The wheels in Trish's head were turning. Denise could practically hear them rolling around, all the way over in Texas. Parents would be pissed if I left the state, but NOLA isn't that far.

*Right*, Denise agreed.

**I could come look. No promises.**

Denise wasn't asking for promises. **No promises.** Just options. Just possibilities. Just a chance to come home, and be home — if that's what this was — and bring somebody she loved along for the ride.

Trish signed off: **Ok then. Good night. Sleep tight. Don't let the ghost-bugs bite.**

Denise told her good night, and then told the other kids the same. It'd been a long day. But tomorrow, she promised everyone, *We'll pick up where we left off.*

She plugged her phone in and flopped back down on her bed. From there, she stared around and realized she needed some wall art. Posters, or pictures, or blown-up pages of comic books that no one ever published. That and a few throw pillows, maybe a couple of cute rugs, and a lamp, and it wouldn't be the world's most embarrassing place to have a guest.

It wouldn't take much. Just a little time, and a little money. Or a lot.

"Good night, Vera," she mumbled sleepily to the room at large. "Thanks for everything."

Then she turned off the lamp and fluffed her pillow, punching it into a shape that worked, and she did not notice the shadow that perched on the window seat. She did not smell any perfume, and she did not hear any music. She didn't even hear a woman's voice, not then. But later, when she checked her messages in the morning, she'd see that someone had turned on the microphone again — and then she would know that she wasn't alone, and this time, that was all right.

Good night, dear girl. Thanks for everything, yourself.

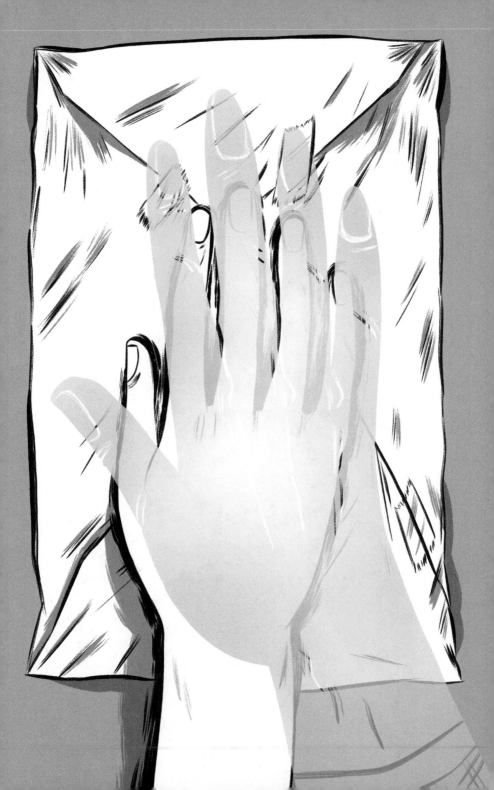

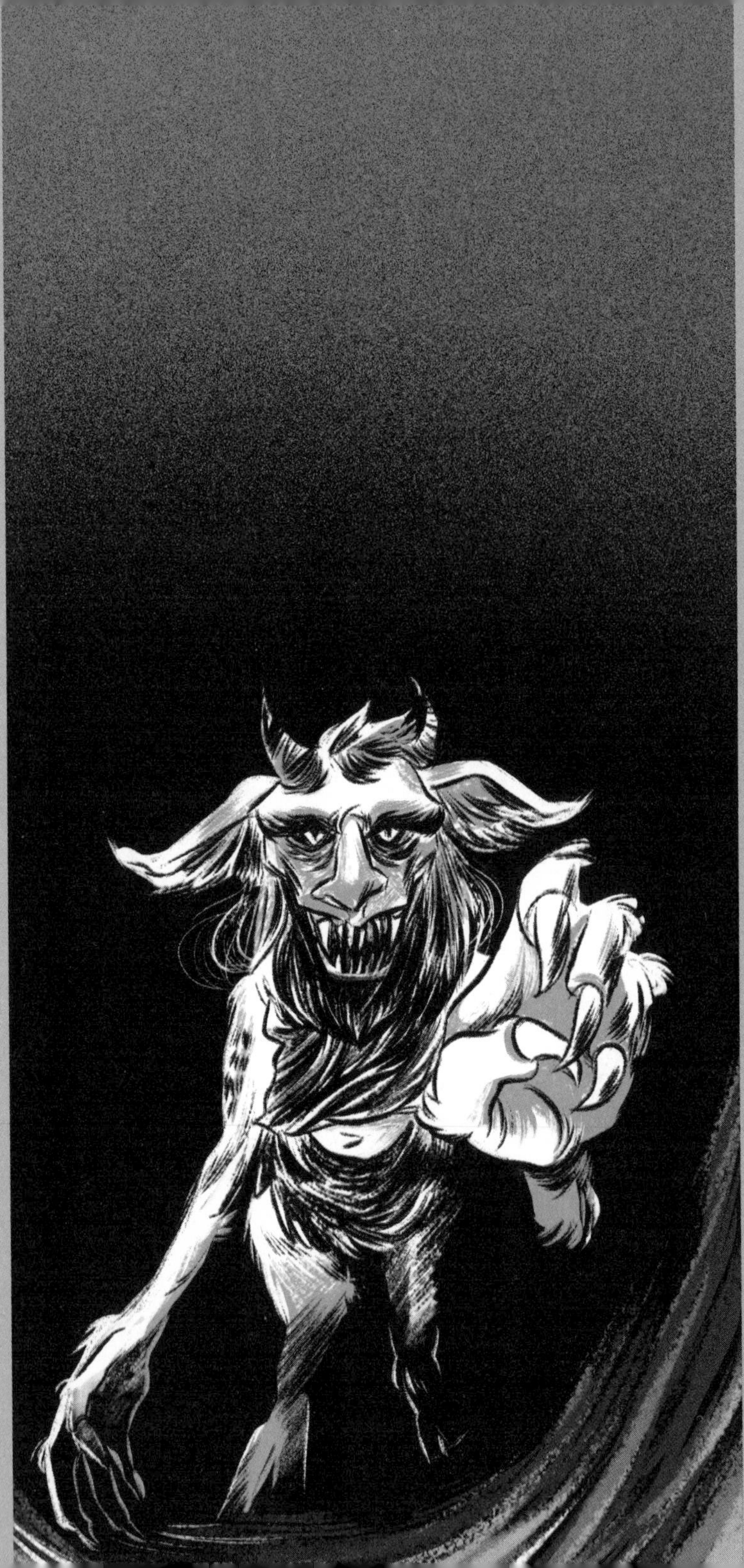

# ACKNOWLEDGMENTS

This book has been a group effort from day one — and it never could've come together without a veritable host of folks including (but by no means limited to) the following great people: Cheryl Klein, the editor who helped me develop *The Agony House* in the first place; editor Nick Thomas, who dove right in to help me pull it together and push it over the finish line; talented and speedy artist Tara O'Connor, who did such a killer job of the comics; art director Phil Falco, who shepherded all the visuals with aplomb; and my outstanding agent Jennifer Jackson. Many thanks to them, and to everyone else who's helped me along this spooky little road.

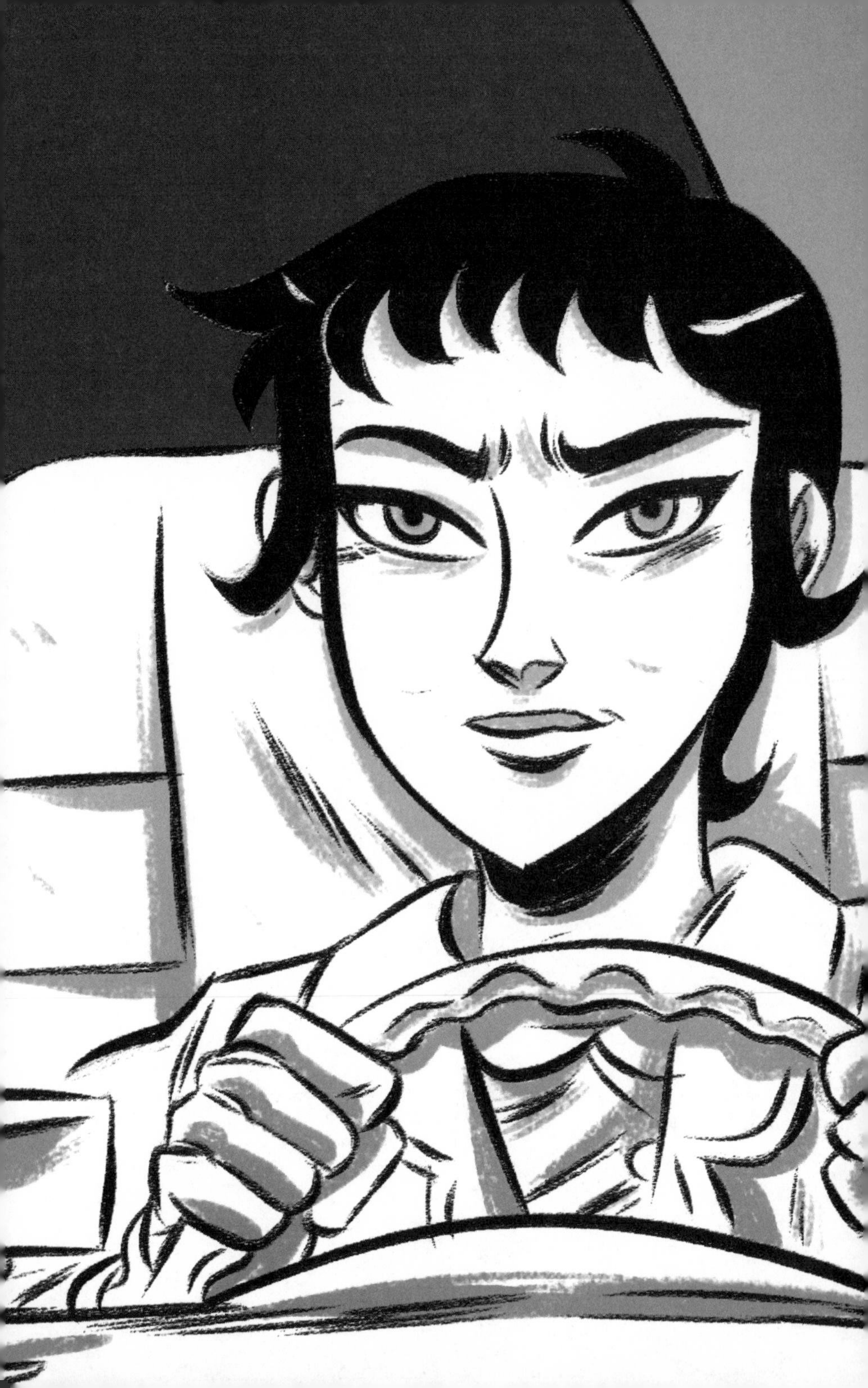

# CHERIE PRIEST

is the author of *I Am Princess X*, her debut young adult novel, which earned three starred reviews and was a YALSA Quick Pick for Reluctant Young Adult Readers. She is also the author of more than a dozen adult science fiction, fantasy, and horror novels, including *Boneshaker*, which won the Locus Award for Best Science Fiction Novel. She lives in Seattle, WA, and can be found online at cheriepriest.com and @cmpriest.

# TARA O'CONNOR

is a comic maker and illustrator currently residing in the New Jersey wilderness. When she's not drawing or teaching comics, she's probably working on an illustration of some sort. She is the author of *Roots* and *The Altered History of Willow Sparks*. You can find more of Tara's art online at taraocomics.com